T0318839

Red

BOOK YOUR PLACE ON OUR WEBSITE
AND MAKE THE
READING CONNECTION!

We've created a customized website just for our very special readers, where you can get the inside scoop on everything that's going on with Zebra, Pinnacle and Kensington books.

When you come online, you'll have the exciting opportunity to:

- View covers of upcoming books
- Read sample chapters
- Learn about our future publishing schedule
  (listed by publication month and author)
- Find out when your favorite authors will be visiting
  a city near you
- Search for and order backlist books from our
  online catalog
- Check out author bios and background informat
- Send e-mail to your favorite auth
- Meet the Kensington staff online
- Join us in weekly chats with authors, readers and
  other guests
- Get writing guidelines
- AND MUCH MORE!

Visit our website at
http://www.kensingtonbooks.com

Red

A TRANSPLANTED TALES NOVEL

KATE SERINE

KENSINGTON
PUBLISHING CORP.

www.kensingtonbooks.com

eKENSINGTON BOOKS are published by

Kensington Publishing Corp.
119 West 40th Street
New York, NY 10018

All Kensington titles, imprints, and distributed lines are available at special quantity discounts for bulk purchases for sales promotion, premiums, fund-raising, educational, or institutional use.

Special book excerpts or customized printings can also be created to fit specific needs. For details, write or phone the office of the Kensington Special Sales Manager: Attn. Special Sales Department. Kensington Publishing Corp., 119 West 40th Street, New York, NY 10018. Phone: 1-800-221-2647.

eKensington and the K with book logo Reg. US Pat. & TM Off.

ISBN-13: 978-1-60183-140-8
ISBN-10: 1-60183-140-4
First Printing: August 2012

ISBN-13: 978-1-60183-018-0
ISBN-10: 1-60183-018-1
First Electronic Edition: August 2012

10 9 8 7 6 5 4 3 2 1

Published in the United States of America

For E.A.S.
Thank you for asking, "What if . . . ?"

Acknowledgments

No novel is a completely solo effort. As such, I offer my gratitude to the members of Team SeRine:

To Zach, Ethan, and Rowan. You are my sun, moon, stars; the guiding lights of my life.

To Mom, Dad, Steve, Rena, Jenny, Cam, Jason, Christen, David, Becky, Amy, Sheila, Kendra, and Tim. Thank you for believing in me and cheering me on.

To Nicole Resciniti and Alicia Condon. Your guidance has been invaluable! Thank you for believing in Red and helping me share her story with others.

And to the writers of IRWA, OKRWA, and MWW, for the advice and opportunities that made this possible.

Thank you all for taking this journey with me and for sustaining me along the way. Your love, support, and friendship make this all worthwhile.

Prologue

What do you get when you cross an egomaniacal fairy godmother, an arrogant genie, and a couple of wandering plagiarists whose idea of cultural preservation is stealing the stories of unsuspecting villagers and passing them off as their own? If I were tossing back a few shots of Goose with the guys at Ever Afters, I might chuckle at such an intriguing setup for what has all the promise of a hilarious punch line—except the punch line of this little beauty isn't funny at all. 'Cause what you get, my friend, is a pissing contest of epic proportions.

Imagine two individuals with almost limitless power, one-upping each other in an effort to prove whose story is the most exciting and thereby win top billing in the aforementioned compilation of plagiarized tales. When magic starts flying, you never know how the story's going to end even on a good day, but toss in a couple of giant egos and one very bored socialite cheering them on for her own amusement, and, well, you know disaster's coming.

And, man, did it ever.

Although supporters and detractors of each side still hotly debate which party was actually responsible, the result is irrefutable: Nearly two hundred years ago, a spell gone awry cast the characters from the land of Make Believe into the world of Here and Now, leaving us to fend for ourselves in an unfamiliar place with unfamiliar realities.

Some of us adjusted and blended in without too much trouble, living among you as perfectly assimilated and productive members of society. Others . . . well, others of us didn't make the transition so easily and still need a hand now and then. And another stubborn few didn't learn a damn thing from the moral of their own stories and have made it their personal mission to exploit and corrupt on this side.

That's where I come in.

When the Fairytale Management Authority, or FMA, has a problem, they call me. I'm an Enforcer—and a damned good one. You might know me by my fairytale moniker of Little Red Riding Hood. But make no mistake, I'm no longer a kid and I ditched the hood when I was twelve—which was long before my little encounter with the wolf, by the way.

Unfortunately, the nickname stuck and followed me into the Here and Now, giving my brethren with more imposing and creative Tale names the mistaken impression they can push me around—that is, until they pop off one too many times and end up meeting the business end of my fist. Then they know I'm not the sweet little gal with the basket of goodies they've read about.

My name is Tess Little. But everyone calls me Red.

Chapter 1

I'd been watching Dave "Pied Piper" Hamelin for a couple of days, waiting for the right moment to bring him in for his most recent screwup. Dave was a registered sex offender who'd reportedly blown the terms of his parole: no kids, no hookers, no booze. Period. And as an Enforcer for the FMA, it's my job to, well, *enforce* the laws of our kind by any means necessary.

Fortunately, Dave hadn't slipped up on the first condition this time—otherwise some other Enforcer would be hunting me down and dragging my ass in for murder. But, too bad for Dave, when he *did* resurface from a prolonged period of flying under the radar, he was bare-assed and shit-faced at a brothel run by one of my best informants.

One thing you learn in this business—keep your friends close and your informants closer. I'd spent decades forming my network of snitches and knew exactly who to go to when I wanted the best inside information. For people like Dave who couldn't control their more questionable proclivities for very long, Happy Endings was pretty much a foregone conclusion. This wasn't the first time I'd picked up Dave here and probably wouldn't be the last.

I checked my watch, noting the time. Seven o'clock on the

dot. Dave's compulsion for punctuality was legendary—he never missed a deadline and expected the same courtesy in return. Knowing he'd be showing up any second now, I scrunched down a little lower in the seat of my jalopy masquerading as a Range Rover until I could just barely see over the dashboard.

Dave and I'd had a few go-arounds in the past, so I knew he wasn't going to be glad to see me and didn't want him to bolt and go into hiding again. Considering that he owned and operated a successful, environmentally friendly, and totally green pest control business and rarely deviated from his highly ordered life, the guy was surprisingly hard to corner.

Squinting against the setting sun that backlit the building across the street from me, I shook my head in dismay as Dave pulled up to the curb in his BMW. He jauntily hopped out, tossing his keys to the waiting valet.

What a dumb-ass.

You'd think someone who'd spent the last couple hundred years nickel-and-diming it in an FMA prison would be a little more careful, but the fact that he'd been visiting his favorite haunt for a little slap and tickle every night for the past couple of days had made him complacent and sloppy. An idiocy twofer.

Rock on.

I got out of the Rover and hurried across the street, grabbing the keys from the valet and pitching them down the chute of a blue mailbox.

"What the hell, lady?" the shocked, freckle-faced teenager demanded. "I'm going to lose my freaking job!"

I paused midstride and gave the kid a bemused look. *"Freaking?"* I repeated. "Kid, if you're going to start something with me, go big or go home."

He screwed up his face at me as I bolted up the rest of the steps and through the brothel's bright red door. The red door was a bit cliché, sure, but as far as these places went, Happy Endings honestly was about as classy as you could get.

A grumpy looking dwarf—no, really, he's a dwarf, long beard and everything—gave me a nod as I passed through the foyer in search of my pal Dave. Seeing me coming, paranoid patrons skittered back into their alcoves and love dens. Knowing me either by sight or by reputation, they were smart enough to get out of my way as I plowed a path to the fantasy suite where I knew Dave would be getting busy.

I was just reaching for the yawning lion's head doorknob when a buzzing at my hip and a strident melody made me jump. Too late, I realized I'd forgotten to silence the ringer on my cell phone. I cursed under my breath at the unforgivable oversight and reflexively hit the button on the side. But the rustling within the room told me that I wasn't the only one who'd heard it.

"Great," I huffed, leaning away from the door and giving it a powerful kick with my battered and worn combat boot. "So much for surprises."

As the door swung open, I caught a glimpse of Dave's back disappearing out the room's emergency exit. A startled, pigtailed blonde pretending to be half her age hastily gathered the sheet over her bare breasts.

"Sweetie, you do this for a living," I muttered as I rushed toward the back door. "Little late for modesty, don't you think?"

I heard Goldilocks call something in the general direction of my departing, but didn't bother trying to decipher it. Probably nothing I hadn't heard before.

"Come on, Dave!" I hollered into the darkening alley I now traveled, my knees pumping as my boots pounded the pavement. "You know how this is going to end."

I paused to catch my breath and listen for movement. Suddenly, something zipped past my face, startling me into a defensive crouch.

"What the hell?"

Not eager to get myself shot, I drew my own weapon and pressed closer against the bricks, creeping more slowly toward where I could hear Dave's ragged breathing.

"You shooting at me, Dave?" I called out, inching farther along. "You're a jerk and a pedophile, but you're not a murderer. Throw the gun on the ground where I can see it."

"Leave me alone, Red!" came the shaky reply.

"You know the drill, Dave. It's no big deal—"

Another wild shot rang out, ricocheting off the brick and sending up a cloud of red dust.

"Damn it, Dave! Watch what you're doing!"

"I mean it!" he yelled back, his voice taking on an edge of hysteria that made me nervous. "You don't understand, Red. I can't let you take me in!"

"You *know* me, Dave," I said, trying to sound reasonable. "I'll make sure—"

This time when the gun fired, the bullet wasn't for me.

One nice thing about being a former fairytale is that we're damned hard to kill—more or less immortal, really, when it comes to the usual ways of buying the farm—but one thing that's guaranteed to get the job done is a bullet to the brain. And Dave had managed it beautifully.

"Damn it, Dave," I muttered, squatting down beside him. "What the hell scared you this badly?"

"Hey ya, Red."

My head snapped up quickly at the sound of a familiar voice. "Hey, Nate," I said with a grin. "You almost scared me to death."

He threw his head back with a burst of mirth that always seemed at odds with this kind of crime scene, but I guess after so many years of collecting the dead as a Reaper, he'd become desensitized to it all.

Nate Grimm came over in the forties and had been so enamored with the post-WWII era he'd never really left it. Let's just say if he'd suddenly faded to black and white and started doing his own voice-over narration in that world-weary raspy voice of his, I wouldn't have been entirely surprised. I'd never seen him in anything except an impeccably tailored wool suit, simple silk tie, and an overcoat that looked like a prop from *Casablanca*. And the fedora that covered his dark hair was such a permanent fixture, I often found myself debating if the shadows shrouding his handsome face were from the hat or some other, more mysterious source.

Nate was the FMA's top homicide detective and, by virtue of his special talents, always knew when one of us had checked out before you could even call it in. Anybody *that* dialed into death was a shade or two this side of creepy, but still, I couldn't help liking the guy—even if in the back of my mind I knew he'd eventually be coming for me, too. There was just something about him that had always intrigued me.

Chomping his gum with the kind of rabid intensity that defined everything he did, Nate ambled over to Dave's body, hands buried deep in his pockets. For a long moment, he studied the gore at my feet, his thoughts churning almost visibly behind his stoic expression. "Offed himself, huh?"

I nodded, knowing that I was still frowning. "Doesn't make any sense, though," I told him, rising to my feet. "I was only bringing him in for a minor parole violation. Nothing serious. But something had him scared enough to dread going back to prison. Any ideas what he'd be so afraid of?"

Nate's bottomless black eyes flashed briefly with a haunting light as he considered my question and mangled his gum with increased vigor. I could practically see the wheels turning. Then, finally, he shook his head. "Nah. I got nothin'."

"Some detective you are," I taunted, casting a wry grin his way and receiving a handsome, good-natured smile in return.

Nate jerked his head toward my hip. "You gonna get that?"

I'd been so caught up in bantering with Nate I hadn't noticed my phone was ringing again. With a groan at the unwelcome interruption, I snatched up the offending device and glanced at the number before answering.

"Hey, Elizabeth."

"Tess! I'm so delighted to have finally caught you," came the slightly husky, softly accented voice of my best—and pretty much only—girlfriend. "Is this a bad time?"

I tried not to sigh. "Uh, yeah, actually," I admitted, edging back toward the opening of the alley and away from Dave's body. "I'm kind of in the middle of something. I'm really sorry—"

"Not at all," Eliza said quickly. "I had hoped that perhaps you'd like to join me for tea this evening. Or perhaps a glass of wine? Darcy is away on business. . . ."

I glanced over my shoulder to check on the progress of the investigation and was startled to see that Nate had followed me. He stood with his arms crossed, grinning smugly while he watched me struggle with abruptly downshifting to girly mode.

"Uh, sure," I relented. "Yeah. I can come by after I finish here. See you soon."

"How *is* the lovely Mrs. Bennet-Darcy?" Nate asked as I pocketed my phone once more.

"Piss off," I snapped. "You're just jealous she prefers my company to yours."

Nate's laugh burst out again, echoing in the alley. "Perceptive as always, Red. Tell me your secret, or I'll have no choice but to unleash my charm."

Now it was my turn to laugh. "And what charm would that be?"

Nate grabbed my arm and spun me around once, dropping me back into a dancer's dip so swiftly it stole my breath. "The same charm you find so irresistible."

Irresistible?

I'd never really thought so until now as I suddenly found myself knocked off balance and held tightly in the arms of Death himself.

My instinct was to make some smart-ass quip, but as I became very aware of his arms wrapped around me, one hand pressed firmly in the small of my back, I was completely enveloped by him. Every sense soaked him in, making it hard for me to breathe—let alone put together a coherent thought. And when he offered me that mischievous wink of his, my stomach unexpectedly danced a little jig.

What the hell?

Nate wasn't a particularly big guy, even though at an inch or so shy of six feet tall he had a good foot of height on me. But he had the kind of strong, broad shoulders you knew you could count on to back you in a fight and an imposing presence that made everyone wary the minute he walked into a room. Everyone but me, that is. I found his presence comforting, soothing—and, at that moment, incredibly and disconcertingly sexy.

My confusion and bewilderment must have leaked into my expression because Nate's altered as well, becoming far more sober than I'd ever seen. For one crazy, mind-numbing moment, I thought he might actually kiss me.

Fortunately, just as things were getting too weird for my liking, my phone went off again, making us both start and practically jump apart. Still rattled by what had just occurred, I reflexively answered the phone, my eyes never leaving Nate's and noting with surprise what looked like disappointment shining there.

"This is Red."

While I listened to my boss's sharp directive, I followed Nate with my eyes as he returned his attention to the crime scene and began to walk a slow, careful perimeter. A moment later, a nondescript black cargo van pulled up at the end of the alley. Two huge dudes in black suits and sunglasses sprang out to guard the entrance to the alley as the forensics team piled out, their unmarked black equipment cases in hand.

"What do we have, Grimm?" Trish Muffet, the coroner and lead forensics Investigator, pulled on a pair of latex gloves with a no-nonsense snap as she approached. Her buttercup yellow ringlets made her seem a lot mousier than she was, but this gal sure wasn't afraid of spiders anymore. Or anything else, I imagined.

As Nate took Trish on a tour of the scene, I gave myself a mental shake and turned my attention back to the irritated voice on the other end of the line. "Yeah, I heard you," I replied. "I'm on my way."

Deciding to leave them to it and get to headquarters as I'd just been commanded, I hurried off toward my worn and battered Rover, mustering all my resolve to keep from glancing over my shoulder to where I knew Nate was watching me go. I could feel his gaze on me, willing me to turn around. In all the times I'd been around him and all the times we'd worked a crime scene together, I'd never noticed that pull between us, but I sure as hell noticed it now.

I shrugged my shoulders, mentally pushing Nate away. I'd felt that kind of a connection to someone before and knew just how dangerous it could be. No way was I going to put myself through *that* again.

Chapter 2

I always hated going in to headquarters. The glossy black marble floors and one-way glass walls sucked the light out of the air and made me feel claustrophobic. Much like the lives the Tales led among our human brethren, or Ordinaries, our law enforcement agency was shrouded in secrecy and shadows.

Blend in. Avoid suspicion. Act human. That was the warning drilled into each Tale after crossing over, and the building's lack of personality was a perfect reflection of this doctrine. In fact, if it weren't for the pixie couriers flitting between offices delivering field intelligence, you would've thought you were in your average, run-of-the-mill, secret government installation.

But it wasn't just the ominous decor that made me twitchy. I preferred to be out on the road, doing my thing and bringing in the bad guys, not sitting in some office, dealing with bureaucrats and politicians as they argued about jurisdictions and budgets and whatever else happened to be the issue of the day.

Apparently, today's issue was more serious than the usual fare, if the hushed tones of conversation and studiously averted gazes were any indication. Not one person I passed was willing to look me in the eye. I certainly didn't have a lot of friends within the FMA, but I wasn't usually the leper I seemed to be today.

If the silent treatment in the hallways hadn't tipped me off that something was up, the Chief's scowl when I entered his office certainly would have done the job.

FMA Chief Director Al Addin was a menacing SOB even on a good day, but today he was flat-out frightening. I was betting whoever had pissed in his Post Toasties that morning had received one serious ass-chewing.

Al was a damned good Investigator and had worked tire-lessly to turn the FMA into what it was today. Considering it was his genie involved in the little kerfuffle that'd landed us in the Here and Now, he felt like he owed it to the rest of us to bring some sort of order to the chaos of our abrupt reloca-tion. Unfortunately, it was a never-ending struggle that had cost him his fortune, his marriage, and his peace of mind. And yet he dragged his ass into work every day to make sure that the rest of us had a chance to live free and happy where fate had tossed us.

That's why I respected the hell out of him. As long as he continued to pay me better than he should have without grumbling too much about the occasional mess I made, I figured the least I could do was put up with a trip to the office every now and then.

"Rough day?" Al grumbled with a scowl as I dropped into the leather chair across the desk from him.

"You have no idea," I muttered, flipping a thick lock of ebony hair over my shoulder and propping my cherry red combat boots on his desk.

(What? The *boots*? Hey, if I'm going to be saddled with the moniker anyway, I might as well rock it right. Besides, a cherry red leather trench coat, while wicked cool, was a bit im-practical in my line of work. Too visible. Mine's black, natch.)

Al's brows lifted a bit. "Oh, I think I might. Get your boots off my desk."

I dropped my feet back onto the floor. "Listen, Al, there was nothing I could do. Dave has never carried a weapon in all the years I've known him. I had no idea he—"

"This isn't about Hamelin's suicide," Al interrupted.

Now it was my turn to be surprised. "It's not?"

Al leaned back in his chair, his already dusky features seeming to grow darker. "We have a problem."

"When *don't* we have a problem?" I joked, trying to lighten his mood and make myself feel better at the same time.

It didn't work.

Al opened a drawer and pulled out a manila folder that he then handed to me. "Take a look."

Warily, I peeked inside and quickly flipped through the crime scene photos, my gut clenching at the violence and gore captured in startlingly vivid detail.

I can't pretend I wasn't disturbed by the carnage I saw in those eight-by-ten glossies. The victims had been ripped apart, savagely mutilated. It wasn't the aftermath of your average mugging gone wrong or even your run-of-the-mill contract hit or crime of passion. I'd seen plenty of those, trust me. No, this was far more personal. There was a rage behind it that was animalistic, inhuman.

"What am I looking at here?" I asked, my voice quivering in spite of my best efforts to seem unaffected.

Al leaned forward, placing his elbows on the desk pad. "Four Tales have been murdered in the last thirty days. There wasn't much left for us to examine, but from what we can tell, they were all killed by the same person."

I glanced up at him in surprise. "A serial killer?"

Al nodded solemnly. "Looks that way."

I pulled out one of the photos and looked at the victim more closely. After a moment, I realized it had once been a man and not a Jackson Pollock gone awry. I cleared my throat of the bile rising there. "Who were these people?"

"Minor characters for the most part." Al took the photos

from my hands and spread them out on his desk. "Julie Spangle," he said, pointing to the first. "She had a bit role in a Restoration Comedy in the sixteen hundreds. She'd been trying to break into the theater scene here in town but was waiting tables to get by."

I scooted to the edge of my seat to get a better look as Al tapped the second photo.

"This one is Dale Minnows. He was an unnamed sailor in *Moby-Dick*. Made a fortune in shipping since coming over but had become a complete recluse over the last couple of years." He slid the third photo forward. "Sarah Dickerson. Ms. Dickerson was the maid in "Sing a Song of Sixpence" and stayed in domestic service after she came over a couple of years ago. She was dropping off dry cleaning for her employer when she was attacked."

I picked up the fourth picture—the one that had nearly made me retch just a moment before. "And this guy?"

"Probably the only name you'll recognize—Alfred Simon."

"Simple Simon?" I said, tossing the photo back onto the pile. "Poor little guy. Last I heard he was holding down a good job delivering soda to restaurants or something. Who'd want to hurt him?"

Al shook his head. "We don't know why anyone would want to hurt any of these victims. There's no discernible connection between them."

"Has anyone talked to the families? Employers? Friends?" I asked.

"They can't give any reasons, either."

"Wrong place, wrong time?"

Al shrugged. "That's what we need to find out."

"Any suspects?"

He took a sudden interest in the notepad on his desk as he replied, "A few."

"What about a murder weapon?"

"Claws," he said, his tone sounding almost apologetic. "Massive blood loss." When he looked back up at me, I was surprised to see true regret behind his expression. "I'm really sorry, Red."

He was *sorry*? Oh, I *seriously* didn't like where he was going with this.

"Any number of creatures could have done this," I insisted, waving my hand toward the pictures. "What about the Jabberwocky? That guy's a certifiable lunatic. Last time I brought him in, he was sucking out goat brains in rural Texas and scaring the hell out of the locals who swore up and down they were being attacked by a chupacabra. As I recall, you had a fun time trying to spin that one. Coyotes with mange, was it?"

"Jabberwocky's still safely in the Asylum," Al assured me, ignoring my acidic tone.

I ran a hand through my hair in frustration and let the heavy locks fall loosely over my shoulders. "What about one of the witches? There are loads of those twisted sisters who could have pulled off something like this using a ritual or a curse."

Al opened his palms to me in a gesture of sympathy. "I already had forensics test the bodies. There's no indication that magic was used to commit the murders remotely."

Now I was just getting pissed off. "How do we even know it's one of *ours*? There were some pretty crazy things hanging out in the Here and Now long before we showed up. What about that Sasquatch guy we dragged in for questioning last year? What was his name? Phil Something. He really rubbed me the wrong way—shifty eyes."

Al sighed but didn't respond, letting me work through everything in my head until I came around to the same conclusion he had. I wasn't quite there yet.

"And what about an Ordinary? They've had their own fair

share of sickos," I reminded him. "Jack the Ripper, Belle Gunness, H. H. Holmes, Jeffrey Dahmer . . ."

"All dead, which you well know. Besides, the Ordinaries have no reason to target us this way." Al's stony expression softened a little and his voice was quiet when he said, "This was an inside job."

"Says you."

"Red—"

"Who found the bodies?"

Al sighed again, apparently willing to indulge me for the moment. "You know who."

"Nate."

Al nodded, then steepled his fingers, looking like an Arabian Sigmund Freud as he leveled his gaze at me. "Nate Grimm would be a damned good detective even without being a Reaper," he reminded me. "You know he doesn't make the kinds of mistakes you were about to suggest."

Al knew me all too well. And, apparently, Nate knew me better than I'd thought. The little dance number in the alley now made perfect sense. He'd been playing me—probably hoping his so-called charm would cushion the blow of the bombshell he was about to drop.

"We need you to bring in the suspects for questioning," Al continued, interrupting the progress of my rapidly growing grudge. "That's all it is for now."

I gritted my back teeth, knowing who would be top on their list without even asking.

I'd told Al that any number of creatures could have committed the murders, but that wasn't entirely true. As much as I liked to think there was a hoard of potential suspects, I had to admit only a few consistently came to mind as I sat there mulling it over. And one of them was Seth "Big Bad" Wolf—the man I'd thought was my Happily Ever After.

I'd been wrong about that, so it was possible I was wrong

about this, too. After all, I'd seen Seth defend himself against a lynch mob of angry villagers and come out of it without so much as a scratch, so I knew firsthand the kind of damage a cornered werewolf could do. But my intuition told me there was no way in hell Seth had committed the murders.

And Al *had* said "suspects," I reminded myself. Plural. More than one. So even though he and Nate had probably already convinced themselves Seth was their guy, they were at least keeping their options open.

I couldn't fathom what would have made Seth—or anyone else—go on a killing spree this savage. But someone had. Someone with a serious ax to grind.

Fortunately, it wasn't up to me to figure out a motive. I'd leave that part to Detective Twinkle-Toes. All I had to do was round up the suspects. Then I could just walk away.

Well, that's what I told myself anyway.

"Okay," I said, holding out my hand to receive the assignments. "Give me what you've got."

Al handed over three thick files. I didn't even bother looking at them as I rose stiffly.

"Red," Al called out, bringing me to a halt as I strode to the door. "I need this one over before the Ordinaries catch wind of it. Something like this could destroy everything we've built here."

I paused, staring at the floor so he wouldn't see the emotions raging war inside me. "I understand, sir."

"Sir?" Al repeated. "You never call me 'sir.'"

I attempted a saucy smile. "First time for everything."

Al let out a long sigh and pushed back from his desk. Knowing what was coming, I tried to open the door and make my escape before he could offer any friendly advice, but he was there with his hand pressing the door closed before I could open it more than a crack.

"I know this one isn't going to be easy," he said gently.

"But you're the best Enforcer I've got. I need to know you're on this."

I didn't immediately respond.

"Red?"

"Yeah," I snapped, wrenching open the door and knocking his hand away. "I'm on it."

Chapter 3

I put on my best Don't Fuck with Me scowl when I left Al's office and kept my head down so I wouldn't have to see all the pitying and anxious looks my colleagues gave me as I barreled down the hallway. It was taking all my restraint not to run toward the nearest exit to escape those stifling corridors as it was—the last thing I wanted was for someone to try to strike up a conversation that might seem well-meaning but was more about getting the latest gossip.

Besides, there was something about this case that was making my skin crawl with apprehension . . . and it wasn't just the prospect of having to haul in my former lover. The whole thing just didn't feel right.

I liked to think I had my ear pretty close to the ground when it came to these kinds of things, but I hadn't heard anything lately that was out of the ordinary. If someone was harboring a grudge this powerful, he was keeping it well hidden. No easy task, I imagine. Hatred that potent has a way of spilling out at the most inconvenient times. Which meant eventually he'd slip up and give himself away. And I'd be right there to drag his ass to jail.

"Another job well done, Red. Bra-*vo*."

Speaking of barely restrained hatred . . .

I stiffened immediately at the one voice that could get my hackles up in an instant. Forcing a smile that felt grotesque on my lips, I turned around and batted my eyes innocently.

"Well, if it isn't Mistress Mary Quite Contrary," I drawled, infusing my voice with my own special blend of syrupy sweetness and pointed disdain. "My visit wouldn't have been complete without bumping into you. Tell me, how *does* your garden grow?"

Mary "Quite Contrary" Smith was so named for a reason. She was the most condescending, abrasive, ball-busting bitch I'd ever met. She also happened to be the FMA's prosecuting attorney and had a hard-on for making me look bad at every opportunity. What was most irritating, though, was that she managed it with the kind of cold, calculating finesse that almost made me want to thank her for the effort.

A little more salt for my wound? Why, yes, thank you— don't mind if I do. Could you give that knife another twist while you're back there? Perfect!

Funny thing was, if I hadn't hated her so much I think we might've actually been friends.

Mary looked down at me from her statuesque height, peering over the top of her naughty librarian glasses to make sure I realized that she was far superior to me—from her perfectly coiffed golden tresses to the tips of her six-hundred-dollar Manolo Blahniks.

"Original as ever," Mary sneered. "Your sense of humor's as stale as your sense of style."

Ouch. That one hurt. I live in jeans and combat boots—so sue me. It's a little hard to do my job in a business suit, no matter what you see on TV. And running in heels? *Please.*

"So, did you stop just to chat about my inability to accessorize," I asked, keeping my expression mildly bored, "or did you actually have something worth saying?"

Mary looked like she would've liked to punch me in the face, but she was far too poised and professional to give in to her baser urges, which was lucky for me. Don't get me wrong—I had no doubt I could wipe the floor with her pretty little buns of steel, but after she picked herself up off the floor she would have had me behind bars in a fairytale minute. And as much as I love to invite authority to bite my ass, I couldn't deny that being stuck in the clink with the very people I hunted might be a bit . . . *awkward.*

"I just wanted to congratulate you on killing yet another criminal," Mary oozed. "What does this make now—four this year?"

Okay, so sometimes things get a little rough when I'm picking up a mark. Tales can get a bit panicky when faced with being confined again after having had a taste of freedom from the stories that'd held them prisoner for so long. Unfortunately, panic makes people stupid, and I really can't be responsible for the ones whose extra dose of dumb-ass sends them running at me with a gun or a knife. That's why there's a "dead or alive" clause in my employment contract. But, honestly, considering how many criminals I bring in every year, my track record really isn't so bad.

"Only three," I informed her. "Suicides don't count. This one wasn't my fault."

Mary's crimson lips twitched at the corners as if she could barely restrain her derisive amusement. "Oh, I don't know," she drawled. "From what I hear, men who come in contact with you have a way of meeting rather bad ends."

My eyes narrowed. "What's that supposed to mean?"

"Have you looked at your most recent assignment?"

Well, no, actually I *hadn't.* It really didn't matter. I'd bring them in, regardless; it was my job. But something about Mary's smirk was enough to make me want to put my hands around her pretty little throat and squeeze. Hard.

"Sorry to steal your thunder," I bit out, my fist clenching at my side to keep it in check, "but I already know Seth Wolf is a suspect."

Mary laughed mockingly as she turned on her stiletto heel and headed toward the elevators. "He's not the only one," she tossed over her shoulder. "It should be quite a lovely trip down memory lane."

The elevator doors slid open in perfect dramatic timing, allowing her to slip inside before I could ask any more questions. But, apparently, *she* wasn't quite finished. Her beautifully manicured hand caught the edge of the elevator door, bouncing it back just long enough for her to stick her head out and offer me a final parting shot.

"Oh—and, Red? Do try to bring in your boyfriends alive—it's not nearly as entertaining to prosecute a corpse."

Boyfriends?

Frowning, I looked down at the thick folders I held in my arms, fanning them out so I could see all the names. A horrible, sinking feeling in the pit of my stomach made me want to hurl—not something I do as a general rule. But Mary wasn't kidding.

Memory lane? Try highway to hell.

"Son of a bitch."

"I hope you're not talking about anyone I know."

I turned the full ferocity of my glare upon Nate as he sidled up to me, which wasn't completely fair, but I was pissed, he was there, and—abracadabra!—instant scapegoat.

"I wasn't," I hissed, punching the elevator button, "but I could be."

Nate moved closer to me, ducking his head a little. "What are you talking about?"

"Thanks for the heads-up," I replied, punching the button several times in rapid succession in case it hadn't gotten the message the first time. "Was that the reason for the little dance number earlier tonight? Trying to distract me from the fact you were about to screw me over?"

Nate jerked slightly at my harsh accusation. "What? What the hell are you talking about?"

"You know exactly what I'm talking about," I shot back. *Punch, punch, punch, punch.*

Nate blinked at me in dismay. "I wish I did. Then I'd be able to defend myself."

What the hell was the deal with the elevator, anyway? It'd been more than obliging for Mary's dramatic exit but was totally ruining mine. Kind of tough to pull off the whole righteous indignation thing when you can't storm off.

Exasperated and annoyed, I cursed under my breath, abandoning the elevator and darting around Nate toward the stairway. I heard him close on my heels as I made the first landing and was just about to take the next set of steps when he grabbed my arm, bringing me up short.

"Want to tell me what this is about?" he asked, his body crowding mine.

I shoved the folders into his chest, forcing him to take them. "You tell me."

Nate's glance flicked down at the files as if he already knew what they were. He confirmed my suspicion when he said nothing in response, just looked at me with a slightly contrite expression.

"Seth Wolf. Vlad Dracula. Todd Caliban," I said, pointing to each of the folders in turn. "Anyone else from my past you want to target? There are a couple of other guys I've slept with who didn't make the list. Want me to bring in Achilles? Maybe Charlie d'Artagnan?"

A muscle in Nate's jaw twitched and his eyes seemed to darken slightly. I'd never seen Nate pissed off, but I had a feeling I was getting close. "Wolf and Dracula were the only two with records of this kind of violence," he countered. "And Caliban's a known hothead with violent tendencies. But, hey, you know Achilles and Charlie better than I do, so maybe we *should* bring them in, just to be on the safe side."

"Go to hell, Nate."

Nate shrugged. "Been there. It's not that exciting."

With a huff, I brushed past him and started down the stairs again, not surprised to hear him still following. "Why them?" I called out. "Why not one of the other monsters creeping around in the shadows? It's not like there's a shortage."

There was a slight pause before I heard Nate sigh. The next instant he was in front of me on the landing, blocking my path. His sudden appearance startled me, making me stumble backward.

"Damn it! Don't do that!"

Nate held out the folders, ignoring my rebuke. "These murders are the worst I've seen in a long time, Tess—"

Ah, hell, he was using my real name. This was *serious.*

"—I need to find the person responsible as soon as possible. And I need your help."

I shook my head, completely confused by his logic. "So, you pulled your primary suspects from my little black book?"

"You've got it backward," he explained. "They really are the most likely suspects, but if you can help me clear them, great—I'll cross them off my short list and we can figure out who's really behind these murders."

"I'm an Enforcer," I reminded him, "not an Investigator. And I work alone."

"Maybe it's time to change that."

I studied Nate for a long moment, taking in every nuance of his chiseled features and wondering what else he wasn't telling me. "Knowing my personal history with these three suspects, wouldn't someone else be a better choice?"

Nate shook his head slowly. "Nope," he said with a grin, the familiar, flirty tone coming back into his voice. "You're the only one for me."

I rolled my eyes. "Come on, Nate."

Nate's expression sobered once more. "Fine. The truth? I asked the Chief to put you on this one. You can get to these guys easier than I can. People tend to panic when Death shows up on their doorstep. I'd rather not have any bloodshed bringing them in."

"Did you forget about what happened earlier tonight?" I asked, averting my eyes in embarrassment. "Bloodshed and me, we're kind of going hand in hand lately."

There was a whisper of motion and I suddenly found myself staring up into Nate's eyes again, my chin held in his grasp. "You help me solve these murders, Red, and I promise we'll get to the bottom of Dave Hamelin's suicide."

Chapter 4

After Nate and I parted ways in the parking garage, I checked my watch and cursed under my breath. I'd planned to make a quick stop in the office, then head over to Elizabeth's, but all the drama had taken quite a bit longer than anticipated and it was now pushing ten o'clock. Still, my conscience nagging me, I gave Eliza a call as I pulled out into the nightlife traffic. I wasn't entirely surprised to find her still awake.

"Sorry for the delay," I told her sincerely. "Do you still want some company?"

"Of course!" she said eagerly. "Shall I brew the tea or uncork the wine?"

"Wine," I said firmly. "Definitely the wine."

"That sounds rather ominous."

Dear Elizabeth—perceptive as always. "You have no idea," I informed her. "I'll tell you all about it when I get there."

Fortunately, Eliza's house was nestled in one of the elite neighborhoods of Chicago's North Shore and so wasn't that far a drive from headquarters. Twenty minutes later, I was standing in her foyer, finding myself the recipient of Eliza's warm embrace.

No matter how often we saw each other, Eliza had a way

of making me feel like she had desperately missed me while we were apart and couldn't wait to hear all about the events of my life.

As I followed my friend into her favorite sitting room, I was struck as always by the tasteful yet opulent decor of the Darcy home and how perfectly it reflected Elizabeth's personality—warm, open, comforting, but exhibiting just enough sass to make it interesting without being pretentious. The moment I curled up on my favorite sofa I had in my hand what I knew would be a fabulous glass of Pinot Noir. As soon as Elizabeth had procured her own glass, she nestled into the opposite corner of the sofa, her dark eyes sparkling with excitement.

"Rough day, dearest?" she asked with a grin as I took a long draft of my wine.

Yep, it was just as good as I'd imagined.

I laughed a little, in spite of how I felt. "You could say that." I took another sip, smaller this time, then let out a long sigh. "One of my marks committed suicide on me tonight."

Elizabeth's lovely face contorted into a concerned frown. "Are you all right?"

Leave it to Elizabeth to be more concerned about my well-being than the details of the story. It was moments like these that reminded me why we were friends.

I nodded, staring down at my wine. "It doesn't make sense, though," I told her. "He was scared to death of being taken in—literally, as it turns out. What would make a person so afraid that he'd take his own life?"

"I'm sure I don't know," Elizabeth told me gently. "But I *do* know that if anyone can discover the truth, it's you."

"That's just how the night *started*," I told her before draining my glass. Without even asking, Elizabeth got up and poured me another. As soon as I was holding the next installment, I continued, "Right after you called I got another call from Al at headquarters, requesting my presence in his office posthaste."

Eliza's brows rose just enough to indicate her surprise. "Oh?"

I let my head drop back against the cushions as I sank lower into the couch. "There's a series of murders the FMA's investigating and they want me to bring in the three main suspects."

"That's not so unusual, is it?" Elizabeth asked, resting her chin on the palm of her hand, waiting for my response.

I shook my head a little, wishing I could tell her more specifics. "No," I replied, "not so unusual. It's just a tough case."

"I imagine so."

We sat in silence for a long while, sipping our wine and listening to the fire in the fireplace crackle, the occasional pop enough to keep me from dozing off in the warm glow of firelight and friendship. Then I heard Eliza's barely perceptible sigh and sat up straighter, suddenly realizing what a lousy friend I was.

"How are *you*?" I asked, feeling guilty for not asking sooner. "Is everything okay?"

Elizabeth gave me a tight smile. "Mmm-hmm. I love being in the Here and Now," she said rather whimsically.

"But?"

"But Darcy . . ."

"Still not adjusting so well?" I filled in.

She shook her head, confirming my suspicions. "I thought it would get easier. . . . It really has been wonderful for us—thanks in large part to the Character Relocation Bureau. Darcy has been very happy with his firm, we have a beautiful home, wonderful friends . . . but he still misses our former life."

"And what about you?" I prompted.

Eliza dropped her eyes briefly, trying to hide the tears that

I knew would be there. After a moment, she looked up to offer me a sad smile. "I miss Jane," she admitted. "Some days I can hardly bear it." She laughed a little through her sorrow and wiped at her cheek, brushing away one of the few tears that had managed to escape. "I even miss Lydia and all of her ridiculous antics. Can you imagine?"

I reached over and gave her hand a squeeze. "Yes, I can."

We've never been able to figure out why some characters come over and others don't. At first, it was just us Fairytales who were affected by the magical duel. But then the Literary and Nursery Rhyme characters began to migrate over— sometimes individually or in pairs, other times en masse.

Elizabeth and Darcy had the good fortune to come over together in the Lit Migration of 2000. They were lucky. Random migrations have shattered the romances of many loving fictional couples over the years. Unfortunately for Darcy and Elizabeth, none of the others from their story joined them—a loss Eliza still mourned and I suspected Darcy did as well.

Eliza's way to cope with the loss of all she had ever known was to embrace her new circumstances, to throw herself into the Here and Now with the same zest for life she had exhibited in the pages of her story. She was beautiful, witty, intelligent, and had the added benefit of her story's enduring popularity among the Ordinaries, who never seemed to run out of ideas for sequels and adaptations for Eliza—a fact that made her the envy of all Tale society. Everyone wanted to know her, be near her, and claim her as a friend.

Darcy, on the other hand, had retreated to his former reserve, unsure how to relate to the twenty-first century and unable to embrace their new life with the same eagerness as his wife. He had enjoyed a tremendous amount of success with his business ventures; having a quick mind and what seemed to be a sixth sense for the ups and downs of the Ordinaries' stock markets had netted him a fortune within a very short time of their migration. But Darcy was a man of his times—cultured, mannered, proud—the very essence of British aristocracy, and as such had a difficult time accepting the ways of contemporary America.

His disdain for modern culture notwithstanding, I had seen the way his eyes sparked with love and desire the moment his beloved walked into a room, and was a little envious of that kind of undying affection. In spite of all their losses, they could at least find comfort in the unshakable love they shared.

"He'll come around," I assured her. "You might just have to nudge him in the right direction."

She gave me a glance that clearly conveyed her doubt. "I fear he does not approve of my more modern ways. I am no longer certain my influence would be eagerly accepted."

"Have you tried including him in some of your activities that are important to you?"

Eliza nodded. "Yes, but he does not share my activist spirit."

"What about something with your kids?" I suggested. "I thought you told me William is going to be starting Little League in the spring. How about that?"

Elizabeth chuckled. "I cannot see Darcy coaching base-ball, I am afraid."

She had a point.

"You'll find your common ground," I assured her confidently. "You two were meant to be together."

"I have always thought so," Elizabeth said with a grin.

I laughed, which was exactly what she had intended. "No, you haven't!"

Playful and teasing now that her fears had been allayed, she laughed with me. "Well, perhaps I had my doubts in the beginning, but I saw the error of my ways." She cast me a searching glance, her eyes sparkling with mischief. "And what of you, my dearest friend? When shall you find the one with whom you are meant to spend eternity?"

I groaned and melodramatically rolled my eyes, as was my typical response. "Eternity?" I repeated. "I'd settle for Saturday night!"

I was gratified to hear my friend's rich laughter but was more than a little surprised when her question brought to mind the image of a certain homicide detective whose dark eyes still haunted me hours later when I finally drifted to sleep.

Chapter 5

I awoke the next day to the wonderful aroma of cinnamon rolls and bacon—and nearly hurled. Wine and I as a rule don't mix so well, but I can never turn it down when it comes as a token of Eliza's hospitality. Maybe one day I'll figure out how to tell her I prefer a good Irish stout or a shot of Goose to the fruit of the vine. In the meantime, my stomach and I were going to have a serious conversation about the evils of fermented grapes from Burgundy.

"Red? Red, my darling?"

I cautiously opened one eye just enough to see the still-stunning silver-haired woman standing in my doorway, then closed it again. On a good day, my eyes were robin's egg blue, but considering the way my head was pounding, I was guessing they were pretty shot with red today. With a groan, I rolled over so that my back was to her cheerful smile. "Go away," I grumbled. "It's too early."

"Pish posh." Gran laughed, gliding into my room and leaving an aromatic trail of jasmine in her wake, which in combination with the cinnamon rolls and bacon brought a whole new level to my agony. "It's already half past seven, my dear."

"Seven?" I mumbled into my pillow. "I've only been asleep for four hours."

Gran gave my rump a swat as she strolled by on her way to my bedroom window. With a quick *swish* she pulled open the curtains, letting the early morning sun assault me. "Rise and shine!"

"Oh, come on!" I protested, burying my face in my pillow. I heard Gran's exasperated sigh, then her jaunty steps as she exited the room. The smell of jasmine began to dissipate, so I risked lifting my head only to see her standing in the doorway once more, arms crossed, her brows raised expectantly.

I let my head drop back down for a moment but then forced myself into a sitting position. Guess it was time to get up whether I liked it or not. I ran my hands through my tousled hair and blinked several times, trying to get my bearings. "Don't you need to be at work?"

Gran's lips parted in an affectionately amused smile. "Don't you?"

I glowered at her. "No."

Gran laughed. "Well, now that you're awake you might as well get moving."

I looked at her with one eye—the other had managed to close again on the sly—and realized she was already in her best suit and makeup, ready to head in to the office. "Who are your guests today?" I asked, hoping that trying to carry on a conversation would force my brain into activity.

Gran's eyes lit up. "Pete and Wendy Panella! Can you believe it?"

My brows shot up. "Seriously?"

Even though I was still half asleep, the magnitude of such famous guests on Gran's television show didn't slip by me. Matilda "Gran" Stuart was something of a celebrity in her own right among the Tales. After we came over, she'd discovered a whole new side to herself, a creativity and sense of unique style that soon made her a highly regarded expert in all things domestic.

Her skills in the kitchen became legendary and eventually branched off into a very successful series of cookbooks, a line of cookware, a home decor business, and now her own talk show, which, in addition to giving tips on how to create the perfect flan or Christmas wreath, featured Tale celebrity guests. Gran was a natural when it came to hosting her own show—there were days when she had the entire studio audience in tears as they listened to some poor character's struggle with adjusting and his subsequent rise to glory and success. She made Ordinary talk show queens look like two-bit hacks.

"How did you manage to get Pete and Wendy?" I asked, my mouth finally catching up to my brain.

The Panellas had come over in the seventies and had had a more difficult time than most. Not only were they completely uprooted but they'd also had to deal with finally growing up. In the end they'd come through okay, eventually married, and after changing their last name—something about copyright infringement—they'd managed to channel their experiences into business ventures that skyrocketed them to success.

Pete was now a motivational speaker, traveling the world and giving seminars to Ordinaries and Tales alike on how age was all a state of mind, and Wendy owned an upscale chain of day care centers that had revolutionized childcare. Getting them to drop by the studio for a sob session on Gran's couch was quite a coup.

"Let's just say I pulled a few strings," Gran said with a wink. "Now, come on—you need to come down and eat your brunch. It's getting cold. And that nice gentleman from the FMA has already eaten, so you don't want to keep him waiting too long."

I straightened in surprise, fully awake now. "What? What nice gentleman?"

"You know," Gran said, her hand fluttering as if my question were an insect making an aerial assault. "The dark and mysterious one. What's his name?"

My already sensitive stomach clenched tightly. I felt my control over its contents beginning to slip as I realized who she meant. "Nate Grimm?"

"Yes!" Gran replied, turning on her heel. "That's the one."

I threw the covers back and stormed down the stairs, brushing past Gran in my fury. I charged into the kitchen, fully expecting to light into Nate about barging into my house—okay, well, not technically *my* house, but still—but when I saw him I slid to a halt, briefly wondering if I'd wandered into a parallel dimension.

Nate had discarded his omnipresent suit jacket and fedora in exchange for one of Gran's pink frilly aprons with a creepily cheery gingerbread man embroidered on the front. His shirt sleeves were rolled up to the elbow, revealing muscled forearms and intricately drawn tribal-style tattoos that were completely out of sorts with the girly cooking attire.

When he heard me come in, he turned away from where he was scrambling eggs with peppers and onions and offered me a wide smile. "Good morning, sunshine," he called over his shoulder.

I intended to stun him with a witty comeback that started with *Piss* and ended with *Off,* but before I got the chance, he added, "Breakfast will be ready in a sec. I hope you like your eggs loaded. I didn't figure you for a cinnamon roll kind of girl, but Gran insisted I whip some up when she heard my recipe."

I blinked at him, now certain about my alternate reality theory. "What the hell are you doing here?"

Nate added some shredded cheese to his concoction and

gently folded the eggs a couple of times before responding, "Thought we'd get an early start."

I hopped up onto one of the stools nestled around the kitchen bar and gave him a wary look. "Start on what exactly?"

"I figured we'd drop in on Wolf," he said. "Get it out of the way."

I felt my stomach flop ominously. Probably just the hangover. "He's nocturnal," I muttered. "Maybe we should wait until later in the day."

"Or we can catch him unawares so he doesn't run," he rejoined.

I bristled a little at his tone. "Seth won't run."

Nate shrugged. "Because he has a history of sticking it out when things get rough?"

"Fine," I snapped, having to admit he had a point. "But he's not the guy."

"So you keep saying. As soon as he's cleared, we'll move on to Caliban."

Nate scooped the eggs onto a plate and arranged a few slices of crisp bacon, perfectly toasted sourdough, and a sprig of parsley around them before setting the lot in front of me.

I stared down at the beautifully arranged food before me and wondered if I should eat it or take a picture of it. My stomach grumbled in spite of its queasiness, which really left only one option. I shoveled a bite of eggs into my mouth and had to stop myself from moaning with delight as Nate set out a glass of freshly squeezed orange juice.

"So what do you think?" he asked, studying me in that über-intense way of his.

"I think Caliban can be an arrogant, foul-tempered asshole," I mumbled around my eggs, "but I don't think he's your perp, either."

Nate laughed. "Not what I meant. The breakfast—do you like it?"

I swallowed, lifting my face from the trough—uh, *plate*—and meeting his gaze. "Yeah, it's great. Thanks."

He gave me a wink and went back to the stove, gathering up the frying pans and utensils and loading them into the dishwasher. Bemused by the decidedly surreal experience, I continued eating and was just polishing off the last of the most delicious cinnamon roll I'd ever consumed when Gran came bustling in.

"Well, I'm off!" she cried cheerily, her cheeks aglow with excitement. "Wish me luck, my darlings!"

Darlings? Plural?

Nate hastily dried his hands on the edge of his apron and shook Gran's hand warmly. "Best of luck, Tilly—"

Tilly?

"—I'm sure your interview will go swell."

Swell?

Gran tittered like a schoolgirl, blushing at Nate's encouragement, then good-naturedly batted at his shoulder. "Oh, Detective, if all my audience was as kind as you, I would never worry about ratings!"

Dear God, it was a morning-person conspiracy.

I groaned at their chipper banter, my nausea returning with a vengeance. "You two are insane."

Gran cast an amused glance at Nate, then came around the bar to smother my face in grandmotherly kisses in spite of my best efforts to dodge her.

"Good luck with your investigation, Red, my dear!" she called as she bustled out of the kitchen once again. "See you tonight!"

I shook my head and turned back around only to find Nate leaning on the counter, his wide smile a little too blinding and cheerful for my sleep-numb brain. "So, you ready to get going?" he asked. "Need to get dressed, take a shower or anything?"

Suddenly aware that I hadn't bothered to make myself

presentable before storming downstairs in nothing but a T-shirt, I felt my face growing warm. I ran a hand through my tangled hair and slid from the bar stool, my legs feeling extremely bare and exposed. "Um, yeah," I stuttered. "I'm going to head back upstairs." I tugged the hem of my shirt down a little, making sure it covered my ass, then took a couple awkward steps backward. "You go ahead and make some coffee or something. I'll, uh, be back in a bit."

As I made my way up the stairs, I heard the coffeemaker grinding the beans and had to smile in spite of myself. A girl could get used to being waited on hand and foot, especially if the one doing the waiting was as drop-dead gorgeous as Nate (no pun intended).

And if his coffee was as good as his cinnamon rolls, I could almost forgive him for being insufferably cheery before noon.

Almost.

Chapter 6

I took another sip of my coffee—which was perfect, damn it all—then cast an angry glance at Nate. "I still don't see why we couldn't take my Range Rover."

"Are you still mad about that?" he asked. "No offense, Red, but I know what they pay you at the FMA. You could afford a better car."

"I don't *want* a better car," I insisted. "That Rover has gotten me out of a jam more than once. I know it's not great to look at, but I've never had to worry about getting stuck in a bog."

"Because we have so many bogs in Chicago . . ." Nate grinned.

I rolled my eyes. "Fine. How about snow? There's no shortage of snow."

Nate sighed, his patience with my petulance apparently wearing thin. "Like I said, when we're on official business for the FMA, I'm supposed to be in my unmarked. Besides, call me old-fashioned, but I think the guy should drive."

"I'll call you a pig for that one," I told him.

Nate grunted.

"Anyway," I went on, "can't you just do that swoosh thing? Why do you even need to drive a car?"

"I don't do that unless it's necessary," he said. "It tends to make people uneasy."

"Tell me about it," I mumbled. When I glanced over at him, he was staring straight ahead, his expression dark even for him.

He shrugged a little and rolled his head, then reached into the breast pocket of his jacket and withdrew a pack of chewing gum. He pulled out a foil-wrapped stick and offered it to me. "Want any? It's spearmint."

"No thanks." I shook my head, wishing I could get up in his head. The guy was a total mystery to me—and not just because he had the whole Death thing going for him. I had the distinct impression that Nate Grimm was a many-layered persona that covered for someone no one really knew.

After a few minutes of dedicated mastication, Nate said, "So, you want to tell me where we're headed?"

I shifted in my seat and took another sip of my coffee before answering. "He's probably still asleep, so we can try his apartment."

Nate took out his phone and started dialing a number. "I'll have headquarters text me his address."

"Don't need to."

Nate's brows lifted. "You already looked it up?"

I squirmed again, squinting against the early March sunlight even through my shades. "I find people for a living," I reminded him. "I've known Seth's whereabouts since we came over."

"Ah."

My head snapped around. "What's that supposed to mean?"

Nate shrugged. "Nothing."

"Listen," I said, turning in my seat to face him, "there's nothing wrong with looking after someone I cared about once upon a time."

"I didn't say there was." He gave me a bemused look like

he didn't know why I was being so defensive. Or maybe I was just projecting.

"I just want to make sure he's doing okay," I explained, "that he's not in any trouble."

Nate nodded. "Sure."

I studied his profile for a few seconds, trying to figure out if he was being serious or just being an ass. When I realized he was on the level, I said in a much calmer tone, "By the way, turn right up here at the light."

Nate dutifully followed my directions, then drove in silence for several minutes before asking, "So, how long's it been since you've actually talked to the guy?"

I shrugged. "Not since our story."

"Not a word?"

I shook my head.

Nate cleared his throat a couple of times, then said, "You realize he's probably not the same guy anymore, right? I mean, deep down, you know it's possible he's changed, yeah?"

I stared straight ahead, leaving Nate's question hanging in the air.

Of course I knew it. That's why I'd stayed away. I needed to believe Seth was the same person I'd fallen in love with, the same person who'd abandoned me, the same person who I was still angry with after all these years. Because if he wasn't, everything I was, everything I'd become, meant nothing. But I wasn't about to admit that aloud.

A few minutes later, we squeezed into a parking spot in front of a dilapidated apartment building that looked like it'd missed the memo on urban renewal. The stone steps dipped in the middle where decades of footsteps had worn a permanent groove, and the paint on the doors and window casements probably hadn't seen a brush since the Nixon era. Several of the windows boasted air-conditioning units even though they wouldn't be necessary for a few months. And, pacing back and forth in front of the building, a strung-out junkie twitched and muttered to himself about the End Times and eternal damnation.

"Nice place," Nate mumbled as we made our way up the steps.

"Seth tends to live in places with a lot of . . . character," I explained, searching the intercom buttons for one that wasn't broken. "It makes his condition easier to hide when there's plenty of other weirdness to divert attention away from him."

Nate glanced around, taking in the rest of the grime and disrepair in the surrounding neighborhood. "Something tells me there's no shortage of drama around here."

As if on cue, a deafening crash and a woman's loud, angry voice sounded from somewhere down the street, making us both turn in time to see a half-dressed man beating a hasty retreat, ducking and covering as a heavy frying pan came flying after him.

"And there goes one of those characters now," Nate drawled with an amused smirk.

I gave him an irritated look, then pressed the button at the bottom of the row. A moment later, a woman's groggy voice said, "Hello?"

"Hey!" I called back like she should recognize my voice. "Sorry to bug you—I lost my keys! Crazy night, ya know? Can you buzz me in?"

"That'll never work," Nate mouthed to me.

The woman giggled over the intercom. "I can *totally* relate! Hope you find your keys!"

When the door's lock sprung open at the sound of the buzzer, I lifted my brows at Nate and ushered him in ahead of me. "After you, Detective Know It All."

The corner of Nate's mouth hooked up in the merest hint of a grin. "I stand corrected."

"How about walking corrected?" I said, casting a glance toward the junkie. "Our pal the prophet is starting to take an interest in us. I think he might recognize you."

The shadows around Nate's face deepened immediately in response. Without even so much as a glance at the junkie, he flipped up the collar on his overcoat and pulled his fedora a little farther down over his eyes. "Let's go."

"So does that happen often?" I asked as the door clicked shut behind us.

Nate's expression was hard to read beneath the shadows. "Often enough."

"Then maybe I should go first."

I stepped over a still-drunk twenty-something passed out at the bottom of the stairs and made my way to the third floor, feeling Nate's presence at my back even though his footsteps were silent on the well-worn wooden stairs. It was oddly comforting to know I had a colleague, a partner, behind me, backing me up. Until that moment, I'd never realized how vulnerable and exposed I'd been in these kinds of situations before when I'd been on my own. Considering what I was about to face—both literally and figuratively—I was glad to have Nate with me.

When we reached the third-floor landing, I motioned down the hall toward apartment 324. Nate gave me a nod and followed me to take up positions on either side of the door. I knocked loudly and waited for a response. When none came, I knocked again, louder. This time, I heard a rustle of movement and the light tread of bare feet upon the floor as they approached the door.

I frowned, double-checking the apartment number on the door. It was the right place, but the wrong footsteps. Just then, the door swung open to reveal a lithe young woman with long, sleep-tousled dark hair wearing a hastily buttoned man's dress shirt.

"Can I help you?" she asked, peering at us with bleary eyes.

My stomach dropped so swiftly to my feet, I couldn't open

my mouth for fear the amazing breakfast Nate had prepared would come launching back up.

"We're looking for Seth Wolf," Nate stepped in, coming to my rescue.

The woman glanced back and forth between the two of us, then said slowly, "He already left for work."

"And where's work?" Nate probed.

The woman narrowed her eyes at Nate, obviously growing more suspicious by the second. "What's this about?"

"Who are you?" I breathed, finally finding my voice.

She turned her large dark eyes toward me and blinked away the sleepy haze as she focused on my face. "Who are *you*?"

"I asked you first," I snapped, inexplicable anger making my voice loud in the close hallway.

Nate smoothly edged in front of me. "Miss, we need to talk to Mr. Wolf regarding a matter of utmost importance. Could you please tell us where we can find him?"

She narrowed her eyes at Nate, studying him intently. "How about you tell me where *he* can find *you*?"

"Tell him Tess Little was here," I said. "He'll know how to find me."

With that, I turned on my heel and practically fled the stifling confines of the apartment building, bursting through the doors and out into the open where I could breathe again. I took in great gulps of cool air, trying to calm my racing heart. When that didn't work, I bent forward, bracing my hands against my knees for a moment, trying to pull myself together before Nate came out.

"Red?"

Damn. Too late.

"Leave me alone," I mumbled, straightening quickly and rushing to the car. I jerked open the door and dropped into the seat. I ran my hands through my hair, then down over my face to regain my composure.

Nate got in a moment later and sat in silence for a few seconds before asking, "You okay?"

"Just go," I ordered. "I just want to get out of here."

Nate obediently started the car but didn't put it into gear. "I've been there, you know."

"Good for you. Now, let's go."

"You don't have a monopoly on broken hearts," he went on in spite of my obvious lack of enthusiasm for the topic.

When it became apparent he wasn't going to start driving unless I started talking, I sighed and said, "Okay. I'll bite. What was her name?"

"Pandora."

This made me blink in surprise. "*The* Pandora?"

Nate put the car in gear and pulled away from the curb. "One and the same."

The wicked little devil on my shoulder snickered and prodded me to make some innuendo-laden crack about Pandora's box, but I resisted. Instead I said, "Are you kidding me?"

He cast an offended glance my way. "Why is that so hard to believe?"

I shrugged. "Well, you're *Death.*"

Nate's grip on the steering wheel tightened. "There's more to me than this job, Red."

I turned my gaze upon him, studying his profile for a long moment. The shadows had dissipated, but the intensity of his expression hadn't. I immediately felt bad for pigeonholing him so unfairly. I'd been struggling to break away from my storybook persona for so long now, I'd forgotten I probably wasn't the only one.

"I'm sorry," I apologized. "Of course there's more to you. I'm learning that more and more with every minute we spend together." When I saw the slight flush on his cheeks and felt my own growing warm, I quickly added, "So, what happened?"

"Nothing."

I frowned at him. "If you didn't want to talk about it, why'd you bring it up?"

Nate glanced over at me and chuckled. "No, I mean, nothing happened. Ever. I was just infatuated with her from afar. She didn't even know I existed—well, you know, not in this form."

"Okay. . . . So what's your point?"

"I guess my point is you can't expect the other person to sit around and wait for you if he doesn't even know how you feel."

"So, we're back to the fact that I haven't talked to Seth since we came over?" I demanded angrily. "I didn't say I expected him to pine for me all these years and not move on. I was just blindsided, okay?"

"That was pretty obvious."

"Besides, it's not like I haven't moved on," I continued. "I've been with plenty of people."

"I'm aware of that."

I jerked back a little at his remark. "What the hell is that supposed to mean?"

Nate sighed. "Listen, I don't mean to offend you or anything. I've just known you for a while now and have never seen you really stick it out with anyone for very long."

"So what?" I demanded.

"Come on, Red," Nate replied, chancing a glance at me. "Don't you want to fall in love, settle down, live happily ever after?"

I cringed before I could stop myself. "I don't believe in happily ever after. Not anymore."

"I know Wolf hurt you," Nate said, "but how can you not believe in happily ever after? You're a fairytale."

"I'm not a fairytale," I snapped. "I'm a parable. A moral. And a misguided one at that. The first time I heard my own story it was being told to a group of young girls as a cautionary tale about the evils of men and sexuality!"

Sad but true. And, honestly, I don't know which part pissed me off more—that Seth was maligned as a villain in the tale, that I was portrayed as a little girl too naive and delicate to decide my own fate, or that all these young women were being spoon fed horrific lies in an effort to preserve their chastity by keeping them dangerously ignorant.

I sat brooding over the tragedy of it all for a long moment before Nate said, "So, if the story everyone's always heard is bullshit, you want to tell me what really happened? Call me crazy, but I'm guessing there was no cross-dressing involved when Seth seduced you."

"No—there was no cross-dressing," I replied, laughing a little in spite of the heaviness in the center of my chest. I let out a long sigh, then said, "I met Seth when I was eighteen. He was a hunter who lived alone in the woods near my village." I felt a grin curving my lips. "The first time I saw him, he took my breath away—he was *wickedly* handsome. But it wasn't just that—he was unbelievably kind, and exceptionally gentle."

"Unfortunately, he was also a werewolf."

"Yeah, there was that."

"I assume that didn't go over so well with your parents," Nate guessed.

I grunted. "To put it mildly. And when the villagers found out the truth about Seth, they went into full panic mode—complete with torches and pitchforks." I turned my head so Nate couldn't see my face as I remembered that horrible night so long ago. "When I heard what they were planning, I went to Seth to warn him. I planned to run away with him, be with him forever, but he thought it'd be safer if I stayed. He promised he'd come back for me."

"But he didn't."

I shook my head.

"Maybe he thought he was doing you a favor by staying away."

"Some favor," I drawled. "My parents disowned me and the village cast me out into the wilderness with nothing but the clothes on my back. I wandered around for a few days until I finally collapsed."

"What happened then?" Nate asked, his voice carrying an edge that made me turn and look at him.

I shrugged. "Don't know. I only remember feeling really cold. And hopeless. I was sure I was going to die—and I didn't much care. Then . . . "

"What?"

"I just . . ." I paused, trying to put what happened next into words. "I felt like someone wrapped his arms around me and held me. It was so warm and peaceful. . . ." My words trailed off and I closed my eyes for a moment, remembering the inexplicable comfort I felt in that dark embrace. I'd never felt anything quite like it before or since.

Suddenly recalling that Nate was sitting next to me, waiting for me to continue, I forced myself to snap out of it. I could feel the blood rising in my cheeks as I said quickly, "Anyway, when I woke up, I was at Gran's. When she heard my story, she insisted I stay. She didn't have any family either, so I became like the granddaughter she never had."

"And the rest is history?" Nate supplied gently.

I shifted in my seat. "Yeah. Something like that."

"You know what I think?" Nate asked.

I gave him a sour look. "Can I stop you from telling me?"

His incredible laugh burst from him, and then he turned those amazing black eyes on me, reading me a lot better than I would have liked. "Whether you like it or not, Red," he said, "there's more to you than your story. You may think it defines you, but it doesn't. And I have a feeling it never did."

Chapter 7

About half an hour after leaving Seth's, we pulled into an underground parking garage that serviced the suite of offices where Todd Caliban filmed his local cooking show.

Like Gran, Caliban had found a sense of purpose in the Here and Now that had been lacking in the rather restrictive story he'd been a part of. *The Tempest* was technically a comedy, but there was nothing funny about the part he'd been forced to play. He'd been treated with derision and contempt—and called a monster because his circumstances pissed him off.

But in the Here and Now, he was an incredibly talented chef and restaurateur who had finally become a nationally recognized rising star in the world of gourmet cuisine, thanks in large part to the success of reality television. He'd come a long way from the greasy spoon where he'd started out bussing tables when he first came over. His upscale café, Tempest in a Teapot, had just earned him a rave review from one of the most renowned food critics in the country.

Unfortunately, as you can imagine, Todd had a lot of emotional baggage he couldn't seem to offload no matter how many therapy sessions and anger management courses he took part in. And, in spite of the way he'd been treated, he still hung with the Shakespeare set. The Willies, as we called them at the FMA, were a group of melodramatic attention whores who couldn't seem to stay out of trouble.

"So, how did you meet Caliban?" Nate asked as we headed toward the elevator.

I grimaced inwardly and adjusted the collar of my leather trench coat. "Stalking case."

Nate blinked at me. "You got involved with a *stalker*?"

"It wasn't like that," I insisted, punching the elevator button with more vigor than necessary. Of course, it stubbornly refused to respond. "Caliban and Miranda had a thing. Her father got pissed about it—nobody's good enough for Daddy's little girl and all that—so she lied about Caliban stalking her to maintain Prospero's delusions."

"When were you two together?"

I glanced at the lights above the elevator, wondering if the damn thing was even in service. "It was after that. He made me dinner."

A smug grin slowly curved Nate's lips. "So, the way to your heart is through your stomach?" he quipped. "I thought that was just a guy thing."

I squared my shoulders and mentally pleaded with the elevator to get its ass in gear. "Girl's gotta eat."

Nate crossed his arms and leaned casually against the wall, regarding me with open amusement. "So since I made you breakfast . . ."

I shot him a deadly look as the elevator finally arrived. "Don't even go there."

Nate chuckled as we stepped inside, but by the time we reached the fifteenth floor he was all business again, his jaw pulverizing a fresh stick of gum.

As the elevator door slid open, a cacophony of noise greeted us. I exchanged a frown with Nate, then picked up the pace as another loud crash sounded from the studio set.

"What the hell is *this*?" roared a furious voice. "I said I wanted pork belly—who was the fucking moron who brought me pork cutlets? What the fuck am I supposed to do with this? Get my producer! I can't work in these conditions! This is ludicrous! Where's Sebille?"

"Ah, the famous rage of Caliban," Nate muttered. "No wonder you found him so charming."

"He was a victim of circumstances," I snapped. "I could relate."

A familiar scene greeted me as we entered the kitchen where Caliban was supposed to be filming. Well, it had once been a kitchen anyway. Pots and pans were strewn about the floor as were various ingredients that had been set out for whatever recipe he'd intended. On the countertop, a lone bowl of shallots had somehow escaped his tantrum. The rest was in shambles.

"I'm sorry, Todd," a smartly dressed woman with titian hair and painfully pointy shoes soothed, stroking his arm. She was pretty in an uptight, corporate kind of way. "It was my fault. I should have made sure that the correct protein was delivered before you came on set."

Caliban ran a hand through his wild mane of tawny hair, reminding me of a caged lion ready to spring on his prey. He cast a frustrated glance around the wreckage of his set and waved away her apology. "It's all right," he said, his voice a lot milder than it had been. "I'll figure something out."

At that moment the woman—Sebille, I presumed—sensed our presence and rushed forward to intercept us. "I'm sorry," she said calmly in spite of the angry flash of her forest green eyes, "but this isn't a good time. Chef Caliban is busy at the moment."

Nate grunted and nodded toward the wreckage. "So we heard."

I lifted my FMA badge. "This is official business, Miss . . ."

"Fenwick." Sebille's eyes narrowed at me as she gave me

the once-over. "You're Tess Little," she practically snarled. "I've heard about you."

I grinned at her, hoping it would get under her skin. "Peachy. Then you know to get the hell out of my way and let me do my job."

Sebille took a step forward, not intimidated by me in the least. *Interesting.* "I don't think I like your attitude," she snapped.

I returned the advance and shoved my face up at hers. "I don't think I like your shoes, so I guess we're even."

Based on the look of outrage on her face, I was about to have a good girly throw-down complete with scratching and hair-pulling, but Caliban stepped forward and placed a hand on Sebille's shoulder before the fun could get started.

"It's all right, Sebille," he said gently. "I have no reason for concern."

The woman instantly dropped back a step. "Of course," she muttered. "I'll be in my office if you need me." She cast a glance toward Todd from under lowered lashes, but his gaze was trained on me, his lips almost curving into a smile.

"Hi, Red," he said warmly. "I thought I might be seeing you."

"I wish it was under different circumstances," I said, meaning it.

His eyes took me in with a sweeping glance, taking on the same hungry look that had first brought to mind the image of a lion. "Me, too."

"We have to take you in for questioning," I told him, not bothering to keep the regret out of my voice. There was no point. Caliban wasn't the monster he was made out to be— which apparently was the theme of my love life. But he'd also been in trouble enough to know the drill.

"I had nothing to do with Hamelin's death," he said, taking off his chef's jacket and tossing it onto the kitchen counter.

"I hired him to get rid of a few rats in my restaurants. That was the extent of our acquaintance."

Nate stepped forward and grabbed on to Caliban's arm, giving him a none too gentle tug toward the hallway. "Not about the Hamelin case."

Caliban's face contorted instantly at Nate's rough treatment, and he jerked his arm away. "Then what the hell *is* it about?"

"Take it easy!" I chastised, glowering at Nate. Then, turning to Caliban, I asked, "How did you know about Hamelin already?"

He shrugged. "Word travels fast. I heard it from an associate."

I raised my brows. "Want to give me a name?"

Todd offered me a genuine smile this time. "No, probably not. It's always more fun to watch you sort it out on your own."

This time I was the one who grabbed his elbow and ushered him off the set. "You know, you'd make things a lot easier for everyone if you just cooperated, Todd."

To my surprise, he swept up my hand and kissed it with a chuckle. "And deny myself these lovely visits from you?"

"Hey, lay off the kissing, pal," Nate growled. Literally.

Caliban and I both jerked back at the harshness of Nate's tone. "Who's the new boyfriend?" Caliban taunted, nodding his head in Nate's direction.

I glanced at Nate just long enough to gauge his reaction to Caliban's question, but he didn't seem nearly as perturbed as I was. "He's not my boyfriend," I replied. "This is Detective Nate Grimm."

At this, Todd paused, glancing between Nate and me, his expression sobering. "Homicide. This is about a murder?"

"Murders," Nate informed him. "Plural."

Caliban looked a little panicked at this revelation and bent toward me, lowering his voice. "I'm on parole."

"For what?" I asked, lowering my volume to match his. "What happened this time?"

He made an impatient gesture with his hand. "Incident in New York City a couple of months ago involving a mouthy hotel clerk and a telephone. It was nothing. But if I get arrested, Red, I'm back in the FMA prison for at least a year. I swear to you I wasn't involved with any murders."

I knew Caliban, had known him for quite a while, and I believed him. But I didn't get paid to make that call. "Just come in quietly with us, Todd, and answer the Chief's questions. If everything checks out, you'll be good to go."

He nodded absently, his thoughts obviously distracted. "I should probably let Sebille know where I'm going. Let her know that I won't be filming today."

"We can bring her with us," I suggested.

"No, no," Todd replied, running his hand through his hair again. "Never mind. She doesn't need to get wrapped up in any of this. She's a good girl."

I made a scoffing noise and urged him forward. "Careful," I warned. "Seems like it's the good girls that get you into trouble, Todd."

Todd gave me a mischievous grin. "Perhaps that's why we didn't work out, Red—you were just too damned *good* for me."

I gave him a shove, refusing to rise to the bait. "Just get going," I grumbled. "The sooner we get this over with, the sooner you can get back to bombarding your staff with f-bombs and condescending tirades."

Caliban laughed and leaned toward Nate conspiratorially. "Don't be fooled," he whispered loud enough that I could hear. "She might pretend to be irritated by my particular brand of charm, but she's never really gotten over me."

I rolled my eyes to the ceiling as we entered the elevator, resigning myself to the fact that Todd was going to play it this way. I didn't know what I'd been hoping for. Although talented and truly kindhearted once you got past the quick temper and

latent rage, his success had made him an egomaniacal dick—
a much maligned, often wrongly accused, and seriously
misunderstood egomaniacal dick, but a dick nonetheless.

As the elevator doors slid closed, I received a sharp smack
on my left butt cheek that stung from the impact. I spun
around, glaring angrily, but Caliban only winked. Which
made me want to deck him. Instead, for the sake of my
paycheck, I hissed to Nate, "Cuff him. For his own safety."

Caliban held out his wrists to Nate. "Yes, Detective, please
do. I wouldn't want to do myself harm."

Nate glanced at me as he clicked the cuffs into place. He
said nothing, but I could see the puzzled look in his eyes as
he no doubt tried to figure out why I'd ever hooked up with
Caliban in the first place.

I turned my back on them both and squared my shoulders.
"Smack my ass again, Caliban, and I'll arrest you for assault."

He sniggered. "Once upon a time you wouldn't have
minded a good smack on the ass. . . ."

I closed my eyes and counted to ten. Twice.

This was going to be a long day.

Chapter 8

I stood on the other side of the one-way glass, listening in on Nate's conversation with Caliban. I had to hand it to Nate, he was good at his job. Caliban had started out with his usual cocky self-assuredness, but after half an hour under the penetrating gaze of Death, Caliban quit jerking Nate around and finally started answering his questions. And he answered them well.

"So, what do you think?"

I glanced over my shoulder as Al entered the observation room. He sauntered up to the glass and crossed his arms, studying me as much as he was studying what was going on in the interrogation room.

"He was with his producer until ten the night of the first murder," I said. "Then she dropped him off at a nightclub where he met up with Falstaff. They closed down the club around two."

"Would his producer confirm his alibi?"

I snorted in a very unladylike manner. "I'm sure she'd say anything to keep him out of trouble, but I think it's legit. Todd takes his career very seriously—it's everything to him. I have no doubt he was going over the plans for the next day's show with Sebille until she took him to the club. Of course, I also have a feeling they weren't just chatting about recipes."

"Girlfriend?"

I shrugged. "Dunno. Maybe. There's something going on there—at least on her part."

I heard Al purse his lips, mulling over what I'd told him. "And the other murders?"

"Alibi for every single one of them."

"With his producer?"

"Yeah."

"Huh."

I frowned and glanced up at Al. "What does that mean?"

"Just odd that he'd have such an airtight alibi for *all* the murders. And that each one would be confirmed by a woman who may or may not be romantically involved with him."

As much as I hated to admit it, Al was right. Todd had an active social and professional life, but even the biggest celebrity took a night off every now and then for some alone time. We hadn't received the tried and true "I was home alone sleeping" excuse for even one of the nights in question.

"Are you saying his alibis are *too* good?" I asked.

Al shook his head. "No," he said slowly. "I'm just saying that innocent until proven guilty is one thing. Overlooking guilt because you *want* him to be innocent is another."

"If you didn't think I could be impartial, you shouldn't have put me on this case," I snapped.

"I know I can count on you to be impartial, Red," Al called over his shoulder as he headed for the door. "I just want to make sure *you* know it."

I was still frowning over Al's remark when Nate left the interrogation room and joined me on the other side of the glass. "I'm going to let him go," he said. "Everything seems to check out."

I nodded absently. "Okay. Good."

Nate gave me a nudge with his shoulder. "You okay?"

I threw my hands up in exasperation. "Yes, I'm fine! Why are you asking?"

Nate blinked at me. "I could be wrong, but I think it has something to do with being polite."

I closed my eyes and took a deep breath, forcing away my frustration. "Sorry."

Nate shrugged. "No problem." He glanced at his watch. "It's just past one. You hungry?"

"I'm not sleeping with you."

Nate laughed in a loud burst, making me smile in spite of myself. "Like you said," he explained, "a girl's gotta eat. It's just lunch—no strings attached."

I thought about protesting, but my stomach growled, ratting me out. "All right. But I get to pick the place."

For some reason the smile Nate gave me as he opened the door made other, more pleasant things happen to my stomach, but that ooey-gooey warmth vanished instantly when I stepped into the hallway and saw who was lurking there.

"Well, well, well," Mary said, breaking out of her highly stylized lounge against the wall to slink toward us. "If it isn't my favorite detective. I've been looking for you."

Huh. So, she wasn't there just to make my life miserable. She'd been waiting for Nate. For some reason that pissed me off more than if she'd been stalking *me*.

Nate gave her a curt nod. "Mary."

Mary took a step closer, pointedly placing herself between Nate and me and blocking my view of his face. "You stood me up, you naughty boy," she reprimanded, her voice taking on a sultry heat I wouldn't have thought possible from a human iceberg.

"Sorry," Nate mumbled. "Had a case."

"Oh, I know all about your case," Mary told him. She ran her fingertip down Nate's lapel, her eyes devouring him inch by inch. "But work has never gotten in the way of pleasure before."

Wow. That was her best line? I groaned out load before I could stop myself.

Mary's head snapped around (and down), her eyes narrowing. "Something to say, Red?"

I batted my eyes at her. "Sorry? What was that?"

"I asked if you had something to say," Mary repeated with forced patience. "I didn't want to be rude and miss the chance to hear your captivating contribution to our conversation."

My lips curved into a wicked smile. So many smart-ass remarks came to mind. It was a pity to have to choose only one. "I was just going to compliment you on your witty repartee." I screwed my face in an imitation of her smug grin the day before. "Well done, Mary. Bra-*vo. . . .*"

Mary's face contorted with such contempt she looked like she could have murdered me, but she apparently thought better of it—considering she was standing next to a homicide detective and all—and quickly draped a patronizing smile across her lips instead. "So good of you to acknowledge my superior skill."

I resisted the urge to roll my eyes, but felt my restraint fading fast.

"Study hard, Ms. Little, and perhaps someday you can be witty, too."

Don't roll your eyes, don't roll your eyes, don't—

"Did you just roll your eyes at me?" Mary sputtered.

Damn. Busted.

I felt Nate take a step closer to me. "I hate to interrupt," he said to Mary, "but we need to get back to work."

"Of course," Mary replied. "Forgive me for keeping you." She gave Nate a seductive smile, then sauntered away, glancing over her shoulder to make sure he was watching the exaggerated sway of her hips—at least, that was my take on it.

And, of course, he was.

I made a noise of disgust and started walking. I didn't

bother glancing over *my* shoulder. A few beats later, I heard Nate hurry to catch up with me anyway.

(So there, Mistress Mary.)

"Where did you want to have lunch?" he asked, as if the encounter with Ms. Sex-in-a-Suit hadn't just taken place.

I glanced at him askance and increased my pace. "Mary Smith?" I muttered. "Seriously? Don't ever talk to me about my love life again."

Nate had the good grace to flush a little. "It's not what you think."

"She didn't leave a lot of room for misunderstanding," I retorted. "God, you could at least be a little more discreet about it."

"I'm not fooling around with Mary Smith," Nate insisted loudly. Then, seeing that he had drawn the curious stares of some of our colleagues in the bustling hallway, he lowered his voice. "She and I were supposed to get together to discuss a case over dinner. I stood her up when Hamelin offed himself last night. I was with you instead."

The knowledge that I had ruined Mary's plans made me all warm and fuzzy inside. The fact that her plans had included Nate was just coincidence, of course. I would have felt the same sadistic glee had her plans involved anyone I even remotely liked and respected. Really.

Nate took hold of my upper arm and pulled me to a stop. "Listen, I know you don't like her, but you might try being a little less antagonistic."

I frowned up at him. "I'm not antagonistic." When he gave me a knowing look, I said, "Okay, I'm a *little* antagonistic. But she started it."

Nate shook his head. "Nice. Very mature."

I huffed and crossed my arms, my bottom lip poking out a bit. I stopped just short of sticking my tongue out at him. "Fine. I'll try to play nice. But I won't like it."

Nate chuckled and put his arm around my shoulders, leading

me forward. "I'm not asking you to like it, or even like her. I'm just asking you to try to be civil."

I sighed, conscious of the arm still around me. "I can't make any promises," I said as we stepped onto the elevator.

Nate pulled me in closer to him so that we were facing each other and looked down at me, his black eyes smoldering with a dark fire I'd never noticed there before. "You have a dangerous job, Red," he reminded me softly. "You need all the allies you can get."

The air in the elevator grew thicker, harder to inhale, and was charged with an electricity that I felt down to my bones. Suddenly, it was hard to breathe and I had to gasp a little. "Yeah? Like you?"

"Tess," he rasped so softly that the sound of his voice made me shiver. "I—"

An annoyingly high-pitched chirp cut him off, startling us both and sending me to the other side of the elevator with an embarrassed flush on my cheeks. I ran my hands through my hair a couple of times, wondering what the hell had just happened, when Nate's cell phone went off again.

He snatched it out of his jacket pocket and barked, "*Grimm.*" His eyes flicked my way in response to whatever he heard on the phone, then glanced away just as rapidly, avoiding direct eye contact with me. "Yeah, I'll tell her."

A moment later, he pocketed his phone again. "Looks like lunch is going to have to wait."

The elevator came to an abrupt halt, and I immediately stepped out, eager to get away from the too-close space. "Yeah, why's that?" I called over my shoulder.

"There's been another attack. About half an hour ago."

This brought me up short. "What? Why didn't you know about it?"

"The victim didn't die," Nate said, his tone oddly gentle.

This news made my eyes widen. "Really? He left a witness? Then let's get going!"

I started toward his car in a rush, but Nate cut me off with his swoosh move. "Red—"

I let out a little yelp of surprise. "Damn it! I hate it when you do that!"

Then I noticed the pained, sorrowful look on his face. Something was wrong. Way wrong. When he took me by the shoulders and brought me closer, I wanted to forbid him to say whatever horrible news he was trying to tell me, but I swallowed hard instead and croaked, "Who is it?"

"It's Gran."

Chapter 9

I read. A lot. I read everything from ancient mythologies to modern literature. In my line of work, I never quite know who I'm going to bump into and need to be prepared. Over the years, I've come across a lot of stories, especially in the Victorian novels, in which the heroine is always gasping and swooning from shock. I never in a million years thought I'd ever be able to identify with such schmaltzy melodrama.

But the moment Nate told me Gran had been attacked by some unknown creature, my world pitched into a disorienting spiral. I didn't *swoon* per se, but the news sure as hell knocked the breath from my lungs and the bones from my legs.

I remember gasping something like "Oh, my God" and stumbling a little when my legs went to jelly on me. But the rest is a blur.

Sometime later, a nurse in pink scrubs ushered me into an Ordinary hospital room where Gran lay against a fluffy white pillow, her silver hair a tangled mess. A bandage had been taped to her forehead and her left arm was in a cast. Numerous bruises and scratches were visible where her skin wasn't already stitched and dressed, and I had a feeling there were other injuries I couldn't see beneath the coarse cotton blanket.

Nate gave me a comforting squeeze on my shoulder, then backed out of the room, giving us some privacy. But I had a feeling if I needed him, he wouldn't be far away.

Sensing my presence, Gran opened her eyes and offered me a weak smile. "Red, my darling." Her voice was rough and brittle, making her seem very old. I had never thought of her that way, even though she'd been written as an elderly woman. She was always just Gran—a perpetual parcel of perkiness that exuded the sort of kindness and energy that was completely infectious. I couldn't imagine who would want to harm her in any way, but I *could* imagine about a thousand ways that I was going to make that person pay for it.

I sat down in the chair next to her bed and took her uninjured hand in both of mine. "What happened, Gran?"

She exhaled a shuddering breath. "I honestly don't know, dearest. I had just finished the interview with the Panellas and had gone to my dressing room to freshen up. The next thing I know, something attacked me from behind. It all happened so fast."

I gently patted her arm. "Did you happen to see who attacked you?"

She shook her head. "No, my darling, not really. All I can tell you is that it wasn't human. I saw . . . fur. And its claws and teeth were so—" Gran broke off, fighting the tears I heard in her voice.

"Don't worry, Gran," I told her gently. "I'll figure out who did this to you."

She smiled and patted my cheek. "I know you will. Just be careful. I am always so afraid for you."

"I'm not working this one alone," I assured her. "I have a temporary partner."

At this, Gran's eyes sparkled. "Indeed? Would it be that handsome detective?"

I let out a short laugh and felt my face growing warm. "Yes, Gran. It's Nate."

She settled into her pillow, her eyelids growing heavy. "I like him. I think he'll be good for you."

I started to ask what she meant by that, but she had already drifted back to her drug-hazed sleep. So, instead, I stood and pressed a kiss to her cheek before pulling the covers up to her chin and making sure she was as comfortable as possible. When I exited her room, I saw Nate sitting in the waiting room chairs exactly where I had expected him to be. He immediately launched to his feet and hurried toward me.

"How is she?"

"Okay," I told him. "She'll be all right after a couple of days, but she's pretty shaken up."

"Did she get a good look at the guy?"

I shook my head. "Not good enough to make an ID. She did say that he wasn't human." I paused before adding, "He had fur."

Nate gave me a sympathetic look and said, "Werewolf fur?"

The look I shot his way made him take a step back. "Just fur, okay? Like I said, she didn't get a good look."

Nate held up his hands in mea culpa. "Sorry. You're right. I shouldn't be drawing any conclusions yet. Seth might have really been at work this morning. We confirm the alibi his girlfriend—"

"We don't know she was his girlfriend," I interrupted.

"Okay, sorry," Nate amended. "We confirm the alibi his *houseguest* provided and all is well. At least we can definitely take Caliban off our list. He was in custody when the attack occurred."

I started down the hospital's hallway, my angry steps drawing the stares of the Ordinary employees and visitors. "We need to get her out of here," I muttered. "Why did her assistant call the Ordinaries? They're going to figure out she's not like them when she starts healing up quicker than humanly possible."

"I've already taken care of it," Nate assured me. "The Chief has people on it as we speak. Our contacts in the Ordinaries' police force will take care of the incident report, so we don't have to worry about them getting involved. And Al's sending over a couple of FMA agents to order Gran's transfer. They'll transport her to our own facility where Tale doctors can make sure she has the proper medical treatment."

I was silent the rest of the way to Nate's car, mulling over what I knew—which was damned little—and thinking about how many ways I was going to rip the head off this thing once I got my hands on it. It wasn't until we were back in his car and on the interstate that I spoke again. "Thanks."

Nate shrugged off my gratitude. "It was nothing."

"Maybe to you," I replied, "but I appreciate it. Gran is everything to me. She took me in when no one else wanted me. I owe her my life."

"We'll get him, Red," Nate assured me. "I promise."

I cringed. "Don't make me a promise you aren't sure you can keep," I muttered. "I've had more than my fair share of those. Just tell me you'll help me, that you've got my back. That's enough."

Nate gave me a tight nod. "Okay then."

Satisfied, I leaned my head back and closed my eyes, too angry for any additional conversation. If Nate was right and one of my former lovers was to blame for the attacks, why had he targeted Gran? Seth didn't know her and Vlad adored her. And even if Caliban hadn't been in custody, I wouldn't have believed him capable of such an attack, either—he'd always had a soft spot in his heart for Gran in spite of the fact that she was his primary ratings rival. There was no way one of them would have a reason to attack her.

Unless it was to get to me.

All the other attacks had seemed random, crimes of

opportunity. But something in my gut told me Gran had been targeted. Was I getting close to uncovering something already? Was it a warning? That theory sounded paranoid even to me.

Maybe I'd know more once I'd had the chance to question Vlad and Seth. If I could clear both of them as easily as we'd cleared Caliban, then we could look more seriously at who might really be behind the attacks.

A little while later, the car came to a stop. Anxious to get back to work, I shoved away my musings to mull over later, but when I opened my eyes I was surprised to see us not at the scene of the crime but at Gran's pale pink Victorian Eastlake. The house was so daintily darling it seemed completely at odds with its more utilitarian bungalow neighbors and had enough fanciful spindle work to make Sleeping Beauty nervous.

"Why are we here?" I demanded. "Don't we need to be at the studio, looking over evidence?"

"The Chief already has Trish on it," Nate said. "You know if there's anything to be found, she'll find it."

"That's beside the point!" I huffed. "Why would you bring me here?"

Nate looked surprised at my anger, which didn't help. "I thought it'd be too hard for you to see the crime scene, considering who the victim was."

"Who asked you? You don't know a damn thing about me!" Mad as hell, I lunged out of the car, slamming the door behind me. I was climbing into the Rover, determined to set off on my own, when Nate caught the edge of the door, keeping me from closing it.

"Don't know you?" he repeated. "I know all about you, Red. You're a loner and a rebel and a beautiful woman with a seriously bad attitude. Then there's this idiotic death-wish behavior of yours. You rush into everything head-on, putting yourself at risk unnecessarily. What I can't understand is why. What exactly are you trying to prove?" Nate ran his hand down his face, visibly bringing his frustration with me back under control. In a much calmer voice he said, "Now, I told you, Trish is on the scene. If you show up there, you'll just be in the way."

I slammed my hand against the steering wheel, knowing he was right, but feeling like I needed to be doing something, *anything.* "I can't sit here and do nothing, Nate—not when this asshole is out there hurting people! I need to be out there hunting him down."

"So where are you going?" he asked softly. When I tried to look away, he leaned into the car between me and the steering wheel, forcing me to look at him. "You said you wanted my help, Red. Where were you planning to go?"

I shrugged, then let my head fall back against the headrest. "I don't know."

Nate held out his hand to me. "Come on. You still need some lunch."

"I'm not hungry."

When I refused to take his hand, Nate grabbed mine anyway and pulled me out of the car. "You're a bad liar," he replied. "I thought you might want to take the rest of the day off, all things considered, but if you're going to insist on being a pigheaded pain in the ass about it, at least eat something first. Then we'll head back out. Together."

I glanced up at him, gauging his sincerity, then sighed. "Fine," I relented, "but you need to stop mixing your metaphors. You're a fictional character, for crying out loud; it's embarrassing."

He laughed and gave my hand a squeeze, bringing a smile to my lips in spite of my irritation. A few minutes later, we were sitting side by side at the kitchen bar, eating roast beef sandwiches and kosher dill pickles.

"Thanks for the sandwich," I mumbled around a mouthful of pure heaven. "This is delicious."

Nate gave me a self-satisfied smile. "Thanks. It's the

herbed mayonnaise. I mixed it myself. If you're nice to me, maybe I'll give you the recipe."

"Don't bother," I replied. "I don't cook."

Nate lifted his brows. "Not at all?"

"Never."

"But you love to eat."

"So does a dog," I retorted. "Doesn't mean it cooks."

Nate chuckled and nudged me playfully with his shoulder. "Stick with me, kid. I'll show you the ropes. Then you won't have to rely on your men to cook for you."

I felt my stomach tighten at his remark, but afraid to read too much into it, I let it go. Trying to cover my sudden onset of nerves, I took a bite of pickle, then wagged the spear at him. "I don't get you."

Nate's smile vanished and he turned away, concentrating on his sandwich. "What's to get?"

"You're an enigma to me," I admitted. "I've known you for decades. We've worked—what?—scores of crime scenes together over the years?"

Nate shrugged. "Yeah, something like that."

"So why are you suddenly so interested in working with me *now*?"

Nate wiped his hands on his napkin, obviously looking anywhere other than at me. "I told you, you're the best one to be on this case. You have intimate knowledge of the suspects."

I let out a bitter laugh. "My love life aside, there are several other Enforcers who could have brought them in."

Nate polished off his lunch and got up to put his plate in the dishwasher. "Call it a professional courtesy, then. I figured you'd want to be involved."

I studied him, knowing that there was something he wasn't telling me, but I didn't have the faintest idea what it could be. Then, a sudden, chilling thought came to me. I was almost afraid to utter the words, but I had to know if my hunch was right. "You're not hanging around with me just because of the murders, are you?"

Nate grabbed a sponge from the sink and began wiping down the countertops. "What are you talking about?"

"There are only a few reasons the Grim Reaper takes a sudden interest in a person," I pointed out. I gripped the edge of my chair, bracing myself. "My number's up, isn't it, Nate?"

Nate hesitated briefly at my question but didn't answer. He didn't need to. I could see the truth etched in the sternness of his expression.

I took a deep breath and asked, "How's it going to happen?"

This time Nate came back to his chair and sat down next to me, lacing his hands together in front of him before answering. "Just because I saw what's coming, doesn't mean it will come to pass. Consider it more of a cosmic heads-up."

"But it has to do with this case," I surmised. "It has to do with these suspects?"

Nate nodded. "I knew that if you found out who our suspects were, you'd get involved on your own, regardless of what the Chief said. So I asked him to put you on the case with me. That way I figured I could keep an eye on you, be there in case I needed to intervene."

"Can you do that?" I asked. "I mean, won't you get in trouble or something?"

At this, Nate finally turned toward me. "I don't usually get this kind of advance warning," he admitted. "Usually I get notified a few seconds ahead of time or even just after. There's a reason I was tipped off this time around. And, well, I like you, Red. A lot. I'd hate to see anything happen to you."

I swallowed hard, trying to process what I'd just heard. I don't know how a person is supposed to react when she finds out she may or may not be dying soon, but for me, it just hardened my resolve to solve this case and bring the killer to justice. If I was going out, I was going out doing my job. That's how I always figured it would happen anyway.

And, no, I hadn't missed the fact that Nate said he liked me. In fact, the words played over and over in my head, somehow negating the pronouncement of my possible doom. Call me a silly little schoolgirl if you want, but knowing Nate cared made me go all fluttery inside. And who wants to die prematurely when she feels fluttery?

When I looked over at Nate again, the shadows around him seemed to have darkened—a by-product of his apprehension and concern, I supposed. Aside from Gran and Eliza, I'd never really known what it was like to have someone actually worry about me. Yet here was this guy I'd rarely spoken to outside a crime scene, putting himself out there to bring a killer to justice and, with any luck, save my life in the process. Somehow, just saying a simple thank-you didn't seem adequate.

I hopped down from my bar stool and took hold of Nate's hand, pulling him to his feet. Then I did something I almost never do to anyone—I slipped my arms around his waist and hugged him. It felt good. No, not just good, great. His arms came around me and held me close against him, making me feel safe and protected. I didn't realize how much I had missed that feeling until that very moment.

Afraid of letting the embrace go on for too long, I stepped back a lot sooner than I would have liked and grabbed my coat off the back of the bar stool. "Come on," I said, trying to make my tone light. "If we're going to crack this case, I guess we'd better get going."

Nate grabbed his fedora and placed it on his head at just enough of a rakish angle to make my heart trip over itself. And if that hadn't done it, the smile he gave me would have. "Lead the way," he said. "I'll be right behind you."

Somehow, that was all I needed to know.

Chapter 10

I pocketed my phone and shook my head. "Still no answer," I told Nate. "He's probably still sleeping off the most recent midnight snack."

"We'll try again later," Nate told me. "With Vlad being one of the walking dead, I can play hardball if I have to. No worries."

I nodded, wondering what exactly it meant when Death decided to play nasty against one of his escapees. . . .

Seeing as how the day was still young and neither Vlad nor Seth were accessible, Nate and I decided to visit the site of Dave Hamelin's suicide and see if we could find any clues as to why Dave would have done himself in.

I knocked on the infamous red door of Happy Endings and waited, knowing it would take a few minutes for someone to answer. Hardly surprising, considering what most of the employees did for a living. Although the FMA tolerated this kind of business as a necessary evil to keep our kind out of trouble and our identities secret, the Ordinary police weren't so willing to look the other way and came poking around every now and then.

Finally, the dwarf I'd run into the previous night opened the door and ushered me in. "Good day, Red. Always a pleasure."

"Hey, Ted," I greeted him with a nod. "How's it going?"

"Busy day," Ted grumbled, flipping the end of his beard over his shoulder to keep from stepping on it. "Lots of people coming and going—so to speak."

"Well, we won't take up much of Snow's time," I promised. "I just wanted to ask her a few questions."

"Who's the stiff?" Ted asked gruffly, with a nod toward Nate.

"Death," I replied.

Ted's eyes widened a little, but he said nothing until we reached a set of French doors that led to Snow's private quarters. "She's with a client," he told us. "She'll be with you momentarily."

"Thanks, Ted," I called as he shut us in.

Nate did a slow turn, taking in the lavish decor in Snow's private apartment. The entire sitting room was covered in rich, lush fabrics of red and gold that went perfectly with the crystal chandeliers, golden candelabras, and intricately carved cornices. Sculptures that looked like they might actually be marble originals of nudes dating back several centuries were set in a series of recesses that lined every wall.

I walked to a beautifully crafted golden serving cart set near a bust of some long-dead Roman and poured myself a shot of Goose in a crystal glass. "You might as well have a seat," I told him, pouring another drink. "Snow could be a while."

"They seem to know you pretty well here," Nate said, sounding a little bemused by it all. "Do you come here often?"

I laughed at the implication of his question and glanced at him over my shoulder. He was still standing in the center of the room, taking it all in. "Here," I said, bringing him my second shot. "Drink this. You look like you could use it."

Nate downed it with a wince and handed the glass back to me. "I've never been in a brothel," he said. "I wasn't expecting . . ." He made a sweeping gesture with his arm.

"All of this?" I asked. "Snow brought some of this with her after the divorce. The rest she has acquired over time. Having lived as a princess all those years, she developed expensive tastes."

Nate sat down on an ornately carved settee. "And she makes enough to cover the cost of these expensive tastes?"

I grinned at his naïveté. "Oh, yeah." When he looked at me, his shock evident, I chuckled and sat in a thronelike wingback chair next to the settee. "You have to keep in mind, Nate, Snow caters to Ordinaries as well as us Tales. You'd be surprised what people pay to live out their ultimate fantasies."

Nate shook his head slowly. "How does a princess fall into this kind of life?"

I grunted. "She has a husband who leaves her for an Ordinary and an ironclad prenuptial agreement that gives her practically nothing in the divorce settlement. She had to do something. And there was a need for this kind of business for our kind. Something safe and anonymous. It keeps a lot of people out of trouble."

"Except Dave Hamelin, apparently," Nate pointed out.

"There's always the ones who are too stupid for their own good," I said. "That's why I have a job."

At that moment, the doors opened to reveal a vision of beauty and elegance. Olivia "Snow" White glided into the room, her chocolate brown curls cascading over her shoulders and down her back, her lovely heart-shaped face flushed, her emerald green eyes sparkling brightly with afterglow. She wore a loosely belted diaphanous white dressing gown—and nothing else. Even I had to blink at the spectacular curves visible through the sheer material.

"Hello, Red," she husked, her voice as soft and silky as her milky white skin. "I haven't seen you in a while."

"Hey, Snow," I said, coming forward to shake her hand.

She lifted her gaze over my shoulder, letting her lovely eyes travel the length of Nate's body with such appreciative hunger he couldn't possibly have mistaken her admiration. "Did you bring a friend for me to play with?" she asked with a mischievous grin.

I felt a stab of irritation at her presumption, but said evenly, "Sorry, not this time. Olivia, this is Nate Grimm—"

Snow came forward and extended a delicate hand. "Detective Grimm," she purred. "I've heard of you. I'm surprised you haven't visited before now."

Nate cast a desperate glance my way, then said, "I'm afraid this isn't a social call."

She offered him a gorgeous pout in response. "Pity. Perhaps another time?"

Nate took a slight step back from her even as she moved closer. "Perhaps."

"Dave Hamelin committed suicide in the alley last night," I said, pointedly interrupting Snow's advances. "I thought I'd see if you'd heard anything about it."

Snow sighed dramatically, then took a seat on the settee Nate had recently vacated, draping her body decoratively across the pillows for our benefit. Her negligee gaped open, giving us a tantalizing glimpse of full breasts that she did nothing to cover. Once she was comfortably seated, she made a dismissive motion with her hand, waving away my question. "Why would I possibly have heard anything about his suicide?"

"He was on parole," I told her, going to the serving cart and pouring her a glass of Merlot. "I was only bringing him in for a minor violation—he got pinched by the Ordinaries soliciting a working girl. He would have been out again in a couple of months."

Snow shrugged as she reached for the wine. "Some people simply cannot handle going back in."

I held on to the wineglass as she tried to take it, forcing her to look up and meet my eyes. She pressed her ruby red lips into an angry line, then let out an irritated huff.

"You gonna talk to me?" I asked, releasing the glass and nearly sloshing wine onto her negligee. A single crimson droplet landed on the back of her hand. With a slow, languid motion, she licked it off, holding my gaze.

"I suppose I might have heard something," she murmured. She took a sip of her wine, then ran her tongue along her lips with a glance toward Nate. "If I tell you what I've heard, what's in it for me?"

I resumed my seat in the wingback chair and smiled. "The contentment of knowing you did the right thing?"

Snow threw her head back and laughed. "Red, you never cease to entertain."

I grinned at her, familiar with the routine. "A regular laugh riot, that's me. Now, what do you have for me?"

Snow abruptly abandoned her stylized pose and sat up quickly, setting down her wineglass with such enthusiasm it sloshed over onto the table's dark wood. I leaned forward, too, eager for her most recent gossip.

She glanced around dramatically, then whispered, "You didn't hear this from me—"

I held up my hands. "I never do."

She grinned, revealing remarkably white teeth. "Ever the soul of discretion, my friend. The word among my girls is that Dave's business was booming. He recently did some work for Todd Caliban."

I nodded. "Yeah, I knew that."

Snow's eyes flashed and she leaned forward farther, motioning for Nate to lean in as well. He hesitated until I gave him a nod, indicating that he should play along. Gamely, he leaned forward, resting his forearms on his knees (and working hard to keep his eyes on the carpet).

"Who else?" I asked.

"The Charmings."

This raised my brows. "James and Cindy?"

Snow nodded vigorously. "Yes! And guess who else!"

"Why don't you just tell me and save me the time and effort," I suggested. I heard Nate choke back a laugh and shot him a warning glance. He gave me an "Oh, come on" look but smothered his grin nonetheless.

Fortunately, Snow hadn't seemed to notice. "Tim Halloran," she whispered. "Isn't *that* interesting?"

Hell, yeah, it was.

"Tim Halloran?" Nate repeated. "The Sandman?"

Snow nodded again. "Precisely. Dave had done such a wonderful job ridding Caliban's restaurant of rats, he was suddenly in high demand among the wealthy. It was odd, really. All of these highly affluent people with their droves of servants and attendants suddenly finding themselves with an infestation of rats?"

"That *is* odd," I said, starting to get a little itch at the base of my spine that told me the whole thing was a little too coincidental. "Do you know of any other interesting clients Dave has had lately?"

Snow shrugged, baring her pretty shoulder. "Those are the only ones I've heard about, but I bet you could get a client list from his office girl. She's a pretty little thing. Tell her to give me a call if she needs a job."

I got to my feet. "Thanks, Snow. I'll pass the word along." I glanced over at Nate, whose gaze had wandered away from the carpet, and snapped my fingers to get his attention. "Coming with me, Grimm?"

Nate lurched to his feet, looking flustered and a little embarrassed. "Right behind you."

I couldn't help but grin a little in spite of a surprising twinge of irritation at his interest in Snow. I really couldn't blame Nate for taking a peek—it wasn't like Snow was doing anything to keep him from it. And, well, by all accounts Nate wasn't exactly a monk.

As we made our way to the door, Snow glided up between us, putting a slender arm around each of us. "He's quite a catch, Red," she purred in a faux whisper. "If you decide you don't want him, *do* send him my way."

I turned toward her to throw back a saucy retort, but that was a mistake. Seeing it as an invitation, Snow pressed into me, reaching up to twine a lock of my hair around her finger. "Or you both could drop by for a visit." With that, she brushed a kiss to my lips, nipping at my bottom lip just enough to make her point. "Then you can pay me in the kind of currency I like best."

"Tempting as always," I told her, edging out the door. "See you around, Snow."

I heard her disappointed sigh. "I could make a mint with her, Detective," she said to Nate as he tried to squeeze past her. "Petite but tough—and those eyes! Have you ever seen any that shade of blue? Like a robin's egg. Some of my clients would pay a fortune for an hour or two with her. Too bad she'd rather play it straight."

I turned back in time to see Nate's face contort ominously. "Nate!" I hissed, interrupting whatever remark he was about to make. "Come on."

He gave Snow a tight nod in farewell, then fell in behind me, his jaw clenched so tightly I thought I heard his teeth creak. When we got back to the car I expected him to start it up right away, but he just sat behind the wheel, his expression shifting so rapidly between different emotions I couldn't even keep track.

"You okay?" I asked after a few minutes of watching the fascinating display.

"What the hell was that all about?" he said at last.

I frowned at him. "What? Snow's little cat and mouse game? That's the usual with her."

"She kissed you."

"Yeah, I know. I was there. So?"

Nate shifted in his seat, adjusting the way his coat was draped around his thighs. "That was . . . It kind of took me off guard. I mean—never mind." A flush of crimson began to creep into his cheeks. "I can't believe she thinks you'd go to work for her."

I tried to hide the grin pulling at the corners of my mouth. The fact that he was so offended for my sake and yet apparently aroused by Snow's coming on to me gratified me on several levels.

"Snow's harmless," I explained. "She knows I'd never work for her. It's just her way of trying to maintain an illusion of control over the situation. If that's what it takes to get the information I need, I don't mind playing along."

Nate looked a little dazed for a moment longer, then shook his head and started the car. "So, what do you think the deal is with the rats? Coincidence?"

"No way," I said. "Rats in Chicago certainly aren't out of the ordinary, but at the Charming compound? Cindy's fairy godmother is . . . well, Lavender's still powerful enough to take care of a few rodents."

"What about Halloran?"

This one made me squirm a little. "He uses magic to keep his operation under wraps," I said. "We all know what he does for a living, but we can't get anything on him concrete enough to put him away. His witches aren't just hacks who like to scare kids in the woods. They're serious nasty. They should have been able to just blast the rats away."

"Maybe the rats weren't there naturally," Nate suggested.

"What do you mean?"

Nate shrugged. "Maybe someone used magic to cause the infestations, magic the Charmings and Halloran couldn't counter."

That uneasy feeling I'd experienced at Snow's came rushing back. "That would be some incredibly powerful magic."

Nate's grip on the steering wheel tightened. "It's out there."

"Okay, suppose you're right," I said. "Let's say for the sake of argument that someone out there is wielding magic potent enough to combat the wards of some of the most powerful magical creatures this side of Make Believe. Why target the Charmings and Halloran?"

"Maybe someone has a grudge against them," Nate said.

"Who doesn't?" I muttered, checking my watch. "The day's not over. Maybe we should take Snow's advice and go visit Dave's pretty little assistant."

"A pretty little assistant, eh?" Nate said as he reached into his suit jacket and took out a stick of gum. He gave me a wink as he folded it into his mouth. "Guess it's time to turn on my charm."

I rolled my eyes and opened my mouth to offer a comment on his self-professed charm when I felt a buzzing at my hip.

"What—no theme song?" Nate teased as I reached for my phone.

I gave him a warning look, choosing not to divulge the fact that I'd kept my phone on vibrate after my last little snafu. "Everyone needs a theme song," I shrugged. "You should consider getting one. Maybe something from the death metal genre."

Nate groaned at my lame joke, so I was grinning as I answered my phone. "This is Red."

"Hello, little one."

Chapter 11

I felt a chill at the sound of the voice on the other end of the line. It was silky and smooth and deadly. And it affected me in ways I hated to acknowledge. I swallowed hard, trying to find my own voice somewhere in the pit of my stomach where it had vanished.

"You're a hard man to catch," I managed to croak out.

A low chuckle replied, making me shiver. "That is the idea."

"Red," Nate whispered, "you okay?"

I glanced over at him, knowing my eyes were wide and my breath shallow, but nodded anyway.

"Did you enjoy your visit with the lovely Ms. White?"

I frowned. "How did you—"

"My informants are everywhere, little one," the voice interrupted. "I am always watching."

I closed my eyes, trying to ignore the fact that the mere thought of his eyes upon me made my stomach flutter. "Then you know why I'm looking for you?"

"I know it has something to do with criminal activity. I know you were assigned to this case specifically. But the rest, I want to hear from your beautiful lips."

I swallowed again and gave my head a shake, trying to

fight off the hypnotic effect of his voice. "Where can we meet?"

"Come to my office."

I frowned at his response. That certainly wasn't what I'd been expecting. Part of me was secretly a little disappointed. "When?"

"Right now."

"I'm on the other side of town," I told him. "It will take a little while to get there."

I could tell he was grinning when he said, "I have nothing but time, my little love. I have been waiting patiently for you to come for me again."

"You mean come *to* you," I corrected.

That silky laugh wrapped around my senses once more. "We shall see."

My heart skipped at his implication. "I'll be there soon."

"I shall count the seconds," he said. "And, Red?"

"Yes?"

"Come alone," he commanded. "Do not bring your new friend. If you bring him along, I am afraid you will find me far less agreeable."

I hung up and shoved the phone in my jacket pocket. My head was spinning, my heart racing. I closed my eyes and leaned my head back, willing myself calm again. God, I hated what he did to me, but was exhilarated and aroused by it at the same time.

"Red?"

I heard Nate's voice as if he were far away. And down a tunnel. And underwater.

"Red? Can you hear me?"

When I opened my eyes again, I noticed Nate had pulled over to the side of the road and was patting me on the cheek, trying to get me to snap out of the trance I was in. It took my eyes a moment to focus.

"I can hear you," I grumbled. "Quit smacking me."

"What the hell just happened?" he demanded, worry creasing his brow. "You totally drifted away from me there."

I took a deep breath and let it out slowly. "We've had a change of plans," I told him. "That was Vlad. He wants to see me."

Nate took hold of my chin and looked into my eyes. "What did he just do to you? Your pupils are dilated. Your cheeks are flushed. Your pulse is racing."

I averted my gaze, embarrassed by my lack of control. "Nate, come on—"

"I'm worried about you."

This brought my gaze back to his and I saw that he was serious. "I'll be fine," I assured him. "It's always like this. Vlad's a vampire, Nate. He has . . . abilities. Let's just say he gets what he wants and there's not a lot a woman can do to resist."

Nate leaned back slowly, taking in what I had just told him. "Is that how you two got involved?" he asked, his expression going dark. "He forced himself on you?"

I shook my head quickly. "No! Good God, no! It wasn't like that at all." I paused, trying to figure out how to explain the hold Vlad had over me . . . or anyone else he desired, for that matter. "He has a way about him, Nate. It's hypnotic. All he has to do is speak in a certain way and his prey can't resist him—they don't *want* to resist him."

"So, he hypnotized you?" Nate concluded.

I gave a little shrug. "Kind of. That first time anyway. Then, well . . . we were what the other needed at the time."

"And now?"

I frowned, a little irritated at Nate's grilling. "You're getting a little personal, don't you think?"

Now it was Nate's turn to shrug. "I think I have the right to ask. He's a murder suspect. If you can't handle being around him—or even talking to him on the phone—then I'll just go by myself."

"No!" I cried, reaching out and grasping his arm before I even realized what I was doing. "You can't!"

Nate looked down at where my fingers were digging into his arm. "Why not?"

"Nate, please," I said, trying to keep my voice calm. "He said he'd only cooperate if I come alone."

Nate scoffed. "No way in hell am I letting you talk to him alone. Not after what I just saw him do to you."

"Listen to me—"

"End of discussion."

I pressed my lips together in an angry line, realizing there was nothing I could do to reason with Nate. "Fine," I relented. "He wants me to meet him at his office."

"Okay, then," Nate said with a sharp nod. Without another word, he pulled back into traffic and made an illegal U-turn, heading back toward the other side of town.

I sat in angry—and worried—silence for the rest of the ride, trying to determine the best way to keep Nate from getting on Vlad's bad side and get himself—or both of them—killed. I reminded myself he had a valid concern about my ability to be impartial on the case. I had argued the same thing when I'd been assigned. Nate was concerned that Vlad could manipulate me in whatever way he wanted to in order to get away with murder—perhaps in a very literal sense. I could understand that, too—mostly because I was worried about the same thing. But there was no way I was going to put Nate in danger because I was too weak to deal with one measly vampire. I liked the guy too much.

When we pulled into the parking garage for Vlad's office, I got out of the car first and waited for Nate to come around to the other side of the car where I was standing.

"Ready?" he asked.

I nodded. "Let me just give him a call and tell him you're coming with me. He doesn't like surprises." I reached into my pocket and pulled out my phone, but it fumbled from my grasp and onto the ground, sliding under the car. "Damn it!"

"Here, I'll get it," Nate said, his chivalry completely predictable.

The minute he bent down to pick it up, I brought my arm down hard, hitting him on the back of the neck. He went down without even flinching. I glanced around quickly, then opened the back door to his car and somehow managed to lift the top half of his body into the backseat. Unable to push him any farther, I ran around to the other side and pulled him the rest of the way in. As soon as I had him situated as comfortably as possible, I picked up his fedora and set it on his chest. Then, on impulse, I reached out and brushed his thick hair away from his brow.

"I'm sorry about this," I whispered. Then, giving in to another impulse, I bent and pressed a kiss to his forehead. "It's for your own good."

Hating to leave him there unconscious and vulnerable, I lingered just a moment more, letting my conscience gnaw at me. I was running my fingers through his hair, marveling at how soft it was, when something caught my eye. I leaned in closer to get a better look.

The same tribal tattoos I'd seen on his forearms were hidden under the thick locks. On closer inspection, I saw they weren't necessarily tribal in origin. In fact, they looked more like black flames licking at the nape of his neck and disappearing down the collar of his shirt. Frowning, I briefly traced the designs, wondering what they meant. I could have stayed much longer, letting my fingertips drift gently across his skin, but footsteps a few rows over made me jerk my hand away and slam the door. If Nate was still speaking to me after this, I'd have to ask him about his incredible ink.

After locking the doors, I fished my phone out from under the car where it had fallen when Nate went down, then headed for the main entrance to the office building where Vlad operated his various business ventures.

I'd met Vlad after he came over in the Great Lit Migration of 1985. He'd been one of those characters who'd had difficulty adjusting and soon had gotten into trouble when it came to his need for blood. That's when he got assigned to me. And let me tell you, it's not an easy task to bring in a guy who could shape-shift, vanish into thin air, and seduce you with nothing more than a look from startlingly pale blue eyes.

Our months-long game of hide and seek was, in a word, *exhilarating*. I hadn't had that much fun in decades! Vlad wasn't the first vampire I'd dealt with—folklore from all over the world is filled with variations on the theme—but he was the first *literary* vampire I'd encountered. And I hadn't been prepared for that. Thanks to the metamorphosis of vampires from monsters to sex symbols, Vlad had undergone a transformation as well. He wasn't the horrible creature Stoker had originally envisioned anymore—he was brilliant, handsome, suave, and sexy as hell. Finally, as eager as I was to bring our game to its explosive conclusion, Vlad had let me catch him.

Fortunately, after Vlad's rehabilitation at my careful (ahem) tutelage, he had managed to find a respectable way to feed and put his talents and charisma to better use, becoming a billionaire within a few short years. Now, in addition to owning the world's largest casket company, his empire consisted of three Fortune 500 companies and numerous other lucrative enterprises. In fact, it was hard to find an industry that Vlad didn't have *some* connection to.

Since our original whirlwind romance, Vlad and I had had an on-again/off-again relationship that would give you whiplash trying to keep up. I think we both knew that it would never really go anywhere. Vlad had an obsessive need to bed as many women as inhumanly possible, and I had an obsessive need to stay unattached. And yet we couldn't seem to get enough of each other. I would break things off, only to give in to his persistent entreaties again a few months later. And there you had it. We were addicted to one another. And that addiction was just as toxic as any drug on the street. Part of any rehabilitation process was staying out of situations where you'd be tempted to backslide. Yet here I was right back where I knew I shouldn't be.

I made my way to the top floor of the high-rise where Vlad kept his private office, preparing myself for the onslaught of sexy I knew I'd be facing down. So when the glass doors opened to admit me into the main lobby, I was a little surprised to see a new girl sitting at the reception desk instead of the matronly assistant Vlad had employed for over twenty years. The new receptionist looked very young—maybe just out of high school. In fact, her blond hair still looked natural. And I could tell at a glance she was an Ordinary.

The girl offered me a genuinely friendly smile as I approached. "Hi," she said cheerfully. "Do you have an appointment?"

"Not on your books," I told her, eyeing her cautiously. "But he's expecting me. I'm Tess Little."

"I'll let the Count know you're here." She hopped up and came around the desk, extending her hand. "Can I take your coat?"

I took a step back, clutching my trench close to my body. "No. No, thanks."

She gave me an indifferent bob of her head. "Okay."

I gestured toward Vlad's office door. "Is he in there?"

She shook her head. "No, he's, uh . . . in a meeting at the moment." Her eyes drifted toward a room down the hall where Vlad often took his long lunches.

I lifted my brows in understanding. "Ah. Got it. So, I'll just wait in his office then?"

She glanced down toward the room again, her hand subconsciously going to her throat where I'm guessing a rather

fresh bite mark was hidden beneath her turtleneck. Based on
the look of longing in her eyes, I'd say she was probably
breakfast and was a little hurt not to be asked to lunch.

"Yes," she said, her smile a little less cheerful this time, but
just as friendly. "Please make yourself comfortable. I imagine he'll be finished soon."

As I shut myself in Vlad's office and took a seat behind his
desk to wait for his grand entrance, I couldn't help but feel for
his new receptionist. She seemed like a nice girl. Maybe she
even could be someone Vlad actually cared about, for all I
knew. Unfortunately, monogamy wasn't his thing. Not that he
could really help it. I knew from experience that he couldn't
feed from the same person for too long without it becoming
problematic. Not only was it a draining experience—in a very
literal sense—but it was also a binding one. The connection
that grew between Vlad and a regular partner was hard to end.

Obviously. All these years later, and I was still trying to
break free.

I propped my feet up on his desk and leaned back in the
wickedly soft leather chair, stroking the luxurious material. It
had probably cost more than I made in a year. I leaned my
head back and closed my eyes, taking advantage of the
moment of decadence.

"Well, if it isn't my favorite color."

My eyes popped open. I hadn't even heard him come in.

"Hello, Red."

The very sound of his voice was enough to make my blood
run hot and cold by turns—a fact Vlad knew all too well. I
had intended to brace myself against the effects, but I hadn't
been prepared to see him again. Not as he was at that moment
anyway—half dressed and gorgeous, his incredible physique
still flush from his recent feeding, his dark hair falling in
waves around his shoulders to frame his stunningly handsome
face. He looked like a god strolling toward me, full of power
and grace and raw sex appeal.

I let my boots fall to the floor and rose to my feet, not about to let him corner me. "Vlad."

As he drew nearer, a wickedly sexy predatory look came into his eyes. Involuntarily, I backed away until my back pressed into the wall behind me.

Grinning smugly, Vlad reached out and ran a finger down the vein of my neck, a move he knew would make my breath go shallow. I tried to move away from his touch, but Vlad pressed his palms to the wall on either side of my head, caging me in.

"I'm here on business," I said, glancing up at him briefly.

I knew better than to meet his gaze for long, but I don't know why I even bothered. In a blur of movement he had me in his arms, my body pinned tightly against his.

"Are you certain?" he demanded. "It has been a very long time since you have let me take from you."

I felt my resolve beginning to shatter. "There's a reason for that," I reminded him, my voice sounding too strained to be convincing. "Remember?"

Vlad chuckled, the deep velvety sound caressing me inside and out, making my heart once more beat frantically. Being a member of the undead, Vlad had no beating heart to clue me in on what he might be feeling, but as his hand slid slowly down my backside to grip my ass and press my pelvis into his, I was assured that another, very impressive organ, was still very much alive.

I groaned—or maybe moaned; I'm not sure which. Either way, I brought my eyes up to his, conceding defeat.

And what I'd thought was off, was very much on again.

Chapter 12

"You're a suspect in several murders, Vlad," I told him as I pulled my jeans on, keenly aware of the bite mark throbbing on my inner thigh. "I have to take you in for questioning. It's my job."

Vlad shrugged, causing his half-buttoned shirt to gape open, revealing his perfectly sculpted chest once more. My libido greedily licked its lips, already hungry for another helping.

Mmm. Yummy. . . .

"I have been a very good vampire," Vlad assured me. "I have not killed a single soul since being *rehabilitated* by you."

"God, Vlad, you make that sound dirty," I grumbled, searching his office for my shirt and missing boot.

I heard him laugh from where he sat perched on the corner of his desk and then in the next moment felt his arms around me as he nuzzled my neck. "Perhaps I need to be rehabilitated a little more," he murmured against my skin. His hunger for me was evident in the barely restrained urgency of his caresses.

With a herculean force of will, I dropped down, ducking out of his hold and snatching up the boot that had been tossed behind a chair. "Sorry," I replied, pulling it on. "This was the last time, Vlad. It has to be."

He sighed, no doubt recalling how many times we'd had the same conversation.

"I'm serious," I said firmly. "I'm tired of being just a midnight snack-n-sack to you."

"Then don't be."

My head snapped up. Too surprised to remember to avoid looking into his eyes, my gaze locked briefly with his. "What are you talking about?"

"You say you are nothing to me, that I simply use you for blood and sex, but when I ask you to stay with me you run away. You have never even slept in my arms, Red."

Hmm. He had a point.

I really was crazy about Vlad—and when things were *on* they were very, very on. But then he'd go on a womanizing spree or I'd find myself getting a little too comfortable with our situation, and one or both of us would become unreachable for a while.

"You're just lonely," I said, finally locating my shirt. "You don't want me, Vlad, you just want *some*body at your beck and call so you don't have to go hunting."

"Red, my own—"

"I'm *not* your own," I interrupted.

Vlad lifted his arms in invitation. "You could be, little one."

Whoa.

Was he seriously asking me to be something to him? Something more than just a lover? If so, what? A girlfriend? I swallowed hard, suddenly feeling panicked. A *wife*?

I must have gone about three shades of white because Vlad rushed forward, easing me down into a nearby chair. "Are you unwell?"

I looked at him cautiously. His face was only inches from mine as he knelt in front of me. "What—" My voice cracked, so I coughed a couple of times. "What are you asking me?"

He laughed, which pissed me off, but he was gentle as he took my hand in his and brushed his lips against my knuckles. "I am asking you to have dinner with me."

"Oh."

Vlad's brow creased into a frown. "What did you think I was asking?"

Flustered, I wiggled out of the chair. "I . . . I don't—"

"To *marry* me?"

I couldn't help flushing, which pissed me off even more than when he'd laughed. "Of course not. You know how I feel about that."

"Indeed I do," he said with a maddening grin. "But I think someday you will change your mind."

I gave him a doubtful look.

"I am asking for nothing you cannot give," he assured me, still smiling with that self-assured, patronizing grin of his. "I know you have not gotten over what that mongrel did to you so many years ago, but I shall make you forget him if given the chance."

I wanted to punch Vlad's handsome face, but I was so hurt by his amusement at my expense I couldn't even channel my rage. I just wanted to run away and forget the entire experience. Keeping with tradition, I started to sprint toward the door, but Vlad caught me up around the waist and brought his mouth down on mine, kissing me until my anger had completely vanished.

When he finally lifted his head, he pressed his forehead to mine. "Will you let me take you to dinner?"

I sighed. "Like on a real date?"

He nodded.

"Where I'm not the main course?"

He grinned. "Not the main course."

"We've never had one of those."

He pressed a kiss to my temple. "I know."

"But you don't eat."

He leaned close to my ear. "I will wait for dessert."

I shuddered, not needing to ask what he meant by *that*. "I still have to take you in for questioning," I reminded him, distracted as his fangs grazed lightly along the curve of my throat.

"Right now?" he murmured.

I gasped as his fangs hit the mark. "No," I breathed, twining my fingers through his hair and pulling him closer. "It can wait a few more minutes. . . ."

When we finally got back out to the car, Nate was awake and pacing in agitated patterns, frowning fiercely. He didn't say a word to me as I loaded Vlad into the backseat and climbed into the front. Nor did he speak when we escorted Vlad to the interrogation room at headquarters for questioning.

His only acknowledgment of my presence was to give me a hard, hurt look as he closed the heavy interrogation room door, pointedly barring me from entering. I thought about observing their discussion, but I knew Vlad would handle himself well. And somehow I knew his alibis would be just as airtight as Caliban's had been. That was just his way.

An hour or so later they emerged, Vlad grinning and Nate scowling. Apparently, the session had gone just as I'd anticipated.

Nonetheless, I asked, "How'd it go?"

Vlad took my hand and lifted it to his lips. "I think I have assured Detective Grimm that I am not guilty of these heinous crimes."

"Oh," I said with an uncomfortable glance at Nate. "Good." I tried to sound unconcerned, but my relief came through in my voice.

Vlad's grin widened. "Well," he said, turning to Nate and extending his hand, "good evening, Detective Grimm. A pleasure as always."

I started at the familiarity between them. *As always?*

Nate shook Vlad's hand and mumbled something incoherent.

"Do you need a ride home?" I asked, but seeing Nate's stormy look grow even darker, I immediately regretted the offer.

"Thank you, but no," Vlad replied. "I have no need. I have a car waiting for me already."

Well, of course he did.

I nodded. "Okay."

Vlad turned my hand over and pressed a kiss to my palm, his eyes holding mine. "I will see you tomorrow night, my own."

I was still shuddering from the heat of Vlad's breath on my skin when I realized he had gone and that Nate was glaring at me.

"What?" I demanded, storming down the hall toward the stairs. I wasn't about to get stuck in an elevator with Nate right now.

"He's a suspect, Red," Nate pointed out, following me into the stairwell.

I started down the stairs. "Not anymore, right?"

"That's not the point."

I abruptly stopped on the landing and turned back to Nate. "I'm sorry," I said. "About earlier in the parking garage."

Nate looked away from me, his jaw tight with anger. "I should have been with you."

"Vlad cares for me, Nate," I told him. "If you had gone with me, he would have seen it as you infringing on what's his."

At this, Nate turned his gaze back to me. "Yeah, well, there's no chance of that, is there?"

I felt a sinking in the pit of my stomach when I saw the look in his eyes. I wanted to reach out and touch him, caress his hair as I had in the parking garage, trace the strange markings upon his skin and see just how far they went.

But, instead, I shoved my hands in the pockets of my coat.
"Nate, I—"

"We've had a busy day," Nate interrupted. "Why don't we
call it quits for now and meet up again tomorrow?"

I nodded, disappointed at the thought of parting ways.
"Sure."

"Do you want a ride home?"

"I think I'm going to head to the hospital and check on
Gran," I said. "Want to come with me? I'm sure she'd like to see
you." I didn't add that I'd like to have him there as well. It just
seemed like the wrong thing to say, no matter how true it was.

Nate looked like he wanted to say yes, but he shook his
head. "Just give her my best."

"Okay."

"Well, I guess I'll get going."

He started to walk past me, but I reached out, grabbing his
hand. "I was trying to protect you," I told him. "I don't know
what else to say. I didn't want anything to happen to you."

Nate's fingers tightened around mine. "I appreciate that.
But I'm a Reaper, Red. There's not much that can hurt me."
He took hold of my chin and forced me to look up at him.
"But there's a lot that can hurt *you.*"

"I'm a big girl, Nate," I protested. "I'm not some dainty
little princess who just sits around all day waiting to be
rescued. It's not my style."

Nate's lips pressed into a frustrated line. "I'm not saying
you're helpless. You removed any doubts of that when you
sucker punched me in the parking garage. I just want to
stick close for a while, keep an eye on you—just in case."
His expression softened, and his tone was gentle when he
said, "I can't protect you, Red, if I'm not there."

Great. We were back to my imminent demise. As much
as it pissed me off, I had to admit I wasn't thrilled about
pushing up daisies any time soon. I'd be damned if I was
going to get caught up in that whole damsel-in-distress

bullshit, but having someone at my back until the danger had passed certainly couldn't hurt.

"Fine," I agreed begrudgingly. "I'll be more careful."

Nate's mouth hooked up in the corner in the hint of a smile. "Good. I can get over you knocking me out for my own good," he said, "but if something were to happen to you— well, I can't make any promises there."

His thumb slid briefly across my skin before he abruptly released me and took a step back. "I'll see you tomorrow."

I watched him go down the stairs, confused by the disconcerting whirlwind of emotions knocking around between my heart and my head. Trying to rid my mind of the image of his eyes gazing so intently into mine, of the feel of his fingertips upon my skin, I ran my hands through my hair, then let out a long, slow breath.

When I was certain I could no longer hear Nate's footsteps echoing in the stairwell, I began my own descent, glad to finally have some time to myself. It gave me a moment to mull over what we'd learned so far about the murders (which was pretty much jack) and Dave Hamelin's suicide (ditto jack). Still, I had yet to question Seth and find out what he knew, if anything.

At the thought of my former lover, a chill began to creep up my spine, reminding me of the same old feeling I used to get whenever he was near. It was so intense I stopped dead in my tracks and glanced behind me—almost certain I'd see Seth standing there. But when I saw the hall was empty I chalked it up to exhaustion and a healthy dose of caution.

Or maybe just wishful thinking.

Chapter 13

I followed the network of tunnels beneath Chicago that connected FMA headquarters to the other key Tale buildings. It took only half an hour of walking to finally arrive at the hospital where they had taken Gran earlier that day, but it seemed like a hell of a lot longer that night. I couldn't shake the feeling that someone else was in the tunnels with me, lurking in the shadows just beyond my sight. Yet every time I stopped to listen or turned around suddenly to face my pursuer, the tunnel was empty. By the time I finally arrived at the entrance to the hospital, I'd never been so happy to see the place.

If you didn't know any better, you'd think the heavy steel door before me was just your average utility access panel or other random portal you'd find anywhere along the city's underbelly. But beyond this particular doorway you'd be shocked to find a bustling center for health and wellness equipped to treat any kind of Tale ailment that might come along—transparency and fading being chief among them. Of course, because we were also susceptible to the same kinds of injuries as our fact-based peers, the physicians were also well-educated in Ordinary medicine, which came in handy for keeping our kind safely hidden away among the hustle and bustle of the big city.

Because we healed a hell of a lot quicker than the Ordinaries did, ending up in the care of Ordinaries like Gran had could be problematic and had to be dealt with swiftly and discreetly. We'd had more than one close call over the years, with some of our brethren making miraculous recoveries and ending up as front-page news.

If accounts of the mysterious ended up in the tabloids like the Jabberwocky incident had, it was much easier to keep a lid on things. But if the story leaked to the Associated Press, the folks in Damage Control at the FMA went into full panic mode. Fortunately, those instances were growing less frequent, thanks in large part to the Internet. Once it would have taken a whole team of PR strategists to handle the situation, but since the emergence of the information super-highway, all it took now to discredit even the most well-documented case was a viral e-mail and a little misdirection, and the story was suddenly branded an urban legend. (If only it were that easy to get rid of the penis enhancement spam . . . Now *there* was a fairytale.)

When I entered the hospital, I flagged down a nurse who directed me to the room where they'd taken Gran after the Chief had ordered her transfer. After a few twists and turns and a trip through the cafeteria, I finally found Gran's room. She was sitting up in bed watching reruns of *One Tree Hill*.

"Ah, Red, my darling," she sighed wistfully as I came in. "I've been watching the most fascinating program. These teenagers are quite dramatic."

I couldn't help but smile. "Everything's a drama when you're a teenager, Gran."

She nodded sagely, folding her hands in her lap. "Yes, I guess I had forgotten. Of course, things were so different during my time. I would never have slept around like these young people do."

I couldn't help but flush a little, wondering what she thought of *my* extracurricular activities. Time to change the subject. "I brought you some dinner," I told her, holding up the bag I carried.

Her eyes lit up. "Lovely! I'm famished!" She nodded toward a discarded tray sitting on the side table. "The food here leaves a great deal to be desired."

I rolled a wheeled tray to her, then pulled out a grilled chicken sandwich, a teacup-sized container of pasta salad, and a perfectly square brownie. "Sorry to disappoint you, but it's from the cafeteria—which I'm guessing is maybe a half step up from what they already tried to foist onto you." I chuckled when she eyed the food with mild horror. "It's all I had time to pick up. Next time you're attacked by some nefarious monster, I'll be sure to call ahead for takeout."

Gran offered me a genuine smile of gratitude and motioned me forward to receive her kiss on the cheek. "I appreciate the effort, my dear. You are always so thoughtful."

As she dutifully ate her subpar repast, I pulled a chair over to her bedside and took a seat. It was then that I noticed the numerous bouquets of flowers that filled the room. "Where did all these come from?"

Gran's eyes widened with excitement. "The wonderful roses are from the Panellas," she said, motioning toward a huge arrangement to her left. "Then that one is from my producer, and that one is from my assistant, and that one is from Detective Grimm—"

"Nate?" I said, my brow furrowing. "He sent you flowers?"

Gran blinked at me. "This troubles you?"

I shrugged. "I was just wondering why he'd do that."

"Well, I imagine it was to be polite," Gran said, her tone bemused. "Should he not have sent them?"

"It just surprises me," I told her.

"Thoughtfulness surprises you?" Gran asked, smoothing her blanket primly.

"Thoughtfulness is one thing," I mumbled. "Ass-kissing is another."

Gran laughed. "Oh, Red. When will you learn to accept kindness without suspicion?"

"Suspicion's kind of my thing, Gran," I reminded her, stealing a small corner of her brownie and popping it into my mouth. "I'm *trained* not to trust anyone."

"Well, I think you can trust the Detective," Gran assured me. "I like him the best of all the men with whom you've been involved."

I started at her presumption, choking a little on the brownie. "What? No, Gran," I stammered. "Nate and I aren't involved."

She lifted her brows at me. "Oh?"

I rubbed my palms on my thighs, suddenly feeling uncomfortable. "He's just a friend. My partner. We work together. That's it."

Gran tried unsuccessfully to hide a smile. "Mmm-hmm."

I glowered at her. "What's that supposed to mean?"

She waved her hand nonchalantly in the air. "Oh, nothing."

"Gran," I huffed, "you might as well say it. You're going to eventually anyway."

Gran lifted the brownie and nibbled tentatively at the edge. "Hmm. That actually isn't terribly disappointing."

"Gran."

She took a more substantial bite of the dessert and shrugged daintily. "I don't know many men who would show up early in the morning just to make a colleague breakfast."

"Nate likes to cook," I said. "He made me lunch today, too."

"Really?" she whispered, clearly intrigued.

I rolled my eyes. "Gran, Seth cooked for me. So did Todd. You see how those relationships turned out. Culinary talent does not true love make."

Gran shot me an irritated glance. "I am just saying that he

has gone out of his way for you. He seems like a perfect gentleman. And he certainly is handsome enough."

"I'll give you that last one," I agreed. "But he's also a Reaper, Gran."

She polished off the brownie and brushed the crumbs from her hands. "Well, we all have our idiosyncrasies."

I couldn't help but laugh. "Idiosyncrasies? Gran, he's Death. Capital D."

"Yes, dear, I *know*. You said that already. What is your point exactly?"

I shook my head, realizing I wasn't going to win this one. "Nothing. Never mind."

"I'm merely suggesting you give him a chance," Gran said, fiddling with the coverlet again.

"Fine," I relented. "I'll keep it in mind." Then, trying to sound casual, I said, "So, I saw Vlad today."

Gran's hands stilled instantly. After a moment's hesitation she sighed. "Oh, Red."

"He was a suspect in the investigation," I divulged, "so I had to bring him in for questioning."

Gran folded her hands on her lap. "And?"

"And we let him go," I told her. "Airtight alibis."

She looked down her nose at me, making me squirm a little. "That is not what I meant, and you know it."

"He asked me out on a date."

Gran's posture eased slightly, but her expression was still guarded. "Before or after you slept with him?"

"Gran!" I shrieked, going probably five shades of red.

"What?" she asked innocently. "I am not nearly the prudish old woman you think, Tess Little. I recall what it's like to have sexual needs."

"Oh, God!" I launched to my feet, covering my ears.

"Do you think only you young Tales have needs and desires?" she demanded. "I might be old, my girl, but I'm not dead. In fact—"

"We are *not* having this conversation!" I groaned. My stomach churned ominously as I desperately tried to keep images of Gran in flagrante with God-knows-who out of my head.

Gran laughed. "All right, all right. I won't torture you any further with the assignations of an old woman."

"Thank God."

Gran held out a hand to me, beckoning me to her. Obediently, I took her hand and sat on the edge of the bed. "I have always respected your choices, my darling," she reminded me, "even if I haven't always understood them. I love you as if you were my own flesh and blood—I ask only that you be careful. Vlad Dracula . . . well, he concerns me. He always has."

I gave her what I hoped was a comforting smile. "It's just dinner, Gran. And I'm choosing the place. He's not even picking me up; he's sending a car for me tomorrow evening and meeting me at the restaurant."

Gran let out a slow breath, then nodded. "Well, I cannot pretend I won't be pacing the floor all night long."

"You're coming home tomorrow?" I asked, surprised yet gratified she was recovering so quickly.

"Did you think I'd stay down for long?" she asked, the old twinkle back in her eyes. "I have an interview with Thumbelina next week. I can't miss out on that."

"What about security measures?" I asked. "Has the studio increased their security in any way since the attack?"

Gran shook her head. "I have no idea, dear, but I imagine they will do something to keep this from happening to anyone else."

I pressed my lips together, not wanting to tell her my theories about her attack not being just a random act of violence. There was no sense in worrying her with conjectures and gut feelings. She had a life to live just like the rest of us and couldn't be kept under lock and key until I sorted out who was killing Tales and why.

"I need you to promise you'll be careful, too," I insisted. "If you feel threatened in any way—even if it's just a bad feeling—I want you to call me. Or Nate. He can be there quicker than I can."

"Of course!" Gran agreed. "I have no desire to repeat what happened to me this morning."

We chatted for a few more minutes until Gran started to yawn, so I tucked her into her bed and made sure she was asleep before I finally crept from the room, shutting the door quietly behind me.

I checked all the rooms near hers but all the patients looked legit and nothing else seemed out of place, so I left my cell number with the night nurse, just in case she needed to reach me. Then I made my way out of the hospital and into the darkening night.

Chapter 14

When I left the hospital, the last place I wanted to go was home, so I caught a cab and headed to my favorite hangout. When it comes to quaint, little-known pubs, Ever Afters is about as hole-in-the-wall as you can get. There's a simple wooden shingle hanging outside the windowless door, which, thanks to a fairy enchantment, reads Coleman Shoe Repair to Ordinary passersby. But the true nature of the establishment is well known to us Tales.

The place was packed as usual when I got there, Tales crammed around tables and standing at the bar, if they were lucky. The unlucky found themselves wedged into any available square inch of open floor, juggling drinks and dodging busy waitstaff. In the back corner on a small stage, the house band, Fiddlers Three, had just struck up a lively rendition of an old Chieftains' tune that set the crowd to clapping and dancing impromptu jigs, thereby sloshing their drinks onto the already sticky floor.

Determined not to be one of the unlucky, I elbowed my way through the crowd and up to the bar, insinuating myself between two guys in suits who weren't making use of the lone vacant bar stool.

"Hey!" barked a sharp voice at my elbow.

So not in the mood for anybody's shit, I turned toward the guy, poised to take him down if necessary, but when I saw who it was, my eyes widened with delighted surprise. "Well, if it isn't Nicky Blue!"

Nicky offered me his lazy grin and held up his arms in invitation. "Hi ya, Red." When I threw my arms around his neck, he hugged me back, then kissed both my cheeks. "It's been a long time, kid."

If Nate had stepped out of *Casablanca,* Nicky "Little Boy" Blue came straight from *The Godfather.* He was about as close as you could get to being a Corleone without actually being ripped from the pages of Puzo's famous tome. In fact, there were times I wondered if maybe Nicky had been Puzo's inspiration for the young Vito.

Nicky certainly wasn't short on good looks or charm, but I knew beneath the suave exterior and relaxed demeanor lay the keen intelligence and brutal resolve of a man who had climbed his way to the top and intended to stay there. Nicky demanded complete loyalty and professionalism from those who worked for him—anything less than the best was unacceptable. He ran his business interests with a deadly efficiency that would have made some of the more hardened dons look like little more than schoolyard bullies.

Fortunately, Nicky tended to stay on the right side of the law when it came to anyone outside his outfit and was in good with the Ordinaries, so the FMA tended to look the other way, for the most part—at least for now. Although I knew what Nicky did for a living, I couldn't help but love the guy. I honestly didn't know what I'd do if *he* ever showed up on my to-do list.

"When did you get back in town, Nicky?" I asked, grinning from ear to ear at seeing my friend so unexpectedly. "I thought you and Jules were still in the Old Country."

Nicky shrugged and leaned casually on the bar. "It was

good to visit, but I couldn't be away too long. Business doesn't run itself. Plus, a little of the in-laws goes a long way."

I could imagine—especially with that querulous lot. The Capulets were always fighting with somebody.

"So what's new with you, kid?" he asked, waving a hand to signal the bartender. "You still hanging out with that dolt Dracula? I'll never forgive that blood-sucking bastard for turning your head away from me."

I gave him a teasing grin. "Ah, come on, Nicky," I said. "You know I never would have been the good little wife you were looking for. Jules is much better for you."

Nicky's eyes sparkled. "Yeah, but we sure had some good times, kid."

Oh, man, did we ever. . . .

"What can I get for you two?"

Relieved at the interruption, I looked up and smiled at Bob "Old King" Cole, proprietor of Ever Afters. Bob was easily the most jolly, jovial man I'd ever met, and with his round belly and thick white hair, he easily could have moonlighted as Santa. His blue eyes held an omnipresent merriment that was completely contagious, and just being in the same general vicinity as Bob could buoy your spirits even on the worst day—which was probably why his business was always booming.

"Hi, Bob," I replied, now doubly glad that I'd decided to stop in. "The usual for me, thanks."

Nicky gave a nod to Bob and tapped his empty glass. "I'll take another, Bob." Nicky waited until Bob had placed our drinks in front of us, then turned back to me. "So what's doing, kid? I can tell you've got a lot on your mind."

I shook my head. "I never could pull one over on you, could I?"

Nicky took a drink of his scotch and gave me a wink. "Not on your life."

I edged a little closer on the off chance someone might

actually hear our conversation over the Fiddlers' current jig, and rolled my bottle of Guinness between my palms. "Dave Hamelin offed himself the other night," I informed him.

Nicky's dark brows shot up. "The Pied Piper? Everything was going well for him from what I heard."

"That's the problem," I replied. "Business was going a little too great, I think. He did some work for Todd Caliban, then suddenly had contracts with the Charmings and Tim Halloran."

Nicky's eyes went a little stormy at the mention of Tim Halloran. "If he fell in with that drug-peddling prick Halloran, then there's no telling what he was into."

I nodded. "That's my concern. And I think magic might be involved. Not with his death, but with the jobs he was working on."

Nicky leaned in a little more so that our shoulders were touching. "You think he was murdered?"

I took a long drink of my Guinness and shook my head slowly. "No, I don't think so. All indications point to a self-inflicted gunshot wound. But he was scared enough to fear being caught and taken in." I took another drink and stared hard at the bottle in my hands. "I feel like there's something I'm missing, that the answer's right there in front of me."

"Let me check into it," Nicky offered. "Maybe there's something my people have heard that wouldn't have gotten back to you."

I turned my head and offered him an appreciative grin. "You'd do that?"

Nicky nodded. "You bet, kid."

I glanced away, watching my fingers peel off the label on my beer. "Can I ask you another favor, then?"

Nicky put his hand on one of mine, stilling my agitated fidgeting. "You know you only have to ask, Red."

"Someone attacked Gran," I told him. "I don't know why, but I think it's connected to another investigation. I want someone to keep an eye on her, make sure she doesn't get attacked again."

"You got it," Nicky said without hesitation. "You know I've always had a soft spot in my heart for your Gran. She's good people. I'll send one of my best guys to look after her."

"Thanks, Nicky," I said sincerely. "I'll owe you one."

Nicky shook his head. "Not on this one, kid." He squeezed my hand and studied me for a moment before leaning over and kissing my cheek. "This one's between friends."

I squeezed his hand back, thinking Jules was a damned lucky woman. "Thanks."

"You tell me if you need anything else, Red," he insisted. "You don't have to go it alone all the time, you know."

"I've been hearing that a lot lately," I said, eyeing him suspiciously.

He gave me a knowing grin. "What can I say? A guy hears things." He got up from his bar stool and tossed back the last of his scotch. As he turned to go, he gave me a wink and said, "Let me know how that new partner works out for you."

As the crowd finally started to thin, I rose from my bar stool and tried to place a few twenties by my row of empty bottles and shot glasses, but Bob pushed the money back toward me. "No need," he said. "Already taken care of."

I frowned. "What? Who?"

Bob nodded toward the back corner where a lone patron sat enshrouded in shadow. The man lifted his glass in salute and inclined his head before setting his glass aside and rising from his chair. I let out a shaky breath as he walked toward me, my heart pounding so loudly I was afraid he might hear it.

"You need a ride home *now*?" Nate asked with a grin.

I blinked at him, mostly because he was a little blurry. "I was going to take a cab." Well, I think that's what I said, but it sounded kind of funny, so I'm not sure if that's how it came out.

Nate tried to hide a smile as he put an arm around my shoulders. "Come on."

Trying to prove that I was just fine, thank you very much, I jerked away from his hold—which was a mistake. In what I suspect was a graceless spiral, I lost my balance and ended up sitting on some woman's lap. "Sorry," I mumbled, flailing about as I tried to stand.

Fortunately, the gal was a happy drunk and thought the episode uproariously funny and didn't take offense at the sudden intrusion into her personal space. As she giggled with her companions, Nate helped me back to my feet.

"You going to let me help you now," he asked, "or should I continue to let you make an idiot of yourself?"

I shot him a dirty look but didn't fight back this time as he supported me to the door. I heard him call a farewell to Bob just as the cold wind hit me in the face, making me gasp a string of curses at the sudden assault on my senses.

"Rough day at the office, honey?" Nate quipped, leading me to his car.

Always quick with the comeback, I retorted, "Shut up."

Nate dropped me into the passenger seat and, because my arms were dancing around like a marionette that had lost its strings, buckled me in. I vaguely remember the car beginning to move and the welcome warmth inside it as the heat finally kicked in, but I must have dozed off for a little while because the next thing I knew, Nate was half carrying me into the house and dragging me up the stairs to my bedroom.

As soon as he helped me stretch out on the bed, the room began to spin, so I closed my eyes, willing it to stop. All of it. The spinning, the pitching, the rolling, the hurting, the aching, the remembering, the regretting, the—

Damn it!

I felt tears on my cheeks but didn't bother to wipe them

away. I was on the verge of devolving into a drunken, weeping mess when I felt a tug on my foot and instinct took over. Without thinking, I kicked. Hard.

I heard Nate grunt as I nailed him square in the chest. He cursed something under his breath, then snapped, "Hold still! I'm trying to take your boot off!"

"I don't want my boot off," I said, feeling that was a perfectly reasonable argument. "Just leave it on."

Nate sighed and gave another tug, nearly pulling me off the bed in the process. "Hey!" I cried. "What the hell!"

"Give me the other foot," he ordered.

I briefly considered being difficult, but my stomach started to roll around again, so I lifted my foot. "Fine."

He peeled off my other boot, then went for my socks.

"I can do it," I protested, but he pulled them off anyway.

"Huh," he said.

I blinked at him. "What?"

"I wouldn't have guessed silver."

I frowned, trying to figure out what the hell he was talking about. Then some inkling of understanding made it through my alcohol haze. "Elizabeth and I get pedicures every couple of weeks. Big deal."

I could feel Nate's grin like it was a charge in the air. "I like it."

I made some kind of noise in response, then curled into a ball on my side. "I don't feel so great."

I had no sooner spoken than my stomach heaved. By some small miracle, Nate was there with the wastebasket. I don't know how long I went on—for five seconds or five minutes—it seemed like forever. When I had finally purged my stomach, I dropped back down on the pillows and closed my eyes, ping-ponging between misery and humiliation.

I heard Nate leave the room and figured he was probably running far, far away after my stunning display, but a moment later, he was back, helping me sit up and holding a glass of cool water to my lips.

"Just a little," he said. When I'd had enough, he eased me back down on the pillows and smoothed my hair back from my face.

My faculties began to return to me now that I'd rid myself of the mass quantities of Guinness and Goose that I'd consumed, and a whole new wave of mortification washed over me. So much for making a good impression on my new partner.

"I'm sorry," I murmured, my body beginning to drift, edging closer to sleep.

"For what?" Nate asked, pulling my covers up over me. The bed dipped a little as he sat on the edge and peered down at me.

"For being such a mess."

I couldn't be sure, but I thought I felt Nate press a kiss to the top of my head—just a light brush of his lips against my hair. Whether real or imagined, that kiss quieted my soul in a way I never thought possible. And for the first time in as long as I could remember, I fell asleep with a smile.

Chapter 15

For the second day in a row, I woke up with a hangover that would've made Bacchus proud. And *that* wine-swilling reprobate could tie one on.

I rolled out of bed and promptly plopped onto the floor with a loud thud, which rattled the glass on my nightstand as well as the throbbing brain in my skull. I winced, glad Gran wasn't there to hear the aftereffects of my ill-advised overindulgence. Then I caught the unmistakable aroma of bacon in the air. I frowned in spite of my stomach growling in eager anticipation. Gran was gone. She couldn't be downstairs cooking breakfast. Which meant—

My eyes went wide. "Oh, my God."

I struggled to my feet, still a little off balance, and lunged for the doorknob. Fortunately, before throwing open the door and racing downstairs, I happened to look down and noticed that I was completely naked. Nude. Sans clothing.

As my synapses began to fire, I tried to put two and two together. Unfortunately, the answer to the equation was all a little fuzzy. The last thing I remember was Nate pulling the covers over me and *maybe* kissing my hair. I rubbed my eyes, trying to banish the last vestiges of inebriation, but there was nothing else. Zip. No other memories of anything after that point. How the hell could I possibly not remember sleeping with someone that hot, for crying out loud? It seemed unfair on a cosmic level.

The sound of pans clacking together downstairs reminded me that sooner or later I was going to have to face Nate even though I had no frigging idea what I was going to say. Should I pretend to remember what happened and say something about how nice it was but we worked together and yadda yadda blah blah blah? Or should I just cop to the fact I didn't remember a thing and hope he didn't take it personally?

Or maybe I should just pretend like nothing happened and see if he said anything first. Yeah. I liked that plan.

Coward, I chastised, pulling my bathrobe from the back of my door and slipping it on before creeping guiltily down the stairs.

The surprisingly welcome fragrances of breakfast grew stronger as I approached, making my mouth water in anticipation. And if that hadn't done it, the sight I came upon in the kitchen certainly would have done the trick.

Nate was standing at the stove with his back to me. His *bare* back. As I had noticed in the past, his shoulders were strong and broad, but my imagination hadn't done him justice. His was by far the most incredible male physique I'd ever seen. He made the chiseled beauty of Achilles and sculpted perfection of Vlad look like rough drafts of the masterpiece.

As I watched him in stunned silence, he moved with a kind of mesmerizingly sinewy grace, his lean muscles bulging and rippling in a carefully choreographed dance. Adding to the breathtaking beauty of his movements were the black flames I'd noticed on his neck and scalp. I was surprised to find they didn't end there but, in fact, started there, fanning out across his shoulders to engulf his biceps, then dancing down his back in intricate designs, licking his skin with fiery sensuality. I had never seen anything so sexy.

Unable to resist the pull of my libido's curiosity, I drifted forward and reached out, compelled to touch him and feel the heat of those flames. The instant my fingertips met his skin, Nate's muscles flinched and his hands stilled. As he slowly turned to face me, my fingers traced the flames around to where they seared his well-defined pectorals and taut belly.

"So incredible," I murmured as my hand drifted lower, determined to discover where the fire ended.

Nate caught my hand in his before I could follow the designs where they disappeared below his waistband. Suddenly realizing what I was doing, I jumped back and snatched my hand away, flushing fiercely.

"God, I'm sorry!" I gasped, averting my gaze. "I just . . ."

I didn't even know how to finish the thought. *I just want to explore every inch of your amazing body . . . with my tongue* seemed a bit too forward.

"Don't worry about it," Nate said, striding over to the dining room table and grabbing up the shirt hanging over the back of a chair. He shrugged into it, covering up the flames and breaking their spell over me.

"They're beautiful," I said, trying to say something appropriate. "Where did you have them done?"

"They're not tattoos," he muttered.

I arched my brows, more curious than ever. "What are they?"

Nate kept his gaze averted. "Penance."

"For what?" I asked before I could stop myself. Realizing how intrusive I was being, I said quickly, "I'm sorry—it's none of my business."

We stood in silence for several minutes while Nate finished dishing out breakfast. Then he set my plate down in front of what was becoming my customary bar stool. "Here you go."

I had climbed onto the bar stool and picked up my fork before I noticed he wasn't joining me. "Aren't you going to eat anything?"

Nate shook his head. "No, I should probably go." He glanced at the plate he'd fixed for himself, then picked it up and started to toss the contents down the sink.

The wonderfully fluffy mouthful of eggs suddenly tasted like ashes. "I wish you wouldn't," I blurted, irritated at the edge of distress that bled into my voice.

He paused at my words, then brought the plate over to me and set it down next to the one I was currently devouring. "You're right," he muttered. "No sense in it going to waste."

My hand darted out, grasping his as he started to back away. "Nate—"

For the first time that morning, his eyes met mine and the emotion I saw wrecked me. He was hurting, agonizing over something. But the moment I caught this tiny glimpse of his inner turmoil, his gaze went dull black again, blocking me from what he was hiding deep in his soul.

"I don't want you to go," I told him, realizing just how true it was. "Will you at least sit here with me?"

Nate hesitated but then came around and sat down with me while I polished off my plate. He didn't say a word, didn't even look at me, but having him there was enough. At some point, I shoved his plate back at him and he obediently picked up his fork.

"Thanks for breakfast," I said. "Again."

"You were in pretty bad shape last night," he said, finally speaking to me again. "I figured you needed someone to look after you."

"That doesn't usually happen," I assured him. I fiddled with the edges of the napkin, folding and unfolding the fabric into a bastardized version of origami. "I think everything just got to me a little more than I realized."

"Then you ran into Nicky Blue."

My head snapped up at this. "Yeah, I did," I said slowly. "And he seemed to know you and I were working together. How'd that happen?"

Nate picked up our plates and took them to the sink. "We go back a long way."

I frowned. "You and Nicky?"

"Long story." Nate quickly buttoned his shirt—damn the luck—and tucked it into his pants.

I leaned back in my chair and scooted his toward him with my bare foot. "I've got time."

Nate glanced down at his watch. "Not really," he retorted. "We need to get moving. We still have to talk to Hamelin's assistant, Halloran, and the Charmings, and track down Wolf. And I want to see what Trish found from the evidence they gathered at Gran's studio."

I nodded. "Yep, we've got a busy day ahead of us." I crossed my arms stubbornly. "But I'm not going anywhere until you tell me how you know Nicky."

Nate let out an impatient huff, then smoothed his hands through his hair. "I came to collect him once."

I don't know if I slid out of my chair or was jolted from it. "What?"

"Long time ago," Nate said, buttoning his cuffs.

I shook my head, trying to figure out when this would have been. Maybe it was after Nicky and I had split up— maybe even while he'd been over in Italy. I only knew of one time that Nicky had been close to death, and I'd been there for that one.

One of Halloran's toughs had shot Nicky over a soured business deal, and Nicky lay bleeding in my arms there in the dark alley until help arrived. I have to admit, I'd been worried there for a while—terrified, really. Of all the guys I'd been with since Seth, Nicky was the only one I'd say I'd been in love with. That's why I'd broken things off after the shooting. I'd already been through loving a guy with all my heart only to lose him. Seeing Nicky there bleeding to death with a gunshot wound to his chest was almost more than I could take. I felt like my heart was bleeding out in time with his.

Even in my grief and panic, if Nate had come for Nicky that night, I would have seen him. I mean, I guess I would have. I hadn't met Nate yet at that point—he wouldn't come over until a few years later. Still, I think I'd remember Death dropping by for a visit.

"So what happened?" I probed. "Why didn't you take him?"

Nate glanced at me, then busied himself looking for his shoes. "I changed my mind."

"Why?"

"Red, every now and then, there's a case that gets to me," he explained. "Something about it will make me want to give the person a second chance, spare him this time, reroll the dice, so to speak."

"And Nicky's dice?" I asked, suddenly nervous for my old friend and former flame.

Nate straightened from his search and finally looked at me. "He's got a very long life ahead of him—as far as I know."

I let out a relieved breath. "He's a really good guy, you know."

Nate gave me a short nod. "Yeah, I know. We've gotten to be pretty good friends since then."

My brows went up again at this. "And?"

Nate gave me a grin. "And he's one hell of a poker player. I'm down about five G's to him right now."

I laughed, suddenly feeling the tension lifting from the air surrounding us. "He won't call it in. Not if you're a friend."

"That's why I keep playing. And losing."

I stared at Nate for a long moment, glad we seemed to be falling back into the easy camaraderie we'd once enjoyed. So, in the spirit of totally ruining a wonderful moment, I said, "So, uh, about last night . . . Did we . . ."

Nate blinked at me. "You don't remember?"

I coughed, stalling for time as I debated how to answer. "Uh . . ."

Nate's laughter burst from him and he gave me a wink. "No,

we didn't. You passed out after I covered you up. I made sure you were okay, then slept in the guest room across the hall."

I laughed a little, trying to hide my mixture of relief and disappointment. "So how'd I end up completely naked?"

Now it was Nate's turn to be surprised. He shrugged. "You got me. I suppose you stripped down while you were sleeping." A broad smile slowly curved his lips. "I guess I should have hung around your room a little longer."

"You're an ass," I teased, taking a swing at his arm as he tried to dart away.

He laughed, rubbing at his upper arm where I'd slugged him. "Ah, but you love me."

I tossed a crooked smile over my shoulder as I headed out of the kitchen. "I *love* your scrambled eggs," I corrected. When I heard him chuckle, I paused and turned around just a little, suddenly feeling nervous. "But I have to admit, I do kinda like having you around."

"Good thing," Nate said, strolling toward me. He leaned a shoulder against the door frame, slouching in such a casual way that his face was alarmingly close to mine.

"Why's that?" I managed to ask, my voice sounding annoyingly breathless.

Nate dipped his head a little lower, and for a moment, I forgot to breathe. But then he gave me a chuck on the chin and offered me that wide, cocky smirk of his. "Because you're taking so long to get ready, I'll be here forever."

My immediate impulse was to punch him in the gut, but if there's one thing I've learned over the years, it's that there's more than one way to make a guy ache.

"Well," I said, arching a single brow, "guess I'd better take a shower." As I strolled to the stairs, I made sure to swing my hips just enough to catch his interest. I could feel his eyes on me, the heat from his gaze, making my bathrobe insufferably warm.

Well, only one way to fix that . . .

I untied the belt as I sidled up the stairs, letting first one side and then the other glide through my fingers. Obediently, my robe gaped open, flowing out behind me as I ascended. Checking my progress, I glanced behind me just as the material slid from my shoulders and pooled at my elbows, and was gratified to see Nate's startled expression. He blinked up at me and swallowed hard enough I could hear it. I didn't bother hiding my satisfied smile.

Men. They're so predictable.

Finally reaching the top of the stairs, I prepared for my final assault. And let my arms fall. The bathrobe followed. Nate probably caught little more than a glimpse of my completely nude backside before I turned the corner to go down the hall, but it was enough. I heard his sharp intake of breath and, although I can't be certain, I'm pretty sure I heard his jaw hit the floor.

Mission accomplished.

Chapter 16

"What?"

It was at least the fifteenth time Nate had glanced over at me since we'd left Gran's house.

Nate's eyes darted back to the road, and he shifted in his seat, suddenly looking uncomfortable. "Nothing."

"Then why do you keep looking at me?" I demanded. "You're starting to creep me out."

Nate's grip tightened on the steering wheel, his expression becoming even more intense. "I just . . ."

I waited for several seconds, but when he didn't continue, I prompted, "You just what?"

He huffed, then said quickly, "I just wanted to say you're beautiful."

Startled by his frank compliment, I jerked a little, not entirely sure how to respond. Besides, the sudden warmth in my cheeks made it a little hard to think. "Um, thanks."

Nate shrugged. "No big deal. You know, just being honest."

I nodded. "No worries. Thanks. I appreciate it."

"Yep."

An awkward silence fell between us for a moment, neither of us entirely sure what to say next. Finally, I decided to just leave it alone and try to get our attentions focused on something else.

"So, Gran comes home later today," I announced.

Nate's shoulders eased a bit. "Good. That's good. I'm glad she's doing okay."

Remembering the surprise I'd received the night before about him and Nicky being old friends, I asked, "So, had you met Gran before yesterday?"

Nate's tension immediately returned. "Once," he said stiffly. "But I hadn't come to collect her. She just happened to be nearby. We didn't really meet—I just saw her from a distance. She didn't even know I was there."

I gave myself a mental smack on the forehead. Of course, he'd seen her before—Gran was a widow. Odds were good she'd been there the day her husband had been collected.

"Is there anyone else you're acquainted with that I should know about?" I asked.

Nate gave me a disappointed look that stopped just short of rolling his eyes at me. "It's safe to assume that I know pretty much everyone you know, Red—it's my job. And if I haven't met them yet, I'm going to."

I flushed a little. "Right." Trying to redeem myself by actually asking an intelligent question, I said, "So, are we Tales the only ones on your client list?"

"Do you mean do I collect Ordinaries as well?"

I nodded. "Yeah. I mean, it's not like Tales are dropping like flies or anything. Statistically, I'd think the Ordinaries would be better business. Supply and demand and all that."

"I don't collect Ordinaries," Nate told me. "Not unless I happen to be there collecting a Tale at the same time."

"Why?"

Nate got that closed-off look as he replied, "I'm on special assignment."

My brows lifted in surprise. "We're a special assignment?"

He cast an irritable glance my way. "It's not like you play by the same rules as Ordinaries, is it? You're fictional characters made flesh. It presents a few unique challenges to collecting you. For one thing, I can't just drop you off in the hereafter."

"I can understand that, but—"

"It's complicated," he interrupted with a finality that clearly indicated I should drop the subject.

I chose to overlook it. "So enlighten me."

Nate's jaw tightened and he didn't immediately respond.

"I'm trying to understand you, Nate," I said sincerely. "I just want to get to know you, to understand where you come from. Is that so horrible?"

I saw his muscles ease just a little, but his voice was quiet when he tentatively asked, "And if you don't like what you find?"

That's what he was worried about?

"Nate," I said with a laugh, "it's not like I don't know about your second job. You're a Reaper. I'm not asking you to give away the secrets of your trade or anything—I honestly couldn't care less about how your job works. That's your business. But I *am* curious about *you.*"

Nate exhaled on a sigh and I knew I'd made some headway. "Okay," he said. "What do you want to know?"

"How'd you get put on special assignment?"

"I asked for it."

"Why?"

Nate shrugged. "Thought it would be interesting."

"Yeah?" I said with a grin. "And what do you think so far? Have we been a huge disappointment?"

"Are you kidding me?" Nate said as he turned off the main street and onto a gravel road leading to a huge complex of warehouses surrounded by a nine-foot-high chain-link fence. "You Tales are so dysfunctional you make the Ordinaries look like one big happy family."

I grunted. "You say that like you're not one of us."

As we reached the entrance to the complex, Nate pulled a

stick of gum out of his pocket and folded it in half before putting it in his mouth. Time to get down to business. "So, do you know which one it is?" he asked, nodding toward the rows of identical square buildings.

"Yeah—third row from the left, eighth building down." Dave Hamelin's pest control company was nestled among the other warehouses and only stood out because of the several white vans emblazoned with the logo of a man skipping merrily while playing a flute, an assortment of rats, roaches, bees, and various other pests trailing along behind him.

"Think the employees know about Hamelin yet?" Nate asked, pulling into a vacant spot next to one of the vans.

"Only one way to find out."

The answer to Nate's question was clear the minute we stepped inside the building. At the reception desk of the office area, a young woman with a chestnut brown bob and wide brown eyes rose to meet us. Her cheeks were streaked with tears and her nose was red and swollen from crying.

"I'm sorry," she sniffed. "But we're closed. I just haven't changed the sign."

"We're not customers," Nate assured her gently. "We are looking into Dave Hamelin's death and were hoping you could answer some questions."

She glanced between us and sniffed a couple more times. "Are you cops?"

"Not exactly," I replied, realizing she was an Ordinary. "More like private investigators."

She nodded and grabbed a couple of tissues from the box on her desk. "Okay then. I can help you with any questions you might have."

Wondering just how cooperative she would've been had we said we were police, I asked, "What's your name?"

"Alice."

"Alice, were you and Dave pretty close?"

A sob burst from her at my question and the waterworks

began anew. Nate gave me a pleading look and jerked his head toward Alice.

"What?" I mouthed.

"Help her," he mouthed back.

I puffed my cheeks full of air, then let it out on a sigh and went around behind the desk, wondering just how I was supposed to console the weeping woman. Dealing with my own emotions was a bit of a stretch—dealing with the emotions of others was completely foreign territory.

"Uh, is there anything we can do?" I asked lamely, putting my hand on her shoulder. "Do you need some water or something?"

Alice shook her head and made a concerted effort to pull herself back together. "No, no. I'll be fine. It's just that"—she hiccuped a couple of times—"Dave was like a father to me."

Nate and I exchanged glances, apparently both having difficulty picturing Dave in the fatherly role, all things considered.

"How so?" I hazarded.

After taking a long, shaky breath, Alice said, "I used to be a street kid, did lots of drugs and all that. Dave took me in, gave me a job, helped me find a place to live. He actually cared about me, you know?"

Actually, I didn't know. In fact, I never would've guessed.

"Alice," Nate said gently, "do you know if Dave was in any kind of trouble?"

She wiped her eyes with the tissue and shook her head. "No. Things were going great. We suddenly had a ton of business—big clients, too. Rich people."

"Do you mind if we take a look at your client list, Alice?" I asked. "Maybe we could talk to some of these folks and see if any of them can help us understand what might have happened."

The poor thing looked at me like I'd just offered her a million dollars. "You'd do that?"

"Yeah, sure." I looked at Nate to confirm the offer.

"You bet," he assured her, giving her one of his killer smiles. "We'll do anything we can to help."

Alice's face lit up as she returned Nate's smile. Then, with a little bit of a bounce in her step, she scurried over to a filing cabinet and rummaged through the folders until she came out with several sheets of paper stapled together.

"Here you go," she said, turning the list over to Nate. "That's the most recent list of clients. I print a new hard copy every couple of weeks, so this one was current as of last week."

"Why keep a hard copy if you have them in the computer?" I questioned.

She smiled a little sadly. "Dave doesn't like me to mess around in the computer, so I don't know the log-in and password. He would log in for me every other Friday and let me catch up on some of the invoice work and print out a new list."

"You seem like a bright girl," Nate told her. "Didn't he think you could handle it on your own?"

Alice flushed a little at his compliment. "It isn't that. It's just that this is his personal computer, too," she informed us, gesturing toward the desk. "He said he was working on some freelance project that was confidential and that he couldn't violate his agreement by letting me accidentally stumble on it."

I'll bet.

I tried not to think about the variety of smut and other illegal content that might be lurking on Dave's hard drive. No wonder he didn't want his darling little protégée to stumble upon anything. Of course, there might also have been some truth to the whole freelance story. Maybe he *was* working on something for somebody on the side—something that he couldn't risk coming to light if I hauled him in for a parole violation and we confiscated his computer.

"Alice," I said, making a concerted effort to smile and seem friendly, "do you think maybe you could let us borrow Dave's computer for a couple of days?"

When she drew back, looking skittish at my words, Nate immediately joined in. "Don't worry, sweetheart. We won't give anything we find to the police. We know people who can hack past his password and find out if there are any clients who still owe you money, that sort of thing."

Alice's eyes went wide, giving her a panicked look. "Oh, God," she gasped. "You're right! What am I going to do now that he's gone? We'll have to close the company. What will I do for a job? I'll end up back on the streets!"

Sensing the dam was about to burst again, I quickly moved forward and put my arm around her shoulders. "Don't worry. I think I know someone you can talk to. She's really good at helping people who've lost their way and need a little help finding it again."

Alice blinked at me with teary eyes and sniffed. "Really?"

I nodded, then went to the desk and hunted down a piece of paper and a pen. I quickly jotted down a name and number and handed the paper to Alice. "Give her a call sometime in the next couple of days. I'm sure she can help you."

In a move that completely took me off guard, Alice threw her arms around my neck and hugged me so tightly I struggled to breathe.

"Thank you," she sobbed. "Thank you so much!"

I gave her a couple of pats on the back. "No problem." When Alice didn't get the hint that she was slowly suffocating me, I sent a pleading look Nate's way, but he was scowling at me angrily, apparently content to let me fend for myself.

I patted Alice again and then gently pried her loose. "It's okay. Just hang in there, all right?" Then, seeing her rather forlorn expression, I reached into the inner pocket of my trench and pulled out a card that had nothing more than my name and phone number printed in simple block letters. "Here. This is my number. Call me if you need anything."

She nodded and sniffed, pocketing both numbers. Taking my cue, I quickly disconnected Dave's laptop from the docking station and tucked it under my arm before she could

capture me again. "Take care," I called over my shoulder as I
headed out the door.

"I can't believe you," Nate hissed, suddenly materializing
in my path.

"What?" I snapped.

"You know what."

I pulled open the car door and stuck the laptop in the
backseat. "No. Sorry, I don't. Care to enlighten me?"

He rushed toward me, crowding so closely I could feel the
heat of his anger. "How could you turn that girl over to her?
After all she's been through, you'd send her right back into
the streets? God, did I have you all wrong."

Now it was my turn to fume. I gave him a hard shove away
from me, then advanced on him this time. "First of all—
Back. The Fuck. Off." I gave his shoulder another shove, but
this time he was ready and didn't budge. Regardless, I spat,
"I don't know what the hell you're so mad about. The kid is
obviously having a rough time of it, so I thought Gran could
maybe—"

"You gave her Gran's number?" he interrupted.

"Yeah," I huffed. "Gran's helped out some other girls over
the years besides me. I thought maybe she could help Alice
find a new job. Hell, I don't know—maybe get her some
counseling or something."

Nate looked suddenly sheepish—well, about as sheepish
as Death could. "I thought you'd sent her to Snow."

For a moment, I could only stare at him, unable to believe
that he had thought me capable of such a thing. Did he really
think that after what I'd been through in my youth that I'd
talk some poor vulnerable waif into a life of prostitution?
I shook my head in disbelief, trying to ignore the ache of
disappointment twisting my heart. With a wounded laugh, I
slammed the car door and started walking.

"Red, I'm sorry!" Nate called after me. I heard his footsteps on the pavement as he hurried to catch up with me, but
I didn't slow my pace until he grabbed my arm and spun me

around to face him. "I said I'm sorry. I should have known you'd never do anything like that."

"Yeah, you should have."

"Will you forgive me?"

I lifted my eyes to his, fully prepared to tell him off again—this time with a little more profanity—but the sincere regret and shame I saw there made me change my mind. "I'll think about it." With that, I turned and started walking again.

"Where are you going?" he asked. "Come back to the car. I know you're pissed but—"

"Tim Halloran's warehouse is in this same complex," I said, cutting him off. "We might as well pay him a visit while we're here, don't you think?"

I heard Nate laugh as he fell in beside me. "You know, you could have just said that's where you were going from the very beginning instead of making me beg."

"It would have ruined the drama," I replied, "and significantly diminished my enjoyment from watching you squirm."

"You're incorrigible. You know that, don't you?"

I cast him a coy, sidelong glance. "And yet here you are."

Nate shoved his hands into his pockets, a slow smile curving his lips. "Here I am."

Chapter 17

Any self-respecting head of an organized crime operation has a successful front business to hide his more questionable activities, and Tim "the Sandman" Halloran was no exception. To most of the world, he was known as President and CEO of a highly respected independent pharmaceuticals wholesaler, Dreamland Distributors.

But, in addition to being the Medical Magnate of the Midwest, Halloran was Chicago's most feared and reviled drug lord. Or so we suspected. We couldn't prove it. Over the years, we'd pinched more than a handful of Halloran's people in drug busts and had seized truckloads of black market pharmaceuticals being smuggled to cities around the country, but we'd never been able to make anything stick to Halloran. Several layers of plausible deniability always seemed to exist between him and prosecution, making him completely untouchable.

It was bad enough that Halloran was dealing in the usual high-end Ordinary drugs like cocaine and other, more difficult to come by products that soccer mom drug addicts wanted to hide from their PTO peers. But he also was the sole provider of fairy dust—or Vitamin D, as it was called on the street—the most addictive and dangerous drug a Tale could possibly ingest.

In small quantities, fairy dust could create a feeling of euphoria, confidence, the belief you could do anything. Tale doctors used it to treat severe depression in their patients, but intake had to be monitored carefully for the safety of the patient. In fact, in order to get their weekly dose of Vitamin D, patients had to visit a fairy clinic to have it administered by a certified fairy dust distributor. The likelihood of addiction was almost guaranteed, and, from what I understood, weaning off it was a bitch, with the withdrawal symptoms sometimes leading to suicidal thoughts or violent rages—even hallucinations and paranoia.

Unfortunately, Halloran was an opportunist who had seen a need in the community and had filled it, peddling D on the street with the nonchalance of a hotdog vendor. He didn't care how many people got hurt or how many lives were ruined as a result of his activities. It was all about making money. And Halloran was raking it in hand over fist.

Putting Halloran away for good and getting his poison off the streets was about the only thing that Mary Smith and I saw eye to eye on (although I'd never admit it to her). One of these days, I was going to take down the son of a bitch, but today I just wanted to know more about his connection to Dave Hamelin.

Not wanting to tip off Halloran and his people to our presence too early, Nate and I came around the side of the building through a loading area shared by Halloran's warehouse and the one next to it. A couple of trucks were parked at the loading docks, waiting to be put into service, but otherwise it was quiet.

"Halloran's office is just inside the main door," I told Nate, motioning toward the front of the building.

"Anybody we should be worried about?" Nate asked.

I shook my head. "Just the usual thugs. His people all carry, so watch for anybody who looks a little too twitchy. Other than that, just don't make any sudden movements or appear too threatening. I don't want them to think we're here to bust them."

Nate gave me a tight nod. "Got it. I'll just follow your lead."

"About time you—" My words were cut off by Nate jerking me off my feet and behind a stack of empty mattress boxes. "What the—"

He held a finger to his lips and looked hard at the side door. I gasped when I saw who was exiting.

"What the hell's she doing here?" I whispered.

Nate shook his head, then nodded toward where Sebille Fenwick was charging down the stairs. Her hair was down and she had traded her business suit for jeans and a yellow turtleneck sweater, but the scowl she'd been wearing the day we'd met her was still firmly in place. She looked flat-out pissed.

A split second later, one of Halloran's people came out of the same door and hurried after Sebille, catching up to her quickly in spite of her angry strides. The guy caught her by the elbow and pulled her to a halt. They had a quick moment of conversation that looked more business than social. Then the guy placed a small package in Sebille's hands. She glanced down at it, then nodded. She still looked angry, but her expression was a little less harsh than before. Apparently, whatever the guy had told her had placated her at least a little.

Sebille glanced around, then said something else before hurrying off and disappearing around the corner of the neighboring building. Halloran's employee went back inside, apparently unaware of our presence just a few yards away.

"What was that all about?" I wondered aloud.

"We should follow her and see where she goes," Nate suggested, coming out from behind the boxes.

"Why don't you tail her," I said, "and I'll go have a chat with Halloran."

Nate gave me a look that told me he was about to remind

me of my promise to be more careful, but I cut him off before he could protest. "Listen, Halloran knows me. He knows that if I was coming to bust him I'd be bringing a fleet of agents with me. He also knows that I wouldn't be stupid enough to come see him without telling someone where I was going. I'll be fine. I'll meet you back at the car."

Nate glanced in the direction Sebille had gone, obviously as curious as I was to know what she was up to. "Are you sure?"

"Yes," I said. "Now get going before you lose her."

He pressed his lips together and looked at me like he wanted to say something else, but instead he just gave me a nod and vanished in a blur of black mist. With Nate gone, I made my way around to the front of the building.

The minute I stepped inside, pain exploded in my head with such shocking force I dropped to the ground, fully expecting to see stars and canaries circling above me. Instead, I saw the face of the man at the loading docks as he peered down at me. Then there was only darkness.

I had no idea how long I'd been unconscious when I finally came to, but I knew for a fact I wasn't at the warehouse anymore. I was lying on a soft bed in total darkness except for a sliver of light that seeped in under the door. I patted my pockets, not surprised to find my cell phone and gun missing.

Groaning at the pounding pressure in my head, I sat up slowly and allowed my eyes to adjust to the light. I could dimly make out the outlines of a chest of drawers and a few other pieces of heavy furniture in the small room, but not well enough to determine to whom they belonged.

Not wanting to wait to find out, I swung my legs over the side of the bed and made for the door, but was jerked off my feet before I'd gone more than a few strides. I cried out in pain, belatedly realizing my right arm was shackled to the bedpost. I cursed under my breath and tried to work my hand loose, twisting and pulling against the heavy iron and trying to ignore the searing pain as my skin peeled away. I was just starting to make some progress when the door swung open, the sudden column of light making me wince.

"Awake at last, Enforcer?"

I glared at the man silhouetted in the doorway. "No thanks to your goon."

Tim Halloran sauntered in, his pale brown eyes glinting with smug amusement. "I'm afraid Aloysius overreacted when he saw you come in. He thought you were a burglar."

I sniffed dismissively. "I'll bet."

"I humbly apologize for my colleague's overzealousness." Halloran offered me a smooth, charming smile, his teeth a little too white and perfect to trust. "And, I assure you, the moment I learned of what had occurred, I insisted you be brought to my home until you awakened."

I held up my arm, indicating the cuff on my wrist. "Yeah, well, your hospitality sucks, Halloran."

He lifted his arms at his sides in a conciliatory gesture. "Again, I must ask your forgiveness, my dear, but it was for your own protection. I couldn't have you wandering around unfamiliar surroundings. You might have come to harm."

I gave him a skeptical look. "In your *house*?"

"Sophia," he called over his shoulder. "Come here, my darling."

On cue, a white Bengal tiger padded into the room and affectionately rubbed her massive head against Halloran's leg. She purred loudly as he reached down and scratched behind her ear.

"Sophia is a docile creature," he explained mildly as the big cat came slinking slowly toward me to investigate, "but she's terribly possessive of me. She doesn't care to have other women infringing upon her territory."

I scooted back up onto the bed and tucked my legs under

me. "You can tell her she has nothing to worry about," I murmured. "You're the last guy I'm interested in."

Sophia sniffed the air around me, then put her front paws up on the bed, leaning closer, all the better to gobble me up. I cringed, edging as far away as the shackles would allow.

"Come, Sophia," Halloran said gently. "She means me no harm. Isn't that right, Enforcer?"

I nodded. "Yep. I just came to talk. That's all."

Sophia regarded me for a moment longer, then let her paws fall back to the floor. As she padded unhurriedly back toward Halloran, there was a shimmer of white light in the air, and where the tiger had been, now stood a beautiful young woman with long white hair, which perfectly complemented the white streaks in Halloran's sandy locks.

She twined her bare body around Halloran, nuzzling under his chin in a disconcertingly feline motion. He stroked a gentle hand down her hair along her back and down her backside, making her arch and purr with delight at his questing touch. She lifted her unmistakably hungry gaze to his and was rewarded with a kiss so deep and passionate, I suddenly felt like a voyeur on the set of an upscale porno. I averted my eyes and coughed to remind them I was still there.

"I will come see to you soon, my darling," I heard Halloran say softly.

I looked his way just in time to see the lovely Sophia drift out into the hallway. "That's, uh . . ." I wasn't even sure what to say. *Disturbing* came to mind. But I figured it was better to just let it go. After all, I was still handcuffed.

"Beautiful, isn't she?" Halloran asked, his admiration of the lovely shape-shifter evident.

"No denying that," I confirmed, figuring agreeing with him on such an obvious fact was pretty safe territory. Then I lifted my wrist again. "So, now that your girlfriend and I have met, you think you can take this off?"

Halloran came forward and produced a key, unlocking the cuff. "There you are. See? No harm meant."

I rubbed the raw skin on my wrist and eyed him warily. "Now you want to give me back my stuff?"

Halloran clasped his hands behind his back and gave me that artificial smile of his. "In due time. But I believe you wanted to talk. Come—let us move to my office."

I followed him out of the room and through a circuitous network of corridors and stairways that had so many twists and turns that by the time he came to the room he sought, I had long ago lost track of lefts and rights, ups and downs, and was hopelessly lost. There was no way I could've found my way to the bathroom, let alone the front door. Which I'm sure was the point.

"After you," he said with a polite sweep of his arm.

I scanned my surroundings as I entered, taking in at a glance the Chippendale furniture, Baccarat crystal, and other finery that would have looked gaudy and showy in a smaller room. I had to admit, Halloran had good taste—or at least his decorator did. I took a seat in the chair across from his desk, forcing him to the other side.

He folded his hands placidly and regarded me evenly, his smile still draping his lips. "Now, how may I help you?"

"I want to know about your relationship to the Pied Piper," I said, coming straight to the point.

"He took care of a rat infestation at my warehouse," he replied. "Quite effectively, I might add. I was very happy with his work."

"He's dead," I told him, watching his reaction closely. He didn't even flinch.

"A pity," he said. "How did it happen?"

"He committed suicide."

Halloran shook his head. "How horrible. Do you know why?"

"If I knew why, I wouldn't be here," I snapped. "Word

has it that Todd Caliban recommended Hamelin to you. Is that right?"

Halloran nodded. "Yes. Caliban had a similar problem at his café and the steak house as well, I believe. He was very happy with Hamelin's work and recommended him to me."

I leaned back in my chair, assuming a casual pose similar to Halloran's. "Remind me how you know Caliban?"

"We are business associates," he said tersely.

I lifted my brows a bit. "Caliban's going into the pharmaceutical business now?"

This time Halloran's smile was a little tighter. "You have it backward. I am going into the restaurant business. I have long thought Caliban to be a very talented chef, and with his television show doing well, I saw an opportunity to invest in his future."

"Meaning what?" I asked cautiously. The thought of Halloran investing in anything concerning Caliban made me nervous.

"There is a chance his show is going to expand into wider syndication," Halloran explained. "He has an offer to move it to Hollywood."

"Hollywood?" I echoed. "He's going to the Ordinary TV networks?"

"Most assuredly." Halloran's smile widened. "With the right financial backing."

"And that's where you come in," I deduced. "You're footing the bill to move his operations to California."

Halloran's eyes glistened with greed. "Not only that, but I will be the main corporate sponsor of the show."

"Free advertising."

"Indeed."

It all sounded like it was on the level, but there was still something about the whole thing that didn't sit well with me. "And that's it?" I asked, still fishing for information. "That's the extent of your business relationship?"

An appreciative smile spread across Halloran's face. "You know me too well, Enforcer. Caliban is to open a new steak house here in Chicago called, appropriately, Caliban's. I anticipate that the popularity of his television show in the local media—which is rivaled only by that of your dear Gran's—will make it an instant success. Add in the potential for opening locations in LA and New York after his show hits the major cable networks, and I will profit quite handsomely for my initial investment."

Now came the million-dollar question. "So where does Sebille Fenwick fit in to this equation? What was she doing at the warehouse earlier today?"

Halloran's smile evaporated, replaced by a furious scowl. "That meddling bitch doesn't know when to mind her own business," he spat, his mask of suavity slipping briefly. "She presumes to know business better than I do?"

"Not a fan of hers, I take it," I drawled.

Halloran launched to his feet and began to pace around the office, his hands clasped behind his back. "She thinks Caliban walks on water," he grumbled. "I admit the man has immense talent, but he can't possibly run his businesses here while he is filming in California."

"And you've offered to run things for him?" I guessed.

Halloran gave me a look that clearly indicated the stupidity of my question. "I haven't the time to deal with that kind of minutia. I insisted that Caliban hire another very talented chef to run the steak house." Here Halloran paused in his pacing and offered me a sadistic grin. "In fact, I believe you know him, my dear. He's an old friend, as I understand it—Seth Wolf. Your infamous first lover, yes?"

My blood turned to ice water in my veins. I stared dumbly at Halloran, which he found immensely amusing.

"Didn't know your former flames were going into business together, did you?" he taunted.

"It's not like I hang out with them much these days," I managed to croak.

Halloran circled around to the back of my chair and bent down until his lips were near my ear. "We never quite get over our first love, do we? Our first heartbreak? Of course, yours was even more tragic than most—being abandoned and ruined at such a tender age. How ironic that he should end up working with Todd Caliban. I imagine they will have a great deal to talk about."

I ground my teeth together so hard I felt my molars creak with the strain. With about as much dignity as I could manage, I rose to my feet and faced Halloran, offering him a strained smile. "Thank you very much for chatting with me, Sandman," I said politely. "It's been a pleasure as always."

Halloran's smug chuckle was almost more than I could bear. I clenched my fists at my sides to keep from popping him in the mouth. Fortunately for Halloran, there was a knock on the office door.

"Enter!" he called.

The man who'd jumped me at the warehouse—Aloysius—entered and handed Halloran my cell phone and gun. "The phone's been ringing off the hook," he complained. Then he turned to me and said, "I like your ring tone."

I frowned at what I guessed was some kind of apology and replied, "Uh, thanks." As soon as Aloysius was gone, I held out my hand to Halloran. "I'll take those now."

He handed them over without comment, then gestured toward the door. "Shall I show you out?"

"If you would be so kind," I ground out, forcing a smile.

We entered the labyrinth of hallways once more and eventually ended up in a cavernous foyer complete with marble floors and crystal chandeliers. At the other end was a set of doors twelve feet high, actual doormen standing sentinel at either side, waiting to perform their duties. As Halloran and I approached, they snapped to attention and rushed forward.

"Enforcer Little is leaving now," Halloran announced. He then turned to me and inclined his head. Had the gesture come from someone I actually liked and respected, I would have felt honored by the little bow. But from Halloran, it just cemented my disgust for the slime hidden beneath his smarmy veneer.

"I'll be seeing you, Halloran." I lifted a hand in farewell as I headed out the door, making sure that I used all five fingers. As much as I would have loved to express my sincere gratitude for my stay at Chez Sandman, there was a hungry she-tiger lurking around, and I wasn't in a hurry to end up as dinner.

I was stepping over the threshold when I snapped my fingers, ready to make my parting shot with the one other question that had been plaguing me. "By the way, Halloran," I drawled, "what did Aloysius give Sebille?"

Halloran's brows twitched ever so slightly. "I beg your pardon?"

"In the alley outside the warehouse. I saw him slip something to her—a small package."

Halloran blinked at me, then gave me a tight smile. "Merely a gift for Caliban, I presume."

"A gift," I repeated, my skepticism bleeding into my tone.

"Precisely."

"You presume? You don't know?"

"Good day, Enforcer Little."

"Guess our conversation's over, then?" I taunted. "Well, don't worry, Sandman. We'll chat again."

"I shall count the hours until we meet again," he sneered.

The minute I stepped onto the porch, the front door slammed behind me, the hollow boom echoing in the twilight. "Wow," I muttered. "Try not to miss me."

Interesting that Halloran hadn't known about the package. Made me wonder what kind of come-to-Jesus meeting Aloysius was in for. Oh well, not my problem.

However, trying to get back home with no mode of transportation *was* my problem. I rubbed my wrist again and glanced around, trying to get my bearings.

Where the hell was I anyway?

I assumed I was still somewhere near Chicago, but I couldn't even really be sure. Groaning at my fabulous good fortune, I took a look at the call log on my phone to see what I'd missed thanks to my unexpected time warp. Twenty missed calls. Damn. No wonder Aloysius was pissed. I'd be annoyed, too.

I paged through them quickly. The first several were from Nate spaced fifteen minutes apart. One from Elizabeth. Two from Nicky. One from Vlad. One from Gran. One from headquarters. Five more from Nate—the last one was only ten minutes ago. At 6:14!

I groaned again. *Great.* The whole day was shot, thanks to my little adventure. But at least it wasn't a total loss. We had Hamelin's computer in our possession, which might yield some answers about why he'd killed himself. And the bit about Halloran's connection to Caliban was certainly an interesting development.

With a sigh, I hit speed dial. The phone had barely connected when I heard Nate's relieved voice. "Thank God!" he said in a rush. "Are you okay? Are you hurt? We've got a lock on your coordinates. I've got six agents with me—we'll be there in ten minutes, but if you need me right now, I'll pull over and vaporize to where you are."

"You can call off the cavalry," I told him. "Aloysius thought I was a burglar and knocked me out."

"Aloysius?"

"Muscley guy at the loading docks with Sebille," I explained. "Halloran brought me to his estate to sleep it off."

"Are you okay?"

"Just tired," I realized. "And my head's killing me. But I found out some information you might find interesting. Go ahead and send the rest of the guys back to HQ. I'll start walking toward the main road—you can pick me up there."

"Are you sure?" Nate asked, sounding hesitant.

I jogged down the steps and started walking down the narrow paved road leading away from the house. "Yeah, I'm sure. I'll just see you soon."

I pocketed my phone and stumbled along the road, surprised at how dizzy I was. I hadn't felt strange at Halloran's house, but the longer I walked, the worse I felt.

A concussion? Great. Just what I needed.

I looked around, trying to find a place where I could sit down for a minute, but there was nothing along the private drive except for the darkening woods. Nothing to do but keep walking, so I forced my feet to move. Unfortunately, the contusion on my head had other plans. The road pitched and rolled, throwing me off balance. Unable to combat the vertigo, I stumbled and fell, hitting the ground hard with my shoulder.

"Damn it," I muttered, trying to force myself to my feet but pitching forward onto my elbows in an undignified sprawl.

I closed my eyes for a few seconds and took several slow breaths, trying to pull it together so that I could try again. If I stayed there on the ground, Nate might drive right past me— or worse, run me over. Dressed all in black as I was, it would be kind of hard to see me against the asphalt in the waning light. I finally struggled to my knees and reached into my pocket to fish out my phone again when a low growl made me freeze.

My heart pounded as I listened, trying to pinpoint the sound. I swallowed hard, slowly surveying the woods surrounding me, but I couldn't make out anything except the silhouettes of trees among the thick shadows. Growing increasingly uneasy, I pulled out my Glock and ejected the clip. *Empty.*

Aloysius must have taken the bullets when he had the gun in his possession.

I mumbled a juicy curse, then, newly motivated, I struggled again to regain my footing. I was just straightening when a branch snapped behind me, making me jump and swivel toward the sound. Ten yards away, a glowing pair of green eyes glared back at me. A low growl drifted toward me again, raising the hairs on my arms.

I slowly backed away, never taking my eyes off those of my feral stalker. "Is that you, Sophia?" I asked softly, my voice trembling. "I'm leaving. See? You don't have to worry about me. I promise."

The creature moved parallel to me, making sure I knew it was still there with every step. Then the glowing eyes dropped lower as the creature prepared to pounce.

I let out a choked, shaky breath. "Oh, shit."

Chapter 18

I'd always imagined that I'd come up with something clever and pithy when it came to my last words, but as I stood there staring at those horrifying eyes, I settled for a little startled profanity.

How embarrassing.

But even more humiliating than my wit abandoning me was my complete and total paralysis. I couldn't think, I couldn't move, I couldn't breathe. I was going to be slaughtered without even attempting to fight back. How the hell did that happen? Either I was more banged up than I'd thought, or some other force was controlling me—something far beyond fear and panic.

What had been a low growl now turned into a deep rumbling snarl. Then the underbrush seemed to explode with the crackling rustle of something powerful and massive and deadly bounding forward. Time seemed to slow as the beast burst from the cover of foliage. I caught the gleam of ferocious teeth in the moonlight as a horrific roar assaulted my ears, filling me with terror.

Just then high beam headlights split the darkness, illuminating the road and the woods surrounding it. As Nate's car came to a screeching halt, the beast abruptly shifted direction, retreating in a blur of motion so swift my mind could barely process what had transpired. The creature howled in frustration and crashed through the underbrush, seeking cover from the sudden intrusion. As soon as it disappeared, my breath came rushing back to me in a gasp.

"Red, you okay?" Nate asked, slipping an arm around my waist to support me and hurriedly looking me over.

"Get in the car," I ordered, looking around frantically. The beast had been scared off by Nate's arrival, but I had a feeling it was only a temporary withdrawal. It'd be back.

"But—"

"Get in the car!"

Without another word, Nate hurried me into the car, then climbed in behind the wheel.

"Let's go," I told him, still monitoring the woods for any sign of movement.

Nate put the car in gear and turned it back toward the main road. He was just accelerating when a tremendous impact against my door sent me flying toward him. I cried out in a combination of horror and pain as my head hit his shoulder.

"What the fuck is that?" Nate yelled, trying to keep control of the car.

"Just go!" I screamed, looking toward the shattered window and the gaping hole that was now there. "Go, go, go, *go!*"

This time Nate didn't ask any questions. He slammed his foot down on the accelerator, tires squealing in protest. We took the winding private road in what I imagined was record time, barely hanging on to some of the hairpin turns as the car slid on gravel and skidded toward a wide ditch between the road and the trees. In a final burst of speed, we broke free of the wooded road and found ourselves on a main highway, still traveling at breakneck speed. We were at least two miles down the highway before Nate let up at all on the accelerator.

The cold wind buffeted my face, stinging and numbing my skin to the point that I didn't realize I was bleeding until Nate reached into his pocket and held out a handkerchief.

"Put that on your forehead," he ordered, his hand shaking as he thrust the folded cotton cloth toward me.

Dazed, I nodded and pressed the thin material to a random spot that seemed sorer than the rest. His face pale and drawn, Nate glanced at me, then adjusted my hand, pressing the handkerchief against the wound more effectively.

"Right there," he said. "Keep it on there until I can get you to the hospital."

Again, I nodded, not able to form a coherent argument against going to the hospital and not sure if I should try. "It was going to kill me," I stammered, edging closer to Nate in an effort to stop the violent shivers shattering my body. "Rip me to shreds. Tear me apart. I couldn't do anything. I couldn't move. What the hell happened to me?"

Nate put his arm around my shoulders and pulled me close. "It's all right now. It's all over. I've got you."

I put my head down against his chest and curled into him, trying to hold on to consciousness. And failing.

When I awoke, I was lying in a hospital bed, surrounded by darkness and the soft beeping and whirring of various monitors and machines. I had an IV in my arm and electrodes taped to my chest, monitoring my heartbeat. Moonlight shone in through the slats of the venetian blinds, cluing me in that it was still night, but the sliver of moon was high, so several hours obviously had passed since the attack.

I closed my eyes again and tried to ignore the pounding in my head, but a rustling in the far corner brought me wide awake. The heart monitor went crazy as my body tensed in preparation to take on whatever was lurking in the shadows. But then I realized the form in the darkness was that of a man—not a beast preparing to strike.

I let out a relieved breath and sank back into the pillows. "Nate?"

The shadows shifted as the man stepped forward into the

moonlight. "Regrettably, no. Detective Grimm had to step out for a moment."

I frowned. "What are you doing here?"

"You missed our date," Vlad replied, coming to the bed to take my hand in his. "Obviously for good reason."

He was smiling at me, but within that smile there was something else. Concern. And, if I wasn't mistaken, anger. No, not just anger. Rage—barely restrained and lying just beneath the surface.

"How did you find out?" I asked, my voice cracking.

"When you did not call, I made some calls of my own," he explained. "Eventually, I reached your dear Gran. She told me you had been attacked and were in the hospital. I came as soon as night fell."

My brows came together and I glanced toward the window. "Are you becoming more sensitive to light? You've never had trouble except on really sunny days."

Vlad smoothed my hair back with a gentle hand, careful not to disturb the bandage on my forehead. "Today was quite beautiful, my little love," he said. "Unseasonably warm, in fact. It's a shame you had to miss it."

I shook my head in confusion. "How long have I been here?"

"Just twenty-eight hours."

"Twenty-eight hours?" I cried, trying to sit up.

Vlad pressed me back down against the pillow. "Do not sit up so quickly," he admonished. "You suffered quite an injury—two injuries in fact. You needed time to mend."

I closed my eyes. Twenty-eight hours. I'd missed an entire day that I could have been out trying to track down the murderer, get to the bottom of Dave's suicide, arrest that bastard Halloran's psycho girlfriend for attacking me. . . .

"Where's Nate?" I asked, my eyes snapping open. "I need to talk to him."

I heard Vlad expel an irritated breath, but when he answered his voice was even. "He left three hours ago to tend to a call. I imagine he will return when he is finished. I was very nearly ready to murder someone myself to get him away from your bedside."

I gave Vlad a sharp look that made him chuckle.

"I jest, little one," he assured me. "I promised you that I would never again bloody my hands with the death of another, and I have kept that promise."

I closed my eyes again, too tired to keep them open for long. "I need to get back to work."

I could tell Vlad was grinning with amusement when he said, "Clearly."

Unfortunately, he had a point. My head was pounding and I was obviously still weak and out of it from whatever glorious painkillers the docs had me on. "Maybe I'll rest a little longer."

Vlad bent and pressed a kiss to my hair. "I think that wise. Shall we reschedule our dinner?"

I nodded, already drifting back to sleep. "Tomorrow?"

"I shall depend upon it."

I heard the hospital room door open and shut and thought Vlad had left until I heard Nate's angry voice demand, "What the hell are you doing here?"

So much for sleeping.

I heaved a sigh before opening my eyes so that I could play referee.

Vlad lifted my hand and pressed a delicate kiss to my palm. "I merely came to visit my darling Red," he murmured as his lips brushed against my skin.

"Well, you've visited," Nate snapped, "so get out."

Vlad's hand reflexively tightened around my fingertips. "I do not believe that is up to you, Detective Grimm."

"She's my partner," Nate ground out, spreading his legs and hunching his shoulders, readying for trouble. "I'll be the one to take care of her."

Vlad blinked at him, unfazed. "As you did last night?" he baited. "Well done, Detective Grimm. With your brand of care, she'll be dead in no time."

Nate lunged forward, grabbing Vlad by the lapels and shoving him against the wall hard enough to rattle the window. Vlad bared his fangs and hissed, returning the attack by grabbing Nate's throat in his hand and squeezing. Nate stepped off and flung Vlad away, breaking his hold and sending the vampire sprawling into a chair. But Vlad wasn't down for long. He sprang to his feet, ready to engage once more.

"Hey!" I yelled, forcing myself to sit up, but they ignored me and began to circle one another warily in the cramped hospital room. I cursed under my breath and stuck my fingers in my mouth, blowing out a shrill whistle that brought their heads up instantly.

"In case you Neanderthals hadn't noticed, 'she' is right here! And I think 'she' can decide who she wants hanging around! Right now, I'm about to kick both your stupid asses out of the hospital, which would really piss me off because my head is killing me, and I'd really rather not exert the effort. So knock it the hell off!"

Both men straightened from their attack stances and had the decency to look contrite for acting like idiots. Nate cast a guarded glance toward Vlad, who was nonchalantly smoothing his clothing as if nothing had just occurred.

"Sorry, Red," Nate muttered.

Vlad gave me a curt bow. "You are quite right, Red—we behaved very childishly, indeed. My apologies as well."

Satisfied that they weren't about to go at it again and rip each other's throats out, I settled back against the pillows. "Vlad, I will call you tomorrow and reschedule. Thank you for your concern—your visit means a lot to me."

Recognizing a dismissal when he heard one, Vlad offered another bow to me and swept elegantly from the room, pointedly ignoring Nate as he did so. Nate's acidic glare as he watched Vlad leave could have burned a hole in the door, but when he turned back to me, his expression had softened.

"How're you feeling—aside from the head pounding?"

"I've had better days," I grumbled. "Did Gran make it

home okay? She tried calling while I was at Halloran's, but I haven't checked my voice mail."

"She's safe and sound back at home," Nate assured me. "Nicky sent one of his guys over—Eddie Fox."

I blinked in disbelief. "Eddie's the best," I said, surprised to hear that the man Nicky had sent to watch over Gran was not just one of his best men—he was his own bodyguard. "Nicky's a good friend."

I watched Nate for a moment as he went about the room tidying up from his and Vlad's play date. When he glanced up and caught me staring, I asked, "So, how are *you*?"

Nate shrugged. "I'm good. A few bumps and bruises thanks to our thrilling adventure, but nothing that won't heal."

I held out a hand to him, suddenly needing to feel him near me. "Nate?"

He eagerly stepped forward and took hold of my extended hand with both of his. "What's wrong?"

"Nothing," I said, pulling his arm even closer and tucking my free hand under his bicep so that I could lean against his shoulder. "I just wanted to say thank you."

I felt him heave a frustrated sigh. "For what? Almost showing up too late to help you? If I'd been just thirty seconds later—"

"You weren't," I interrupted, lifting my eyes to his. "I'm fine. But I want that bitch arrested."

Nate frowned at me in confusion. "Which bitch?"

"Halloran's girlfriend," I hissed. "I almost got killed because his pretty little pussy didn't like me."

Nate's thumb smoothed across the back of my hand. "I'm not so sure his girlfriend is to blame."

"Why's that?" I asked, not liking the shadows accumulating around his face. They reminded me of gathering storm clouds—the kind that brought down the wrath of the heavens upon those too foolish to get the hell out of the way.

"The call that took me from the hospital a few hours ago— it was out at Halloran's estate. His doormen were mauled almost beyond recognition trying to keep something out of the house. And Sophia was seriously injured trying to protect Halloran from the same creature. They brought her in while I was collecting the doormen. She's down the hall."

"What does our murderer want with Halloran?" I questioned. "If he was specifically targeted, that kind of blows my wrong place, wrong time theory."

Nate shook his head hesitantly. "Maybe," he said slowly. "Maybe not. I want to talk to Halloran and Sophia as soon as they're up for it."

"Sounds good," I agreed, trying unsuccessfully to hide a yawn as I snuggled back down into the pillows. "Maybe in the morning?"

Nate grinned knowingly. "Morning?"

I yawned again. "Well, maybe afternoon."

"Deal."

"Hey, Nate?"

"Yeah?"

"Don't sneak off again, okay?"

I don't know why I asked him to stay. I felt kind of silly doing it, actually—like a little girl who's still afraid of the dark. But the thought of him watching over me while I slept, keeping me company in the darkness, was immensely comforting.

Nate tucked the covers up around me as I curled up on my side. "I'm not going anywhere."

A moment later, the guttural screech of wood against the floor told me Nate was dragging a chair toward the bed. I heard him sit down and shift around, trying to find a comfortable position, apparently without much success. I opened my eyes and saw him stand and take off his jacket and tie and drape them over the back of the chair before trying again.

"You can share with me if you want," I offered, scooting back against the rail of the bed.

"I'm good," Nate assured me, looking decidedly uncomfortable in spite of his words.

"It's no big deal," I told him. "If you're going to stay here, you might as well try to get some rest, too. Unfortunately, I didn't have the foresight to call ahead and get one of the larger private rooms with the fold-out couch, so you'll have to make do with sharing the bed."

Nate studied me for a long moment, his lips pressed together in a tight line. "Okay. But I'll stay on top of the covers."

I rolled my eyes. "For crying out loud! Keep one foot on the floor, open the door—whatever makes you feel better. Just get the lead out. I'm tired and you're keeping me awake."

Nate walked stiffly to the bed and eased down beside me. He shifted around awkwardly, trying to find a comfortable position without infringing upon my space, but then apparently gave up trying. "Here," he sighed, slipping his arm under me and rolling me into his embrace. "This okay?"

I nestled into the hollow of his shoulder, curling up against him, then nodded. "Mmm-hmm." I would have said more, but with my heart pounding so hard I could barely breathe, it was all I could manage.

Nate's arms tightened around me, holding me so close I could feel his own heart pounding in time with mine, could feel the rise and fall of his chest with each tense breath. I desperately wanted to turn my eyes up to his to see if that dark fire I'd seen before was smoldering in his eyes now, but instead I tucked in closer and concentrated on the peaceful warmth of Nate's body and let the soothing darkness of sleep drift forward to claim me as its own.

"Sweet dreams," I heard Nate whisper from the edges of the darkness.

As I snuggled in closer, I couldn't help but grin, somehow sure that in spite of the horrors of the last couple of days, my dreams this night would be sweet indeed.

Chapter 19

My head had healed up nicely overnight, but it was still a little tender the next day as I lathered it with shampoo in the hospital room's shower. I stood under the spray for who knows how long, keenly aware that Nate was still sitting vigil in the other room just feet away from where I stood completely naked. In spite of the heat of the water, I felt cold down to my bones. It was a chill I couldn't put a name to, and I had the distinct impression that the only cure for it had nothing to do with turning up the heat of the water and everything to do with turning up the heat with the man in the other room.

It would've been so easy to turn my face up to his during the night, to press my lips to his and see where that took us. I shook my head, pushing such thoughts away. In all the years I'd worked with Nate, I'd never allowed myself to go there—regardless of the obvious mutual attraction. So why was I going there now? It had to be the stress of the situation, knowing that my number had been drawn. I was getting distracted and letting my guard down. And that had to stop. Nate was my partner. Off limits. End of story.

I squeezed my eyes shut and leaned my head against the tile, stalling for as long as I could. Finally accepting there was nothing in the tiny shower that could warm me in the way I needed, I turned off the water and grabbed a thick white towel. I dried off quickly, shivering so hard my teeth chattered, then wrapped the towel around my body.

"Hey, Nate," I called as I came out into the room. "Did you see where they put my bra? I thought—" I screeched loudly and jumped back, clutching the towel closer around me when I saw Nate was no longer alone in the room.

A tall, silver-haired wall of muscle in a navy blue suit and sunglasses stood just inside the room, his hands clasped in front of him. Eddie Fox—Nicky's personal bodyguard. No one really knew where Eddie came from. He just showed up one day not long after Nicky's brush with death and offered his services. I never understood why Nicky trusted him right away, but he did. And Eddie had proven his worth on numerous occasions in the decades since.

I gave Eddie a rather dazed nod in greeting. He nodded back, then studiously averted his eyes, staring at a point on the wall over my shoulder as Gran bustled forward carrying an overnight bag.

"I sent your clothes to the laundry," Gran explained, thrusting the bag at me, "and brought you some fresh ones." She leaned toward me and lowered her voice, but not nearly low enough, as she said, "I had difficulty finding panties, though, dear. Those little scraps you wear get lost in your delicates drawer."

I saw Eddie try to hide a smile, then glanced at Nate, who didn't even bother. "Thanks, Gran," I mumbled, taking the bag. "I'll just go change."

"Yes, do, my darling," Gran said, brushing my damp hair back from my eyes. "You will feel better once you're back in your own things. These hospital gowns are so uncomfortable, especially with the back hanging open—of course, you don't seem to mind your backside hanging out if your style of undergarments is any indication."

"Gran!" I groaned.

"You think these gentlemen care what kind of panties you wear?" Gran said, shooing me into the bathroom.

I glared at the guys, daring one of them to go there. Fortunately for both of them, they just looked away, pretending not to hear the conversation. I spotted my missing bra hanging over the back of a chair, so I snatched it up and ducked into the bathroom where I quickly pulled on the panties, jeans, and black turtleneck Gran had brought for me.

When I emerged from the bathroom a moment later, Gran was chatting animatedly with Nate and Eddie, telling them all about how Pete Panella had broken down while talking about his childhood during their interview the other day. Eddie in particular looked completely enthralled.

"I'll be certain to watch the interview when it airs," Eddie said sincerely. "It sounds captivating."

Gran seemed flustered by the compliment and ducked her head a little, flushing. "Well, thank you, Mr. Fox. I hope you will not be disappointed."

Hello. What the hell was this?

I cocked my head to one side, watching the scene play out. I had never seen her so discombobulated. Was it possible that Gran was attracted to Eddie? He was obviously flirting with her.

Eddie offered her a smile that was genuinely warm. "I can't imagine you ever disappoint, Mrs. Stuart."

Gran suddenly seemed years younger to me as she flushed a little deeper. "Mr. Fox!" she tittered. "You are such a flatterer!"

I stepped forward quickly, suddenly uncomfortable with the sly fox putting the moves on my Gran. "Gran, should you be up and about so much this soon?"

She cast me an amused look. "Perhaps you are right, my darling. I might have overdone it a bit today."

I put my arm through hers. "Why don't you head on home and get some rest? I'll be fine. Nate and I have a lot of work to do, so we need to get going anyway. Don't worry about me. Really."

Gran nodded, although somewhat reluctantly. "If you are certain . . ."

I smiled and patted her arm. "Of course I am." Then I turned my attention to Eddie. "Can you take her home and make sure she gets some rest, Eddie? I don't want her working on anything today."

Including her flirting skills, I added silently.

Eddie gave me a tight nod. "Mr. Blue has given me leave to watch over Mrs. Stuart until you are satisfied she is out of danger. I will do whatever is necessary to ensure she is well."

I briefly wondered if sending Gran home with Eddie was the best idea, but she seemed relieved at being ordered to rest, so I sent her on her way with reassurances that I would be careful and look after myself as well.

As soon as they were gone, I grabbed up my trench coat and strode for the door. I was reaching for the latch when I realized Nate was still lounging in his chair, studying me contemplatively. "What?"

He shook his head and rose to his feet. "Nothing. I just like seeing the softer side of you now and then."

I frowned at him in disgust. "Softer side? What are you talking about?"

He shrugged and picked up his fedora from the end of the bed. "The way you are with Gran—so protective and caring."

I bristled at his words. "Yeah, well, don't think the way I am with Gran means I couldn't kick your ass if I needed to."

Nate came forward and put his hand over mine on the door latch. "Caring about someone isn't a sign of weakness, Red."

I pressed my lips together angrily. "I know that."

"Do you?" he pressed, moving a step closer.

"Of course I do." I looked up at him, prepared to meet his penetrating gaze defiantly, but as I stared up into those bottomless pools of darkness, my anger drifted away, replaced by a tingling sensation that began in the center of my stomach and radiated outward.

Ah, yes. There it was. That warmth I'd been craving . . .

The air between us suddenly became charged and primed. One little spark was all it would have taken to set off the kind of explosion that could bring us both to our knees. And I was completely and utterly terrified. I couldn't look away. Didn't want to. In fact, what I wanted was—

Nate's phone suddenly sprang to life, making us both jump. And just like that, the charge was diffused, leaving a vast empty void where it had been. Nate opened his mouth as if to say something else to me, but then he shut it again and reached into his jacket for his phone.

As he put the phone up to his ear, I grinned, realizing that I was hearing music and not the annoying chirp that I'd heard before.

Nate looked irritated as he gruffly barked, "Detective Grimm."

I glanced down to where his hand still covered mine, liking the way his fingers curled around my own so lightly. On impulse I moved my hand, planning to lace my fingers with his, but he snatched his hand away. Perhaps he'd mistaken the movement, thinking I was trying to rescue my hand. Or maybe I was the one who'd been mistaken.

"Sorry," he mumbled, hanging up the phone and pocketing it once more. "That was the hospital trying to reach me. Apparently they didn't realize I was still here."

Ah. Back to work then.

"What did they say?"

"Sophia's condition has been upgraded. Looks like she's going to pull through."

"Well," I said, "let's go have a chat then, shall we?"

We both reached for the door at the same time but jerked our hands back, avoiding the other's touch. I was the first to move a second time and pushed on the latch, opening the door.

"So, Benny Goodman," I mused as we strode down the hall toward Sophia's room, glad to focus on a lighter topic.

Nate chuckled. "You said I needed a theme song."

I cast a hopeless glance his way. "Yeah, but 'Sing, Sing, Sing'?"

"It's quintessential Benny Goodman!" Nate argued. "Plus, it kind of goes with my look."

"Oh, you have a *look* now, do you?"

"You know I have a look," he defended. "I've always had a look."

I gave him the once-over. "No offense, Nate, but it's a little dated."

"What's wrong with looking a little dated?" he demanded. "I think it suits me. Very dark and mysterious. Dramatic even."

I shrugged. "I guess."

He nudged me with his shoulder. "Admit it—you think the fedora is pretty dashing."

I snorted dismissively. "No way am I saying the word *dashing* in any context."

No matter how true it might be.

"Okay, so how about the suit?" Nate asked. He came to a stop in the middle of the hallway and began to strike various runway poses, oblivious to the strange looks and muffled giggles we received from the hospital staff that passed by.

Laughing, I grabbed Nate by the shoulder and spun him around, giving him a shove forward. "Fine! Fine! You're *dashing*," I said, falling into step beside him. "Happy?"

He grinned down at me. "Almost."

I looked away quickly, trying not to read anything into that one simple word, and held up my hand. "Let me have your phone."

Nate obediently drew out his phone and handed it over. "Why?"

"Well, Mr. Dark, Mysterious, and Dramatic, if you're going to have a *look,* you need a better theme song." Nate made a grab for his phone, but I held it away, then cocked my head to one side, pretending to study him. "Let's see . . . what would really capture the true Nate Grimm?" I nodded, giving the question due gravity. "I'm thinking maybe some Anne Murray or Karen Carpenter. . . ."

Looking horrified, Nate snatched the phone from my grasp.

"What? You don't like Anne and Karen?"

"They're fine if you're in an elevator," he grumbled.

I nodded gravely. "You're right. You need something more funereal. How about 'Amazing Grace' on the bagpipes?"

Nate shot me a warning look. "Over my dead body."

I blinked at him in mock astonishment as we came to a halt outside Sophia's room. "Nate, was that a *pun?*"

He groaned. "Let's just chat with the tigress, what do you say?"

I motioned toward the door. "Lead the way, funny man."

Nate rolled his eyes as he brushed past me and entered the room.

Sophia was asleep in the bed, and considering she was wrapped in so many bandages she looked like an extra from some long-lost Ed Wood mummy movie, I'm guessing the deep slumber was probably by design. Halloran sat in the chair next to her bed, his head in his hands. Upon hearing our entrance, his head snapped up, and the look of despair and concern on his face rapidly morphed to one of pure rage.

"Get the fuck out of here!" he roared, advancing on us— me, specifically.

Nate stepped in front of me, blocking me from Halloran's fury. "Back off, Halloran!"

"We're here to help, you idiot!" I snapped, talking over Nate as I tried to get past him to defend myself.

Nate's arm came back, wrapping around me to keep me behind him. "You need to settle down," he said—though I wasn't sure if he was talking to me or to the notorious crime boss glaring daggers at me.

"She was at my estate," Halloran seethed, jabbing an accusatory finger in my direction. "I offered her assistance when she was injured"—I thought about correcting him but decided against it—"I told her what I knew about Hamelin. And this is how I am to be repaid?"

"As hard as it must be for you to believe," I hissed, "this isn't about you, Halloran!"

He pushed closer, forcing Nate to slide me around in a waltzlike shuffle. "I discovered that you were attacked— probably by the same creature—the evening before. A strange beast nearly kills you not a mile from my home and none of you assholes at the FMA thought it worth mentioning?"

As much as I hated to admit it, he had a point. My defensiveness deflated and I grabbed Nate's arm, easing out from behind him.

"You're right," I admitted. "Someone should have said something. I assumed Sophia had come after me to either kill me or warn me off permanently by scaring the shit out of me. I should have had someone look into it."

Halloran and Nate both gaped at me like flying monkeys had just shot out of my ass.

(Hey, I've never claimed to be good at apologizing. In fact, I do it so rarely I get very little practice.)

"Listen," I said, "you're the last person I want to help, Halloran, believe me. But if the thing that came after Sophia is the same murderer we've been following on another case, we need to figure out why you were targeted. Otherwise the next time it comes for you, you might not be so lucky."

Halloran seemed to consider this for a moment. Then, with

a glance toward Sophia, he ran his hands through his sandy hair and let out a long sigh, his shoulders sagging. "I have no idea who could have done this."

Seeing that Halloran was no longer a threat, Nate's tension eased a bit. He stuck his hands in his pockets, taking on a more casual stance. "You're a pretty powerful man," he observed. "Powerful men tend to make powerful enemies. There's no one you can think of who'd want you dead?"

Halloran let out a short laugh. "On the contrary—I can think of plenty of people. But I know of no one who controls such a creature."

I crossed my arms over my chest. "So start naming them and let us sort out which one might be behind it."

Halloran shook his head. "They're other businessmen, other professionals—competitors."

Nate took out a notebook and pen and began jotting down notes. "And they'd kill you to become the new pharmaceutical king?"

Halloran shifted a little in his chair. "It is not the pharmaceutical distribution business that is so competitive."

"Fairy dust?" I guessed.

He looked at Nate, then back at me. "Off the record?"

I cursed inwardly, damning my luck. I had Halloran in a corner, finally ready to admit to the kinds of crimes that could put him away for years. It was the perfect chance to take him down. But if he had anything on the murders, I had to know. "Yeah," I agreed grudgingly. "Off the record."

"There is no one who would dare challenge me on that front," he boasted. "It would be suicide to even attempt such a coup. There are, however, other ventures in play in this city that will change everything. You cannot even begin to fathom the implications, Enforcer."

"So, why don't you enlighten us?" Nate prompted irritably.

"Does this have anything to do with your recent investment in the restaurant business?" I asked, going on a hunch—

although how being part owner in a successful restaurant could have a transformative effect on Chicago was beyond me.

Halloran shrugged. "That is only a minute piece of it."

The surprise I felt at actually having hit on something with my hunch must have shown.

Halloran's eyes twinkled with amusement. "It's much, much bigger than one person—or even one investment," he went on. "And those of us in positions of power are vying for control in a true winner takes all situation."

"Control of what?" Nate interjected.

Halloran's lips curved into a taunting smirk. "I am afraid I am not at liberty to discuss that at this point."

Nate returned the smirk mockingly, clearly frustrated with the Sandman's evasiveness.

"Are the other Tale crime lords involved?" I asked, trying to keep Halloran from skittering back behind his reticence. "Are they the powerful people you mentioned?"

Halloran's brows lifted at my frank question. "Do you mean people like your friends Vlad Dracula and Nicky Blue?" When I only glared in response, he said haughtily, "I imagine you know far more about their activities than I, Enforcer."

"You going to keep jerking me around, Sandman," I drawled, "or do you want to help me catch who did this to Sophia?"

Halloran's eyes sparked with anger, but he let out a long sigh and eased back in his chair. "I can honestly say I have no idea who the other players are in my side ventures. We deal anonymously through an intermediary."

"Fine, then tell us the name of the intermediary," Nate demanded.

Halloran spread his hands in an apologetic gesture. "No name has ever been given. That is the truth."

"Can you give us anything to go on at all?" Nate asked

with forced politeness. "Any reason why someone would want to target you or someone you care about?"

Halloran gave Nate a bored look. "Detective, it would be less time-consuming to give you a list of those who do *not* wish to bring harm to me."

"You told me you and Sebille Fenwick are butting heads over how to run Todd's show," I said. "Any chance someone's trying to send you a message to step off?"

Halloran shrugged. "I cannot imagine Sebille would be idiotic enough to go to the mattresses with me over a difference in opinion. However, although I am Todd Caliban's largest investor, I am not the only one. I suppose it is possible another would like to squeeze me out. That being said, anyone who would attempt to murder me must have known that I would respond mercilessly if I survived—quite a gamble, wouldn't you agree?"

I inclined my head with a shrug. "Okay. So what's your point?"

"My point, my dear Enforcer," he sighed, his tone patronizing, "is that I would have expected my professional colleagues to use a more adroit method than a werewolf assassin to eliminate me. It's hardly efficient, is it? A shot from a rooftop sniper or a car bomb would have been more in line with our idiom."

"Dead's dead, Halloran," I pointed out. "What's the difference how an assassin goes about killing you?"

"The occasional assassination is a business necessity," he replied. "And, like any other business transaction, should be conducted efficiently and effectively. This was neither."

I frowned, trying to read between the lines. "So what are you saying? This is a newbie?"

Halloran shrugged. "Perhaps. Or perhaps just hoping to appear so."

Recognizing that we'd pretty much gotten all we were going to get from the Sandman, Nate closed his notebook and tucked it into the inside pocket of his jacket. "Regardless of whether this is a seasoned professional or a new kid in town, you need to let us handle this, Halloran."

Halloran sneered at him. "One does not rise to power by being an idiot, Detective." He folded his hands placidly across his abdomen, resuming that cool, calculating demeanor I knew of old. "I intend to protect my investments by any means necessary."

"We can help you," I pointed out, "but you can't go all vigilante on us."

He merely smiled at me.

"Think of Sophia," I pleaded, gesturing toward the sleeping woman.

He didn't even glance her way. "I will send her away to a safe place to convalesce. She will be guarded."

I pressed my lips together in an angry line. "Tim—"

Nate gently touched my arm. "Come on, Red. We've got all we're going to get."

I cast one last look at Sophia, feeling guilty that my presumptions had led to her condition. Then I followed Nate from the room, hoping the pretty shape-shifter's jackass of a boyfriend didn't end up getting her killed.

Chapter 20

"So, where to next?" I asked as Nate led me through the hospital's underground parking lot.

"Want to take a trip to the morgue?" he replied, fishing a set of keys out of the pocket of his trench.

"Not especially," I said warily. "Why? You have friends in town?"

Nate gave me a cockeyed grin. "Not at the moment. I just thought we could drop in on Trish and see what she's come up with from the various crime scenes."

I shrugged. "I guess now's as good a time as any. How do you plan to get there? Last time I checked, your precious unmarked was barely drivable."

He stopped in front of a dun-colored sedan that looked like it had been a shining star among the American auto industry sometime during the Regan administration but had lived long past its prime. The paint had flecked off over the years, creating a liver spot effect that added to its weathered, aged appearance. A jagged crack started in the upper left corner of the windshield and zigzagged diagonally across the glass, ending in a starburst in the center of the passenger's line of vision. A sizable dent marred the front fender and the dings and scratches from years of being victimized in parking lots just like this one were too numerous to count.

Nate made a sweeping gesture across the front of the craptacular heap of junk and looked at me expectantly.

I stared at him. "What?"

"Your chariot awaits," he announced.

"No, really," I laughed. "Where's your loaner?"

Nate gestured toward the car again. "This is it. This was the only one available at such short notice."

I pulled open the passenger door and climbed inside, cringing at the persistent stench of mildew. "Don't ever say anything about my Range Rover again," I mumbled as Nate coaxed the jalopy to life.

We sputtered, grumbled, and rumbled out of the parking garage and into the drizzle of the late morning. Nate switched on the car's windshield wipers, but only one of the blades actually touched the window as they arced to and fro across the glass.

He hunched lower over the steering wheel in order to get a clear view of the road. "Not a word," he ordered with a glance my way. "Not a single word."

"I didn't say anything," I assured him, grinning wickedly. "I think the car can pretty much speak for itself."

Nate gave me a sour look. "Don't you have something to do besides making snide remarks about the car?"

"Sadly, yes," I confirmed. "I should probably return some of the calls that came in before the attack. Fortunately, about fifteen of the twenty were from you."

Nate stiffened defensively. "I was worried about you," he reminded me. "And for good reason, as it turned out."

"No arguments there," I replied, dialing Nicky's number. "But, for future reference, if you don't get an answer after the first five or six calls—odds are good I could use a hand."

"It's about time you called," came Nicky's voice in my ear, cutting off whatever remark Nate had planned.

"Sorry," I apologized. "I've been a little busy."

"Eddie told me you were attacked," he said. "You okay?"

"Been better." I glanced over at Nate, somewhat wistfully. "I'm just lucky Nate got there when he did, or it could have been a lot worse."

Nate glanced away from the road, his gaze holding mine for a moment before turning away again.

"Want to talk about it?" Nicky asked.

Part of me wanted desperately to talk to Nicky about the whole thing—especially the part about the crazy thoughts I was having about Nate. But now definitely wasn't the time. "Nah, nothing more to tell at this point. I saw you called a couple times—did you find out anything?"

"A whole lot of nothing," Nicky told me.

"What's that tell you?"

"It tells me people are trying too hard to keep quiet. There's usually at least a few rumors floating around. This one's airtight."

"You aren't involved in any way?" I asked.

Nicky chuckled, understanding exactly where my head was. "Believe it or not, Red, I don't have a hand in every business in town. There are some things even I won't touch, and people know better than to ask."

"Sorry," I said. "You think it could have something to do with Vitamin D?"

"Got me. You thinking it does?"

I frowned to myself, mulling over the various conversations I'd had with the Sandman. "Halloran tells me no," I replied.

"You believe him?"

I let out a sharp sigh. "I'm still on the fence. His girlfriend Sophia was attacked last night and nearly killed. I'm thinking the thing that attacked us is the same creature we're trying to find on a few other murders. He thinks it has to do with this super secret deal going down."

"Super secret seems about right," Nicky muttered. "I don't like it when something's going on in my town and I don't know about it."

"Tell me about it." Then a thought struck me and I glanced into the backseat of the car. "Hey, Nicky—do you still know that computer guy?"

"Yeah," Nicky said slowly. "He's still a friend of mine."

"Are you insane?" Nate suddenly interjected. "Hamelin's hard drive is evidence. If we tamper with it at all, it'll be in-admissible as evidence against anyone involved. Mary Smith will have our heads."

"Yeah, like I'm worried about Mary Smith," I shot back. "She can bite my much shapelier ass."

I heard Nicky chuckle and returned my attention to him. "So can you have your guy take a look at something for me?"

"Your ass or the computer?" Nicky retorted.

"The computer, smart guy."

Nicky chuckled again. "Anything for you, kid. Just tell me where you want me to pick it up."

"How about the morgue?"

The FMA morgue really wasn't a morgue as such. It was more a forensics laboratory with an autopsy table and a couple of freezers for storing bodies. And, all things considered, it was actually pretty cozy. Trish had completely redecorated when she took over, covering the walls with prints of the work of Ansel Adams and other, more contemporary photographers like Christopher Burkett and Charles Cramer, to take away some of the closed off, sterile feel of the room, which was otherwise filled with steel furniture, gleaming glass, and various high-tech gadgets and gizmos that looked like they belonged on the set of *Star Trek*.

When Nate and I arrived, Trish was elbow deep in an autopsy of what I assumed was one of Halloran's doormen, if the scraps of blood-soaked clothing spread out on the countertop for analysis were any indication.

"Suit up!" Trish called out, not bothering to look up from the dead Tale's chest cavity.

Nate and I obediently grabbed surgical garb and gloves from a nearby shelf and pulled them on before heading over to take a look at the remains on Trish's table. I immediately wished I'd stayed by the door. Even through the masks, the stench of blood and flesh assaulted my nostrils, making me retch. And if that hadn't done it, the sight before me would have. Although the crime scene photos I'd seen in Al's office were horrific, they were nothing compared with seeing one of the victims up close.

"Great God," I murmured, glad I hadn't eaten anything yet that day.

"You should have seen the other guy," Trish replied, lifting the man's heart out and placing it on a scale. "At least this one's still recognizable as having been a person. The other one came to me in chunks."

I swallowed a couple of times, keeping my nausea from overtaking me. "Got it. Thanks. End of story."

Trish glanced my way, and I could tell she was grinning at me behind her mask. "Sorry. I forget not everyone's as used to this kind of thing as I am. Don't feel bad. Even my photographer had to take a break a few minutes ago—and Mike does this for a living."

"Have you found anything useful?" Nate asked, annoyingly unaffected by the grisly autopsy.

"Yeah, I think so," Trish said, her excitement unmistakable. "I found a sample of hair on this one's uniform. I've compared it to a sample I found at the scene of Matilda Stuart's attack and of the murder of Julie Spangle—the first victim."

"And?" Nate prompted.

Trish stripped off her gloves and tossed them into a biohazard container. "Come take a look," she said, motioning us over to her table of microscopes.

Nate bent over the first one and peered at the prepared slide. "What am I seeing here?"

"This is the sample from Julie Spangle's murder."

Nate moved to the next. "And this one?"

"Matilda Stuart's attack."

"And this last one is the current case, I presume?"

Trish nodded. "Notice anything?"

"They're different," Nate said, straightening from the third microscope with a puzzled frown. "I expected them to be the same."

"So did I," Trish admitted. "The modus operandi for each crime is identical. The wounds are the same even down to the depth of the claw marks. And yet the hair samples, while similar, are definitely different."

As Trish spoke, I took a look at each of the samples, noting the very minute differences between them. "So does this mean it's more than one werewolf?"

"Possibly," Trish said, turning back to the autopsy table and drawing a sheet over the remains. She then pulled down her mask with a frustrated sigh. "Unfortunately, we're just really starting to understand the science of lycans. There are dozens of species and they vary in origin from those born into the condition to those who have it forced upon them through a curse to those who choose to become wolves on their own volition."

"What's your gut feeling on this one?" Nate questioned.

Trish crossed her arms over her chest and shrugged. "Best guess? You're either dealing with a close-knit family of lycans so similar in their physiology as to be almost indistinguishable—which, statistically, would be almost impossible—or there's magic involved in the transformation, which would explain the very slight deviations in composition. Because the change to wolf isn't at a true genetic level, there are variations so minute you can only see the difference under the microscope."

I pulled off my mask and gloves and tossed them into the trash. "Damn it."

Nate glanced at me, meeting my tortured gaze. "Seth's condition is a curse, isn't it?"

I nodded. "Yeah. He went afoul of some witches long before we met. He's been searching for a cure since then, but obviously hasn't had any luck."

"If we were to get a sample from a suspect," Nate said, turning back to Trish, "could you analyze it at the genetic level and tell us if it's like the samples from the crime scene?"

Trish shrugged. "Yeah, sure. If you think you can get close enough to a werewolf to get some of his hair, I can take a look. But good luck with that. I don't know anyone crazy enough to try it."

I sighed. "I do."

Trish opened her mouth to respond, but I heard the door to the lab open behind us, and saw her face transform with a combination of surprise and embarrassment. Visibly flustered, she smoothed the front of her surgical scrubs, then tucked an errant ringlet behind her ear, leaving a smudge of blood on her cheek. She flushed a little when she asked, "May I help you?"

"Just looking for a friend of mine."

I caught a glimpse of Trish's disappointment as I turned to accept the kiss Nicky dropped to my cheek. "Thanks for coming," I said, returning his embrace. When he'd finished shaking hands with Nate, I gestured toward Trish. "Nicky Blue, this is Trish Muffet."

Nicky stepped forward with a grin. "The cleanup lady," he drawled. "I've heard of you."

Trish's face flooded with color. "I've heard of you, too, Mr. Blue."

Nicky laughed. "Nothing good I'm sure." He leaned forward and said in a low voice, "Don't believe everything you hear. Red can tell you I'm not such a bad guy."

"That I can," I agreed. "Speaking of which, we have the project out in the car."

Nicky gave me a tight nod, then turned back to Trish. "A pleasure to meet you, Ms. Muffet." Then he reached into his suit pocket and withdrew a handkerchief. "Here you go. You have a little something there on your cheek."

Trish took the handkerchief and wiped at her cheek. "Thank you."

She started to hand it back, but Nicky folded her fingers around the material. "Keep it."

Trish blinked at him and offered him a shy smile. "Thanks."

I rolled my eyes and gave Nicky a nudge toward the door. "Come on, you charmer."

"Thanks, Trish," Nate called as we headed outside. "We'll be in touch."

When we were safely out of earshot, Nicky let out a low whistle. "That is one beautiful gal right there," he said with an appreciative shake of his head.

"Yes, she is," I agreed. "And you have another one just as gorgeous waiting for you at home."

Nicky laughed, then turned to Nate. "Any wonder why I loved this gal?" he said. "Always so quiet and submissive. Never one to speak her mind, that Red."

Nate's laugh burst from him, making my heart trip over itself, so I gave each of them a punch in the shoulder. "When you two are finished yucking it up, you think we could get some work done?"

I pulled open the car door, which creaked and groaned in protest, and reached in to grab Hamelin's laptop.

From behind me I heard Nate mutter a startled curse and started to back out to find out what was going on when I suddenly felt a pair of strong hands on my ass. But before I could voice the angry protest on my lips, the hands shoved me into the car headfirst.

"Hey!" I cried as I fell into a heap on the backseat. "What the—"

"Go, go, go!" Nate yelled.

I whipped around to look out the back window just in time to see Nate running toward the building, gun drawn.

The next thing I knew, Nicky was jumping into the front seat and gunning the motor, his Glock in one hand as the other threw the car into gear.

"What the hell is going on?" I demanded, somehow staying upright in spite of Nicky spinning the car around so hard the force threatened to throw me into the opposite door. "What are you doing? Where's Nate?"

"We've got company," Nicky called over his shoulder as he sped out of the parking lot. "We saw it at the same time and Nate shoved you into the car and went back into the building to get the coroner."

"We have to go back for them!" I cried, swiveling around to try to see what was happening behind us.

"Red, honey, if anyone can handle whatever that was, Nate Grimm can," Nicky assured me. "Plus, he'd kick my ass if I let anything happen to you. Once he has Trish, he'll be in touch."

"You act like you two have done this before," I seethed. "You moonlighting a little, Nicky?"

He cast a glance over his shoulder at me, but didn't say anything more.

Angry at being kept in the dark and worried for Nate and Trish, I punched the back of Nicky's seat, letting out a loud scream of frustration.

"This is bullshit!" I yelled. "*Bullshit!* I need to get back there and help them. Nate's my partner—I can't just leave him on his own."

Not twenty seconds later, Nicky's phone rang. "Yeah."

I listened, scowling, trying to hear the conversation, but

the loud banging and growling of the engine prevented any meaningful eavesdropping.

"Okay," Nicky said with a nod. "Where?" There was a pause then, "You got it."

"Was that Nate?" I demanded the second he hung up, my nerves wound taut with apprehension.

Nicky's head bobbed once. "Yeah, that was him."

I leaned forward over the seat, eager for more information. "Is he okay? What about Trish? Was she hurt? Did Nate see who it was? Did he get a good look at the creature?"

Nicky gave me an annoyed glance. "Nate and Trish are both fine. He's taking her to headquarters and putting her into protective custody. We're supposed to meet him there."

I let out a sigh of relief and collapsed against the backseat, closing my eyes as I felt my adrenaline rush dissipating. "Damn it. I had no idea I'd be putting Trish in danger by going to the morgue."

"If what Nate said is true," Nicky said, "it wasn't after you."

My eyes snapped open. "What are you talking about?"

"It ransacked the lab, destroyed everything," Nicky informed me. "And probably would have torn that pretty little coroner to shreds had Nate not gotten to her first."

"Oh, God."

Nicky glanced over his shoulder at me, his brow furrowed. "What the hell have you gotten yourself into, Red?"

I ran my hands through my hair, then down over my face, trying to make sense of it all and not having any luck. "Apparently, a lot deeper shit than I'd thought."

Chapter 21

The door to the Chief's office slammed into the wall with such force it left an inch-deep hole in the drywall.

"Where is he?" I demanded.

Al blinked up at me from his paperwork. "You're paying for that," he said calmly, with a nod toward his wall.

"So bill me," I shot back. "Where's Nate?"

"He took Trish to the cafeteria to get some coffee," he said. "She was pretty shaken up by the attack."

Without a word, I turned and stormed into the hallway, intent on tracking Nate down and giving him quite a substantial piece of my mind.

"Red, you need to calm down," I heard Nicky warn as he jogged a little to keep up with me. "Nate was just trying to protect you. He cares about you."

I shot a glance Nicky's way. "No offense, Nicky, but what the hell do you know about it? You're poker buddies."

"I know plenty," Nicky snapped. "Trust me. Do you have any idea—"

"Hey, where's the fire?"

The sudden sound of Nate's voice behind me stopped me dead in my tracks. For a full thirty seconds, I stood there with my back to him, clenching and unclenching my fists as my

impulse to punch him in the face for ditching me warred
with my impulse to throw my arms around his neck in relief
because he was unharmed.

"Glad to see you're okay," I heard Nicky say. "How's
Trish?"

"She'll be fine," Nate told him. "A few cuts and scrapes
from flying debris but she's more shaken up than anything.
And after seeing the creature up close and personal, she's
even more determined to ID it."

Nicky chuckled appreciatively. "That's one tough dame."
There was an awkward stretch of silence before Nicky
coughed and said, "Well, hey, I'll let you two kids get back to
it. I'll just grab that laptop, Nate, and leave the keys in the car.
I doubt anyone'd want to steal that junk heap."

"Thanks, Nicky," Nate replied, clearly distracted. "Just
give us a call when you find out something."

"Will do." I felt Nicky's hand on my arm. "I'll see you
soon, Red."

I gave him a nod, still refusing to turn around. As soon as
Nicky's footfalls had faded, I felt Nate take a few cautious
steps toward me.

"Red? You okay?"

For some reason, the softness of his voice, the concern I
heard there, was the trigger that released the full force of my
anger. I whirled around, my right hook connecting squarely
with his jaw.

"You bastard!" I yelled as Nate staggered backward.
"We're supposed to be partners! How dare you ditch me
like that?"

"Ditch you?" Nate repeated, his own anger bubbling to
the surface. "I didn't ditch you! I was protecting you. You're
welcome, by the way!"

"And who would have protected you?" I demanded.

Nate huffed in exasperation. "Red—"

"Yeah, yeah, I know. You're *Deeaath*," I mocked in my

spookiest voice, waving my hands in the air. "I get it. Maybe that creature couldn't have *killed* you, Nate, but it could have hurt you enough to knock you off your game. And who would have protected Trish then?"

This seemed to give Nate pause. He stood there glaring down at me, his expression unreadable. Then, pressing his lips together in a grim line, he glanced quickly up and down the hall and grabbed me around my waist with one arm, scooping me off my feet.

"Hey!" I protested, squirming to get free of his hold. "What the hell, Nate?"

Without a word, he dragged me with him into an empty conference room and dropped me unceremoniously in the middle of the floor. He muttered a juicy curse under his breath and kicked the door closed, then turned back to me, hands on his hips.

"You're right," he ground out, his voice still tight with anger.

I scrambled to my feet and straightened my clothes, glaring at him. "Of course I'm right," I snapped. Then, frowning, asked, "About what?"

Nate stared at the wall, focusing on some point well above my head and refusing to look at me. "I let the way I feel about you interfere with the job," he said, his word clipped. "It won't happen again."

The heat of my anger instantly faded, replaced by a different kind of heat—one that started in the pit of my stomach and worked its way up to my cheeks. "The way you feel about me?" I echoed softly.

Nate's gaze darted down at me so briefly I almost missed it. But he recovered quickly, shoving his hands deep into his pockets and giving an indifferent shrug. "We've been colleagues, friends, for a while now," he said evasively. "In case you haven't caught on yet, I care about you."

"Ah." I swallowed my disappointment at his very benign,

platonic admission, wondering what exactly I'd been hoping he'd say. I lifted my eyes to his, finally catching his gaze full on, and gave him a gentle shove. "Well, the feeling's mutual, so stop being a dumb-ass. It'd really piss me off if something happened to you."

Nate laughed in a loud burst, then inclined his head in a bow of acquiescence. "I'll do my best," he replied, his grin returning. "And I'm sure you'll be there to pull me back in line if I slip up."

"You bet your ass."

For a moment, we stood there together, the heavy silence deepening as a palpable tension began to build. I took a step forward, not sure what I had intended by the movement. I think I was going to maybe slug him in the shoulder or something equally flippant, but instead, I grabbed his lapels in both fists and brought him close to me, pressing my forehead against his chest until his arms came around me.

"This was so much easier when I was on my own," I mumbled into his shirt.

Nate pulled back enough to grin down at me. "Yeah, but if you were on your own, who would you dazzle with your sparkling wit and endearing irascibility?"

I gave him a sour look. "Bite me."

"See," Nate chuckled, putting his arm around my shoulders and guiding me toward the door, "this is exactly what I'm talking about. Those clever one-liners would go unappreciated."

"Well, I suppose having you for a partner does have its advantages."

"Nice right hook, by the way," he complimented as we stepped back into the hallway.

I couldn't help but smile, rather proud of how I'd gotten the drop on him. "Thanks. You like that, you should see my uppercut."

Nate's laughter rumbled deep in his chest. "I'd rather not; thanks all the same."

"So, you up for another visit?" I asked, glad to have the pressing matter of a murderous werewolf and a questionable suicide to distract me from more pleasant thoughts of black flame tattoos and sculpted pectorals. "I'd kind of like to drop by Seth's restaurant, see what he's been up to this afternoon."

Nate cast a sidelong glance my way. "A little less convinced of his innocence?"

I shrugged. "No, but I'd sure love to hear that he was at work this afternoon and couldn't possibly have trashed a certain forensics lab."

"Speaking of the forensics lab," Nate said, "seems a little too coincidental that the creature should attack and tear the place apart just when Trish was close to a breakthrough with the crime scene evidence."

He had a damned good point. "Lucky guess?" I posited. "Everyone knows where crime scene evidence goes when Tales are involved. Isn't it possible that the person behind this just got a little worried and didn't want to take a chance on Trish finding something that would give away his identity?"

Nate scowled in response. "Maybe. But if he was trying to destroy evidence that would reveal his identity, why attack while we were there and risk getting caught?"

My steps slowed while I thought over what Nate had just said. It *did* seem a little too coincidental. And risky. It would have been a lot safer for the creature to ransack the lab after hours when there was no chance of being caught or killed.

"Unless he wanted us to see him," I said aloud. When Nate gave me a quizzical look, I explained. "Sorry. I was just thinking—maybe this was all for show."

Nate blinked at me. "Why go to all the trouble?"

"Bait and switch?" I guessed.

Nate shook his head. "A diversion? From what? If anything, it's only made us more intent on finding Seth. Sorry," he said, holding up his hands in front of him to ward off the sharp look I sent his way. "I just mean that after this attack, it's even more imperative that we find the killer—it attacked us in our own forensics lab, for crying out loud. And, I hate to say it, Red, but Seth's our remaining suspect at the moment."

I gave him a tight nod. "I know."

Nate took hold of my elbow and drew me to a stop. "I know I asked you in on this case, but if you want me to try to talk to Seth on my own, I will."

I shook my head and squared my shoulders. "No, I'm good."

Nate's brow furrowed with concern. "Are you sure? You've been through a lot in the last few days."

"I'm fine!" I snapped. Then, feeling guilty for biting his head off, I said in a softer tone, "Trust me, okay?"

Nate studied me intently for a long moment. "Okay," he said with a tight nod. "Your call. So, as long as you're up to it, what do you say we go grab a late lunch at Seth's restaurant?"

My mouth began to water at the mere thought of food. "God, yes! I'm starving!"

With food on the line, I hurried down to the parking garage with Nate on my heels. "Why don't you let me drive?" I offered. "I can get us there faster."

Nate looked down his nose at me. "Just get in the car."

The entire car shuddered and shook when Nate started it up, making my head pound in time with the high-pitched whistle coming from under the hood. I sat on my hands, re-sisting the urge to make a smart-ass remark.

Nate glanced over at me. "This thing is a piece of shit, isn't it?"

"Yep."

He sighed and turned off the car. "Okay, so what do you say we take a cab?"

"To the restaurant?" I asked.

"To Gran's," Nate replied. "We'll pick up your car, then go have a chat with Mr. Wolf."

Chapter 22

"Let me run in and check on Gran," I said, hopping out of Nate's car as soon as it came to a stop in the driveway.

"I'm sure she's fine," Nate called after me as I sprinted up the front steps. Nonetheless, he followed me in, nearly barreling into me in the living room where I'd come to a dead stop. "What the—" His words died on his tongue when he saw the shattered lamp lying on the floor.

I glanced around the room quickly, noticing the overturned piano bench and stack of magazines scattered on the carpet. Suddenly, Gran's cry pierced the silence, snapping me into action. I bolted toward the stairs, drawing my gun as I went, fear giving me an injection of speed as I hit the first step.

"Red, wait!" I heard Nate yell after me. "Don't go up there!"

Like hell! I scoffed inwardly. No way was I going to hang back and let some psychotic werewolf tear my Gran apart. The woman had taken me in when no one else cared. She was the only family I had, and I'd be damned if I was going to let anyone take that away from me.

Another scream rent the air as I reached the top landing. Without pausing to consider what manner of beast might be lurking within, I slammed my shoulder against her partially closed bedroom door, throwing it out of my way so I could level my gun on Gran's attacker.

A startled cry burst from me before I could stop it, and I fumbled my gun, barely avoiding shooting the parties within. For a moment, I could only stare, my feet turned to stone by the sight before me. Even now words fail me, the scene far too disturbing to describe. After a split second of pure, unadulterated horror, the magnitude of the situation struck me in the gut, forcing the wind from my lungs in an agonized gasp and sending me stumbling backward out of the bedroom. Without a word, I whirled around and raced down the steps, shoving my gun back into its holster.

I heard Gran calling my name, but there was no freaking way I was going back up there.

"Go!" I yelled at Nate, motioning him toward the door. "Go, go, go! Get out of the house!"

I bolted down the steps and toward my Range Rover, hopping into the driver's seat and slamming the door. Shaking, I put my head down on the steering wheel, trying to banish the images seared into my retinas.

I heard Nate get in and close the door. For a moment, he sat in silence. Then the laughter started. Low at first—little more than a quiet chuckle, really. Then it built into a guffaw that filled the confines of my SUV.

"Shut up," I mumbled, too nauseated to do more than cast a sidelong glance his way.

"I told you not to go upstairs," he chortled, wiping tears from his eyes. "Maybe you'll listen to me next time."

"Piss off."

"Didn't you notice the clothes on the floor of the living room?" Nate asked.

"Oh, God!" I cried, covering my ears. "Don't talk about it!"

Nate's laughter started anew, doubling him over as he gleefully enjoyed my discomfort.

Humiliation suddenly overcoming my nausea, I started

the Rover and tore out of the driveway, angrily careening down the street. As soon as I hit the interstate, I pulled out my phone and scrolled through my contacts.

"Who are you calling?" Nate asked, still struggling to keep his amusement in check.

"Nicky," I hissed. "I'm telling him to call off his hornball bodyguard before I cap his ass."

Nate leaned over and jerked the phone out of my hands. "Leave it alone, Red."

I gave him a furious glare, then turned my attention back to the road. "Eddie was—" I paused, swallowing something dark and acidic in my throat, and lowered my voice to a whisper. "He was *fornicating* with my Gran! That image will be burned into my brain forever."

"Fornicating?" Nate repeated, choking on the word. To his credit, he tried valiantly to hide his grin, but I knew it was there. "Red, come *on!* Tilly is a grown woman who is more than capable of making her own choices. Besides, in all these years, has she ever interfered in *your* love life?"

I pressed my lips together, refusing to answer, mostly because I would have had to admit he was right.

"Apparently, she likes Eddie," Nate reminded me. "And he's definitely taken with *her*. Instead of being upset you should be happy for her. Don't you think she'd be happy for you if the situation were reversed?"

I heaved a heavy sigh of resignation. "No fair being reasonable."

Nate grinned at me. "Sorry. Bad habit."

My phone buzzed in Nate's hand, so he handed it back to me. Expecting it to be Gran calling to check on me after I barged in on her and Eddie, I frowned when I saw the number on the caller ID wasn't hers. "It's Snow."

Nate's brows lifted. "Think she's heard something?"

I shrugged, then answered, "Hey, Snow."

"Red!" she gasped, her voice strained. "I'm so glad I caught you!"

It took a lot to rattle Snow, but I could tell by the tremor in her voice that something had definitely unsettled her. "What's going on?"

There was a slight hesitation, as if Snow were weighing her words carefully. "One of my girls has shared some information with me that I thought you might find useful."

"What did she tell you?" I asked, sending Nate a significant look. He leaned toward me so he could listen in on the conversation.

There was another hesitation. "Have you visited Dave Hamelin's assistant yet?"

"Yeah," I said slowly. "Why?"

"Did she tell you the names of any other clients?"

"She gave us a list of clients," I told her, "but we haven't had a chance to look at it yet. It's been a little crazy."

Snow exhaled slowly, a sure sign that she was stalling—whether her reservations were real or just for dramatic effect, I couldn't tell. "Red, it appears there are some odd business dealings going on. My employee didn't know any of the names of those involved, but she said Dave had mentioned that he was going to be set for life as soon as his boss eliminated some complications."

Nate and I exchanged glances. Dave Hamelin's suicide and the murders were starting to dovetail a lot more than I would have liked.

"Red?"

"Yeah, I'm here," I replied. "Thanks for the information, Snow. It's more helpful than you know."

"There's one other thing," Snow said quickly. "Red, please be careful. After you left the other day, Ted thought for sure he saw . . ."

"Saw what?"

Snow cleared her throat daintily. "He said it looked like

you were being tailed. I am afraid you might have stumbled onto something quite dangerous."

That was an understatement.

"Thanks, Snow," I replied, choosing not to divulge to either her or Nate that I'd felt someone watching our every move for a while now. "I'll be in touch."

I'm not sure what kind of expression I was wearing after I hung up the phone, but whatever it was must have given away something of the thoughts whirling around in my head.

"How long have you known you were being followed?" Nate demanded drily.

I shrugged. "Pretty much from the beginning. It started after Gran's attack. I felt someone in the tunnels with me."

"Why didn't you say anything?"

I lifted my shoulder again. "I thought maybe this whole thing just had me on edge. I didn't want you to think I was being paranoid."

"And now?"

"And now I think I never would have forgiven myself if the creature had hurt Trish," I admitted. "It's bad enough that the evidence is compromised."

Nate didn't immediately respond. When he did, it wasn't what I was expecting. "You couldn't have known the creature would attack her. You said yourself that anyone would have known where to go looking for the evidence that Trish had collected."

"That's it?" I asked, surprised at his lack of reprimand.

"What do you mean?"

"You're not going to scold me, tell me I was being reckless, demand that I be more careful?"

Nate gave me a lopsided grin. "It doesn't do any good, so why waste the breath?"

I couldn't help but laugh. "Point taken."

"Besides," Nate continued, "it's not like I can chastise you when I felt it, too."

My eyes went wide as I glanced his way. "You did?"

"Uh, yeah," Nate said, coming just short of rolling his eyes. "I didn't get to be a Reaper by ignoring my instincts."

"How *did* you become a Reaper?" I asked, glad to segue to a different topic. "I don't think I've ever asked."

Nate's face immediately shuttered. "It's not a very exciting story."

"We have a few more minutes before we get to the restaurant if you feel like sharing," I told him, trying to keep my tone indifferent even though I was dying to know the origins of his position among the ranks of the afterworld.

Nate suddenly took an inordinate amount of interest in the pleat of his slacks. "Let's just say I fit a certain profile."

"Okay, so you were recruited," I commented. "Not so different than me."

This brought his gaze up to me briefly before he turned his attention to a loose string on the cuff of his trench. "Not exactly."

I couldn't help the slightly exasperated sigh that escaped me. "Is having this conversation going to be this laborious the entire time, or at some point are you going to participate without me prying it out of you?"

"It's not something I've ever shared with anyone," he admitted.

My brows shot up. "Not even Al?"

Nate shook his head. "He never asked."

"Is that a not so subtle way of telling me to mind my own business?"

Nate exhaled slowly. Then, without turning to look at me, he said, "If there's anyone I'd share my story with, Red, it's you."

Touched by his words, I felt my cheeks flooding with warmth and offered him a shy smile. "Thanks, Nate."

"What, no witty comeback?" he teased.

The weight of his gaze made me shift a little uneasily in

my seat and adjust my hold on the steering wheel. "I just appreciate you feeling that way," I told him with a shrug. "That's all."

We drove in silence for a few miles, and I had just resigned myself to the fact that Nate wasn't going to tell me anything more, when he suddenly blurted, "I used to be human—an Ordinary."

Those words hit me like a punch to the gut. I think I even gasped with the impact. My head began to spin, making the road ripple and bow in front of me. Feeling like I was about to hurl, I swerved over to the shoulder and threw the Range Rover into park.

"Red? Are you okay?"

I turned in my seat and stared at him for a moment before I could bring my brain back under control enough to speak. "How could you have been an Ordinary? You're a Tale like me."

Nate shook his head. "I never told you that. You just assumed it like everyone else. I only told you I was here on special assignment."

I ran my hands through my hair, trying to stay calm. I don't know why it bothered me so much that Nate had been an Ordinary, but it did. Maybe it had something to do with the fact that he'd had a real life at one point, an existence that hadn't been dictated by some storyteller's imagination. I had only experienced that kind of freedom since coming over to the Here and Now, but Nate had always known it. Maybe I was just jealous. And afraid. I mean, what if he woke up one day and decided he didn't want to live as a Tale anymore? What would I— What would the *FMA* do then? We'd be without our best detective.

"You said you *were* Ordinary," I pointed out, still dazed by the revelation. "Does that mean you were truly alive at one point?"

"If you want to call it that," Nate replied. "I lived during ancient times. I was a soldier. Then a slave."

I gaped at him, my heart clenching at the thought that

he'd belonged to someone else. Perhaps I'd been too quick in my jealousy. "What happened?"

"Like I said, I have good instincts," Nate said, his tone flat like he was just commenting on the weather. "My master used my talents to ferret out his enemies—and if their treachery was confirmed, I took care of it."

I jerked back a little, startled by the sudden truth. "You were an assassin."

Nate inclined his head a degree, confirming my suspicion. "And a damned good one."

"So, how did you die?"

He gave me a brief, sardonic smile. "There's always someone better."

I blinked at him in disbelief, trying to reconcile the Nate I knew with the murderous slave he'd once been. "And then you became a Reaper?"

Nate gave a tight nod. "Like I said, I fit a certain profile."

"And how did you find out about us?" I asked, my voice strained.

"I literally stumbled upon you." Nate turned toward me, his eyes darker than I'd ever seen them, deeper somehow, and filled with that same pain and longing I'd caught a glimpse of once before. "I knew this was where I needed to be."

I didn't know how to respond to his revelation. Part of me wanted to say it didn't matter a damn where he'd come from and what he'd been before. All that mattered was what he was now. But another part of me was angry as hell for having been led to believe he was something he wasn't. Of course, that seemed to be a running theme when it came to the people I cared about. Why should Nate be any different?

Indecision and confusion still plaguing me, I decided to do what I did every time I found myself in a situation that threatened to make me feel more emotion than I would have liked.

Without another word, I put the Rover in gear and pulled back into traffic.

"Red?"

"Yeah?"

"We okay?"

I gave Nate an indifferent shrug. "Sure. Yeah."

"It doesn't change anything, you know," Nate assured me. "I'm still your partner. Your friend."

"Okay."

"You asked, remember?"

I gave him a tight nod. "Yep."

"I can't change my past but, trust me, I paid the price for what I did." He jerked up his sleeve, revealing the tattoos on his forearms. "My penance? Having these seared not just into my skin but into my soul. And it's done slowly, painfully. You think a burn on your skin is agonizing, try a burn to your soul."

I swallowed hard, trying not to imagine what he'd been through—it made my heart ache far too much and I wanted to stay pissed for a while longer. "You were forced to be an assassin," I told him. "I understand that. You're not that person anymore—obviously."

"You're upset because I'm not a true Tale?" he cried. "You've got to be kidding me! I was worried about confessing about having been an assassin, and you're shitty because I used to be an *Ordinary?*"

I shot him a furious look, my betrayed feelings bubbling up whether I liked it or not. "You lied to me," I spat. "You lied to all of us. You made us believe you're something you're not!"

"And what about you, 'Red'?" he asked, complete with finger quotes around my name.

My brows snapped together. "Excuse me?"

"You pretend to be this rough, tough, ass-kicking Enforcer," he explained evenly, his tone maddeningly condescending. "But beneath it all you're just a scared little girl who's still running from the Big Bad Wolf."

If we hadn't been driving down the road at breakneck speed, I would have clocked the son of a bitch. Instead, I jerked the wheel to the right and skidded to a halt, sending up a roiling cloud of gravel and dust.

"Get out," I ordered, my grip tightening on the steering wheel until my knuckles turned white.

Nate sighed and removed his fedora so that he could run a hand through that midnight black hair of his. "Tess, I'm sorry. I didn't mean—"

"Get. The Fuck. Out."

He cast a crestfallen look my way, then opened the door and climbed out. I didn't even wait for him to slam the door closed before I peeled out, leaving him standing there by the side of the road.

I was pulling into a parking spot down the street from Seth's restaurant twenty minutes later before I realized my cheeks were wet with furious tears. Damn Nate for daring to challenge my image of him and damn him again for what he'd said about *me*. I don't know what pissed me off more—that he saw right through me, or that I cared enough about that to actually cry.

Disgusted with myself for devolving into a bullshit emotional wreck, I slammed my palms against the steering wheel and let out a loud scream.

On the sidewalk, a woman walking her dog glanced my way, then quickened her pace, obviously anxious to put as much distance between herself and the deranged lunatic screaming her lungs out in the dilapidated Range Rover.

I hastily wiped my tears and took a few deep breaths, trying to get a grip. I had to get it together. The last thing the FMA needed right now was me bringing down a shitload of attention on the Tales because I couldn't deal. Oh, yeah, Al would *love* that. As if he didn't have enough of my bullshit to put up with on a daily basis, now I was going to give him one more mess to clean up?

Screw that.

I checked my reflection in the rearview mirror and, after

confirming that my eyes and nose weren't so swollen that I should consider moonlighting with Ringling Brothers, I got out of the car and headed toward the steak house where Seth was the executive chef.

As my fingers closed around the heavy brass handle of the restaurant's door, my stomach twisted painfully. I swallowed hard and pulled, telling myself that the aching feeling deep in my gut was merely due to the fact that I was so damned hungry. And as I stepped across the threshold and caught the delectable aroma of charred meat, I almost believed it.

Chapter 23

The waitress who came to my table took one look at me and whirled around, scurrying in the opposite direction.

Well, damn.

I'd really been looking forward to a nice filet, too.

With an irritated huff, I hurried after her, catching her just as she was about to burst into the kitchen and announce my presence. "Hi, there," I said, putting on my best fake smile. "I almost didn't recognize you with your clothes on."

She glanced around frantically, then gave me a pleading look. "He's not here," she whispered. "Please, don't make a scene. I need this job."

"They don't know you're sleeping with Seth?" I asked loudly.

She looked like she wanted to sink through the floor. "I'm not sleeping with Seth!" she hissed. "He just let me stay at his place as a favor."

The look I gave her clearly conveyed my disbelief.

"Look, are you hungry?" she asked.

I shrugged. "Maybe."

She glanced around again. "I have a break coming up. Go

back to your table and I'll bring you something—on the house."

I narrowed my eyes, trying to look as menacing as possible. "How do I know you're not going to bolt?"

She sighed. "Because Seth is my friend and I think he's in trouble. You look like the kind of person who could help him."

I stared at her for a few seconds, trying to figure out exactly how I should take that. In the end, I decided it was probably some kind of compliment. "Okay," I relented. "But if you're not out here in five minutes, I'm coming to look for you. And I won't be quiet about it."

She nodded and hurried away, so I went back to my table. True to her word, a few minutes later she brought out a filet with steamed veggies and a Caesar salad.

"Here," she said, sliding the plates in front of me and taking a seat at my elbow. "I wasn't sure what you'd wanted. I hope this is okay."

"It's fine," I said, lifting my fork. "Thanks." I ate a few bites of the steak, savoring the special brand of seasoning that was Seth's signature blend. The moment the first bite hit my tongue, I pictured the simple cabin in the woods near my village where Seth would often roast venison or rabbit or create some other delectable dish for me, sharing glimpses of his soul through the food he created. But it was the night he'd prepared a particularly delicious steak from the gift of beef I'd brought him that I learned the full range of his talents— from the kitchen to the bedroom.

After making her wait for several minutes while I finished off my steak, I finally asked, "What's your name?"

She gave me a tentative smile. "Molly."

"Other than the fact that I showed up at Seth's door looking for him the other day, Molly, what makes you think he's in trouble?"

She leaned forward a little. "He's being recruited away from here to go work for that pompous jackass, Todd Caliban."

I blinked at her, wondering just how much she knew about Seth's new gig. "Why would that bother you?" I asked. "It sounds like an incredible opportunity. And lucrative, too." She waved away my comment. "Seth doesn't care about the money! He just loves what he does."

I polished off the veggies and paused to wipe the corner of my mouth with my napkin. "If he's working in Caliban's flagship restaurant, he'll get the chance to really exhibit his talents, put the restaurant on the map in the culinary world."

"That's what Seth thought, too," Molly admitted. "I told him he'd be miserable working with Caliban—that guy's *such* an asshole to everyone. But Seth says he can get along with anyone."

Generally true. Unless the village Welcome Wagon showed up loaded with torches and pitchforks, Seth was about the most affable guy you'd ever meet.

"But something's bothering Seth about the deal," I guessed.

Molly folded her hands together and fidgeted with the cuticle on her thumb. "Seth told me he was concerned about the investors, that he didn't trust them. He was worried they'd be too controlling when it came to the actual running of the restaurant that Seth is supposed to manage while Caliban's filming his show in LA."

I lifted a shoulder half in agreement. "If these people are sinking a lot of money into Caliban's future—and Seth's by extension—I'm guessing they'd have some expectation of involvement."

Molly's mouth turned down into a frown. "Within reason," she returned. "There's a difference between being involved and being intrusive."

"No arguments there," I agreed. "I take it these investors have already been putting on the pressure?"

Molly nodded. "Seth is being told the investors want complete creative control over Caliban's enterprises—not just his show but all his restaurants as well. But I don't really think it's the investors making those demands."

I lifted my brows. "No? Why's that?"

"A couple of weeks ago, Seth got into a huge screaming match with that producer of Caliban's—what's her name?"

My mouth suddenly went dry. "Sebille," I supplied, trying to keep my dislike for the woman from seeping into my voice. "Sebille Fenwick."

Molly gave me a quick nod. "That's the one."

"What was the argument about?" I asked.

Molly didn't bother trying to mask her true opinion of Caliban's assistant. Her lovely features contorted with disgust as she said, "That bitch had the nerve to demand Seth sign over all the rights to his recipes."

I blinked at her in disbelief. "What?"

"The original contract stated he'd retain all creative rights to his dishes," Molly told me, "so Seth told her to piss off."

"And Sebille didn't take too kindly to his response," I filled in.

Molly rolled her eyes. "You can say that again. She was furious. Seth said she threatened him, but he wouldn't tell me what she said. I imagine it had something to do with contracts and lawsuits."

I shook my head. "She totally went Ordinary on him," I muttered under my breath.

Molly gave me a quizzical look. "Pardon?"

I stiffened, reminding myself that I was talking to an outsider.

Unless the FMA intervened in a situation and forced interested parties to settle their differences amicably, Tales tended not to waste time on litigation the way Ordinaries did. You piss off a Tale, you should probably start checking your garden for toads and other harbingers of retribution. Fairies and witches are a dime a dozen and can whip up a quick revenge spell or curse for a few bucks in today's market.

"So, you think Sebille's request is just Caliban being a dick and wanting all the glory for himself?" I asked, guiding the topic away from my ill-advised remark.

"I honestly have no idea," she admitted. "You'd have to ask Seth. I *do* think something else is going on, though—behind the scenes. One of the investors showed up here a few days ago to talk to Seth."

"Who was it?" I asked around a mouthful of steak. "Did you catch a name?"

"No," she said. "I'm sorry—Seth didn't say. But I'd recognize the guy if I saw him again."

Unfortunately, that didn't help me a whole lot. I couldn't exactly start parading a bunch of investors through the restaurant for Molly's viewing pleasure—for one thing, with the exception of the Sandman, I didn't know who any of them were.

"So what happened with the investor?" I prompted. "Did Seth have an argument with him, too?"

Molly shook her head. "No. It was a very civilized, polite conversation. But Seth was definitely rattled by the visit. He said the guy warned him that he should be careful, that he was dealing with dangerous people. Seth's been lying low since then, staying at the apartment most of the time when he's not at work."

"How long have *you* been staying at Seth's apartment?" I asked, trying to keep the hostility out of my voice.

Molly turned her eyes up to the ceiling for a moment, apparently calculating the days on her internal abacus or something, considering how long it was taking. "Two weeks."

"Are you sure?" I wiped my mouth with the napkin and slid my plate away. "You had to think about it for quite a while."

"My boyfriend and I had a big fight, and Seth said I could crash on his couch for a while." She averted her eyes, studying her fingers again. "It's not the first time I've needed a place to stay."

I leaned forward toward her and rested my elbows on the table. "Molly, has Seth been around while you were staying at his place?"

She gave me a nervous smile. "Of course."

"If you want me to help him, Molly, I need to know the truth," I told her quietly. "I need to know if he left home at any point during the last couple of nights."

Molly shifted a little and glanced toward the tables surrounding us, ensuring no one was listening in. "Okay, he went out a couple of times," she admitted, adding quickly, "but it was just for a little while! He said he had some things to take care of."

I felt my very full stomach sinking. "Did you see or hear him come back home?"

Molly opened her mouth to answer but closed it again. She slowly shook her head. "He was there by morning, that's all I know."

I pinched the bridge of my nose and squeezed my eyes shut, trying to block the headache I felt coming on. It also gave me time to figure out how to ask my next question. "Molly," I said cautiously, "do you know anything about Seth's . . . *condition?*"

Molly inhaled sharply, her face going disturbingly pale. After gaping at me for a long moment, she finally nodded, tears filling her eyes. "He suffers so much. He needed someone to talk to."

"Yeah," I said, my throat growing tight. "I know."

"I don't want anything else to happen to him," Molly said, her voice cracking.

"Me, either."

She hastily wiped away a tear that had rebelliously made its way to her cheek. "When I told Seth you'd visited, the look on his face . . . He was in love with you once, wasn't he?"

I nodded.

The look Molly gave me was so full of longing and heartbreak, I felt like I was looking in a mirror. "What was that like?" she whispered. "To have him love you?"

I blinked at her, wondering how long her love for Seth had tortured her, coloring every aspect of her life. Molly seemed like an intelligent woman and there was no arguing that she was beautiful. I got the sense that she could do anything or be anyone she wanted, but that she was waiting, holding out for something she wasn't sure would ever materialize. Hope could be both a blessing and a curse. And Molly's was definitely of the latter variety. Clinging to that cursed hope had bound her to Seth, keeping her right where she was no matter how miserable it made her.

Feeling an unexpected kinship to the Ordinary woman beside me, I squeezed her hand comfortingly. "Seth obviously thinks enough of you to share his secret. He has trusted you with his life, Molly. Tell him how you feel. My guess is he might feel the same way."

Her face brightened at this and she squeezed my hand back. Then, without another word, she hurried toward a patron just taking his seat. Her smile was so radiant and glowing when she greeted him that he couldn't help but smile back.

I grinned a little myself as I left the restaurant. As much as it pained me to admit it, I liked Molly. I liked that she loved Seth so much she had the nerve to stand up to me to protect him. And I liked that she had the same disdain for Caliban's little sergeant-at-arms, Sebille.

At the thought of the woman, my grin turned into a frown.

The more I heard about Sebille Fenwick, the less I trusted her. And the thing that bothered me most was that in all my readings, I'd never come across her name. Even though she obviously was a Tale, I couldn't place her in any story.

As I headed down the street to where I'd left my Range Rover, I took out my phone, planning to dial headquarters and have the guys run Sebille through the Tale registry. But I hung up the moment the line connected. Putting her name on their radar might raise some flags that I wasn't quite ready to raise.

No, I'd have to look into this one on my own for now. Problem was, I wasn't quite sure where to start. I could make a trip to the public library, but it would take days to comb through their stacks without a jumping-off point. What I needed was someone as well-read as I was who could help me brainstorm on Sebille's possible origins, someone who would enjoy the kind of mental gymnastics of such a challenge. And only one person—or, I should say couple—came to mind.

Chapter 24

No sooner had I entered the foyer of the Darcy home than forty pounds of energy and vivacity slammed into my legs in the form of a four-year-old boy. I laughed as I stumbled backward, windmilling my arms to keep from falling over.

I looked down to see Collin, Elizabeth and Darcy's youngest son, smiling up at me, golden brown curls in disarray, a smudge of mud marring his dimpled, cherubic face.

"Hello, Aunt Tess!" he said cheerfully.

I scooped him up into my arms and gave him a healthy squeeze. "Hello, monkey! Where's your mum and dad?"

"They're in the sitting room. Would you like to see my frong instead?"

I frowned slightly. "Frong?"

My curiosity was rewarded when a rather hefty amphibian suddenly appeared an inch from my nose. "This is my frong, Nigel."

Nigel gave me a rather resigned croak and, I swear, heaved a huge sigh.

"That is one handsome guy," I said with a laugh, wondering just how long Nigel had been benefiting from Collin's loving care.

"Collin, take your frog outside. Father said you cannot keep him."

When I set Collin back on his feet so that he could scamper away, an extremely handsome lad of six years stepped forward and offered me a very polite, proper handshake. "Good day, Aunt."

I grabbed William's hand and pulled him forward to receive a bear hug and a showering of kisses on his still-chubby cheeks.

"Good day, Aunt. Good day, Aunt," I mimicked, eliciting a hearty laugh. "You act like I'm some stuffy old cow." I smothered his face with another smattering of kisses, then released him.

"Yuck!" William groaned, pretending to wipe my kisses away.

"Your brother is useless as a butler," I joked, nodding in the general direction young Collin had gone. "Could you take me to your parents, Master William?"

Will nodded eagerly and took hold of my hand. "I think you will find I am a very good butler, Aunt."

I smothered a grin. "Most assuredly so," I agreed. "However, I imagine your mother and father have other aspirations for your future occupation."

Will gave me a very solemn nod for one so young. "Indeed. Father believes I shall make a very fine businessman one day."

"Well, your dad does have a good head for those kinds of things," I told him. "He might be right."

Will was positively glowing with pride as he ushered me into the sitting room. The moment we entered, both his parents looked up from their current activities, their eyes brightening at the sight of their darling boy.

No lack of love in this house, I reflected, warmed by merely being in the presence of such a family. I had told Nate I had no dreams of ever settling down, having a family, living happily ever after, and that was mostly true. Except for moments like these.

"Tess!" Elizabeth cried, coming toward me and taking my hands in hers. "I was not expecting you! What a delightful surprise."

"Good day, Ms. Little," Darcy greeted. "A pleasure to see you."

I gave them a rather contrite smile. "I wish I could say it was just a social call. Truth is, I need your help."

"Will, darling," Eliza said, casting an apprehensive glance my way as she spoke, "why don't you run along and discover where Collin has taken his frog."

As soon as Will was safely out of earshot, Darcy gestured toward a chair. "How can we assist you, Ms. Little?"

"Well, I—" My cell phone suddenly sprang to life, cutting off my words and earning me a rather disapproving look from Darcy. I flushed and silenced the ringer. "Sorry."

Elizabeth cast an amused glance at her husband. "I am afraid Mr. Darcy disapproves of the modern insistence upon constant communication with one's colleagues," she teased. "Do not think his irritation is directed at you, Tess dear."

"Sure," I stuttered, intimidated as ever by Darcy's powerful presence. I often had the impression I earned Darcy's disapproval for a great number of reasons—hardly surprising, all things considered—but to his credit, he indulged Eliza's affection for me and was never anything but cordial and welcoming.

"You were about to say?" Darcy prompted.

"Yes, sorry. I'm trying to determine the origin of a Tale named Sebille Fenwick."

"Could you not just check the Registry?" Eliza asked.

I nodded. "I could, but I'd like to keep my inquiry private at the moment."

"What is her current occupation?" Darcy questioned.

"She's the personal assistant to Todd Caliban and the

producer of his cooking show," I explained, silencing my cell phone once again. "She has connections to a lot of people in two different ongoing investigations. That's a lot of involvement in our world for a Tale no one's ever heard of. I'd just like to know a little more about her."

"Is it possible she is from *The Tempest*?" Elizabeth suggested. "A minor character, perhaps?"

I shrugged. "Possibly. Prospero had his fair share of unnamed fairies at his disposal. She could be one of those. It certainly would explain how she and Caliban met. But I don't want to overlook any other possibilities."

"Do you know if Sebille Fenwick is her given name?" Darcy asked. "Is it possible she chose an alias when she came over as so many others have done?"

"Entirely possible," I admitted, suddenly feeling like this was going to be tougher than I'd thought and wishing I had a certain detective at my side to help guide the investigative process. As if on cue, my phone rang again.

"Do you need to answer that, dearest?" Elizabeth asked.

I shook my head absently. "No, it's fine. So, let's operate on the assumption that Sebille Fenwick is her real name."

"The name Sebille could be a distortion of *sibyl*—one of the oracles mentioned in ancient mythologies," Elizabeth suggested.

Darcy nodded. "Indeed. Have you considered this possibility?"

"I don't know," I said slowly. "Sebille doesn't strike me as the oracle type."

"A thorough search through literature could take a considerable amount of time, Ms. Little," Darcy pointed out. "How urgent is your inquiry?"

"Very, I'm afraid." I took out my cell phone and turned it off this time. "Anything you can find for me by tomorrow would be great. I can't really bring Sebille in for questioning until I have something to ask her about."

"Could you not speak to Mr. Caliban directly?" Elizabeth suggested. "Could he not just tell you how he met Ms. Fenwick and what he knows of her?"

I shook my head. "Not without raising suspicion about why I'm asking. We already brought him in for questioning once, so I'm reluctant to do so again without a good reason. And at the moment, my interest in Sebille is just curiosity."

Elizabeth and Darcy exchanged a glance. "What if you were to bump into Mr. Caliban in a social setting?" Eliza asked, her eyes brightening.

"That would be different," I conceded. "Just casual conversation. But it's not like Todd and I run in the same circles these days, so the chances of just bumping into him are pretty slim."

Eliza grinned. "Perhaps we can increase the likelihood of such a happy coincidence."

I lifted my brows, admittedly curious. "How so?"

"The Charmings are to have a party tomorrow evening," she explained. "As Mr. Caliban is well known to be Cindy Charming's particular favorite, he no doubt will be present." Elizabeth's eyes twinkled with mischief. "Regrettably, Mr. Darcy and I shall be unable to attend, so we shall send you in our stead."

"I don't know," I said warily. "If I show up at the Charmings' compound, even with an invitation in hand, I'd probably get booted at the door."

"Nonsense!" Eliza protested.

"It's not like I keep an evening gown hanging in my closet." I waved my hands down the length of my body. "Dressing up for me is wearing leather instead of denim."

Of course, even as I expressed my hesitation, I had to admit that in addition to giving me an opportunity to corner Caliban, the party would also be a good chance to get an audience with the Charmings and question them about their association with Dave Hamelin.

Elizabeth laughed. "I certainly can find something in my wardrobe that would suit you."

I eyed Elizabeth's hourglass figure and ample bosom and somehow doubted that I'd be able to fill out any evening gown as well as she did, but I suppose it was better than showing up looking like I'd ridden in on a Harley. "Okay. What did you have in mind?"

"If you will excuse me," Darcy interjected, rising from his seat with an amused grin, "I shall leave you ladies to discuss wardrobe accommodations as I fear I would be of little assistance."

Elizabeth rose to meet him as he strode toward the door. Smiling lovingly, she extended a hand, which he eagerly grasped and swept toward his lips. I heard him speak softly to her, and although the words were too quiet for me to hear, the effect was unmistakable.

As soon as Darcy had closed the door behind him, I said, "I take it you and Darcy have once more found common ground?"

Elizabeth gave me a wry look. "You are incorrigible, Tess."

"People keep telling me that."

"Then perhaps you should listen."

I waved her comment away. "Nah—ignoring sound advice is one of my more endearing qualities."

Eliza's musical laughter rang out once more. "Someday, someone will come along and educate you in ways you never thought possible, my dear friend."

I started to tell her that there weren't a whole lot of mysteries left in this world for me, particularly when it came to the opposite sex, but instead I decided to get back to a safer topic. "So, should I just come by tomorrow night and try on a few dresses or something?"

Elizabeth gave me a look of mild horror. "Oh, no, my dear. You will need more time than that. Be here at two o'clock—that should give us plenty of time to find something suitable."

"Two o'clock?" I cried. "Are you kidding?" I glanced down at my watch to calculate how many hours of sleep I'd be losing, when I noticed the time. "Damn it!"

"Is there a problem, dearest?"

I sighed. "I'm running late. I have a date at seven and need to run home—"

"A date?" Elizabeth echoed, trying valiantly to hide her incredulousness, but failing miserably.

"Don't sound so surprised!" I said with a laugh. "It's not totally out of the realm of possibility that a man would want to take me out."

"Forgive me," Eliza said, smothering a smile. "You misunderstand. I only meant that you seldom take time off from your work to enjoy yourself. I am delighted!"

I grimaced. "Well, don't be too delighted just yet."

Eliza's lovely brows lifted. "Why is that?"

I squirmed a little, knowing what was coming. "My date's with Vlad."

Chapter 25

Elizabeth's stubbornness was legendary, but I'd never seen it firsthand until now. She stood with her back to me in front of the picture window facing the meadow behind their home, her chin lifted at a haughty angle.

"This is an unspeakable error in judgment," she said firmly.

I blinked at her, too stunned to immediately respond. "Elizabeth, you're my best friend," I reminded her. "If you don't understand, who will?"

She crossed her arms over her chest and lifted her chin even higher. "I care not."

I exhaled in frustration. "I know you don't approve of my relationship with Vlad, but—"

"Relationship?" Eliza interrupted, finally turning to face me. "You have no relationship—you have . . . *relations.*"

"You're in the twenty-first century now, Lizzie," I said. "It's okay to call it sex."

She flushed and strode to the fireplace, irritably stoking the fire. "He uses you."

"I use him, too," I admitted. "It's always been like that between us. But he's wanting to try to have an actual relationship."

"So he says," she mumbled.

"I have a *date*," I reiterated. "An actual date."

She stowed the fire poker in its proper place, then came to where I was sitting. After a moment of hesitation, her expression altered from anger to concern as she sat down next to me.

"Tess, dearest, I just want what's best for you."

I nodded. "I know."

She sighed and leaned back into the pillows. "I want you to be happy. I want you to know the kind of love that I have known with Darcy." She took my hand in both of hers, her brows coming together in a frown. "What if you have misread Vlad?"

"Mis*read* him?" I drew back a little, beginning to catch her drift. "Vlad's pretty well ingrained in the cultural consciousness as he is now."

"So you say," Eliza replied, "but I have read his story, Tess. He may be a perfect gentleman now, but he once was a vicious fiend. One can alter one's appearance, but one cannot change who one is in the essentials."

"He was a victim of circumstances," I said, inwardly cringing at how often I'd used that excuse lately.

Eliza's brows lifted. "Are not we all? The difference is in how we react to our circumstances. When *you* encountered adversity, you became stronger for it. Vlad became a monster."

Suddenly uncomfortable with the implications of what she was saying, I lurched to my feet and began to pace, chewing on the edge of my thumb as I mulled over her words. I understood the question she wanted to ask but was too polite to put into words.

"Even if things don't work out between us, Vlad wouldn't devolve into that version of his character again," I said, not sure which of us I was trying to convince. "He's come a long way since he was written."

Elizabeth nodded. "I make no argument against that," she conceded. "But his transformation has been due in large part to your influence as much as changing perceptions of his story."

I shook my head. "You give me way too much credit. He'd be okay if I weren't in the picture. He'd find someone else who could love him and help him through the difficult times."

Elizabeth sighed. "Oh, Tess. Your affection for him makes you blind. Vlad cannot help what he is anymore than you or I. He must consume blood to survive. You have only so much to give. What happens when he must go to another? Will you lie awake in your bed, wondering if it is only blood he takes from another while you wait for him in the darkness?"

I couldn't deny I'd had the same thought more times than I cared to admit, but I laughed it off. "Come on, Lizzie!" I replied. "It's just a date! Don't you think we're overanalyzing this a bit? He asked me to dinner! I promise I won't get mixed up in something I can't handle."

She gave me a pleading look but said nothing.

Trying to allay her fears, I dropped down on the sofa beside her and gave her a playful nudge. "Come on! When have you ever seen me bite off more than I could chew?"

"It isn't *your* bite that concerns me."

"I can handle him, Lizzie," I assured her. "Really. You have to trust me, okay?"

Elizabeth exhaled with a little huff but nodded. "All right. I shall refrain from further lecture. But, Tess, do promise me you will take care. I could not do without you."

I hugged her tightly and kissed her cheek. "I promise."

Friends once more, Eliza agreed to walk me to the front door, but the moment she opened the sitting room door, my feet turned to stone.

"What the hell are you doing here?" I demanded angrily and, admittedly, somewhat breathlessly, when I caught sight of a familiar fedora.

Nate nonchalantly turned from his conversation with Darcy. "You didn't answer your phone," he pointed out. "You said I should assume you were in trouble if you didn't answer by the fifth or sixth call."

I opened my mouth to argue, but snapped it shut again, hating that he kind of had me on this one. Breaking free of my stupor, I marched toward him. "Well, as you can see, I'm fine."

He nodded. "Yes—Mr. Darcy assured me of your safety when I came barging in his front door."

I cast Darcy an apologetic look. "I'm sorry for my partner's intrusion."

"This is the Detective Grimm you mentioned the other night?" Eliza interjected, coming forward to warmly welcome her guest.

Nate cast me a smug grin as he extended a hand to Eliza. "One and the same."

I rolled my eyes, then grudgingly called up my rusty manners. "Detective Nate Grimm, may I present Mrs. Elizabeth Bennet-Darcy?"

Nate suavely lifted Eliza's hand to his lips. "Delighted to finally make your acquaintance."

"Detective Grimm and I were just discussing Ms. Little's request for our assistance," Darcy explained to his wife.

Nate gave me a subtly chastising look. "Yes, indeed. Quite interesting. I can't wait to hear your theory, Red."

I narrowed my eyes at him. "Well, you'll have to wait. I'm on my way out."

"Where are you going?" Nate asked, his brows drawing together in a frown.

"I have plans," I reminded him haughtily. "And they don't include *you*."

Nate's expression immediately soured. "Oh, that's right," he said, spitting the words out as if they were rotten sewage. "You're seeing the vampire."

"That's right."

Nate shook his head slowly. "He's all wrong for you."

I stepped forward, jutting my chin up at him. "It's none of

your business. You lost the right to an opinion when you lied to me, *partner.*"

Nate stepped closer, his eyes stormy. "I explained that," he hissed quietly. "What else do you want me to say?"

"Tess, dearest," Eliza interrupted gently. "Would you and Detective Grimm prefer to chat in the parlor?"

"No," I said quickly, holding Nate's angry gaze long enough to make a point. "I'm leaving." When I heard him sigh in defeat, I turned to Elizabeth and hugged her good-bye. "Thank you both for your help. I'll see you tomorrow afternoon."

I bolted from the house and down the steps but was pulled to a stop by Nate's grasp on my arm. "Red, please listen to me," he pleaded softly.

I looked up at him, ready to tear into him about following me to Elizabeth's, but the expression in his eyes stilled the words I'd intended. Instead, I said, "You have until I get to Gran's. But you're not talking me out of going tonight."

He nodded and got into the Rover. I waited in tense silence for him to say something as I drove, but we were a good ten minutes on the road before he finally spoke.

"I don't know how to convince you that I only had good intentions."

I pressed my lips together for a moment, keeping my hurt and anger in check. "You could start by telling me the rest of the truth," I suggested. I glanced over at him to gauge his reaction and saw that I'd hit the mark.

"I'm not quite ready to share everything," he replied. "Soon. I promise. You'll just have to trust me until then."

"Yeah, well, trusting people isn't exactly my strong suit," I reminded him.

Nate let out a long breath. "Okay then, I'm just going to have to trust you."

"What do you mean?"

"I've shared information with you that could get me fired

from the FMA," he pointed out. "Information that could get me ostracized from the Tale world forever."

"I'm not going to turn you in," I said irritably. "You know that."

"Do I? I have no guarantee." He reached over and pried my right hand from the steering wheel, then ran a finger down the center of my palm. "You hold a lot of power, Red. You could completely destroy me with what you know. I just have to trust that you won't."

I didn't respond. Mostly because I didn't know what to say. He was right, of course. If the rest of the Tales knew they'd been duped by a former Ordinary, every door would close to Nate. No one would trust him again. He'd be an outcast, a pariah. He could go back to being a normal Reaper, I assumed, but it sounded like there might be issues there, too. Which left the Ordinary world. And they'd proven time and time again just how accepting *they* were of anyone who was different.

We were still suffering through an uneasy silence when I pulled into Gran's driveway and turned off the engine. For a moment, I just sat there, staring out the windshield, my emotions and my bruised ego in a pitched battle for dominance. Finally, I sighed, forcing them to call a truce.

"There's a party tomorrow evening at the Charmings'," I said at last. "It'll be a good opportunity to talk to them about Dave Hamelin and to see if Caliban can tell us anything about Sebille Fenwick." I paused, clearing my throat a couple of times. "Do you want to come with me?"

I didn't have to look at Nate to know his brows were lifted in surprise. "You mean, as your date?"

I turned toward him to throw out a saucy retort but saw that he was grinning, obviously anticipating my response. "Something like that," I groaned.

He gave me a wink. "Love to."

"It's black-tie," I told him, trying to ignore how much

his wink devastated me. I shoved open the car door and climbed out. "Can you come up with something to wear on short notice?"

Nate chuckled as he caught up with me. "Yeah, I think I can handle it."

"I'll see you tomorrow, then," I called over my shoulder. "You can pick me up at Eliza's at seven."

"Red."

I paused on the porch steps and turned around, finding myself at eye level with Nate, my face only a few inches from his. "Yeah?"

He reached up and tucked a strand of hair behind my ear, his thumb grazing my jaw as he let his hand fall away. "Be careful tonight."

I nodded, momentarily forgetting where I'd misplaced my voice.

Nate gave me a rather sorrowful smile, then leaned forward and brushed his lips against my cheek. It was little more than a flutter of sensation against my skin, but it was enough to steal my breath as my lids fluttered closed.

I stood there for a few seconds, unable to respond as I seared into memory the feel of Nate's lips on my skin. But then, realizing how ridiculous I was acting by letting such a simple, meaningless kiss shake me to the foundation of my resolve, I gathered together the crumbling edges of my willpower and opened my eyes. Expecting to see him standing there with a self-satisfied grin on his face, I was rapidly preparing a smart-ass remark in response, but to my disappointment, he had vanished, taking the warmth in the air with him.

Shuddering from the sudden chill, I went inside to prepare for my date, wishing my intended companion was not the in-your-face-sexy vampire I was going to meet but rather the shadowy enigma who had so recently darkened my doorstep.

Chapter 26

The house was dark and still when I arrived home, but considering my earlier trauma, I wasn't about to take that for granted. Praying I wouldn't stumble upon Gran and Eddie again, I proceeded cautiously, letting my senses feel out the house for any sign of the randy seniors. Finally confirming I was in the clear, I headed into the kitchen to check our message board and saw Gran's elegant handwriting there as expected.

Dearest—
  Have gone to meet the lovely young woman you sent my way.
  Then out to dinner with Mr. Fox. Don't wait up!
                                                              Gran

I reread the note, trying not to let my imagination wander. I *seriously* didn't want to think about what they'd be doing that would keep them out all night. *Don't wait up?* Was she kidding me?

I groaned aloud, but it ended on a sigh. At least their date included a visit with Alice. I felt bad for the kid. It was tough enough to be in her situation, but being an Ordinary, she had no clue how dark and treacherous our world could be. But if there was anyone who could steer her clear of the shitstorm of Tale drama, it was Gran.

Speaking of drama, I reminded myself that I had an honest-to-God date in a little less than half an hour and needed to get my ass in gear.

I hurried upstairs and grabbed my red leather pants and matching jacket from the closet—I wasn't kidding about the whole denim-to-leather thing—and quickly stripped out of my work clothes. I was just squeezing into my pants when a blur of movement out of the corner of my eye brought my head up.

Startled, I whirled toward the window. "What the hell?" I muttered, grabbing up my jacket and shrugging into it as I cautiously approached the window.

Standing to one side, I pulled back the curtain and peeked through the small opening, scanning the rapidly darkening night. Not seeing anyone lurking around in the shadows, I checked the lock on the window, just to be on the safe side.

"Weird."

Still trying to shrug off the heavy feeling of someone's eyes upon me, I went back to my closet and grabbed my red stiletto boots. I'd just finished pulling them on when the hair on the back of my neck began to rise in warning. Pretending to be unaffected, I sidled over to my dresser where I'd set my Glock. Keeping it low at my side, I went back to the window to take another look.

Nothing.

The only movement was a gentle breeze swaying the leaves of the maple tree just outside my window.

"Little twitchy tonight, Red?" I said aloud, hoping the sound of my voice would check the rush of adrenaline pumping through my veins. Unfortunately, whatever calming effects it had were negated when the floorboards creaked behind me.

I spun around, leveling my Glock at the empty shadows just outside my bedroom door. I cursed under my breath and stood completely still, listening intently for even the slightest sound, but none came.

Regretting sending Nate off so soon, I snatched my phone and keys from my dresser and stole silently along the hall and down the stairs, my gun at the ready. With each step, the darkness within the house seemed to deepen, taking on a disturbing solidity as it crept ever closer and threatened to completely envelope the house in opaque shadow.

I edged closer to the front door, quickly surveying every corner as I went. Just as my fingers closed around the doorknob, I heard a faint scrabble coming from the living room. Clenching my jaw to keep from crying out, I whipped my gun toward the direction of the sound, my eyes straining to see in the darkness.

"I'm armed!" I barked. "Come out with your hands where I can see them!"

When there was no response, I slid my hand along the wall until I found the light switch and flicked it on, hoping to momentarily blind the intruder and give me just enough of an edge to get the drop on him.

It worked. The intruder burst forward, knocking into the coffee table and sending a porcelain vase crashing to the floor. I swung my gun toward a blur of motion and nearly fired off a round when a creature as big as a cat lunged toward me, red eyes blazing maniacally.

I leapt out of the way with a startled scream, my stiletto heels slipping out from under me and bringing me down hard on my ass. The impact jolted my gun from my hand and sent it skimming across the foyer toward the front door. Fortunately, the rat wasn't having any better luck. It hit the tile in the foyer and slide across the floor with a desperate scraping of claws, trying to get its feet under its body once more.

I managed to get back on my feet first, and grabbed an

umbrella from the nearby stand. Brandishing the makeshift weapon like a sword, I swiped at the offending rodent, catching it in full swing as it made another leap at me. The blow sent it flying into the wall with a thud.

I lunged forward and threw open the front door, then charged the rat again, intent on booting his ass outside. As I swung, the rodent hissed, baring surprisingly long, pointy teeth. Instead of making another assault, it bolted toward the door of its own accord, vanishing into thin air before reaching the threshold.

"What the fuck?" I blurted, my skin creeping with goose bumps.

The rat was far larger than an ordinary sewer rat and had looked like it was there on a mission—though what that mission was, I could only guess. But my gut told me it had some connection to Dave Hamelin.

One thing I *did* know for sure—that rat was conjured, sent by someone with some seriously powerful magic. There was no mistake about that. I shuddered, wondering what the creature would have been capable of had it gotten the drop on me instead of the other way around.

At that moment, Vlad's limo rolled into the driveway, the headlights cutting through the darkness. Far more relieved than I would have liked to admit, I locked the door behind me and hurried to the waiting car, hopping into the back before the driver could get out and open the door for me.

The minute I was safely inside, I took several slow, deep breaths and ran my hands up and down my thighs to calm their trembling. My pulse was just beginning to slow to a respectable tempo when the divider window slid down to reveal a bright, cheerful face. "Hi, Ms. Little! Where to?"

I blinked in disbelief. "Amanda?"

The pert little blonde's smile widened at the fact I'd remembered her name. "Sorry to surprise you! Renfield has the night off."

I frowned, trying to remember when Renfield had *ever* had a night off. Vlad got a little testy if one of his flunkies wasn't immediately at his beck and call. Letting his number-two guy (whose unwavering devotion went way beyond creepy) have a night off seemed completely out of character. "Where am I taking you?" Amanda prompted, casting an anxious glance at her dainty gold wristwatch. "I promised the Count I would call him with the location as soon as I picked you up." She chewed her lip, obviously anxious when I didn't respond. "He can be a bit impatient, Ms. Little. I'd rather not make him wait."

Still perturbed by Amanda's presence, I rattled off the first restaurant that came to mind. Her eyes widened a little at my choice, but she placed the call to Vlad, offering me a tentative smile while she waited for him to answer. A moment later, I heard her say something softly before hanging up.

"The Count was a little . . . *surprised* by your choice," she said, placing her phone on the seat beside her. "But he said to tell you he 'shall endure the experience so long as he can enjoy the pleasure of your company'—or something like that."

Not too long ago, such a debonair compliment would have brought a flush of color to my cheeks, but now it just made me want to roll my eyes at the over-the-top cheesiness of it. Amanda was watching my reaction in the rearview mirror, though, so I resisted the impulse and offered her a tight smile instead.

"So, how did you get tagged for car pool?" I asked, trying to divert the conversation away from me.

The girl lit up with delight. "The Count said I was the only one in his employ he trusted enough to transport you."

"Really?" I replied, my frown deepening. Vlad was never the trusting sort—too many close calls with stakes and holy water over the years. "That's quite an accomplishment."

"I know!" she cried, bouncing a little in her seat. "I think this is a *huge* step forward for us!"

I eyed her reflection in the mirror, mentally high-fiving myself for pegging her interest in Vlad when I'd first met her. She was so into him, I could almost see the outline of her body fading as her identity drifted away.

"How did you meet Vlad, Amanda?" I asked, genuinely curious.

Her smile widened to the point of almost being grotesque. "A friend of mine introduced us. She had belonged to him for a while, but her boss didn't like their relationship and demanded my friend break things off.

"So your friend's boss actually knew about Vlad?" I questioned, surprised to hear that anyone knew the names of Vlad's snacks. He tended to keep such things on the down-low.

Amanda nodded. "Oh, yeah! Her boss is the Count's mistress."

Mistress?

I'd always known Vlad had quite a few other women on call for room service, but I'd never heard of any of them being serious enough to label as a mistress. Even when things were at their hottest and heaviest between us, we'd never gone as far as defining our relationship with monikers. Maybe I was just reading too much into what Amanda was saying, but it sounded like this boss-lady was committed to Vlad in some way. Which made me wonder where the hell he thought I was going to fit in to all this.

"Who is this mistress?" I asked, still digging.

Amanda shrugged. "No clue. The Count makes me call her just 'the Mistress.' Anyway, my friend got fired when the Mistress got pissed about how much time Vlad was spending with his other women."

"And he let your friend go, just like that?" I queried, knowing all too well that Vlad didn't just let his women walk away. In fact, aside from me, I didn't know of any others who'd tried to break things off. His bite was far too addictive.

Amanda shook her head, confirming my suspicions. "The

only way Vlad would release her was if she brought him someone else."

That sounded more like the Vlad I knew.

"And your friend was okay with you stepping in?"

Amanda's expression seemed pained and a little guilt-ridden when she said slowly, "No. She was devastated. She thought it would be easier if she knew her replacement, but I think it was even harder. She kept trying to get Vlad to take her back. It was so sad! But she seemed to do a little better when she started her new job."

"New job?"

"She went to work for Jack Something-or-other," Amanda informed me. "He owns a pie company or something here in Chicago."

"Jack Horner?" I suggested, trying to figure out where I'd seen his name recently.

Amanda's lovely face registered surprise. "Yes!" she cried. "How did you know?"

"We go back a ways."

She shook her head, grinning. "Small world."

Too small.

"I think she likes working for him," Amanda continued. "But even after getting the new job she still struggled to get over Vlad for a while. A few weeks ago, she showed up at his house, demanding to see him. She and the Mistress had a *huge* fight. Yelling, screaming, throwing stuff. The Count had to break things up."

"Were you there for the argument?"

Amanda grimaced. "For a while. He sent me away to his bedroom while he dealt with the two of them. I don't know what he said, but it must have worked. I haven't seen my friend since then."

"What about the Mistress?" I probed, starting to feel uneasy. "Do you still see her?"

Amanda's face contorted in disgust. "Unfortunately. She's

always so mean to me! I don't think she likes to share. I mean, who does? I don't like it either, but I guess that's the price you pay to be with Vlad."

I snorted. *Maybe some of us did.*

This date was becoming less and less palatable all the time. Thinking about the bevy of women who'd apparently been frequenting Vlad's bed made me want to puke. It also made me wonder why he thought it necessary to add me to the mix when he had a veritable smorgasbord of nookie at his disposal.

"Amanda," I began cautiously, "do you know anything about *my* relationship to Vlad?"

She glanced over her shoulder and nodded. "Oh, yeah! Of course! He told me all about the two of you. I think you're one of his favorites."

I looked at her through hooded eyes. "One of?"

Her head bobbed up and down excitedly. "Uh-huh! You should be *so* honored. The competition is pretty fierce."

I resisted the urge to smack the poor girl upside the head to knock some sense into her, deciding it probably wouldn't have worked anyway. She was too far gone. Instead I said, "Amanda, have you considered the possibility that at some point Vlad might choose just one woman to be with?"

Her face fell a little. "I try not to think about it too much," she sighed, nonchalantly double-parking in front of the restaurant. "I just hope that maybe it'll be me. Of course, I'd be okay if it was you. I like you the best!"

"Amanda—"

"Ms. Little," she interrupted, turning around in the seat to face me, "could I ask you something?"

I eyed her warily, put on my guard by her sudden shyness. "Sure."

"If the Count . . . If Vlad *does* choose you, would you . . . I mean, if he still needs someone to feed from . . ."

"Would I consider you?" I finished for her.

Her face flushed with color and unabashed hopefulness as she nodded.

I shrugged, mentally mapping out the many ways I was going to tell Vlad to go fuck himself. But I didn't have the heart to crush the poor kid's woefully misguided aspirations. "Sure," I sighed. "Why not."

With a gleeful squeal, she clapped her hands and probably would have turned a back handspring had she not been sitting in the car. "You are so *awe*some!"

Before I could respond, she hopped out of the car and opened my door. As I stepped onto the sidewalk she cried, "Oh, I love your boots!"

I blinked at her, taken aback by the exuberance of her compliment. "Uh, thanks."

She leaned forward and squeezed my arm. "If we are both Vlad's mistresses, we could maybe even share clothes!" she whispered. "Wouldn't that be *so* much fun?"

I took in her fluffy pink sweater and micro-mini and felt a little frightened at the thought. "Dear God."

Unfortunately, my reaction seemed to only fuel her excitement. "We could be like *sisters*! That would be *so cool!*"

Now, truly horrified, I just gave her a placating and noncommittal smile. "Uh-huh, okay." I peeled her fingers from my arm. "Well, I'd better get going. Can't keep Vlad waiting."

She gasped. "Oh, my gosh! You're right!" She gave me a little shove toward the door, then waved cheerily. "Buh-bye, Ms. Little! Enjoy your dinner!"

I gave her a tight smile and waved, ducking a little into the collar of my jacket in an effort to shield myself from her enthusiasm. I didn't look back for fear she'd take it as an invitation to cement our newly established bond of sisterhood with a super-duper hug or something else equally nauseating.

It took all I had not to sprint to the door.

Chapter 27

After my decidedly surreal exchange with Amanda, ducking into the crowded, too warm hole-in-the-wall Italian restaurant was a relief.

"Hey, Tony," I said to the portly, balding owner of the establishment. "What's doing?"

Tony's round, friendly face brightened with a good-natured smile. "Tess! I haven't seen you in weeks!"

"Sorry," I told him sincerely, my mouth watering at the familiar aroma of garlic and oregano. "I've been busy."

Tony took me by the shoulders and gave me a hearty kiss on each cheek. "You're here now, that's all that matters. I've got some fabulous veal on the menu tonight."

I smiled at him, warmed by his unfailing hospitality. "Thanks, Tony." I shoved my hands into my pockets and peered out into the dining room. "I'm supposed to be meeting a friend of mine. Has anyone asked for me?"

Tony rubbed his very round belly, pondering my question. "No, no one has asked for you. But we had a guy come in and ask for a table in the corner. Longish dark hair—looks like a friggin' rock star."

"Pasty white skin?" I added.

Tony snapped his fingers and pointed at me. "That's the guy."

"Lucky me," I drawled.

Tony eyed me knowingly. "You don't sound so happy to see him. You want me to have my guys throw him out?"

"No, that's okay," I replied, heading into the main dining room. "I got this."

I walked straight back to the shadowy corner where I knew Vlad would be sitting. As I expected, he was reclining patiently in his chair, hands folded in a deceptively placid manner. As I approached the table, he rose and came to meet me, brushing a kiss to my neck as he pulled out my chair.

"Good evening, my own," he said, his voice low and sultry in my ear.

"Yeah, about that," I began, scooting my chair in. I reached for a chunk of bread already waiting in the center of the table. I methodically broke it into several pieces, using those moments to draw up all my mental strength, then looked up at him through lowered lashes to mitigate the power of his gaze. "How serious were you about giving things between us a go?"

Vlad's lips curved into a sensual smile, revealing the tips of his fangs. "Extremely."

I nodded solemnly. "Really . . ."

"Indeed." He lifted a glass of what I assumed was red wine and brought it to his lips. "I simply must have you, Red. I will not be thwarted in this."

I started to say something snarky in reply, but a lovely young waitress suddenly appeared at my elbow.

"Can I take your order?"

Vlad smiled at the girl, visibly affecting her when she got the full-on glory of his stunning good looks. "I believe I have all I require at the moment." He turned his gaze to me as he added, "I will have a bite later."

I held his gaze, daring him to give it a try, and said to the

Kate SeRine

waitress, "I'll have the veal scaloppini. Make sure the chef adds extra garlic."

"Garlic?" she repeated, frowning. "Are you sure?"

I arched my brow defiantly at Vlad. "Yep. Load it up. I want it to *ooze* from my pores."

He let out a low, angry hiss, but his expression remained placid. As soon as the waitress turned away with a shrug, his face grew hard, anger distorting his gorgeous features and transforming them into something bordering on hideous. "You must forgive me if I do not know the rules of the game you play this evening, Red."

I popped a piece of bread into my mouth and gave him an indifferent shrug. "Right back at ya."

I saw him flinch ever so slightly. "I beg your pardon?"

I leaned back in my chair, mimicking his nonchalance. "How many women do you have on retainer right now, Vlad?"

He studied me for a moment as if trying to divine the trajectory of my inquiry. "You know I cannot feed from the same woman for very long without harm coming to her."

"True," I conceded. "But you only need to sleep with one. Who's it going to be?"

His eyes narrowed. "You obviously have something to say. You might as well proceed."

"I don't like to share," I said, grabbing another hunk of bread and dipping it in olive oil. "And, apparently, neither do your other booty calls."

"Ah, I see," he drawled. "You object to my more libidinous needs. I must say, this shade of green is very unbecoming on you, Red."

"Oh, I'm not jealous," I told him calmly. "I'm just laying it down for you. You really want me around, you'll have to pink-slip the others."

The muscle in his jaw twitched ominously. "Like it or not," he said slowly, his voice growing deeper, "I shall be the one to decide with whom I lay. I shall not have my *dinner* dictate my choices."

I cocked my head to one side. "And who would that be? I mean, seeing as how I'm just icing on your fuck cake and all, some other lucky gal must be this *dinner* you speak of." Watching his expression darken ominously, I leaned forward, resting my elbows on the table, and glanced around as if to make sure no one was listening in. "Come on—you can tell me. Who's the main dish?" I gasped theatrically. "Wait a minute—is it the *Mistress*?"

Vlad stared at me for a long moment, his expression an unreadable mask except for the blazing fury in his eyes. Finally, he said, "To whom have you been speaking, my dear girl?"

"Who's the Mistress, Vlad?" I pressed, ignoring his question.

Vlad took another sip of his wine, his eyes never leaving my face. He swallowed slowly, savoring the taste, then licked his lips. "Tell me what you want from me," he said at last, "and I will comply. Consider it a show of my affection for you, a pledge of my sincerity."

I popped the last bit of bread in my mouth. "Is that right?"

He inclined his head. "Say it, and it will be so."

"Oh, so now it's okay for your food to talk back to you?" I replied, pretending confusion. "Because, you know, I wasn't sure."

Vlad darted forward in a blur of motion, his eyes glowing, his cool facade slipping. "You have never been just sustenance to me," he hissed through clenched teeth. "You know how I crave you."

I nodded. "Is that what you tell the Mistress, too?"

"That woman is . . ." He paused, searching for the words. "She is merely an associate. We have a mutual understanding about the nature of our acquaintance."

"You sure about that?" I challenged. "Sounds like she doesn't much like the competition. She fired one of your other women because you were enjoying her too much, right?"

Vlad's face registered surprise at my knowledge of that event, but he quickly recovered, barely missing a beat. "She was a dear girl. It was a pity to have to let her go."

"I bet. So, if I were to tell you to get rid of all your other women, what would you say?" I tested. "Would you do it? For me?"

"Red, it would not be safe for me to feed only from you," he replied, evading the question. "We have discussed this before."

I shrugged. "I'm good with having a spare blood donor. That girl Amanda seems willing. I'd be okay with her being on the menu. She's a sweet kid."

Vlad's mouth curved down into a frown. "Yes, she is. A darling. I have enjoyed her immensely."

I chuckled, shaking my head. "You talk about her like she's a nice Bordeaux."

Vlad's scowl morphed into condescending indifference. "Well, in a sense, she is."

"She's a *person,*" I hissed quietly. "And an *Ordinary* one at that. The Ordinaries won't turn a blind eye to your activities the way Tales do, Vlad. They will never say, 'Oh, he's a vampire. That's just his way.'"

"Being a vampire was a valid defense once upon a time," he pointed out, reminding me of a technicality that had been his saving grace in the past.

"For a Tale," I retorted. "You're treading on some dangerously thin ice by spending so much time with an Ordinary, Vlad. What if she decides to out you to her kind? We'd have a full-scale panic on our hands."

Vlad lazily waved away my concern. "Amanda would never do such a thing—she is far too enamored with me."

"You are one arrogant bastard," I said, shaking my head and wondering how the hell I'd ever found that so charming.

"You aren't untouchable, Vlad—no matter what you think. But if you're going to completely disregard the risks to yourself, you might stop and consider the risks to Amanda."

"What risks?" he asked, a harsh edge to his voice. "Do you believe I would harm her?"

I shrugged. "I don't know what to believe about you anymore," I told him, unable to hide my sorrow at that fact. "But I was referring to this Mistress of yours. My gut tells me she wouldn't mind if your darling little Amanda met an unhappy end to clear the way for herself."

"You say this as if you know her," Vlad said.

"Maybe I do. Tell me her name, and I'll let you know."

Vlad gave me a tight smile. "I shall handle my own affairs, I assure you."

"You're doing a bang-up job so far," I retorted. "The Mistress has already made you get rid of one of your favorites. What's to keep her from convincing you to send someone else packing?"

"She would not dare defy me where *you* are concerned, my own." He took my hand in his and brought it to his lips, pressing a kiss to the center of my palm. His fangs gently grazed my skin, sending a lightning bolt of desire up my arm and down my spine.

I met his gaze and felt that old familiar hold tightening around me, dragging me closer to a dangerous precipice. It would have been so easy to allow him to pull me over into the darkness below. It would have been so easy to fall into his arms once again and lose my mind to the bliss I knew awaited there.

"Now, forget about her," he cooed softly. "I would prefer to focus on you."

My eyes fluttered shut as his lips pressed against the hammering pulse in my wrist.

So easy . . .

Fortunately, I was never one to do anything the easy way.

My eyes snapped open, and I snatched my hand from his grasp. "Then focus on my back as I head for the door," I snapped, shoving my chair from the table. "I'm outta here."

"Red, you're being unreasonable," Vlad hissed through his teeth, his voice losing its hypnotic gentleness. "You shall belong to me. You shall be mine. You cannot deny me."

I met his gaze and slowly leaned down onto the table so that my face was only a couple of inches from him. "Vlad," I said in a low whisper, "this is me, telling you, to fuck off."

I turned to go, but his hand closed around my wrist like a vise, and he jerked me down so hard I lost my balance and fell forward, knocking into the table and sending his wineglass sailing to the floor.

"Do *not* resist me," he warned, his voice little more than a growl. "I am offering you my devotion, my protection. I do not do so lightly."

I glared at him angrily, seeing him more clearly than ever before. "So noted."

"You silly little fool—"

I wrenched my arm from his grasp and straightened, peering down my nose at him. "Thanks for a lovely evening, Vlad," I said haughtily. "It's been illuminating."

As I stormed out of the dining room, I passed the waitress carrying my dinner on her tray. "Are you leaving?" she asked. "Should I box this up so you can take it with you?"

I shook my head. "Nah, give it to him," I told her, jerking my head toward where Vlad still sat fuming. "He *loves* garlic."

Chapter 28

I got out of the cab and warily took in my surroundings, watching the shadows for any movement as I strode to the front door. The house was still and dark, cluing me in that Gran and Eddie had yet to return. Entering the empty house after the little rat episode didn't thrill me, but I sure as hell couldn't stand there out on the porch forever where any and everything could take a crack at me.

I took a breath and went inside, relieved when nothing fanged and furry jumped out at me from within the shadows. I rolled my shoulders, releasing the tension that had been waiting there ready to uncoil at the sign of an intruder, and felt a little ridiculous for having been so uptight in the first place. It was just a rat, for crying out loud. Sure it was a huge, glowing-eyed, vanishing-into-thin-air mutant rat, but a rat nonetheless. What harm could it really do?

Still, I flipped on a couple of lights as I made my way up the stairs to my room, glad to call it a night.

As I climbed the steps, I replayed the evening, frowning as I remembered the way Vlad's face had transformed with fury when I'd called things off. It made me wonder what I would've been walking into had Amanda not been my driver tonight. I liked to think I would have refused him anyway, that my instincts would have warned me off, but I couldn't be sure. I'd tried to resist him before—even just a few days ago—and had always ended up right back in his bed.

So what was different this time?

Sure, I was pissed about the whole thing with the Mistress, but that alone wouldn't have been enough to give me the strength to resist his hypnotic call. It was like some invisible barrier had sprung up, protecting me from the effects of Vlad's talents. Maybe it was just that for the first time since I'd met him, I could see through all the bullshit.

Exhaustion settled into my bones, making my feet heavy and my ears ring as I entered my bedroom. I frowned, suddenly feeling disoriented and off balance. I grasped the door frame to steady myself, then shoved off, forcing my feet to keep moving. A flash of heat washed over me only to be followed by a wave of arctic cold that made the hairs on my arms stand on end. I stripped off my jacket and absently tossed it on the ground as I studied the gooseflesh pimpling my skin.

"What the hell?" I murmured with a shudder. If I hadn't known any better, I would have thought—

Every muscle in my body stiffened, suddenly on alert. In one swift motion, I drew my gun and spun around, leveling the weapon at the silhouette leaning back against my headboard.

"Unless those bullets are silver, you might as well not even bother."

I gasped, instantly recognizing the soft, gentle voice. As the shadows parted, the intruder rose to his feet and walked cautiously toward me.

I swallowed hard. "Seth."

He offered me the gentle half smile I had always adored. "Hello, Red."

I stared at him as he slowly edged toward me, not daring to believe he was standing just a few inches from me. My hand trembled so violently, the Glock slipped from my grip and fell to the floor with an ominous thud. Seth bent and retrieved the weapon, then set it on top of my bureau for safekeeping.

His pale green eyes glinted with a feral light as he warily returned my gaze, feeling me out. His thick waves of golden brown hair were cut shorter than the last time I'd caught a glimpse of him, and a day's growth of stubble covered his powerful jaws, but other than that he hadn't changed at all in appearance since the day we'd met.

But in demeanor, he was almost beyond recognition. Gone was the peaceful spirit and quiet optimism that had hung about him like a palpable force in the air. The Seth Wolf who stood before me now was wary, toughened, and hardened by centuries of being hunted. If he hadn't already shattered my heart, it would have broken now at the sight of him.

"I hear you've been looking for me," he said, his words cutting through my shock.

I blinked, then shook my head, clearing away the haze of long-buried emotions trying to overtake me. "I have a few questions for you," I replied, my voice little more than a whisper.

Seth nodded grimly. "I thought you might." He lifted his hands, wrists pressed together. "Go ahead."

I jerked back a little. "What are you doing?"

"Isn't this where you arrest me?"

I sighed and pushed down on his arm with my fingertips. "Don't be ridiculous. I know you didn't murder anyone."

Seth's brows arched. "Do you?" he asked with a bitter laugh. "Well, then could you convince me? Because I'm not so sure."

We sat side by side on my bed, leaning against the headboard as I took in what Seth had just told me.

"How long do the blackouts last?" I asked.

He shrugged. "It varies. Some nights they're just a couple of hours. Other times it's the whole night and into the day."

"And when you come out of them?"

Seth's breath was shaky as he exhaled slowly. "My entire body aches like I've taken a beating and I'm covered in blood. And I'm always completely naked."

"Naked?" I repeated, shaking my head. "With your type of curse you don't have to strip down to transform. Why would you be naked?"

Seth gave me a hopeless shrug. "I have no idea. Side effect of the blackouts, maybe? None of it makes any sense to me."

"That doesn't mean you murdered anyone," I insisted, my hand instinctively covering his. "It means you need some help to sort things out."

Seth clasped my fingers and turned his head toward me. "I've missed you," he said softly, his voice thick. "Every single day my heart ached for you."

I tried to swallow the tightness in my throat, but my voice was still strained when I asked, "Then why didn't you come back for me? Or come to me after we came over?"

Seth looked away again, staring intently into the shadows that filled the corners of my room. "I didn't want you to suffer anymore because of me. I was trying to protect you."

"God!" I cried. "What *is* it with you men? I'm so sick of all of you *protecting* me and making me miserable in the process! Save the gallantry for a princess. I don't need it."

Seth's mouth curved up in one corner, betraying his amusement at my reaction. "So I've heard," he admitted. "You know, you're quite a legend among the Tales these days. Everyone knows you, fears you—and hates me for what I did to you."

"Everyone but me."

When sorrow twisted his features, I reached out and cupped his cheek. "Someone recently reminded me that we write our own stories, Seth. I've been blaming you all these years for what happened to us, for getting dumped into the Here and Now, for what my life has become. But, the truth is,

I *chose* to fall in love with you. And I've *chosen* my life as
an Enforcer. I'd make the same choices again, if given the
chance."

Seth covered my hand with his. "Are you happy, then?"

I nodded, smiling a little as I remembered asking the same
question of someone else just a few days earlier. "Almost."

He laughed bitterly. "Then you're further along than I am."

"What's holding you back?" I asked.

Seth leaned forward and pressed his forehead to mine. "I
can't seem to stop thinking about you."

I closed my eyes, wishing he had told me such a thing
years ago—or even a couple of weeks ago. It would have
made all the difference. Now . . . Well, hearing his confession
made me feel peaceful, complete somehow. But more than
anything, I felt . . . ready. For what, I wasn't sure, but at that
moment I knew some critical barrier to moving on had just
been breached.

"I wanted to see you after I came over," he continued. "I
wanted to apologize, see if you'd forgiven me and, I don't
know, maybe even still loved me a bit. I knew you were
watching over me—I could feel it every time you were near."

I pulled back enough to frown at him. "Why didn't you say
anything?"

Seth looked down, averting his gaze. "Once a coward,
always a coward, I guess."

I shook my head. "Seth, you're—"

My words were suddenly cut off by his lips upon mine.
They were as soft and gentle as I remembered, even as he
took my face in his hands and deepened the kiss. But as nice
as it was, kissing Seth no longer filled me with the heat and
desire it once had. Something had changed.

Apparently, he felt it, too.

After a moment, he drew back and let out a sigh heavily
laden with sadness. "I waited too long, didn't I?"

I nodded slowly. "I'm so sorry," I told him, genuinely pained to say so. "But I actually think there's someone else." He sighed again, then pressed another kiss to my forehead. "I'm the one who's sorry, Red. For everything. If only—"

Seth's head snapped up abruptly, nose raised. I heard him sniff a couple of times, catching a scent in the air.

"What is it?" I whispered, knowing such tension in his muscles all too well.

Seth held his finger to his lips, then slid lithely from the bed. As he moved, a faint shimmer encased him as the spell that bound him to his curse transformed him into the pale white wolf I remembered. Although he was easily three times bigger than any normal wolf, he moved silently as he slunk toward my closet.

I crawled to the end of the bed on my hands and knees, anxious to see what he was tracking. Just as I made it to the edge, the mattress protested under my weight, creaking loudly. I grimaced and cursed under my breath.

The sound might as well have been a gunshot for the effect it had. Seth lunged forward with a ferocious snarl just as something dark and shadowy burst from my closet. He snatched the creature up in his powerful jaws and swung his head in a quick motion, snapping the intruder's neck, then trotted over to me and dropped the furry mass at my feet. He looked up at me expectantly, awaiting my response.

I ran my hand lovingly through his fur, then crouched down to get a closer look. "Another rat?" I gasped, reeling from the realization that the creature had been lurking in the darkness all along.

Seth transformed at my words and stayed in a crouch next to me. "Another one?"

I nodded, watching the nasty little beast at my feet, half expecting it to dematerialize. "Or maybe the same one, I don't know. I had one come at me earlier tonight. It vanished into thin air before I could kill it."

"A familiar," Seth announced, rising to his feet.

I frowned at him. "What? Do you mean like a witch's familiar?"

"Exactly. Someone sent it here," he told me. "I can feel the magic on it. It's similar to how my curse feels. It's probably a real rat but has been enchanted."

I shook my head, confused. "Why?"

He shrugged. "No clue. Maybe as a spy."

I closed my eyes and let my head fall forward on my shoulders as I mentally rotated pieces of the puzzle, trying to get them all to fit together in a picture that made sense. "Shit."

"What?"

I opened my eyes and stood up so I could level my gaze at him. "Please tell me you don't know Dave Hamelin."

Seth shrugged. "Not really. I just met him in passing when he did some work for Caliban at the restaurant. I was there for a meeting with Caliban and a couple of the investors but we had to call off the meeting when Caliban went ballistic because he saw a rat slinking around—apparently, he'd been having some trouble with them. Anyway, he called Hamelin in to take care of it. Kind of creepy."

"Dave or the rats?" I drawled.

Seth gave me a cockeyed smile. "Take your pick. He had a cute little apprentice with him, though. She seemed nice enough."

"Apprentice?" I'd never heard anyone mention that Dave had an apprentice. Not even Alice had said anything about it when we talked to her.

"Yeah," Seth said, poking the dead rat with the toe of his running shoe, "she and I talked for a couple of minutes while Dave went over the bill with Sebille. I guess she was just learning the ropes. Had been a waitress or something but needed better money so she could concentrate on her acting career."

"What was her name?" I asked, not liking where the trail was headed.

Seth's brow furrowed as he tried to recall the woman's name. "Sorry. I can't remember. Julie something."

I ran my hand down my face as another piece of the puzzle fell into place. "Was it Spangle, by any chance?"

"Yeah," Seth replied quickly. "How'd you know?"

I exhaled slowly. "Because it just fucking figures."

"I'm not following."

"Julie was the first murder victim," I told him.

Seth's eyes widened. "What?"

"And Dave Hamelin committed suicide," I continued. "We thought it was unconnected to the murders, but I'm beginning to think otherwise."

"I had nothing to do with their deaths," Seth protested. "I barely knew either one of them!"

"How about a guy named Dale Minnows?" I asked, my heart sinking a bit.

"The reclusive billionaire?" Seth said. "He's one of the investors in Caliban's business ventures, but there's something going wrong with the deal, I think. I overheard Caliban ranting to Sebille about Minnows wanting a larger share of profits than what they'd originally agreed to."

"Oh, God, Seth," I breathed. "Tell me you've never met Minnows."

Seth swallowed hard. "He came into the restaurant a couple of weeks ago and asked to see me. Nice guy. He wanted to taste my food for himself to make sure I was the right person to run the steak house while Caliban was filming in LA."

"He was the second victim."

Seth was visibly shaken by the news. "Oh, God."

"What about Alfred Simon?"

Seth shook his head, his expression a little panicked. "Everybody knows him. He makes deliveries to all the restaurants in town."

"He's dead, too," I announced, my voice cracking.

The blood drained from Seth's face. "I hadn't heard."

"Have you been living under a rock?" I yelled, my fears for him getting the better of me.

Seth gave me a frustrated, angry glare. "Excuse the hell out of me for keeping my nose out of everyone's business!" he spat back. "I've been brought in so many times by the FMA, I've lost count. You guys have a hell of a knack for profiling, in case you haven't noticed. Old Mother Hubbard's dog is missing? Oh, the werewolf must've eaten it. Some princess reports a Peeping Tom? Well, hell, let's drag in the werewolf—had to be him! It's not just the little shepherd boy who likes to cry wolf, Red."

"Seth, this isn't just about you being harassed!" I yelled even louder. "Up until now we haven't been able to link all the victims together in any way. We couldn't connect all of them to any one person. It seemed random. We could only choose our suspects on their criminal histories. But now, I can connect almost all of them to you!"

"That doesn't mean anything," Seth said quickly, grabbing my arm. "Caliban knows them all too, right?"

"He has airtight alibis," I told him.

Seth laughed, sounding a little wild. "Oh, I'm sure he does!"

"What is that supposed to mean?"

Seth leaned toward me, his face close to mine. "Sebille has created a wall of protection around him," he said bitterly. "He's destroyed his cooking show set dozens of times. He's threatened all the investors at some point. He's been charged with assault and battery too many times to count. And yet, he's still strutting around town, free to piss on whoever he pleases."

My eyes narrowed a little. "That sounds a little harsh."

Seth pinched the bridge of his nose and squeezed his eyes shut, calming himself. After a moment, he said, "Listen, I know you cared about Caliban once—"

I jerked a little. "You do?"

He gave me an exasperated look. "It's not like your affair with him was a secret, Red." I felt my cheeks growing a little warm as he went on. "Anyway, all I'm saying is that maybe you should take another look at Caliban's story. Double check what Sebille's telling you. She'd do anything to protect her precious Caliban."

"Like lying to the FMA to keep him out of trouble?"

"In a heartbeat."

"Okay," I relented. "I'll look into things a little more, but we still have the problem of your association with the victims. Caliban's not a werewolf. He couldn't possibly have harmed these people himself. And we know the attacks weren't perpetrated by a human."

Seth's brows came together. "Caliban's a completely different person when his temper takes over. Are you sure it couldn't be him?"

"Positive. The forensics team confirmed it and was hoping to make an ID off some DNA evidence gathered from the crime scenes."

Seth's eyes brightened. "So then compare my DNA to the other samples. Then we'll know for sure about me," he urged. "I'll lick a stick, piss in a cup, whatever you need. But I gotta know, Red."

"The evidence was destroyed," I said with a grimace. "The creature attacked the coroner in broad daylight and destroyed the lab. The samples were contaminated. They're unusable."

Seth paced a panicked circle, pulling his hands roughly through his hair. "This can't be happening," he mumbled. "Not after all this time. Not after all I've built here."

I stepped forward and took hold of his arm, pulling him to a stop. "Seth, unless you can give me something to work with here, you're looking like the most likely suspect."

"You said I was connected to *almost* all the victims," he pointed out. "Who are the others?"

"The most recent two are Tim Halloran's doormen," I told

him. "His girlfriend, Sophia, was also attacked, but she should pull through. I think the Sandman was the real target. And I know you're acquainted with Tim—he already told me it was his idea for you to run the steak house."

"Exactly!" Seth cried. "He's one of my most loyal customers. Why would I want to kill the guy who was giving me a shot at something bigger?"

Luckily, he had a point. Still . . .

"Stranger things have happened."

"Who's the last victim?"

"Her name is Sarah Dickerson. She was a maid." I pegged him with a don't-bullshit-me glare. "Do you know her, too?"

Seth's breath burst from him, his relief almost palpable. "No. I can honestly say I don't know her."

I plopped down on the edge of my bed and put my head in my hands. He said he didn't know Sarah, and I believed him. After all, he'd readily copped to knowing the others. But that didn't necessarily mean anything. I still didn't know a motive, so I couldn't just disregard the other connections. For all I knew, there could be some connection I just wasn't seeing yet.

"And what about my Gran?" I asked, lifting my eyes to his. Seth stared at me, unblinking. "What do you mean?"

"She was attacked in her studio."

He sat down next to me on the bed and clasped his hands together between his knees. "I would never do anything to hurt the woman who took you in, Red. You have to know that."

I nodded. "I know that, but others don't. If you were trying to scare me off your trail, it would make sense to hurt someone I love as a warning of what you could do. Or maybe Gran was a threat to Caliban's business deals because her ratings are better, so you tried to take her out to eliminate the Tale competition. Your rising star is hitched to Caliban's, Seth. His profit is your gain."

Seth closed his eyes, realization dawning on his features. "And his loss is my loss."

"Precisely."

"Then I'll just get someone to vouch for me. A character witness."

"Like who?" I threw back at him. "It's not like you've gone out of your way to make friends in the Here and Now, Seth."

"I have friends."

I pegged him with an expectant look.

"There's Caliban."

"He'd sell you out in a hot second to save his own ass," I told him.

"Tim Halloran is a fan."

"Of your food, not of you," I said. "Plus, he's a known criminal—not exactly the best judge of character."

"There's Molly."

"She's an Ordinary, Seth."

"But she knows me, knows my affliction," he insisted. "How could I live with a woman and not harm her if I was a murderer?"

I shrugged. "Happens all the time. You really *have* been living under a rock, haven't you?"

"Damn it." Seth rubbed the back of his neck in a quick, agitated motion. "I'm totally fucked on this one, aren't I? What am I going to do?"

If I was any kind of Enforcer, I would have arrested Seth and thrown him into the clink where he could have sat awaiting trial while we let the lawyers sort it all out. After all, that was my job. That's what I'd been told to do.

But I couldn't. Not this time.

I pressed the heels of my palms against my eyes, knowing Mary Smith wouldn't need to show a connection to Sarah Dickerson to get a conviction for Seth. I'd seen her put guys away with much less. She'd have no trouble convincing the Tribunal, who were already gunning for Seth, that being connected to the other five was enough. After all, they'd pegged Seth as a mindless, bloodthirsty killer centuries ago. They just hadn't been able to catch him in the act yet in the Here and Now. Mary wouldn't even need to suggest a possible motive when everyone thought Seth killed just for shits and giggles anyway.

I ran my hands through my hair in frustration.

We might be living in the twenty-first century, but the villagers were still lining up with torches and pitchforks, waiting for the opportunity to assign blame for the evils of the world, clinging to fear and prejudice instead of truth and logic and calling it justice. And with that kind of mob mentality working against him, Seth would either end up on the executioner's block or rotting in the Asylum for the rest of his days. He didn't have a chance. Unless I gave it to him.

"You need to leave," I said, abruptly getting to my feet and pulling him up with me. "Get out of town, hide out somewhere for a while. I don't want to know where you're going— if I don't know, I can't find you—at least, not right away."

Seth frowned at me. "What are you talking about? You said you believed I was innocent—"

"I still do," I interrupted. "But do you really want to put my gut feeling up against circumstantial evidence that everyone wants to believe no matter how flimsy it is? I can tell you which one is going to hold up in a trial with Mary Smith prosecuting."

Seth stared at me for a long moment before he said, "I can't hide out forever."

"It won't be forever," I told him firmly. "I'm close to figuring this out. And I think someone else has noticed. Why else would somebody send rats to spy on me? But I need more time. If they bring you in on this, I'll be off the case and there won't be anything else I can do."

Seth looked at me, his expression serious, and a little afraid. "What if your instincts are wrong?"

"They aren't."

"But what if they are?" he pressed. "What if I *am* dangerous?"

I pressed my lips together in a grim line. "Then the next time you see me, there'll be silver in my gun."

Seth gave me a solemn nod. "I'll leave tonight."

A sudden thought occurred to me, and I said, "Take Molly with you."

Seth shook his head in confusion. "Why?"

I sighed, wishing it still didn't hurt so much to let him go. "She loves you, Seth. You already walked away from love once. Don't do it again."

A slow smile curved his lips. "You are one of a kind, Tess Little," he said. "I hope you find the kind of happiness you deserve."

I returned his smile, hating that our first hello in so many years was to be followed so soon by good-bye. "You, too."

Chapter 29

"What do you think?"

Trish rubbed her eyes and blinked a few times. "It's a rat," she said matter-of-factly. "A big one."

I huffed impatiently. "Come on, Trish. I wouldn't have woken you up in the middle of the night to look at just some ordinary rat."

She pushed her curls back from her face, then slid her glasses a little down her nose to get a clearer look at the carcass lying on the conference room table. "I can't really do any sort of real autopsy while I'm cooped up in here," she grumbled. "However, I don't see any outward signs of magic."

"There has to be," I pressed. "Seeing a rat vanish into thin air earlier tonight, then having one just like it jump out of my closet doesn't scream coincidence to me, Trish. There's got to be someone behind it. I think it's a familiar."

Trish straightened, her eyes wide. "A familiar? What makes you think that?"

I shifted uncomfortably on my feet, not about to admit that my source was our prime suspect in the serial murders—the same suspect I'd just let go free, by the way. "Call it a hunch." When she gave me a doubting look, I pleaded, "Just go with me on this for a minute."

Trish shrugged. "Okay. Fine. For argument's sake, we'll say it was a familiar. But I can't *prove* that, Red, unless I'm able to conduct some tests and determine if there's any magical residue clinging to it."

"What do you need for that?" I asked anxiously.

She crossed her arms over her chest and gave me a sour look. "A new forensics lab."

"There's *nothing* you can do without your equipment?" I pressed. "I need this, Trish."

Trish's expression was sympathetic. "It would be little more than guesswork. I'm really sorry."

"Damn it!" I kicked one of the conference room chairs, sending it rolling across the room and into the wall. The impact sent an irritatingly inspirational poster featuring a sweat-soaked, grimacing athlete crashing to the ground. I cursed roundly at the mess of shattered glass. With a sigh of frustration at my lapse of self-control, I bent next to the glittering pile and gathered up the larger shards in my hand before pitching them into a nearby wastebasket.

At least this time the glass hadn't shattered because my skull was cracking against it, I thought wryly. I winced, remembering the pain that had blasted through my skull as the creature had slammed into Nate's car that night on the winding road leading away from Tim Halloran's estate—

I glanced up at Trish. "What if I can get you a makeshift lab? What's the absolute minimum you'd need?"

Her eyes narrowed. "Where would you possibly get equipment for a lab?"

I shoved my hands in my jacket pockets and shrugged evasively. "I know a guy."

Trish studied me for a long moment, her green eyes suspicious. But she finally sighed and raised her arms in surrender. "All right. You make the arrangements, and I'll see what I can find."

"Text me a list of equipment," I called over my shoulder as I headed for the door. "I'll have it here by morning."

"Red?"

I paused in the doorway and turned back toward her, feeling a little uncomfortable under the intensity of her scrutinizing gaze. "Yeah?"

"Are you okay?" she asked gently. "You seem a little . . . out of it."

I looked pointedly at the rat. "I didn't bring you the were-wolf hair you wanted, but you might find some interesting DNA on that thing."

As I left the room, I heard Trish make a wordless noise, an unasked question lingering in the sound, but I didn't stop walking. I wasn't anxious to explain my late-night chat with Seth to anyone—and certainly not the brilliant forensics Investigator whose loyalty was to the FMA and not to the pain-in-the-ass Enforcer who'd let her emotions get in the way of doing her job.

In spite of whatever misgivings she might have had, Trish texted me a list of equipment before I even made it out of the building. I scanned through it quickly, then made a call. The phone rang only a couple of times before a gruffly basso voice answered. It wasn't the one I was expecting, but it would do.

"Hi there, Aloysius," I said cheerfully. "Is your boss around?"

There was a moment of hesitation. "No."

"Oh, come on . . . I'm not calling to harass him," I assured him. "In fact, I might have some news he'd find interesting."

"News? About what?"

I let out a slow breath to keep my bitch switch from tripping. "About who might have hurt Sophia. Do you think maybe the Sandman could spare a sec to chat?"

There was another pause, longer this time. "All right. I'll wake him up."

I waited for several minutes, pacing up and down the

quiet halls of headquarters until I heard the muffled sound of movement on the other end of the line. A few seconds later, Halloran's angry voice hissed, "This had better be damned important."

I barked a little laugh. "Well, hi to you, too, sweetums."

"Do not toy with me, Enforcer. Aloysius said you had something to tell me."

"I had a rat in my house tonight," I told him, cutting the bullshit.

"Tragic. Call an exterminator."

"The only good one's six feet under," I retorted. "But here's the thing, Sandman—I think he might have somehow been involved in the rampant rat infestation to begin with."

"I beg your pardon?"

I leaned my back against the wall, crossing my legs at the ankle while I thought out loud. "I think the rats were used as familiars, spies to gather information. Then Dave would come in and clean up the evidence before anyone caught the rats and figured it out."

"An interesting theory, Enforcer," Halloran drawled, "but do you have any proof?"

"I will if you can help me out."

I could hear the smug grin in his voice as he said, "Is that so?"

"I need a lab for our forensics Investigator," I told him. "The beast that attacked Sophia destroyed the FMA's lab and we won't have a new one set up for a couple of days."

"I fail to see why you need *my* assistance," he replied.

"If my furry little pal was enchanted, Trish needs to run tests before the magic residue fades," I informed him. "If we wait until the FMA has the new lab set up, the evidence we need could be gone."

"And how exactly does the FMA's ineptitude concern me?" Halloran demanded, his tone annoyingly condescending.

I could've strangled the bastard through the phone. "Do you want me to catch the creature that did this to Sophia or not?" There was a pause. "If I provide the equipment you need, I will expect some favor in return."

"I figured as much. What do you want?"

"Nothing immediately comes to mind," he taunted. "But I am certain I will have need of your assistance someday."

I ground my back teeth together, wanting to tell him to shove his favor up his ass, but there was no one else who had access to the kind of equipment Trish needed on such short notice. "Just make sure to have everything here by morning."

"Send me the list of items you need," he said, all politeness now that he had something to hold over me.

"Fine."

"And, Enforcer?"

"Yeah?"

"I do so look forward to working with you again soon."

Without replying, I hung up, desperately needing a shower after making such a filthy deal, but with no time to spare for such a luxury, I forwarded Trish's list to Halloran and received an immediate response, assuring me I would have the materials I'd requested.

With nothing more to do but wait until morning, I leaned my head back against the wall and closed my eyes, hoping to rest for just a moment before heading back home.

"Enforcer!"

No such luck.

I sighed and opened my eyes to see Alex McCain, one of the newer Investigators, running toward me. As far as Fucking New Guys went, he wasn't bad, but seeing him now made me want to knock his teeth down his throat. "Where's the fire, McCain?"

"The Chief wants you in his office A-sap," he gasped breathlessly, sliding to a halt. "There's been an incident."

I frowned slightly. "What kind of incident?"

McCain shook his head. "Something about an Ordinary."

This brought me fully alert. "What Ordinary?"

"No clue," he replied. "The Chief heard you were in the building and said for me to bring you to see him. He's also called in Detective Grimm."

I shoved away from the wall and walk-jogged down the hall as quickly as my stiletto boots would allow.

"Enforcer Little!" I heard McCain calling to me. "Wait! I needed to tell you—"

"Thanks, McCain," I called over my shoulder. "I got it from here."

I picked up the pace as I neared Al's office, a knot of apprehension tightening around my gut. Turning the corner at a dead run, I collided with a solid wall of muscle that sent me staggering backward.

"Don't you ever sleep?" Nate teased, his arm darting out to steady me. He was grinning but the strain in his eyes betrayed the depth of his concern.

"Not lately," I mumbled, squeezing his arm briefly before hurrying on my way again.

"Nice outfit," Nate said, falling in beside me. "You're looking very Elektra tonight."

I snorted. "Don't tell her that. She's not a member of my fan club."

"You have a fan club?" He grinned when I cast him an annoyed glance.

"It's not very big," I said, opening the Chief's door. "Trust me."

I expected the Chief to be scowling and surly when we walked in as was his custom when calling me to the carpet for some infraction. I never expected him to be sitting at his desk, his face slack, his arms hanging loosely upon the arms of his chair.

"Al?" I said cautiously, trading a worried glance with Nate.

Al's eyes lifted from the documents on his desk, flashing

with recognition when he saw us standing in front of him. "Shut the door."

Nate quickly complied, then came to stand beside me. "What's going on?"

"There's been another attack," Al told us, his voice worn thin. "As I feared, the creature has taken the life of an Ordinary, bringing our problem to the attention of the Ordinary authorities."

"I've almost cracked the case," I said quickly, taking a step forward. "In another couple of days—"

"That won't be necessary," Al interrupted. "We've caught the Tale responsible for the murders. He was still at the scene when our people arrived to try to control the damage."

"That's great," Nate said slowly. "So, why the midnight meeting?"

"I didn't want either of you to hear about it through the grapevine," Al replied. He leveled his gaze at me. "Especially you."

Oh, shit.

"What are you talking about?" I croaked, my breath stuck in my lungs.

"We've taken Seth Wolf into custody," Al announced bluntly.

I shook my head quickly. "No, that's not possible. It can't be him."

"I'm really sorry—"

"Who's the victim?" I cut in, knowing the answer in my gut even if my brain wasn't ready to acknowledge it.

"An Ordinary woman named Molly O'Grady."

"Oh, God," I moaned, my knees buckling under me. I grabbed onto Nate's sleeve and slowly sank down into the chair. "I know her."

"So did Wolf," Al announced. "Apparently, she was a waitress at the same restaurant where Wolf worked. She was staying in his apartment."

"This is a mistake," I mumbled. "Seth wouldn't have hurt her. She loved him."

Nate gave me a curious glance as he took a seat in the chair next to mine and squeezed my forearm, but didn't ask any questions of me. "Are you sure it was Wolf?" he said to Al instead.

Al nodded. "He was holding her body in his arms when the Ordinary authorities arrived. His clothes were covered in her blood. Mary Smith will file the notice of his guilt with the Tribunal first thing in the morning."

Al's words cut through my stupor, bringing my head up. "It wasn't him."

"Red," Al said patiently, "I understand that this is difficult for you. . . ."

I shook my head. "No, that's not what I mean. He cared about her. If he came home and found her, of course he would have tried to help her. Her blood on his clothes looks bad, but it isn't proof." Plus, it didn't fit the MO of Seth's blackouts. This one was different. Someone had very much wanted it to look like Seth was the murderer, frame him up nice and tight so that we'd stop looking anywhere else. A perfect bait and switch.

"She has a point," Nate chimed in. "If Wolf had killed her, why would he have stuck around to get caught?"

"We still know of no motive for these murders," Al reminded us. "Perhaps he didn't realize what he'd done until it was too late. I'm sure it'll all come out when we get his confession recorded."

"Has anyone talked to him?" Nate asked.

Al shook his head. "No. He says he won't speak to anyone but Red."

I felt Nate's questioning gaze upon me once again, but I kept my composure. "Then let's go."

"Red," Al called sternly to my back as I strode to the door, "he's guilty. You need to accept that."

I paused, clenching my jaw, weighing my options. Then I said, "What was the time of death?"

I heard Al sigh. "I don't see—"

I clenched my fists. "What. Time."

"We won't know for certain until Trish can process the evidence we confiscated from the Ordinary authorities," Al said, "but they were placing the time of death around ten o'clock."

I turned around. "Then it couldn't have been Seth."

Now it was Nate's turn to console me. "Red, you have to listen to reason. . . ."

"Seth couldn't have killed Molly at ten o'clock," I said, closing my eyes. "He was with me.

Chapter 30

When Al finally stopped screaming at me, I opened my mouth to defend myself, but he jabbed an angry finger in my face. "Not a word," he growled, the vein in his forehead bulging ominously. "Not a single fucking word."

I was hardly a fan of being berated like a child even on a good day, so seeing as how the last few days had pretty much buried the needle on the suckometer, my ability to quietly take my lumps was rapidly evaporating. "Al—"

"Shut your pie hole, Enforcer!" Al roared. He shoved his furious face in mine. "I've put up with a lot of your shit over the years, Red. But you crossed the line on this one. You're goddamn lucky I don't arrest you for being an accomplice."

"Accomplice?" Nate repeated from the shadows where he'd been banished after trying to calm Al down. "If the guy just showed up at her house like she said, it's not like she willfully went against protocol."

"No," Al retorted, "that happened when she let him go!"

I narrowed my eyes, my own anger flaring now. "I *told* you—if I'd had any doubts about Seth's innocence, I wouldn't have let him walk out of my house. There's more going on here than you think, Al. Someone is trying to throw us off the trail by making it look like Seth's guilty. Hell, he even half believes it himself!"

Al's brows lifted. "Is that so?"

I cursed inwardly at the slip, but met Al's furious glare without flinching. "I can prove it."

Al sat down on the corner of his desk and crossed his arms. "Oh, well, in that case, show me the evidence you've been holding back."

I shifted a little, the temperature of the hot seat growing uncomfortable. "I don't have any evidence yet."

Al nodded. "Uh-huh."

Now it was my turn to go on the offensive. I launched up from my chair and crossed the ground between us in one stride. "When have I ever let you down?" I demanded. "Name one time that I've failed to deliver what I promised."

Al blinked his eyes once slowly, regarding me in stony silence.

"Give me two days—three, tops," I pleaded.

Al held my gaze a moment longer, then turned his head toward Nate. "Grimm?"

Nate rose slowly to his feet and came to stand beside me. "It'd take that long to get the execution order anyway," he pointed out. "You might as well give her the chance to clear him."

"And you'll continue on as her partner until this is settled?" Al asked.

I looked up at Nate, familiar enough with his expressions by now to know he was righteously pissed off. I wouldn't have blamed him if he'd hung me out to dry, but instead he nodded. "Yeah. I'm in."

"Then get out of my office," Al ordered. "You have three days, Red. Mary's filing the paperwork tomorrow. If you don't have results by the date of Wolf's audience with the Tribunal, there'll be nothing I can do to stop his execution."

* * *

Nate said nothing at all to me as we made our way to the holding cells, but I could feel his anger like a palpable force in the air between us.

"Thank you," I said.

"For what?"

I grabbed his hand and pulled him to a stop. "For backing my play with Al. I appreciate it."

He shrugged, keeping his gaze trained on the wall above my head. "You're my partner, right?" He looked down at me and said pointedly, "We're supposed to be in this together."

"I'm sorry," I said sincerely. "I guess I should have called you the minute Seth showed up, but . . ."

Nate stared at me expectantly, waiting for me to continue.

I sighed wearily and ran my hands through my hair. "I needed to talk to him, Nate. And not just about the murders. There were some things I needed to say, things I needed for him to hear."

Nate's expression became less haughty. "And?"

I dropped my gaze, the intensity of his making me suddenly nervous. Noticing his tie was askew, I reached out and adjusted it, smoothing my fingertips down the silk. "And I think I've finally made peace with things."

Nate's hand covered mine, his fingers curling around my own. "I'm glad."

I looked up at him cautiously through my lashes. "Me, too."

Nate's arm slid around my shoulders and pulled me close as he led me forward. "Go talk to Seth," he said. "I'll be here when you're finished."

I was grateful for Nate's arm around me when we arrived at Seth's cell. Otherwise I don't know that I would have been able to bear the heartbreaking sight before me. Seth sat on the cot, his wrists securely shackled, the cuffs attached to a chain that led down to the shackles around his ankles. His face was blank, his eyes vacant from shock. His clothes were splattered with crimson stains that had darkened as they dried into the fabric. Smudges of blood marked his hands, neck, and face where I supposed he had cradled Molly's lifeless body in his arms. They hadn't even bothered to clean him up yet before dumping him in the cold, dank enclosure deep beneath headquarters.

"Seth," I said softly, leaving the warmth of Nate's arm to move toward the steel bars. "Seth? Can you hear me?"

When he didn't answer, I looked over my shoulder at Nate. "I need to get in there. Could you get a guard to open this up?"

A few minutes later, a yawning guard appeared with a heavy set of keys in his hands. "You've got five minutes," he said sleepily, opening the door for me.

The ominous clank behind me as I approached Seth assured me I was locked inside the cell with him.

"Seth, honey," I tried again. When he still didn't respond, I sat down on the cot next to him and gently touched his arm. "It's me. It's Red. Do you know what happened?"

At this he finally turned his head toward me. "Molly's dead."

I nodded. "I'm so sorry."

"Did I kill her?"

The pain in his eyes devastated me. "No," I assured him, shaking my head vehemently. "I know it wasn't you. I'm going to prove it."

Seth looked away. "Don't bother."

"Seth—"

"I don't care anymore, Red," he interrupted. "I only bring suffering to the people I care about. It's better this way."

"But you're innocent!" I insisted.

He lifted a shoulder and let it drop again. "Maybe. Maybe not. Either way, Molly's dead because of me."

"No," I said sternly, taking his face in my hands and forcing him to look at me. "She's dead because some sick bastard wanted to make you look guilty. I'm sure of it. I think you were right about the familiar. I think whoever sent it heard our conversation and knew I was determined to prove your innocence. I think that person had to do something drastic so you'd take the fall and divert attention away from the truth."

Seth's eyes began to glisten as he looked at me. "I was going to take her with me," he said, his voice strained. "I was going to go to the Northwest, hide out for a while in the mountains, give things a go with her and see what happened."

Unable to speak past the lump in my throat, I pulled him close and held him tightly, rocking just a little while his shoulders shook with silent sobs. I pressed my trembling lips against his hair, wishing there was more I could do to alleviate his pain. All too soon, I heard a polite cough behind me and saw the guard and Nate standing outside the door.

"I'm sorry, Enforcer," the guard said. "Time's up."

I lowered my head and pressed another kiss to Seth's hair. "I'll see you soon," I murmured. "Everything will be okay. I promise."

I tore myself away and strode quickly from the cell before I changed my mind about going quietly. I was in enough trouble as it was. If I was going to help Seth and bring the real killer to justice, I needed to get moving.

"Let's go," I said when I heard Nate's footsteps keeping time with mine.

"You going to be okay?" he asked.

"Yep," I replied too quickly.

"Red—"

"Just drive me home," I said, cutting him off. "These frigging boots are killing me."

Thankfully, Nate didn't bother trying to talk to me on the drive to Gran's. And when he pulled into the driveway, he turned the car off without a word. He even walked me up to the front door in complete silence.

It was only when I reached for the door that he finally said, "Hey."

When I turned around, he traced some kind of design on his shoulder with his finger.

I frowned, not understanding. "What was that?"

"Your name," he said with a sad smile. "Whenever you need it, this shoulder's yours to cry on."

I nodded, so touched I wasn't even sure what to say. So I just said, "Thanks. I'll keep that in mind."

He gave me a wink, then tossed my keys in a low arc. "See you tomorrow."

He vanished before the keys even landed in my hand. Sighing, I went inside, wanting nothing more than to get out of my clothes and fall into bed.

"Red, is that you, my darling?"

I heard Gran's jaunty footsteps hurrying toward the foyer, but I kept moving toward the stairs.

"Dearest, I met with young Alice," Gran rattled cheerfully. "She's a dear girl. I've set her up with a job at the library. She seemed eager—" I heard Gran gasp a little when she saw me. "What's happened?"

I paused on the steps. "I'm fine. I just need to get some sleep," I told her. Then I frowned, noticing that Eddie wasn't with her. "Where's Eddie?"

She came toward me, joining me on the stairs. "He's sleeping," she said, her forehead creasing with concern. "Why do you ask?"

"I just want to make sure you're safe," I told her. "There was a rat in here earlier tonight."

Gran's eyes widened. "Oh my! I'll set out some traps first thing tomorrow."

"Good," I said, even though I knew it wouldn't matter a damn if another familiar came calling. "If you see any, though, just leave the house and let me know. I'll handle it."

"Of course, dearest," she said. "But I get the distinct

impression the rat isn't the only thing troubling you. Will you share willingly or shall I pry it out of you?"

Knowing I was too worn and weary to evade her inquiries if she decided to really start laying it on, I dropped down onto the steps and put my head in my hands. "I screwed up, Gran," I told her. "I screwed up big time."

She sat down beside me and ran a tender hand down my hair. "Oh, my dear," she said softly. "We all make mistakes. You are too hard on yourself."

I shook my head. "Not this time. I'll be lucky if I can keep my job after this one."

Gran clucked her tongue. "Al Addin lets you do whatever you want and then gets angry if you make a mess of things. His management style is both a blessing and a curse to you, I'm afraid. However, if anyone can set things to rights, it's you, my girl. You will prevail in the end."

I lifted my head. "How is it you have so much faith in me?"

She offered me a loving smile. "I could tell you were a fighter when I found you clinging to life that day in the woods," she said. "I don't think you could give up if you tried."

I laughed a little, wondering if that was always a good thing. Sometimes it would have been nice to just say, "To hell with it." And maybe someday I would.

But not today.

Chapter 31

I slept for only a few hours. Nightmarish images of Seth and Vlad and Caliban and Dave Hamelin and Sebille Fenwick and the various victims of the creature plaguing our kind stubbornly haunted my sleep and finally became so intrusive I cast my blankets aside and gave up trying.

After showering for twice as long as usual, I made my way downstairs and heard Gran and Eddie chatting happily as they bustled around the kitchen together. I stood in the kitchen doorway for a few minutes, just watching them. They seemed so comfortable, so at ease in each others' company already, I couldn't help smiling. There was a new radiance to Gran, I realized. Something even brighter and more enchanting than usual—which was saying a lot. As much as I hated to admit it, she was falling in love with the enigmatic bodyguard. And, if the tender expression in Eddie's eyes was any indication, it seemed mutual.

"Good morning," I said, finally announcing my presence.

They both offered me words of greeting as I took a seat at the bar.

"You're up early, dearest," Gran said, her tone chipper and unconcerned even though I could see the question in her eyes.

"Couldn't sleep," I told her. "I figured I might as well get up and get moving."

"I've got coffee, if you're interested," Eddie announced. It was odd to see him there, but he seemed to fit in somehow.

I bobbed my head once. "Load me up."

Eddie set a steaming cup in front of me a moment later. He glanced over his shoulder to see that Gran was occupied with breakfast, then leaned toward me over the bar. "Nicky called this morning," he said in a low voice. "He said to tell you he's got the information you were after."

I gave him a quick nod, then lifted the cup to my lips, taking a generous sip. It wasn't as good as the cup Nate had made for me a few days before, but it was just as warm and soothing as it traveled the path to my stomach. "Thanks, Eddie."

"You got it, doll."

Now it was my turn to glance over at Gran. Seeing her still busily engaged with folding crepes, I said, "And thanks for taking care of Gran."

This made his lips curve into a smile, crinkling the skin around his eyes in a very pleasing way. "Tilly's some dame," he said, shaking his head slowly, as if baffled by the depth of his admiration. "That gal's got me but good."

I took another sip of my coffee, my eyes never leaving his. "As long as she's happy, I'm happy. You feel me?"

He gave me a wink. "That makes two of us."

I was just taking another sip of my coffee when my phone started ringing. I checked my watch with a frown. Seven a.m. Aside from Gran—and, apparently, Eddie—only one other person I knew was crazy enough to get up that early voluntarily on a Saturday morning.

"Good morning, sunshine," I answered with a grin.

"Good morning, indeed."

My heart seized at the unexpected sound of Vlad's voice. "Why the hell are you calling me?" I hissed, hurriedly hopping down from the bar stool and taking my coffee into the other room.

"I wanted to repeat my offer," Vlad replied lazily. "I thought perhaps a good night's rest would bring you to your senses."

"Well, I didn't get a good night's rest," I spat. "And even if I had, I'd still tell you to piss off."

"Take care, little one," Vlad warned, his voice taking on a razor-sharp edge. "Consider your decision carefully."

I retreated into the living room, further out of Gran and Eddie's collective earshot. "I don't need to consider anything, you smug son of a bitch."

"Is that so?" Vlad drawled. "Perhaps you should consider the dangers of ending our association."

"Thanks, but I'll take my chances."

"A pity about your little lapdog. So horrible what happened to his lovely friend."

I couldn't help the sharp intake of breath he'd startled out of me. "How do you know about that?"

"That is unimportant."

"Like hell it is!" I snapped. "So help me, Vlad, if you were in any way involved—"

"Do not threaten me, my lovely," he interrupted, his tone mocking. "I think you know of old how well I respond to your threats."

I ground my teeth together, hating that he was right. I could put up a good fight, but when it came down to it, my strength was nothing to his. He'd *let* me catch him before, plain and simple. And we both knew it.

"Did you kill Molly O'Grady?" I demanded.

"Of course not," he replied so innocently I got the impression he was batting his eyes on the other end of the line. "You know such carnage is not my style. I like to play with my food, Red, not torture it. I simply was making a point that one never knows what horrible creatures might be lurking in the shadows, creatures from which I could protect you."

I swallowed the rage burning my throat but I couldn't quite keep the apprehension out of my voice when I asked, "Why would I need protecting?"

"You were attacked once already," he reminded me. "Do you think that Reaper can protect you from another such attack? He is not with you every moment. He does not know the heat of your blood like I do. He does not sense your every heartbeat."

I could feel the tendrils of his voice beginning to work their way under my skin and shook my head to clear the growing haze before it could take hold. "I'd trust Nate with my life," I insisted. "And that's a hell of a lot more than I could say about you."

Vlad hissed something dark in his native tongue, raising the hair on my arms even though the words were foreign to me, then snarled in English, "You have no idea what you are doing!"

"I know exactly what I'm doing," I assured him. "Don't call me again."

Without waiting for his response, I hung up and stared down at my phone for a moment, half expecting it to ring again. When it didn't, I sighed, a little sad at the way things were finally ending.

I'd always known our relationship couldn't go anywhere—at least not anywhere healthy. But I'd always hoped it would end on good terms, that someday we'd run into each other at a party and reminisce about old times, laugh about how crazy we'd been about each other once upon a time.

So it goes.

I took another sip of my coffee and closed my eyes for a few seconds, wondering when exactly my life had gone from being an action-adventure to a two-bit melodrama. Hell, I would have even settled for a romantic comedy. But seeing as how there were no happy endings immediately in sight, I'd at least do whatever I could to rewrite the story in which I'd unwittingly been cast. That meant clearing Seth and bringing in the real killer. And the clock was ticking.

Taking a chance that my impression of Nate's morning routine was dead on, I dialed his number and grinned when I heard his raspy voice drawl, "I'm surprised to hear from you so early."

"What are you talking about?" I returned. "I've been up for hours."

He chuckled. "Liar."

"Okay, *an* hour," I admitted. "But still. I think it might be an all-time record."

There was a slight pause before he asked, "Couldn't sleep?"

I sat down on the sofa in the living room and frowned at the carpet. "Got a lot on my mind."

I heard him inhale and let out his breath in a slow, measured exhale. "Anything I can do?"

God, was there ever!

A barrage of mouthwatering images of him shirtless hit me so hard I had to close my eyes for a second to steady my pulse. I would have liked nothing better than to press my lips to the flames that seared his skin and feel their heat for myself. But there was work to do, so I gave my libido a good smack upside the head.

Down, girl.

"You can come with me to chat with Alice," I suggested, sticking to business. "I want to find out what she knows about Dave's apprentice."

"What apprentice?"

"Precisely."

"That sounds ominous."

"I'll fill you in on the way."

"I can be there in twenty."

"Make it ten."

"On my way."

"Hey, Nate?"

"Yeah?"

I wanted to tell him about Vlad's call, his offer of protection, and get his take on it. But seeing as how he was already nervous enough about my number being drawn, I didn't want to add to his concern. Vlad didn't like being told no, but he'd get over it. Not like there weren't scads of other women clamoring to be one of his bed bunnies.

"Never mind," I said, shrugging off my uneasiness. "I'll just see you soon."

Chapter 32

Calling where Alice lived an apartment was a gross overstatement. It was little more than a minuscule box with just enough room for a twin bed, a small chest of drawers, and a plant stand that held an ancient black and white thirteen-inch TV with one broken antenna. There was a tiny sink tucked along one wall between a stove and refrigerator small enough to fit into a child's playhouse. A lone window covered by venetian blinds yellowed by age (and who knows what else) let in just enough light to hide the worst of the dinginess ground into the carpet. The walls were bare but for a single framed photo of verdant rolling hills and a little red farmhouse nestled peacefully among them. There was no toilet or bathtub to be seen, so I could only guess that they were located somewhere down the hall to be shared with the other residents.

Nonetheless, Alice invited us in with such delighted pride she might as well have been a princess welcoming us to her palace. "I'm sorry for the mess!" she called over her shoulder as she kicked a pair of shoes under the bed and straightened the well-worn coverlet. "I've never had visitors before!"

It broke my heart to see the kid living in such a hovel. If she'd been a Tale, I would have immediately called the

Relocation Bureau and demanded they get off their collective
asses and find the poor girl someplace livable. As it was, all
I could do was smile graciously when she offered me a
drink of water in a chipped teacup.

"Thank you again, Ms. Little," she gushed. "Your grandma
was so sweet! And her boyfriend was *totally* hot for an old
guy."

Nate shot an amused grin my way in time to catch the
cringe I couldn't quite prevent at the word *boyfriend*. "Yes,
Mr. Fox is very charming," I agreed. "I'm glad you liked
them."

"Sorry I don't have much furniture," Alice lamented,
waving her arm toward the bed with a nervous, jerky motion.
"But you can sit down there if you want."

When Nate immediately took her up on her offer, Alice
curled up on the floor with her legs folded in front of her and
grinned up at us. "So, what brings you by? Did you get the
invoice information from Dave's computer?"

I sat down next to Nate, carefully balancing my teacup of
tap water as the bed dipped a little in his direction and wedged
me up against him, my thigh and hip pressed into his.

"No, not yet," I told her, scooting away a couple of inches
so that I could actually focus on the conversation. "But soon.
We did have a couple more questions for you, though, if
that's okay."

Alice's face brightened to the point of beaming. "Are you
kidding? If it weren't for you, I'd be on the streets again! Now
I have a job at the library, which is really cool, and Mrs. Stuart
even mentioned helping me get my GED so I can maybe go
to college. Can you believe that?"

Actually, I could. Dear Gran.

I offered the kid a genuine smile, touched by her excitement and actually glad that I had played a part in it, however
small. "I'm really happy for you, kiddo," I told her. "I hope
everything works out for you."

"So, what did you want to ask me?" she prompted.

"We were wondering if you knew anything about a woman named Julie Spangle," Nate said.

Alice nodded enthusiastically. "Sure! I knew Julie. She was *super* nice. I wish she would have stayed with the company, but she didn't really like it much."

"Exterminating pests or working for Dave?" I asked.

"Definitely the exterminating," Alice replied. "It's not for everyone. I mean, she did okay on the first job—that was at the restaurants—but when the rats started popping up a lot of places, she *totally* freaked out."

"Freaked out how?" Nate asked, leaning forward as we traded a glance.

Alice twisted her mouth as she thought about the question. "I don't know what set her off, but she was yelling at Dave and stomping around the office. They got into a big screaming match right there in front of me. She was all like, 'There's no way in hell I'm going to be a rat catcher for some snooty witch!'"

I frowned. "Did she actually say 'witch'?"

Alice rolled her eyes, then laughed. "I know! I'm nineteen—it's not like I haven't heard somebody called a bitch before."

"Do you know who Julie was talking about?" Nate asked.

Alice shrugged. "Dunno. One of the clients, I guess. We had a bunch of snooty bitches on the client list after the rat infestation started, you know? Anyway, she stormed out."

"What happened after that?" Nate questioned.

Alice pulled her knees up to her chest, her expression turning a little sad. "Dave went after her and they were yelling at each other in the parking lot for a few minutes. He was really pissed when he came back in. He tried calling her a bunch of times but he finally gave up and left early that day."

"Is that it?" I asked.

She nodded. "Yep. I haven't heard from Julie since then.

Not even to get her paycheck for the few days she worked for Dave."

I didn't have the heart to tell her Julie wouldn't be collecting anytime soon. I tossed back the last of my water and got to my feet. "Thanks for all your help, Alice," I said, holding out my cup while she scrambled to her feet.

She shrugged and offered me a disconcertingly adoring smile. "Oh, sure! Anytime you guys want to stop by, feel free!"

"Uh, thanks," I said. "If you think of anything else we should know, give us a call, okay?"

She nodded enthusiastically, then threw her arms around my neck and hugged me tightly. "You are so awesome!"

I patted her back a couple of times. "Okay. Okay, thanks."

When she finally released me, I quickly strode to the door and pulled it open before I could get ensnared in another embrace.

Nate was grinning as he waved a final good-bye to Alice and followed me into the hall. "I think you have another member in your fan club."

"Shut up," I grumbled.

"No, seriously," Nate taunted as we made our way downstairs. "I think she could be president."

I sent an acerbic glance his way. "She'll get over her adoration, trust me."

"Oh, why's that?"

I pushed open the door to the outside and lifted my face briefly to the warmth of the spring sunshine. "Because everyone does."

"I don't know about that," Nate mused. "Seems like a few of us still love you."

My head snapped toward him. "What?"

He blinked at me innocently. "What?"

I huffed, exasperated by his feigned ignorance. "What you said. What did you mean by that?"

The corner of Nate's mouth lifted just a little, but before he could continue with whatever smart-ass reply he had planned, his expression suddenly morphed into a deep frown. "What the hell?"

I quickly turned to follow his line of vision and was jolted by the sight before me. The roof of my Range Rover had been ripped to shreds as if by massive claws. Huge dents the size of softballs—or an enormous fist—covered the side. And the tires were flat down to the rims, ragged gashes in the rubber visible even from a distance.

Speechless, I walked slowly toward the ruined vehicle, hoping my eyes betrayed me, but the damage actually was worse on closer inspection. The dents I'd seen continued on the hood and around the other side. All the lights had been shattered, the amber, white, and red shards of plastic littering the ground. And the windshield was completely demolished but for bits of jagged glass that hung tenaciously to the edges of the frame.

I stood staring at the wreckage for a long moment, a million questions racing through my brain. "Why didn't we hear anything?" I managed to whisper.

Nate's hand rested heavily on my shoulder. "I'm sorry, Red," he said gently. "Want me to call it in to headquarters? See if they'll send someone to take a look? Maybe Trish could lift some prints."

I squatted down to get a closer look at the dents and tentatively ran my fingertips along the edges of one, mentally calculating the diameter. "They won't find any." I walked a slow perimeter around the vehicle, noting that all the dents were exactly the same size. Exactly as I'd suspected. "No one was here."

Nate's face betrayed his disbelief. "In case I missed one hell of a hailstorm, I'd say someone had to have done this intentionally."

I nodded. "Oh, it was intentional all right. But look," I

said, pointing to the dents. "They're perfectly symmetrical. If someone had hit this with a weapon or his fist, it would vary, at least a little bit depending on the force and angle of each blow, right?"

Nate frowned. "Okay, sure, but—"

"And the glass from the windshield and the lights are all on the outside of the car," I continued. "There's not even any debris inside the headlights. It's like they exploded outward."

Nate squatted down in front of the car and peered into the shell of the headlight. "I'll be damned." He squinted up at me. "Are you sure you're not an Investigator?"

"I'm beginning to think I'm a better one than you," I shot back.

He let out a short laugh and rose to his feet. "Yeah, well, I'm used to dealing with dead bodies," he reminded me, "not vandalism."

"Touché."

"So, what are you thinking? This was done using magic?"

I nodded. "I'm guessing it was the same Tale who's been using the rats as familiars. Looks like someone's trying to send me a message."

"I'd say it came through loud and clear," Nate quipped. "But you know what bothers me most about the whole thing?"

I gave him a wry look. "That we have to go back to driving *your* piece of shit now?"

"No," Nate said, drawing out the word patiently. "That no one knew we were here. No one knows we've been talking to Alice. I sure as hell didn't tell the Chief that we've involved an Ordinary in this mess."

"Neither did I," I said, wracking my brain to figure out who might have known. "Gran and Eddie are the only ones who even know about Alice."

"Wrong."

"Excuse me?"

"Did you forget about Snow?" he reminded me. "She's the one who mentioned Hamelin's assistant to us in the first place."

I groaned. "So much for my future in investigations."

"Wanna pay Snow a visit, see if she's had any pest control problems lately?"

"How exactly do you plan to get us there?" I gestured toward the Rover. "In case you hadn't noticed, we're sans transportation at the moment."

He sent a wink my way, then walked slowly down the sidewalk, letting his hand glide over each car he passed. Finally, he stopped next to a Dodge Charger that was probably one of the first ever made, if the rust spots were any indication, and opened the passenger door.

"Hop in, sweetheart."

I lifted my brows, not sure if I was more surprised by his new nickname for me or the fact that he was proposing we steal a car. "Come again?"

He made a sweeping motion with his arm. "Let's go."

I glanced around quickly, checking to see if anyone was nearby. Fortunately, it was early enough in the morning that most people were still inside finishing up breakfast and whatever else normal people did on Saturday mornings.

"That's stealing," I hissed.

He nodded matter-of-factly. "Yes, it is. So get in the car before someone reports us and we end up spending the day at the local police department trying to explain who we are and who we work for."

"We could just call a cab," I reasoned, nevertheless taking angry strides toward the waiting car. "Or call headquarters and have them bring us another one."

"That would take a ridiculous amount of time and red tape," he pointed out. "Now get in."

"Nate—"

"When did you suddenly become the cautious one?" he

demanded, the shadows beneath the brim of his fedora growing denser as his patience began to wane. "What happened to act first, think later and who gives a damn about the consequences?"

I shoved my face close to his. "This is different and you know it."

The sound of approaching sirens cut our argument short.

"Someone's probably called in about the damage," Nate speculated, glancing up and down the street again. "Get moving."

I huffed and flopped down onto the seat, glaring straight ahead as he got in and fished around under the dashboard. A moment later, the car roared to life and we were on the road. Just as we turned, I saw the first police car pull up to the curb behind my Range Rover.

"It's just a car," Nate said after several minutes of the silent treatment.

"Yes, but it's *someone's* car," I snapped. "And that someone is going to be some kind of pissed off when he finds out his car's gone. It's not like the people in this neighborhood have a lot of money."

"I guarantee you the guy who owns this car won't miss it."

"How can you be so sure?" I cried, growing more furious with him every time he opened his mouth.

"Because he passed away peacefully in his sleep last night from a massive heart attack," Nate informed me. "His daughter drives in from the suburbs every Monday, Wednesday, and Friday to check on him, so she won't find him until two days from now. By then, the car will be safely returned. That's why I chose this one."

"Oh," I said, still conflicted but feeling a little better knowing that no one was going to be inconvenienced.

"Are you ever going to trust me?" Nate asked. His tone was light, but there was an underlying note of seriousness that I didn't miss.

I turned and studied his profile for a long moment, tracing every angle, every line with my gaze, wishing I could come up with some kind of witty remark to toss back instead of the heavy phrase weighing down the tip of my tongue. I opted for something in between. "I do trust you," I told him. "I've got to. It's not like I have much of a choice, right? I mean, I've got some unknown Tale killing people and sending me a very clear message that I'm not untouchable, that no matter where I am or where I go, he can find me."

Nate's grip on the steering wheel tightened when he caught my drift. "You're worried about your number being drawn."

"Aren't you?"

"I wish I'd never told you about that," he ground out. "I should have kept it to myself."

I shrugged. "Yeah, well. 'Should be should buzz,' to borrow a phrase from the Willies. What's done is done, so don't worry about it. Let's just find this bastard so everything can get back to normal."

"Normal?"

I snorted. "Yeah. Whatever the hell that is."

Chapter 33

"Hey there, Ted," I greeted when Snow's dwarf answered the door. "We're here to see Snow."

Ted looked up at us through bleary eyes. "She's not available," he grumbled. "Come back later."

When he tried to close the door, I stuck out my boot, blocking his attempt, then shoved hard, sending him stumbling backward. "You know, Ted, you and I have always gotten along," I said, advancing before he could try to block our way again. "It'd be a shame if we couldn't be friends anymore."

The bouncer glared at me, then flipped his beard over his shoulder. "I told you she's not available."

"Then make her available," Nate ordered. "We're not leaving until we have the chance to chat."

Ted looked back and forth between us as if gauging if we were bluffing, then finally huffed in exasperation. "Fine. Follow me," he said, biting off the words.

Instead of taking us to the usual sitting room to await Snow's entrance, Ted took us to the madam's bedroom and knocked lightly upon the door. When no one answered, Ted shrugged dismissively. "Sorry. She must not be in after all."

"Yeah, well, I'll just take a look for myself," I said, making to move past him.

Ted stepped in front of the door, blocking my path, but Nate grabbed the man's shoulder and pulled him firmly to one side. "I wouldn't interfere if I were you, my friend."

I shoved open the door and strode in. "Rise and shine, Snow!"

In response, there was a frantic flurry of movement as the occupants of an elaborately canopied bed scrambled from beneath the covers and to their feet. A wide-eyed Snow snatched the sheet from the bed and clutched it to her bare body, her eyes darting about like a rabbit caught in a snare. Out of the corner of my eye, I saw another blur of movement as her companion made a dive for the bedside table.

I was still drawing my gun when I heard Nate yell, "Drop it!"

The man immediately tossed his own gun to the ground and slowly straightened, arms raised.

My eyes went wide when I realized who it was. "Aloysius?"

Tim Halloran's second-in-command flushed slightly at being recognized—or maybe because he was standing there with his goods on display. Either way, he gave me a polite nod in greeting. "Enforcer."

"Red, please don't speak a word of this to anyone," Snow pleaded, wrapping the sheet more securely around her body, her usual haughtiness disconcertingly absent. "I beg you. I will do whatever you ask, but no one must know Aloysius was here."

I traded a bemused glance with Nate.

"What's to tell?" I replied, turning back to my old friend. "I've never asked about your personal client list."

Snow raised her hand in a conciliatory gesture as she slowly edged around the bed toward Aloysius. "Please, put the guns down. Don't hurt him."

My frown deepened. "We weren't planning to," I assured her. "We were just stopping by to chat. Although, I have to say, seeing a bare-assed criminal going for his gun when I enter a room has a way of piquing my curiosity."

Snow pressed her lips together in a tight line. "I'll explain everything," she said, finally reaching her lover's side and slipping her arms around his waist. "I give you my word."

I looked to Nate to gauge his response. When he gave me a curt nod, we both holstered our weapons.

Snow gestured toward a small sitting area nestled in a corner of her bedroom where the morning sunlight filtered through the blinds. "Please, have a seat. Ted," she said, turning to her faithful servant, "please bring in coffee for all of us."

After the dwarf made his exit, Snow grabbed a dressing gown from the end of her bed and slipped into it before taking a seat on the settee. Aloysius, having pulled on a pair of silk pajama bottoms, joined her a moment later, taking her hand in his and pressing a kiss to her palm.

"Okay," I said, crossing my arms over my chest once we were all seated. "I'm listening."

"Aloysius and I have been lovers for quite some time now," Snow admitted.

"Congratulations," Nate drawled.

"And this is a problem why?" I prompted.

"I want Snow to quit the business," Aloysius announced. "Or at least quit taking clients of her own."

I looked at them expectantly, still not able to connect the dots. "And?"

"In order to cover the money I would have made, Ally has been . . ." She paused, glancing his way. "He has been moonlighting without Halloran's knowledge."

"Moonlighting how?" Nate questioned.

"Selling under the table," I deduced, finally understanding. "You're undercutting his business, aren't you? Skimming just enough product for him not to notice and selling it on the market to create a nice little nest egg for the two of you. Am I right?"

They both nodded.

"When we have enough set aside, Ally's quitting," Snow

explained. "We want to start a life together, Red. But if the Sandman finds out what's going on, he'll kill Ally. You know he will."

"That's why you clocked me in the warehouse," I realized. "You didn't think I was a burglar—you were afraid I was coming to out you to Halloran."

Aloysius dipped his head. "Sorry about that. You'd already seen me in the alley with Sebille. I figured if the Sandman thought you were trying to sneak in and steal information, he'd be less likely to trust you—or anything you said."

Now it was my turn to feel bad. "Yeah, about that," I began. "I might have mentioned your back-alley deal to Halloran already. He seemed surprised. And I get the impression he doesn't like surprises."

Snow gasped, her milky white complexion going a shade paler with sudden panic, but Aloysius slipped his arm around Snow's shoulders and pulled her close, dropping a kiss to the top of her hair. "It'll be all right, baby," he murmured. Then he lifted his eyes to mine. "The Sandman cornered me about it already. I told him Sebille was demanding something to help Caliban sleep. He seemed to buy it."

"What *was* in that package?" Nate asked.

"About six ounces of D," Aloysius said.

"Six ounces?" I cried. "That much D floating around would have the fairies in an uproar!"

"No shit," he agreed. "That's why Sebille comes to me. Caliban's habit is out of control. If he doesn't slow down he's going to end up in the Asylum."

I shook my head in confusion. "His habit? What are you talking about? How long has Caliban been on D?"

"Couple of years," Aloysius informed me. "It was after you guys were together. After Sebille started running things. His businesses were really ramping up, getting pretty stress-ful, I guess. Sebille got him to go to the fairies to get a dose now and then to keep his temper on the level. But he built up a tolerance quicker than most and the usual doses weren't good enough anymore."

"Good God," I breathed. "He's got to be using every day."

Aloysius nodded solemnly. "He's pushing himself too hard. The Sandman is furious with Sebille for getting him addicted in the first place and wanted her to start backing Caliban off the stuff; he's worried that the money he's invested is going to get pissed away if Caliban starts losing it from the side effects."

Side effects, I repeated silently.

Seth had tried to tell me I didn't really know Caliban anymore. Was it possible that his drug-induced paranoia would lead him to hire a werewolf to kill for him? I pushed such thoughts away, not liking where they were taking me.

"Thing is," Aloysius went on, "Halloran wasn't the only one who'd caught on to Caliban's problem. At least one of the other investors was getting skittish, too. Was thinking of backing out unless he was guaranteed the operations here wouldn't suffer while Caliban was in LA."

"Dale Minnows," I realized.

"Yeah," Aloysius said. "How'd you know?"

"Long story."

"I don't get it," Nate interjected. "Sebille seems to care about Caliban. You'd think she'd want him to get clean."

"You would think," Snow interjected. She cast a meaningful look at Aloysius. "Any *decent* woman would do anything for the man she loves."

Aloysius's arm tightened around Snow. "I think she believes she's helping him. When I gave her that package in the alley, I tried to tell her that she was going to end up killing him—or making him crazy—if she didn't get him some help. She told me to mind my own business or she'd make sure Halloran found out about me and Snow."

"She's blackmailing you," Nate concluded.

"Not just him," Snow spat. "Both of us."

My brows shot up. "What would she possibly want from *you*?" Immediately regretting how that sounded, I said, "Sorry, I meant—"

Snow waved away my explanation. "We've known each other far too long, my friend. I take no offense. She demands to have the pick of my girls whenever she likes."

"For herself or for Caliban?" I asked, feeling my stomach go a little queasy and wishing Ted would show up with that coffee.

"Neither," Snow replied. "She said they are for an associate. They are doing business in trade, apparently."

"And who's this associate?" Nate probed. "She give you a name?"

Snow shook her head. "No. She insists I not ask any questions. I send her the girls when she asks and they return to me a day or two later. They are never harmed and seem to enjoy their time with whoever it is. The only stipulation is that I never send the same girl more than once a month."

"And the girls can't tell you anything about Sebille's associate?" I asked, wondering if Caliban's addictions weren't confined to fairy dust. "No description?"

"Unfortunately, no," Snow said. "He's a Tale like us, but that's all I know. They seem to have only a vague recollection of events upon their return."

"Like they're being drugged?" I suggested.

She shook her head thoughtfully. "No, I think not. More like their memories had been altered."

"How many Tales do you think have that ability?" Nate asked me. "We could check the Registry."

"There are several ways to alter memories," I told him. "Any number of magical entities could pull off something like this. As long as the girls are coming back unharmed, there's nothing we can really do."

Nate turned to Snow and Aloysius. "Do you want to press

charges against Sebille?" he asked. "We can bring her in for blackmailing you."

Aloysius laughed. "Are you fucking crazy, man? If we did that we'd have to admit to all our . . . activities. If Halloran didn't kill me for skimming profits, you can bet your ass he'd kill me for ratting him out to the FMA."

I let loose a juicy string of curses under my breath, hating that Caliban's controlling bitch of an assistant seemed to have everyone by the balls no matter where we turned. She was making damned sure Caliban was going to make it to the top and to hell with whoever suffered on the way. I was beginning to think maybe Seth was right about taking a second look at Caliban's alibis. If Sebille Fenwick had him hopped up on D to keep him level, who knew what kind of fucked up shit was going through his head at any given time. If he had hired a werewolf to kill for him, would he also have hired a witch to send familiars out to be his eyes and ears?

Suddenly feeling uneasy, I glanced around Snow's bedroom. "Snow, you seen any rats around here lately?"

Snow's brows snapped together. "I beg your pardon?"

"Rats," I repeated. "Big ones."

Snow shook her head. "No."

I frowned, wondering why my instincts were smacking me in the back of the head. "Are you sure?"

"Positive," Snow insisted. "Dave Hamelin took care of them before he died."

Chapter 34

I sat scowling as Nate drove us to the chichi neighborhood of Rockwell Crossing where we'd be picking up Todd Caliban for another round of questioning. We had enough circumstantial evidence now to bring him in again for a second chat. I was hoping, if nothing else, he could back his now-suspect alibis with something a little more concrete and set my mind at ease.

Sebille obviously was doing everything she could to cover up Caliban's addiction to D, even going as far as blackmailing his drug supplier to keep things quiet, but that could be chalked up to trying to protect the man she loved, not necessarily complicity in murder. The Tribunal would probably let her off with probation.

But there'd be no wrist slapping for Caliban. Although there was no way he was actually committing the murders himself, there was enough circumstantial evidence to make the Tribunal believe he was masterminding them—which did nothing to help Seth. I could just see Mary Smith standing before the Tribunal, painting a lovely picture of two of my former lovers being partners in the worst murders in Tale history.

Fortunately for us, Caliban would sell out his best friend to save his own ass, so maybe he'd start spilling his guts as soon as he found out his alibis were falling apart. I just had to hope that when he did, I wouldn't hear Seth's name on his lips.

"You okay?" Nate asked, as we turned onto Caliban's street.

I nodded. "Yeah, it's just—"

The sudden sound of sirens cut across my words as an ambulance sped past us. I twisted around in my seat to catch a glimpse of the brake lights as it turned the corner and disappeared.

"That was one of ours," I gasped. "What the hell?"

My question was answered the minute we pulled up in front of Caliban's place and saw Sebille Fenwick hurrying down the steps.

"What's going on?" I demanded, jumping out of the Charger and rushing to cut her off.

"You again," she hissed, her eyes narrowing. "Leave us alone!"

"Where's Caliban?" I said. "Was that him in the ambulance?"

Sebille clenched her fists at her sides and stepped closer to me. "Yes, it was. Now get out of my way. I need to get to the hospital."

"Did he finally OD?" I spat. "You give him a little too much D this morning with his tea and biscuits, Sebille?"

Sebille's eyes flashed with fury as she took a menacing step toward me. "I said, *get out of my way.*"

I pushed my face up at hers. "Make me."

For a split second, I thought she was actually going to give it a go, but then she took a measured step back and glanced over my shoulder as Nate came up behind me. "I am sorry to be rude," she said with forced politeness, "but I really must get to the hospital. Caliban needs me right now."

"Let her go, Red," Nate said.

My head whipped around so that I could ask him if he'd lost his freaking mind, but the look he gave me assured me his faculties were all in working order.

I bit my tongue until Sebille had sped off after the ambulance, then I let loose. "What the hell?" I demanded. "We should have taken her in!"

"For what?" Nate pointed out. "We came here for Caliban. I'll call Al and have him put guards outside Caliban's hospital room. If he survives, we'll question him then."

"If he survives," I repeated, disgust seeping into my voice. "Damn it!"

"Red—"

"He's hooked on D, Nate!" I yelled. "How could we not have noticed? How could *I* not have noticed? I've known the guy for years!"

"You heard what Aloysius said," Nate reminded me. "He didn't start using until after you were together. Caliban's a grown man. You can't blame yourself for choices he's made."

I let out an exasperated sigh and ran my hands through my hair. "Let's just get out of here. Nicky called this morning about Hamelin's computer. Maybe he's got something for us."

"Come on," Nate said with a jerk of his head. "I'll buy you some lunch. If memory serves, I still owe you one."

"I'm not hungry," I lied.

Nate took me by the shoulders and steered me back toward the car. "You're always hungry. Come on; you can call Nicky on the way."

I tried calling Nicky three times while we drove but didn't get an answer on his cell. Finally, I tried his landline at home, on the off chance he'd actually be there. He wasn't, of course, but he'd had the forethought to leave a message for me with the housekeeper.

"Nicky can't meet us today," I told Nate, pocketing my phone. "I'm supposed to come by the house for brunch tomorrow morning and pick up the info from Hamelin's computer. I don't know why he couldn't just send it to me."

"I'm sure he has his reasons," Nate said, apparently sensing my apprehension about Nicky's insistence on delivering the findings in person.

Changing the subject to something more pleasant, I asked, "Where should we head after lunch?"

"Don't you need to go to Elizabeth's to get ready for tonight?"

I let my head drop back against the headrest and groaned. "God, that's right. The party."

"We don't have to go," Nate said. "Cornering Caliban for a chat was pretty much our only reason for going."

I shook my head. "When else would we have the chance to mingle with the Who's Who of Tale society without dragging their asses downtown? I'm guessing just about everyone from Hamelin's recent client list is going to be there."

"I looked over the client list," Nate informed me. "It's pretty much just the usual muckety-mucks. I have a feeling they're going to tell us the same story about the rats as everyone else has. And it's pretty clear Caliban was using them for spying on people who could help or hurt him in some way. The only thing we need to know is who has been helping him eliminate the latter group, and I doubt any of those folks are going to be able to tell us that."

"I'd still like to hear what's being said," I told him. "Besides, having Caliban absent from the party might be a great opportunity for people to gossip a little."

"Do you think they'll talk to you, knowing who you are?"

"I hate it when you get all logical on me," I mumbled. "Still, it can't hurt to try. Besides, you don't need me to get them talking. You could just unleash that charm you're so proud of."

Nate gave me a thoughtful look. "This is true," he said slowly. "Considering I'll be adding formal wear to my arsenal, those poor women don't have a prayer."

I punched Nate in the arm, eliciting the burst of laughter I was hoping for. If he hadn't been so damned disarming in his arrogance, I would've slugged him harder. As it was, I just needed to hear him laugh. It had the desired effect on my amped-up nerves as did the deep dish pizza we split at a little hole in the wall joint where my love affair with Chicago's famous pie had begun.

When he dropped me off at Elizabeth's a couple hours later it was with the promise to return at the appointed time looking even more "dashing than usual" (his words, not mine). As much as I was looking forward to seeing what that entailed, it made me feel a little nervous about how I'd measure up.

Fortunately, Elizabeth immediately set my mind at ease when she greeted me at the door, a look of unabashed delight in her fine eyes. "Tess!" she cried, taking my hands in hers and pulling me inside. "I see the concern in your expression, but you needn't worry. All is prepared, and I guarantee you shall look breathtaking when Detective Grimm arrives this evening."

"Breathtaking?" I echoed. "I'd settle for believable."

Eliza laughed good-naturedly and linked her arm with mine as we made our way into the study. "Would it help if I told you Darcy and I might have found some information on Sebille Fenwick for you?"

My brows shot up. "That was quick."

Elizabeth's eyes twinkled. "I do believe Mr. Darcy has acquired a liking for investigative work."

"Really? Maybe he could do a little moonlighting for the FMA. They always need good researchers."

Eliza squeezed my arm. "I shall mention it to him. Perhaps such an activity would make him feel more a part of the Here and Now. This could be exactly what he needed."

I almost didn't recognize Darcy when I entered his study. His rather reserved expression was so visibly altered by excitement he looked like a different person. Gone were the lines of sadness and concern that had creased his brow for so long.

With a friendly smile, he strode toward me and offered his hand in greeting. "Ms. Little. A delight to see you as always."

"Darcy," I said, shaking his hand. "Eliza tells me you might have found something."

"Indeed." He ushered us over to his desk and waited for us to take a seat before perching on the corner of his desk and turning his laptop around for us to see.

"There were literally hundreds of instances of sibyls—the oracles of ancient mythology that Elizabeth suggested. However, after discarding those accounts, I discovered an obscure reference in Arthurian texts to Sebille l'Enchantress, who by some accounts was Queen of the Sidhe and friend to Morgan le Fay."

"No way," I said, giving him a grin. "You're kidding, right?"

"I would not jest about such matters," he assured me, his tone grave. "If Sebille Fenwick is the enchantress mentioned in Arthurian legend, then she is a most powerful foe indeed."

I stared at Darcy for one long, bemused moment. "How is it I've never heard of her?"

"Her story appears in only the most obscure texts," Darcy explained. "And, as with most figures associated with the lore of the great king, there are numerous inconsistencies, depending upon the text in which her story is found. By some accounts, she was merely a pagan queen."

"My God," I breathed. If what Darcy was telling me was true, Sebille Fenwick was potentially more than just a put-upon underling in love with her boss. If she had come over as the Enchantress version of her tale, Sebille actually could be the one sending out the familiars and controlling the werewolf. And if she was powerful enough to hang out with Morgan le Fay, we were in some seriously deep shit, magically speaking.

"Would you guys excuse me for a sec?" I said, launching to my feet and rushing toward the door. "I need to make a call." I paused at the door and turned back. "Thanks, Darcy. I owe you one."

I hurried across the hall to Eliza's sitting room and shut the door behind me before dialing Nate's number.

"Miss me already?" he asked by way of greeting.

"You have no idea," I shot back. "Where are you?"

"On my way to drop off the Charger. Why?"

"Sebille Fenwick is quite possibly a cohort of Morgan le Fay."

There was a long pause before Nate said, "Damn."

"Yeah, no shit." I started to pace, my mind racing. "Do you think she's still at the hospital with Caliban? Maybe if someone can apprehend her there, she'll behave herself."

"Because cornered sorceresses are usually so docile?" Nate said drily.

"There you go being logical again," I huffed. "Got a better idea? This one's above you and me, Nate. Even *I* don't go up against people like her alone if I can help it."

"I'll call it in to the Chief," Nate offered. "He can send in someone from Special Forces to pick her up for questioning."

I stopped pacing and pressed the heel of my hand into my eyes to stop the pounding pain beginning there. "She could be behind the familiars, Nate. She could be sending the werewolf. God, Nate, she could even be behind Seth's blackouts. What if he *was* the werewolf doing this?"

"Even if he was, he wasn't doing it willingly, right?"

"Yeah."

"So then he'll be fine."

"You sound so sure."

"I *am* sure," Nate said. "I know you don't like Mary, but she's reasonable, Red. If we give her Caliban and Sebille, she'll let Seth off the hook."

I sighed, hoping he was right—especially since in handing over the dead rat, I might have given them all the evidence they needed to pin the murders on Seth. "What a frigging mess," I mumbled. "I don't get it. Why would Sebille help Caliban murder these people?"

"I have no idea, sweetheart," he said gently. "Maybe she's just trying to protect him, keep his career moving forward in spite of his addiction issues. People don't always think clearly about their choices when they love someone."

I felt a lance of pleasure at his words and would have liked to stand there listening to that raspy voice of his go on for hours. Hell, he could have been reading stereo instructions and I would have begged him to keep talking.

"Red? You still there?"

I coughed a couple times, gathering my scattered wits. "Yeah, I'm here."

"I'm going to call the Chief," he went on. "Why don't you give Trish a call and see what she's found."

I nodded like he was standing there with me. "Okay. Talk to you soon."

"You bet," he replied, his voice losing some of its heaviness. "I'll see you this evening."

"We're still on?"

"Wouldn't miss it."

When I called Trish she answered on the second ring. "Red!" she said somewhat breathlessly. "This specimen you gave me is remarkable!"

I frowned at her enthusiasm, wondering if her idea of remarkable was the same as mine. "So, you find anything?"

"Did I ever!" she said quickly. "There's definitely magical residue. But the signature—my gosh, it's amazing! I've never seen anything like it. *Very* powerful stuff."

"Fabulous," I murmured. "Did you find any matches to it in the Registry?"

"Not one," Trish replied. "It has to be someone who came in under the radar. The folks at the Relocation Bureau must have completely missed that this Tale had abilities."

Great. So Sebille was able to cloak her powers. This just got better and better.

"What about the werewolf DNA on the rat?" I asked. "Did you find anything there?"

"Yep. It's unusual, too."

My frown deepened. "How so?"

"The magical signature is completely foreign to me," she explained. "It's very intricate. Definitely a curse behind it, but it's not your run-of-the-mill job. Whoever cursed this werewolf was crazy good with spells."

I swallowed hard, preparing myself to ask the burning question. "Can you tell if the person controlling the familiars has also cast a spell on the werewolf?" I asked, not sure what answer I was hoping to hear. As much as I wanted to prove Seth was completely innocent of the crimes, I was willing to settle for being able to prove he was under the control of an evil sorceress and couldn't be held accountable for his actions if it would keep him off the executioner's to-do list.

Trish hesitated. "I can't say definitively," she hedged. "There were traces of that magic in the wolf DNA, but that could have been cross-contamination from biting the rat. I'd need to run some more tests to completely rule out this particular werewolf as a suspect."

"Do whatever you need to do," I told her.

"You do realize it's Saturday, right?" she said, her tone weary.

"I'll owe you big time," I promised. "You know I'm good for it."

I heard Trish let out a long, slow breath. "All right. But I'm going to hold you to that favor someday."

"Trish, you get me the answers I'm looking for, and I'll be your best friend for life."

Chapter 35

"There," Elizabeth said proudly, turning me to face the full-length mirror in her dressing room. "You are an absolute vision."

I admit I had to blink a couple times before I realized I was the woman staring back at me. Her figure was shapely and sleek and filled out the elegant black Vera Wang cocktail dress much better than expected. A surprising amount of cleavage peeked out of the deep dipping V-line bodice, and when I turned my body around and looked over my shoulder, the woman's bare back was in stark contrast to the darkness of the material. Her hair, which was as black as the dress she wore, was piled high on her head in a loose chignon that accentuated the gentle sloping curves of a delicate bone structure and revealed in full brilliance the remarkable blueness of her eyes.

"Whoa," I whispered. "I look . . ."

"Breathtaking," Elizabeth supplied, her smiling face joining mine in the mirror. "The only thing you lack is the proper jewelry, but I believe I have just the thing."

Eliza went to a cabinet sitting atop her dressing table and opened the glass doors. After looking through the contents for a moment, she emerged with a simple blue teardrop diamond pendant hanging from a white gold chain and matching earrings.

"I can't borrow those," I protested. "Anything that sparkles that much makes me nervous. What if I lose them?"

Elizabeth laughed and fastened the pendant around my neck. "Then we shall consider it a sacrifice for a worthy cause. You simply could not wear anything else with this dress. Simple elegance suits you."

"I think you're projecting," I mumbled, nevertheless putting on the earrings with great care.

Her cheeks dimpled with an affectionate smile. "I think you do not take enough credit for your loveliness, my friend. But I hazard a guess you shall not be able to escape it this evening."

I wobbled a little on the black sling-backs as I turned and walked toward the chair where I'd discarded my clothes and other belongings. I tried to ignore the nervous fluttering in my stomach while I gathered them together and looked about absently for what to do with them next.

"Do not concern yourself with those," Eliza said. "I shall have our man deliver your things to you."

I dropped the clothes back onto the chair, then picked up my gun, FMA badge, and cell phone. "Where am I going to put these?" I wondered out loud, glancing briefly at my cleavage. "There's no hiding anything in this dress, that's for damned sure."

"You could carry a reticule," Eliza suggested.

I gave her a sour look. "Like hell."

Eliza laughed again. "Very well, then I suppose you must leave those as well. I can have them sent along with your clothes."

I cast a glance at the items in my hands, then, after a brief moment of misgiving, set them down with my clothes. "Nate will be carrying, I guess, so it should be okay."

A staccato rap on the dressing room door sounded, making

me jump. One of Eliza's maids opened the door and dropped a polite curtsy. "Detective Grimm has arrived, madam."

"Thank you, Ann," Eliza said, then turned to me. "Shall we?"

I hung on to Elizabeth's arm as we made our way down the stairs, as much for balance as support, and kept my eyes firmly on the steps to ensure I didn't miss one and go tumbling down in a gloriously graceless spectacle. So when we reached the bottom of the stairs and I looked up, I wasn't quite prepared for the expression of unabashed admiration I saw on Nate's face. I felt my cheeks going warmer and warmer the longer he stared without comment.

"You look quite lovely this evening, Ms. Little," Darcy said with a slight bow to me.

I gave Darcy a grateful smile and nervously smoothed the front of the dress. "Thanks, but it's all Elizabeth's doing."

"Does she not look beautiful, Detective?" Elizabeth prompted Nate, rescuing me from my self-conscious embarrassment. "Have you ever seen her look lovelier?"

Nate's lips curved into a slow smile. "Only once," he said with a meaningful wink.

As I flushed to the roots of my hair, I averted my eyes, affording me the chance to take in the sight of Nate in what had to be a vintage 1940s doubled-breasted black tuxedo. He had left his fedora at home, so his waves of dark hair hung about his head and neck in a carelessly debonair way that would have given any one of the silver screen stars a run for his money when it came to flat-out sexiness.

Eat your heart out, Cary Grant. . . .

"Well," I said, forcing my gaze back to his, "don't you look *dashing*."

With a burst of laughter at the inside joke, he held his elbow out to me. "Shall we?"

After wishing Elizabeth and Darcy a good evening, he

ushered me outside to where a burgundy 1940 Lincoln Zephyr Continental awaited us.

I blinked in dismay when he opened the door. "Where did you get this car?" I demanded, concerned he might have pinched another one especially for the occasion.

"It's mine," he replied. "You didn't think I was going to take you to the Charmings' party in that clunker the FMA gave me, did you?"

I actually hadn't even considered how we'd get there—I was far more concerned with how I was going to stay upright in these shoes—but I wasn't going to admit that to Nate. "I figured you'd come up with something."

As we drove to the party, I filled Nate in on what Trish had told me earlier. I still hadn't heard back on the rest of the tests I'd asked her to run, which was starting to make me a little nervous. "Even if we can prove Caliban and Sebille are behind the murders, we still can't prove Seth wasn't their murder weapon."

"She could have chosen any werewolf to use," Nate pointed out as we pulled up to the gated estate where two stoic men stood sentinel, checking invitations before allowing cars in. "Why would she choose Seth?"

"Got me," I replied, squinting a little to see if I could make out who was in the Rolls Royce in front of us. "I'll be sure to ask her that when we go visit her in prison. Did the guys have any trouble picking her up at the hospital?"

Nate squirmed a little. "About that . . ."

I sat up straighter in the seat, my heart pounding. "What happened?"

"She wasn't there," Nate said. "The hospital staff said she hasn't been there at all since Caliban was brought in."

My stomach sank into my borrowed shoes. "Damn it! We should have stayed on her when we had the chance."

"We'll get her, Red," Nate assured me. "You know we will."

"Before or after she has anyone else killed?" I muttered.

Nate's brow furrowed as he produced our invitation and rolled down the window to show it to the guard. My question was rhetorical, but his expression was a response nonetheless. He was worried about it, too.

The guard shone a flashlight upon the invitation, then on each of us in turn, then back on the invitation as if questioning the authenticity. Finally, he handed it back to Nate and waved us in with a shrug.

As Nate pulled through the gates I glanced into the rearview mirror and saw the guard lift his radio to his lips and speak rapidly.

"Great," I said. "He's outing us before we even get in there. Good luck getting any uninhibited conversation now."

When we pulled up to the front of the Charmings' manor, a young man in pale blue livery came hurrying toward us and had opened the car door for me before Nate had even put the car into park.

"Enforcer Little," the boy said with a slight bow as he extended a hand to help me out of the car. I was just perfecting my wobbly stance on Eliza's shoes when I heard a loud snort of laughter.

"Well, would you look who has graced us with her presence!"

I turned around to see the speaker and had to do a double-take. The woman's pale violet hair was piled atop her head in what must have been a fashionable style at one point but had come loose and was now leaning precariously to one side. The pearls that wound through the tangled mess made her look like she'd had a fight with a fishing net and the net had won. Her evening gown was askew, one strap hanging loosely off her shoulder. Lovely wide eyes the same shade as her hair were glassy and distant and her cheeks were a bit rosier than they should have been.

"Hello, Lavender," I said warily to Cindy's fairy godmother. "I'd ask how you're doing, but that's pretty clear."

Lavender tittered drunkenly as she wobbled toward me.

"You know me," she said, her speech slurring, "always the life of the party." She swung a slender arm in a wide arc and let it land around my shoulders. "Who's the stud you brought with you, Red?"

I gave Nate a pleading look, then said, "Nate, this is Lavender, Cindy's fairy godmother and the reason all of us are here."

Lavender gave me an offended pout. "Red, I'm so hurt! You know that stupid genie is the one to blame, the worthless jackass." Lavender swayed a little, making me stumble. She wrapped her other arm around my neck and pressed her forehead to mine. "He should have known better than to challenge a fairy. That never ends well."

"Lovely to meet you," Nate said, gently extricating me from Lavender's hold. "Would you like some help into the house?"

Lavender blew a raspberry and waved away his offer. "I'm *fine,*" she assured him loudly, drifting a few steps as she spoke. "Oh, look! There's the band. 'Bout damn time. Better go tell them where to go." She stumbled away, hitching up the hem of her dress as she went.

"Good lord," Nate mumbled, pulling my hand through the crook of his arm. "Is she always like that?"

I nodded. "Pretty much. Let's just say she's more firmly bound to the bottle than Al's genie ever was."

Nate shook his head. "Sad."

I nodded. "If it weren't for Cindy's own guilt-trip over the whole thing, I don't know what would have happened to Lavender. She'd probably be living on the streets, just another homeless drunkard."

I'd never been inside the Charmings' home before that night. I'd heard about it, even seen pictures of it. But nothing could have prepared me for the splendor and opulence of the real thing. Hand-carved marble floors and crystal chandeliers in the foyer were just the beginning. As a doorman led us into the grand ballroom, I couldn't help but stare in awe at my surroundings.

I'd never seen so many original works of art in any one place outside a museum. Picassos, Dalís, Rembrandts, Chagalls . . . I think I even saw a Renoir or two. I would have gladly skipped the party and gone on a tour instead if I hadn't had a reason for being there.

"I'll be damned!"

I whirled around at the familiar voice. "Nicky?" I grinned. "What the hell are you doing here?"

Nicky came forward and shook Nate's hand in greeting before kissing my cheek. "I could ask you two the same thing. Thought you were working tonight."

"We are," Nate confirmed. "I hear you have something interesting to share that could help in that regard."

Nicky took hold of my arm and drew us out of the main flow of partygoers milling around in the hallway. "Don't broadcast that," he whispered to us. "I don't want all these schmucks thinking they can come to me for favors. You think any of these assholes would be associated with me if my wife wasn't a Willie?"

"Where is Jules?" I asked, but the minute I uttered the question, an exquisitely beautiful woman slid up to Nicky's side and slipped her arm through his.

"Hello, Red," she said, her voice as delicate and lovely as the rest of her. "I'm surprised to see you and Nate here tonight."

I offered her a smile. "It was kind of last minute."

I liked Juliet. She was sweet, smart, pretty, kind . . . everything good and decent that a person should be. She'd come a long way since leaving her story behind. Gone was the wide-eyed innocence and naïveté of Shakespeare's tragic teen. This Juliet was perceptive and wise, and although she knew the extent of my past with Nicky, she tolerated our friendship with grace and quiet resignation.

"I do hope you enjoy yourself," she said. Then she turned

her eyes to her husband and placed a hand possessively on his chest, silently but pointedly reminding me what I had given up. "No business tonight, Nicky," she told him softly. "You promised. Red will obtain what she requires of you tomorrow as agreed."

Nicky shrugged at Nate and me. "I guess it'll keep, right? Not like Hamelin's going anywhere."

I glanced at Nate as the four of us headed into the ballroom, joining the throngs of guests already inside. He returned my glance, obviously sensing my discomfort. I felt the stares of those around me as we made our way to an area of the room a little less crowded than the rest, but random whispers still made their way to my hearing.

"Is that Tess Little? In a *dress*?"

"Dear God, I didn't know she had a figure. She always wears that dreadful *trench coat.*"

"Doesn't Red look pretty? Who knew there was a woman under all that leather?"

Abruptly I pulled Nate to a halt. "This was a mistake," I told him. "No one's going to talk to us. They all think I'm a joke. And they're right. This isn't me. I don't belong here."

Nate lifted my chin with the knuckle of his finger and forced me to meet his gaze. "You're just as beautiful as any of these women, no matter what you're wearing. And I know we're here to find out more info, but would it kill you to have a good time for a little while? Relax. I promise I won't let these harpies rip you to shreds."

"I'd be more worried about the harpies, if I were you." I gave him a saucy grin, then turned my head to the closest offender and pegged her with a knowing gaze. "'Cause if I hear one more catty remark, I'm going to shove my fist down somebody's throat."

When the woman and her companion started and scurried off to rake someone else across the coals, Nate laughed loudly. "Ah, yes," he mused, slipping an arm around my waist. "There's the Red I know and love."

I swallowed hard. There was that word again. He'd used it twice now. I was trying to assure myself that it didn't mean anything, that I was reading too much into an innocent remark, when my thoughts were sidelined by the sudden blare of trumpets announcing the arrival of our esteemed hosts.

On cue, James and Cinderella Charming ascended to the stage set up at one end of the room, all smiles and slick manners. Cindy was easily four inches taller than her Prince and cut an impressive figure in her brilliant red sheath evening gown as she took up the microphone and handed it to her husband, her smile wide and well rehearsed.

"Thank you all for coming," James said. His voice surprisingly lacked the deep timbre one would expect from a man who'd become one of the most formidable movie and TV producers in the world. "Cindy and I are delighted to have you as our guests. Please, enjoy yourselves!"

With that, he handed the microphone back to his wife, offered a wave to the crowd, then descended the steps to greet a pair of pretty ingenues, tucking one under each arm. Cindy's smile faltered a little, but then she gracefully stepped away from the stage to make way for the band and busied herself saying tremulous hellos to her guests.

"Looks like there's some trouble in paradise," Nate observed.

A loud snort on the other side of Nate made me bend forward to see who was listening in. Lavender stood at his elbow, weaving a little as she grabbed a glass of champagne from a passing waiter. "Trouble in paradise doesn't even scratch the surface," she slurred.

My brows lifted, sensing an opportunity. "You don't say?" I maneuvered around Nate and slipped my arm through Lavender's. "You look like you could use something a little stronger, Lav."

Lavender rolled her eyes. "God, yes!" She glanced around, then leaned toward me conspiratorially. "Come with me. I'll show you where they keep the really good stuff."

I cast a grin over my shoulder at Nate as Lavender led me away. Maybe the night wouldn't be a total waste after all.

Chapter 36

I blew out a puff of air and glanced at the clock. I'd already been sequestered in the upstairs sitting room for the better part of an hour, listening to Lavender's drunken ramblings about her life with the fabled Prince and Princess, and all indications were that she was far from finished.

"I'm so sick of being treated like a servant!" she seethed. She tossed back a shot of tequila and slammed the glass down on the table where we sat. "That bastard thinks he's still a prince, thinks he can order everyone around. It's always 'Whip up a spell for me, Lavender;' 'Cast a quick curse for me, Lavender;' 'Find the next starlet for me to bang, Lavender.'"

My eyes widened a bit. "James sleeps around on Cindy?"

Lavender's answering expression assured me I was a naive idiot. "Are you kidding? He's getting a new piece of ass every week. And Cindy just turns a blind eye, pretends he's the paragon of virtue she married. Paragon of bullshit, maybe. It makes me *sick* when I think about what I went through to bring them together. She would have been better off married to a nice farmer—or maybe a footman. Anyone's better than that arrogant asshole."

"It looked like something was eating at Cindy tonight," I

pointed out. "Maybe she's not ignoring his extracurricular activities as much as you think."

Lavender poured another shot, sloshing some of the liquid onto the table. "She's worried about her little pet, Caliban. Word is he OD'd on fairy dust earlier today."

I shifted a little in my seat at the reminder. "So I heard."

"I told her he was bad news—once a monster, always a monster—but she wouldn't listen to me. No one listens to Lavender." She turned around to face the door and bellowed, "I'm just a fairy *freaking* godmother—what the hell do I know?"

I glanced nervously toward the door, but when no one came rushing in to respond to her outburst, I said, "I'm betting you know a lot more than they give you credit for."

Her face brightened and she leaned over to give me a sloppy hug. "I knew I liked you," she gushed, her face so close to mine the stench of tequila on her breath made me cough a little.

"Okay, okay," I said, patting her on the back. Then, extricating myself from her hold, I asked, "So, how does James feel about Caliban?"

Lavender made a face and rolled her eyes. "He can't stand him. Thinks he's an arrogant jackass and he sure as hell didn't want to back his TV show, but Cindy kept badgering him until he caved."

"Seems like Cindy is pretty concerned about Caliban's future," I observed.

"Well, she would be, wouldn't she?" Lavender said, tossing back her shot. "Can't have her lover being just another chef, now can she? That wouldn't be good for her image."

I blinked rapidly in surprise. "Lover? I thought Caliban was involved with his assistant, Sebille."

Lavender laughed. "He is—well, to some extent. That's part of the problem. Cindy and Sebille have very different ideas about Caliban's career trajectory. Cindy wants him to be respectably famous. Sebille wants to build an empire and place herself at the helm. That conniving bitch sees Caliban as her ticket to power and control. It's all about control with Sebille. I pity anyone who tries to wrest that control away. . . ."

"Dear God," I breathed. "It all makes sense now."

Lavender pulled a disgusted face. "Glad it does to someone! Nothing in this freaking place makes any sense to me." She met my eyes, her own filled with sadness and heartbreak that went far deeper than the maudlin ramblings of drunkenness. "I'd give anything to go back, Red. To put things right again. Wouldn't you?"

I stared at her for a moment, considering the question. "No," I said finally. "No, I wouldn't go back to my story. I like it much better when I can write my own."

Lavender's eyes glistened with unshed tears. "I want to write my own, too," she confided. "But I don't even know where to start."

I stood up and offered Lavender my hand. "Come on. Why don't you start by sleeping this off?"

Lavender allowed me to pull her to her feet and put her arm around my shoulders as I led her from the sitting room and into the hall. "Then what?" she asked. "When I wake up in the morning and am still trapped in the same shitty story?"

"Then you scrap it all and start over."

I closed Lavender's bedroom door behind me and made my way down the hall to where I assumed the stairs would be. The sound of the band playing downstairs filtered up to the second floor, filling the hallway with music, so I figured I had to be heading in the right direction. I came to an intersection of hallways and paused to listen, trying to get a feel for which way I should go.

"Freaking rich people," I mumbled. "Why do they have to build such damn big houses?"

Suddenly, a door behind me flew open and the sound of angry voices seeped into the hallway.

"You son of a bitch!" a woman yelled. "You never can admit when you're wrong!"

"That's because I never am!" a man roared back. "I told you that jackass was going to screw up. I told you he was on D, but you just *had* to help him. You just *had* to keep nagging me to push him out to Hollywood. If he's fried his brain on the dust, I'm out *millions!*"

I couldn't see who was talking, but based on the topic of conversation, it had to be James and Cindy. I glanced around me, trying to figure out where to go. The last thing I wanted was to be discovered roaming around their house. The voices grew louder, and I saw Cindy backing out of the room into the hallway.

I cursed under my breath and dove for the nearest door. A small lamp on a desk across the room was the only light in what appeared to be a study. I closed the door most of the way, leaving it open just a crack so that I could hear the rest of the argument.

"It's always about money with you, isn't it?" Cindy demanded, her voice thick with tears as she stormed down the hall toward the room where I was hiding. "You don't give a damn about how I'm hurting."

"Hurting about that loser you're screwing?" James shot back. "Are you kidding me?"

"Don't pretend you care about anything I do," Cindy screamed. "All you care about is making the next business deal or nailing the next piece of tail!"

"This conversation's over," James said, standing just on the other side of the door. "Go down and play princess with your friends. Maybe they'll give a shit about your pathetic problems."

"You asshole," Cindy sniffled. "I'm through with you."

"You know how to find the door."

I heard Cindy sob and hurry off down the hall. James

sighed and muttered something under his breath, then grabbed the doorknob and started to push the door open. Panicked, I backed away into the shadows and held my breath, but the door didn't swing in any farther.

"What are you doing here?" I heard James say to someone else in the hall. "I told you not to come here again."

I heard a low voice, a woman's voice, but it was too quiet to place. James let out a frustrated huff in response to whatever she said.

"Fine," he said tersely. "But this is the last time."

I crept back toward the door and listened, straining to hear their receding footsteps.

"That was a close one."

With a startled scream, I spun around, my heart racing. The shadows around the desk parted as Nate leaned forward with a grin.

"What the *hell* is wrong with you!" I hissed. "You scared the shit out of me!"

He chuckled softly. "Sorry. I couldn't exactly say anything when you popped in unexpectedly, what with James and Cindy right outside the door."

"What are you doing in here?" I asked, still whispering.

Nate shrugged. "Snooping around. When you didn't come back, I decided to do some exploring."

I lifted my brows. "Find anything?"

Nate pushed a document forward on the desk pad. "Found the bill for Dave Hamelin's exterminating services."

I took a look at it and whistled softly. "Damn. I'm in the wrong business."

"You and me both. What did Lavender tell you?"

I quickly filled him in on my conversation with the forlorn fairy.

Nate shook his head. "Just goes to show the rich can be just as screwed up as the rest of us."

"Let's get out of here," I said, looking over my shoulder at the door. "I don't want to get caught where we shouldn't be."

"Works for me."

We quickly made our way out of the room and down the hall without incident. The band was still going strong and the partiers were deep in their cups at this point, their voices loud in the crowded ballroom.

"This place is giving me a headache," I called out to Nate over the din.

Nate nodded and pointed to a set of French doors leading to a garden. "Let's go outside."

The moment we stepped outside, I inhaled deeply, letting the night air fill my lungs and clear my head of all the dissonance so that I could think clearly.

Nate came up to stand beside me, resting his forearms on the waist-high garden wall as he stared out into the darkness. We stood in silence for several minutes, the strains of lively big band standards and the fragrance of early spring flowers drifting to us on the breeze, reminding me that sometime within the last couple of days we must have crossed into April. The realization that I'd been so consumed by recent events that I'd lost track of the days made me feel nostalgic for the time when I only had to worry about sex offenders, drug dealers, and thieves.

I leaned back against the wall, watching the partygoers through the glass doors. They danced and laughed as if there was no evil in the world, no wickedness stalking them at every turn. Just once I would've liked to be that ignorant and naive again.

"I'd offer a penny for your thoughts," Nate said, "but I have a feeling they're worth more than that."

"Sorry," I replied on a sigh, offering him a distracted smile. "I was just wishing . . ." I shook my head, leaving the thought unfinished, not wanting to let on how lost and lonely and tired I felt.

"Wishing what?" Nate pressed.

"Nothing," I said, waving away his question. "Never mind." I pushed off the wall and headed toward the doors. "Why don't we take off? I think we got what we came for."

He grasped my hand, pulling me back toward him. "I didn't."

I swallowed hard as he pulled me close, cradling my hand up to his chest while his other arm went around my waist. His hand splayed across the small of my back as he pressed my body up against his.

"What exactly *were* you after?" I asked, liking all too well how nicely my curves fit against his in all the right places.

Nate's mouth hitched up in one corner. "I was hoping to share at least one dance with you tonight. It *is* a party, after all."

I averted my gaze, trying to hide the blood rising in my cheeks. "I'm a lousy dancer," I murmured, attempting to extricate myself from his hold.

His grasp on my waist tightened. "Don't worry. I'll lead."

He pulled me in a little closer so that every inch of our bodies pressed together, then began to sway ever so slightly, letting me get a sense of how his muscles felt with each step, his hip nudging mine just enough to indicate which way I should move.

"That's not so bad, is it?" he asked softly.

I shook my head, finding it hard to breathe. "No, it's not bad at all."

We moved together in silence until Nate began to hum quietly with the music, his deep rumble bringing goose bumps to my flesh. I tried to ignore the heat building in the pit of my stomach and follow Nate's lead, but it was growing increasingly hard to concentrate. Suddenly assaulted by a treasonously libidinous image of tearing open Nate's shirt, I stumbled, coming down hard on his toes. He chuckled as we tripped over each other and nearly careened down the stone steps that led into the garden.

"Sorry," I groaned. "I'm not used to letting someone else take control."

Nate's gaze locked with mine. "Trust me, Red," he said, his voice deeper than I'd ever heard it before. "Just close your eyes and let go."

I nodded, then tucked in closer to him, resting my head against his chest and closing my eyes. The steady hammering of his heart kept time with mine as we began to sway again, moving in a slow, meandering path. For a moment, wrapped in Nate's arms, I felt a perfect peace. There was a quiet stillness in my soul like none I'd ever known. And when the final blast of horns signaled the end of the song, I didn't pull away, and Nate's hold on me didn't lessen.

The next song started—a jazzy, upbeat number that was twice the tempo of the one before, but Nate and I remained still but for our increasingly ragged breathing. And when I could no longer deny the tension between us, I turned my face up to his, anxious to see if he sensed it, too.

Nate's hand came up to cup my cheek. As his thumb smoothed lazily across my skin, he pulled me a little closer, lifting me up onto my toes and pressing me more tightly against him.

My head began to spin and I leaned into him for support, my fist tightening around his lapel. Staring up into those dark, bottomless eyes, I felt like I was drowning, drifting away on a wave of heat that saturated my body with blissful, healing warmth. And suddenly I had to touch him, had to press my fingertips against the planes of his face and bring more of that warmth close to me.

I let my fingertips drift down the line of his jaw toward soft, full lips, then under his chin, gently urging him closer. At the same moment, Nate's hand slid around to the nape of my neck, tilting my head back just a little.

My eyes fluttered closed as Nate's lips found mine in a slow, unhurried kiss, his mouth pressing against mine so tenderly it stole my breath. I gasped a little as his lips brushed mine again, a tentative feint, followed by a more certain advance.

I kissed him back, my body flooding with heat in great crashing waves with each pass of his lips, my heart hammering in my chest. At some point, my arms went around his neck, and his arms wrapped around my waist, holding me so tightly I could barely breathe. But I didn't care. Nothing in the world mattered at that moment but the taste of him, the warmth of his breath against my skin as his mouth left mine to press a line of kisses down the curve of my throat.

When his path led him to the sensitive juncture where neck and shoulder met, I gasped, twining my fingers through his hair to keep him where he was. And for a moment he obliged. But then with a groan, he abruptly released me, stumbling back a few steps to put distance between us. He stared at me for a horrible, confusing moment, his chest heaving.

"God damn it," he muttered under his breath, his voice strained and thin.

"What's wrong?" I asked, bemused by his sudden withdrawal. I shuddered, chilling without his body to warm me.

He raked his hands through his hair a couple of times, then took a hurried step to his right, then back to his left like he wanted to bolt but wasn't sure which direction offered the best route for escape.

"Nate?" I took a step toward him, extending my hand to stay his agitated pacing. "What's going on? I thought—"

He halted and gave me a pained look, cutting off my words. "I want you," he ground out, his voice shot with desire. "I want you so badly, I could press you up against the garden wall and take you right here, right now."

I blinked at him a few times, startled—and undeniably aroused—by his frank confession. My own voice was little more than a breath when I asked, "So, what's stopping you?"

Nate's shoulders sagged and his expression went from pained to agonized. "The rest of the truth."

Chapter 37

My heart sank at his words. I could only hope that what he wanted to tell me wasn't as ominous as his tone suggested. I straightened to my full height and smoothed the wrinkles we'd created in the front of my dress.

"Well," I said, lifting my chin, "I guess now's as good a time as any. Spill it."

"Why don't we head home," Nate replied, his steps purposeful as he strode toward the doors to the ballroom. "We can talk there."

"Afraid I'll make a scene?" I called to his back.

Nate's steps halted, and his head hung down between his shoulders.

"Damn," I mumbled. "I was only joking. This must be a real pisser."

"I'm in love with you," Nate blurted.

I swear I didn't breathe for a good thirty seconds. When I finally exhaled, it burst from me as, "Oh."

Nate turned back around and took a couple of steps toward me, but stopped short of arm's length. "I have been in love with you since the moment I saw you," he confessed. "I just wasn't sure what to call it back then."

I frowned, remembering the day I'd met him all those years ago. "You fell in love with me in the FMA cafeteria?"

Nate chuckled. "I remember that day. I bought you a piece of cake."

I nodded. "Chocolate with raspberry jam between the layers."

Nate's head tilted to one side, a smile curving his lips. "You remember."

"It was damned good cake."

His laugh erupted from him, making me feel a little more at ease, but then his brows drew together in a frown. "I wanted so badly to talk to you, to be near you," he confessed. "I had waited so long."

"What are you talking about?" I asked warily. "You'd just come over."

Nate sighed and shoved his hands into his pockets. "I wish that were the case. But that day wasn't the first time we'd met."

I blinked at him, trying to figure out if he was joking. "I think I would have remembered meeting you before, Nate." I laughed a little. "I mean, a girl doesn't forget someone as *dashing* as you, right?"

Nate lowered his head, averting his gaze for a moment. "Tess—"

"You know I've always been drawn to you," I interrupted. "I would've remembered that kind of . . . *pull* between us if I'd felt it before." I placed my hand lightly on his arm. "You—you feel it, too. Don't you?"

He lifted his eyes, his expression one of longing. "Hell yes, I feel it! I've felt it from the minute I found you lying in the woods clinging to life."

I shook my head a little, involuntarily taking a step back from him. "What are you talking about?"

Nate advanced, not letting me put any additional distance between us. "I wasn't supposed to even be there that day," he said. "It was a scheduling mistake."

"Knock it off," I ordered, not liking where he was going with this. "This isn't funny."

"When I knelt to collect you, I put my hand on your heart," he continued, ignoring my protests, "and suddenly I was privy to all you'd suffered, all you'd endured. And you felt my presence. You *saw* me, Tess. No one had ever *seen* me before—not like you did. They usually just sense my presence, feel me drawing near. But not you. You looked up at me, your eyes so clear and resolute, so fearless. And you saw into my soul just as I had seen into your heart."

"Shut up, Nate!" I barked, my voice cracking. "I'm serious!"

He took another step toward me. I took two in the opposite direction. "I expected you to plead with me to spare your life like anyone else would have," he went on, "but instead, you took my hand and said only, 'I understand.' I couldn't collect you after that. How could I end the life of the one person who'd ever seen me for what I really was?"

I pressed my lips together, growing more furious with each word he uttered. "Oh, I'm seeing you all right," I spat. "You're a lying son of a bitch—I just can't figure out *why* you're lying to me about something like this!"

Nate sighed. "It's the truth. I swear it."

"Prove it."

"Ask Nicky," Nate replied. "He'll confirm the story."

I frowned in confusion. "How the hell would *he* know anything about it?"

"Because the bullet in his chest that night in the alley was meant for you," Nate confessed. "After that day in the woods, I couldn't just walk away and never look back. I checked in on you whenever I could, watching over you from the shadows when I wasn't collecting Ordinaries."

My eyes widened. "You were *stalking* me?"

"No, no," Nate said hurriedly. "It wasn't like that. I was just . . . curious. I'd never come across anyone like you before. I wanted to try to figure you out."

"And you just happened to be there that night in the alley?" I asked, not bothering to hide my skepticism.

"Actually, yes," he retorted. "I happened to pop in that night just in time to deflect the bullet away from you. It hit Nicky instead. But when I saw the pain and fear in your eyes as he slipped away, I couldn't take him. For your sake, I broke with protocol once again and gave Nicky a second chance—but only on the condition he'd help me look after you and never reveal what I'd done."

I couldn't believe what Nate was saying. It was too fantastic to believe—even for a Tale. Still . . . something about his story brought back glimpses of shadowy images, half-remembered memories that chilled me and comforted me at the same time.

"When my boss decided to assign a full-time Reaper to the Tales a few years later," he continued, "I requested the assignment, but because of your unique life force signatures it meant giving up my immortality and taking on corporeal form again. In order to stay grounded in the Here and Now as one of you, I had to claim connection to a specific Tale." His gaze locked with mine. "I chose you."

The news hit me in the gut as sure as if he'd punched me. "What?"

"My life, my very existence is tied to yours," he explained. "When you finally die, it will be my last collection. We'll cross over together."

I walked backward another couple of steps until I bumped into the garden wall and nearly tumbled over the top of it. I sat down on the cool stone, my knees too weak to support me. "I don't believe this," I whispered.

Suddenly, the fact that he was a Reaper, a dealer of death, was all too real to me. He was to have been my executioner that day in the woods and would have torn my soul from my body without a second thought had my reaction not made him hesitate. But what he took to be fearlessness was actually hopeless resignation to my fate. In truth, I'd never been more terrified than at the moment when I'd stared Death in the face. To know that that horrible glimpse of darkness was the man before me struck me so violently I wanted to hurl.

Nate sat down beside me. "Something happened to us that day in the woods," he told me. "You said yourself you've always been drawn to me. You belong to me in a way you could never belong to anyone else. Why do you think you could never commit to anyone?"

I scowled at the ground, my mind racing. I had commitment issues, sure, but tons of people had the same problem. Considering what I'd been through with Seth . . . I shook my head, pushing away the thought before I'd even completed it.

Seth was an excuse. A cop out. In fact, there for a while—

"There was Nicky," I blurted. "I loved him. I could have been happy with him." But as soon as I said it, I knew it wasn't true. I closed my eyes and said softly, "Something changed after that night in the alley."

"After I visited him, you couldn't be with him anymore, could you?" Nate guessed. "It felt wrong, didn't it?"

I squeezed my eyes shut even tighter. "This is crazy."

"I wanted to tell you," Nate said. "I kept waiting, hoping you'd get to know me first. I guess I hoped someday you'd fall in love with me, too."

My eyes snapped open, all the better to glare at him. "You've been playing me this whole time."

"It wasn't like that." He brought his hand up to caress my cheek, but I reflexively smacked it away.

"Don't touch me!" I hissed. "You're a lie. Everything about you has been a lie! You attached your life to mine without my knowledge or permission, Nate! How can I trust anything you say after knowing that? And I actually thought—" I bit off my words, fighting back furious tears. I cleared my throat, forcing the tears away. "I actually thought that I was falling in love with you. Now I know it's nothing more than the connection you *forced* on me."

"Tess—"

"Shut up!" I snapped, launching to my feet, feeling defiled in a way I never imagined possible. "I can't listen to any more of this." Once more, I strode toward the French doors, but Nate swooshed into my path, blocking my escape. When I tried to dart around him, he took me by the shoulders, keeping me where I was.

"You have to understand—"

"I don't have to understand a goddamn thing!" I shot back. "I'm done, Nate. I don't ever want to see you again."

Nate's hands dropped to his sides. "What?"

The part of me that only recently had come back to life felt like it was dying all over again as I said, "Don't come near me. I don't want to see you again until you come to make that final call."

The look of heartbreak on Nate's face was almost enough to make me cave. "Red, let's talk about this."

"There's nothing to talk about," I hissed. "We're done here."

I turned my back on him and rushed toward the ballroom, but as a thought occurred to me, I paused and turned to look over my shoulder at him. "You know, Nate, you should have just let me die there in the woods. Because Seth's betrayal? It's nothing compared to yours."

I didn't bother to wipe away the tears of disappointment that made their way to my cheeks as I jerked open the doors to the ballroom and pushed my way through the crowd. I vaguely heard a litany of protests as I bumped into intoxicated partygoers, but, in keeping with tradition, I was determined to run away as far and as fast as possible before full-blown emotion set in.

I was nearly clear of the crowds when I heard someone calling my name, but I didn't even bother looking to see who it was. Instead, I kicked off my shoes and scooped them up before racing for the door. The last thing I wanted was to stop and chat with some two-faced asshole pretending to give a shit about me just to get the latest gossip and blab it to the rest of Tale society.

I'd almost made it to the front door when the sound of hurried footsteps behind me on the marble alerted me someone was tailing me. I swung around, ready for a fight, but Nicky grabbed my fist before I could take a swing at him.

"What's doing?" he demanded. "Where's Grimm?"

I jerked my hand from his grasp. "Rotting in hell, for all I care," I spat. "Feel free to join him, you bastard!"

Nicky gaped at me in startled confusion.

"You should have told me," I hissed.

Nicky's expression went slack as realization dawned. "So you could tell me to go piss up a rope?" he replied. "If you'd known about my deal with Nate, you wouldn't have let me hold up my end of the bargain."

"You're damn straight! But I didn't have a choice, did I?"

"I didn't have a choice, either!" he shot back. "I loved you, Red! You think I wouldn't have agreed to Nate's deal? I wanted to take care of you. How many times did I ask you to marry me?"

I huffed angrily. "Six."

"A guy doesn't keep trying if he doesn't give a damn," he pointed out. "The only reason I gave up is because you hooked up with someone else. Kind of got the point across."

I crossed my arms and pointedly looked away from him, knowing that my anger was misplaced. It wasn't Nicky's fault that I was in this mess. "I'm so sorry, Nicky," I finally said, my throat tight. "I didn't mean to hurt you. I didn't understand—" I shook my head, not knowing what else to say.

There was a long moment of silence before Nicky said, "Did Nate tell you everything?"

I shrugged. "How the hell would I know?"

"He's in love with you, you know."

I turned my gaze back to Nicky. "So he said."

"Red—"

"Spare me the lecture, Nicky," I interrupted.

He sighed, then ran his hand gently down my arm. "Want me to take you home?"

I shook my head. "No, I don't want to go home. Nate might come by to talk to me, and Gran doesn't need to get sucked into the drama. I just want to go hole up in a hotel or something."

"Like hell," Nicky said, taking out his phone. After a quick conversation with someone on the other end of the line, he opened the front door for me. "Come on. I'll take you to my place. You can stay with us tonight."

I started to protest, but he put his hand on my back and ushered me out the door to the waiting limo, closing the front door behind us. "Get in before I throw you in the trunk—and you know I will."

"What about Jules?" I said. "You can't leave her here."

"I'll come back and pick her up after I get you settled."

"Nicky, I—" My words were cut short when I heard the door to the house opening again and glanced over my shoulder to see a woman standing in the doorway, the light from the foyer illuminating her fiery red hair until it seemed to sizzle. "Sebille."

Not pausing to think, I broke free from Nicky's hold and rushed her, intent on taking her down and dragging her ass in, but she gave me a slow, taunting smile and vanished into thin air just as I reached the top step.

I screamed a wordless curse and glanced around, frantic to pick up any kind of trail. "Where'd she go?" I shouted. "Nicky, did you see where she went?"

Nicky had drawn his gun at my reaction and now grabbed my hand, pulling me back toward the car. "No, I didn't. Get in the car, Red. Let me get you out of here."

"But I—"

"Are you carrying?" he snapped. When I didn't answer, he ordered, "Then get in the damn car!"

With one last look around, I scrambled into the limo, Nicky behind me. He pounded on the glass and the car lurched forward.

"You know about Sebille," I guessed.

"No," Nicky said, "but the fact you went ape shit when you saw her tipped me off."

"I need the information from Hamelin's hard drive," I told him. "What did your guy find?"

"Nothing," he told me. "He just handed over the files he retrieved. I went through the data myself—it was mostly business records and a shitload of porn—but I finally came across a document labeled 'Side Jobs.' Turned out to be a record of a scam he was running. He'd use rats to spy on wealthy Tales and gather information he sold to somebody. Then the same Tales would pay him to go in and kill the rats."

"Does he say who he was working for?" I asked, my heart racing. "Does he name names?"

Nicky shook his head. "Dunno. I didn't have a chance to read the whole thing. When we get to the house, I'll give you the flash drive and you can read it for yourself."

I leaned across the seat and pressed a kiss to Nicky's cheek. "Thanks," I said sincerely. "For everything."

Chapter 38

Nicky flipped on the light in the guest room. "Here you go."

I set my shoes next to the nightstand, feeling a little awkward, and offered him a tight smile. "Thanks."

"I'll grab you some of Juliet's clothes to put on if you want to change," he said. Then he nodded toward a desk in front of the window where a desktop computer sat. "You can use that to look at Hamelin's files. I'll grab the flash drive out of the safe."

"Take these, will you?" I asked, handing him Eliza's jewelry. "I don't want to lose them."

Nicky's fingers closed around the jewelry as he held my gaze. "You looked beautiful tonight, Red."

I gave him a weak smile. "Just a little girl playing dress up," I scoffed. "Just ask Nate."

Nicky's brows drew together in a frown. "What do you mean?"

"He told me once that I was just a scared little girl still running from the Big Bad Wolf," I explained. "Except when he said that I thought he was talking about Seth."

"But he wasn't."

"Nope."

Nicky offered me a rather sad, sympathetic smile, but didn't say anything. What *could* he say? He'd seen my emotional duck and cover routine firsthand.

"Do you know what bothers me most about what happened between us tonight?" I continued. "I'm not sure if I ran out on Nate because I was angry—or because I was afraid."

Nicky gazed at me for a moment, then took a step forward and grasped my chin gently with his fingertips. "The fact that you're even asking that question should tell you something, kid." He sighed somewhat wistfully. "It certainly tells *me* something." With that, he bent and pressed a kiss to my forehead, then turned and left the room.

A few minutes later, he returned and handed me a pair of gray leggings and a voluminous black sweater. "I'm going to head back and pick up Jules," he announced, going over to the desk and setting the flash drive beside the keyboard. "I still give the staff the night off on weekends, so you need anything, help yourself."

"Are you sure Jules won't mind me staying here?" I asked.

Nicky laughed as he backed out of the room. "She'll get over it, if she does. That dame's forgiven me for a whole lot worse than helping out a friend."

I lifted my brows, curious to know exactly what Nicky was referring to and hoping like hell he wasn't about to admit to something I'd have to arrest him for, but he just gave me a wink and shut the door.

As soon as he was gone, I wiggled out of Elizabeth's dress and hung it up in the closet, then pulled on the clothes I'd borrowed from Jules. She was a few inches taller, so the sweater came almost to my knees, but it was warm and comfy and made me feel a hell of a lot more at ease than a cocktail dress.

I was just booting up the computer when my stomach growled, reminding me I hadn't eaten anything in a couple of hours. Deciding to make myself a quick snack before looking at Hamelin's journal, I made my way downstairs and into the kitchen. Moonlight streaming in through the kitchen window illuminated an industrial-sized stainless steel refrigerator, catching my eye and making my stomach sing with joy.

I flipped on the kitchen light and began rummaging around in the fridge, finally grabbing some leftover turkey and other random ingredients for a sandwich. I tried not to let my mind drift while I sliced the tomato, but couldn't help thinking about the lunch Nate had prepared for me a few days before, which led to thoughts of the kiss we'd shared and of what he'd confessed to me.

I set aside the knife and added the tomato slices to the other ingredients, frowning with indecision. Part of me wanted to call Nate, give him the chance to explain why he'd done what he had, let him convince me to forgive him. The other part of me wanted to kick his lying—although admittedly sexy—ass.

I sighed and closed my eyes, trying not to think about the way his kiss had electrified me, how incredible his arms had felt around me.

But it was no good.

I glanced at the phone hanging on the wall, toying with the idea of giving him a call. But what the hell was I going to say?

"Gosh, Nate, I know you're a lying bastard and all, but I've been thinking about what you said about the garden wall. . . ." somehow seemed a little hypocritical.

I might as well just come right out and say, "I'm pissed as hell you played me and I'm not even sure I can forgive you, but, hey, I wouldn't mind sleeping with you. . . ."

Of course, that was if he even took my call. I mean, *I* was the one who'd said I never wanted to see him again, wasn't I? For all I knew, he'd tell me to piss off before I'd get the first sentence out of my mouth. Probably better to just walk away and never look back, forget anything had ever happened.

Yeah, right. Easier said than done.

The thought of never again seeing that cocky grin of his, or hearing his infectiously uninhibited laugh, or feeling the comforting weight of his arms wrapped around me, was far more terrifying than anything I'd faced in all my years as an Enforcer, that was for damned sure.

And, yet, damn it! He'd *lied* to me. He'd manipulated my relationships, my heart, my fate. . . .

The hurt and sorrow in Nicky's eyes when he reminded me how much he'd loved me made me wonder what would have happened had Nate not showed up in the alley that night so long ago. Would I have ended up with Nicky after all? Or would I have just bled to death there in his arms when the bullet meant for me struck home?

I pressed my lips together in a stubborn line and gave myself a hard mental shake. It was pointless to dwell on the what-ifs. Especially when it was becoming increasingly clear to me that what really lay at the root of my indignation wasn't so much what Nate had done to be close to me as it was the realization that I wasn't as in control of my own destiny as I'd thought.

I'd always fancied myself to be quite the author, penning my story the way *I* wanted it to read, no longer at the mercy of the scribes, but such a naive attitude was just fucking stupid. I couldn't be in control of everything all the time. No one could. Life wasn't a series of plot complications that conveniently followed the Aristotelian model to a tidy resolution. That really *did* only happen in the fairytales. If anything, the jacked up series of events of my life made me even more Ordinary than Tale—which, when I got right down to it, was what I'd been going for all along, wasn't it?

I blew out a quick breath and shook my hands before picking up the phone, then snatched up the receiver before I could change my mind again. But my thumb hovered over the numbers as my pride reared its head.

"Mmm. Humble pie . . ." I muttered, shoving my pride aside with a resigned sigh. "Tasty."

I had dialed the first three numbers when the impact of what felt like a ton of muscle slammed into me so hard the phone flew from my grasp and clattered onto the floor. I sailed through the air landing hard on my hip and elbow as I struck the ground and slid to a stop against the back door.

What the hell?

Pain lanced through my leg and back when I tried to push myself to my feet, eliciting an involuntary moan. I had just made it to my knees when another blow struck me in the ribs, sending me crashing into the bar stools surrounding the kitchen island.

Dazed and disoriented from the pain, I scooted out from under the wreckage and rolled over in time to see a great mass of fur and claws swiping down in a savage arc. With a startled cry, I swung the remains of the bar stool, blocking the attack before the razor-sharp claws could rip out my esophagus.

The beast howled in fury and swung again, knocking the stool from my hands and sending it smashing into the stove.

Not pausing to observe the damage, I scrambled on hands and knees around to the other side of the island and heaved myself to my feet, snatching up the carving knife from the counter.

"Is that the best you can do?" I taunted, trying not to wince as my damaged rib cage sent a new stab of pain through my gut.

The creature rose up onto its hind legs and shimmered briefly, the white fur and thick muscle fading away in a haze of light to reveal a completely nude Sebille Fenwick, her perfect teeth bared, her green eyes blazing with rage.

I gasped, the truth knocking the wind out of me. "You," I whispered, pressing a hand to my side to stave off the pain enough that I could order my chaotic thoughts. "You weren't using Seth to commit the murders. It was you all along."

"Little slow on the uptake, Red," she sneered, prowling slowly toward the island. "I'm *so* disappointed. I was told you'd be a threat, that you'd be the one we'd have to worry about putting all the pieces together."

I inched to my left, mirroring each step she made, careful to keep the island between us. "Well, I think I've got your number now, Sebille." Relying on a Tale villain's compulsion to recount a nefarious plot to buy me some time, I said, "Mind if I throw out my theory, see how it sticks?"

She gave me a smile so cold it made me shiver. "By all means. Go ahead and dazzle me with your intellect."

I sighed inwardly, grateful Sebille was as egomaniacal as any other villain I'd met. Once a Tale, always a Tale, I guess.

"You and Dave had cooked up a scheme to spy on the wealthy, gather info to blackmail them into doing what you wanted," I said, kicking debris aside so I wouldn't trip over it. "It was all going great until Julie figured it out and wanted no part of the scheme. When Dave called and told you what had happened, you knew you'd have to take Julie out."

I saw her eyes spark and knew I'd hit the mark with that one.

"And Dale Minnows was threatening to pull his support, wasn't he? He knew Todd was too volatile, a risk even in Hollywood," I went on. "You took him out to keep him from complicating negotiations—after all, you already had his money, why would you need his influence? You had the same problem with Tim Halloran—you and he didn't see eye to eye on how to run things. He insisted on having a hand in management and badgered you into putting Seth in charge of the operations here."

"Very good, Red," she cooed. "Go on."

I continued circling, glancing down to see if I could spot the phone in the process. "I'm thinking Gran was a warning to me—or maybe just a red herring to throw me off the trail."

Sebille's mouth lifted in one corner as she hunched a little lower, her eyes beginning to glimmer with a predatory hunger. "Well, you *are* a smart girl. Maybe I underestimated you. How about poor little Simple Simon? Have you figured out that one?"

"I'm guessing Simon overheard something he shouldn't

have while making a delivery," I said. "Did he come across you in wolf form? Overhear you plotting? You might have to help me out on that one."

"He discovered me calling my little spies," Sebille said with a pitying sigh. "Terribly sad, really. I *did* like Simon."

I stepped over a fallen bar stool and felt the phone hit my bare foot. "And the attack on Trish at the lab," I continued, sliding the phone around with me as I shuffled another couple of steps. "You had to destroy the evidence before we figured out the werewolf wasn't Seth. But when you found out he'd visited me, you had to kill Molly to put him back in our crosshairs."

Sebille shrugged nonchalantly. "Not quite, but close enough."

"The only one I can't figure out is Sarah Dickerson," I admitted with a glance at the phone, noting its exact location. "Why her?"

Sebille's face transformed with a violent rage. "Sarah," she spat, "was *personal*."

"And now me," I said calmly. "Am I the last loose end?"

I'd made a full circle and now had my back to the kitchen entrance.

"No," Sebille said slowly. "Sadly, I am forbidden to kill you. My real target should be arriving home with his lovely wife any moment now."

The truth hit me square between the eyes. "Nicky."

By asking for his help in retrieving the data from Dave Hamelin's computer, I'd put him in danger. After all he'd done, after all he'd meant to me, I had signed his death warrant. Except Nate had assured me Nicky would live a long life, that he was protected. So, if Nicky's number wasn't up . . .

Well, shit. Guess it was mine. Didn't that just suck a big one?

Even so, there was no way I'd let Sebille hurt people I cared about. I'd save them or, apparently, die trying. "You'll have to get through me first," I hissed.

Sebille's eyes narrowed menacingly. "If you insist."

"What about your orders?" I jeered. "Mustn't make the master angry."

Sebille's face distorted with fury, but her voice was deadly calm when she said, "I am beginning to see my orders as nothing more than a sentimental attachment that should be severed. However, give me Dave Hamelin's hard drive, and I will perhaps reconsider."

"I don't have the hard drive," I said, warily backing away from the island toward the kitchen doorway.

Sebille edged a little closer. "Of course you do. Mr. Hamelin's lovely little assistant told me all about how kind you've been and how you had offered to get the customer data for her."

"Alice is just an Ordinary," I hissed. "She doesn't know anything."

Sebille gave me a reproachful look. "Come now—do you really think I've accomplished this much by being stupid? As soon as I learned that you'd be poking around, asking questions of Alice, I sent a few of my little spies to keep watch over little Alice."

So, that's how she'd known we were at Alice's apartment.

"Even now my little friends await my command, ready to perform whatever task I set them to," Sebille continued, a sadistic gleam in her eye. "It's really quite shocking how vicious they can be."

"Leave her alone, you bitch," I growled.

"Or what?" she taunted. "You'll arrest me? That'll be tough if you're dead."

"You won't get away with this, Sebille," I told her, tightening my grip on the knife. "Even if you take me out, Nate will track your ass down and haul you in."

"The *Reaper*?" She chortled. "He will track down your killer, all right. He has suspected Seth all along, and after Seth killed that poor Ordinary woman, it was only a matter of time until he came after you—the one Tale who could bring him down."

I blinked at her, trying to keep my surprise from registering. She didn't know Seth had turned himself in. She thought she'd be in the clear once Nicky and I were eliminated. Sebille had made a critical misstep, and now it was my turn to pounce.

"That would have worked," I told her, a grin growing on my lips, "except that Seth is sitting in an FMA prison cell awaiting a hearing with the Tribunal Monday morning."

Sebille's face fell, the realization of how colossally she'd miscalculated hitting her with full force.

Taking advantage of her momentary panic, I snatched up the phone from the floor and bolted. I was already racing out of the kitchen and dialing Nate's number when I heard Sebille's roar of rage. In a split second it morphed from her voice to something far more guttural and terrifying.

I ran as hard as I could, not sure where I was going or how I planned to get Sebille away from the house. I just knew I had to move. And quick.

I had just made it as far as the foyer and was lunging for the front door when it suddenly swung open. I slid to a horrified stop when I saw Nicky and Jules framed in the doorway.

"Get out!" I screamed, waving my arm that held the knife. "Go! Go!" But when I saw Juliet's eyes widen, heard the scream building in her throat, I knew there was no time. I didn't bother turning around; I knew what was coming.

Nicky's expression was deadly as he pulled his gun. I dropped to the ground to get the hell out of the way. He fired off several shots, nailing Sebille in the chest, but the assault came too late. Several hundred pounds of muscle slammed into them, knocking Nicky through the open doorway and sending Jules to the foyer floor.

Juliet's head hit the marble with a sickening *thwack*.

"NO!" I screamed, the sound burning my throat as it split

the air. Without thinking, I dropped the phone and charged at Sebille as she attempted to claw her way back to her feet. I landed on her back and plunged the knife deep into her flesh.

Sebille reared onto her hind legs with a furious cry, throwing me off her back and into the wall. I felt the drywall dent behind my head and shoulders, but quickly shook off the pain.

Apparently thinking I was out of commission, Sebille prowled toward Nicky, who'd dragged himself back to Jules's side. A low growl rumbled in Sebille's throat as she hunched over, preparing to strike, but Nicky didn't hear, his attention focused on trying to revive his wife in spite of the thick pool of blood creating a crimson crown around her head.

"Nicky!"

His head jerked up just in time to see what was coming. With no time to get off another shot, he dove out of the way, taking only a savage swipe from Sebille's claws instead of the full assault, but the blow was enough to rip through his clothes and slice open his abdomen as it spun him in midair. Nicky landed hard on his shoulder and rolled to his ruined stomach. He tried to push up on his knees, but collapsed again with a choked cry of pain.

Not waiting for Sebille to go in for the kill, I launched myself at her, barreling into her side and taking her down to the ground. I plunged the knife once more into her thick fur, this time planting it firmly in her chest and ripping down. Blood gushed from the chest wound and spurted from her mouth as I struck again and again.

But she wasn't going down easy. She let out a roar and gnashed at me with her massive jaws, her teeth grazing my arm. I yelped and reflexively caught her with a left cross, then struck again with my blade.

It took several minutes and countless blows before I realized she had gone still and that the shimmering incandescence of transformation had begun.

Trembling uncontrollably, I let the knife fall from my

grasp and scrambled toward where Nicky and Jules lay. Two separate pools of blood crept slowly toward one another, finally intermingling and becoming indistinguishable.

"Oh, God," I moaned. "No, no, no." I went to Jules first, putting my arm under her neck and lifting her up so I could check her injury with my other hand. What I found when I pulled my hand away made me heave. Knowing there was nothing I could do, I gently set her back down before quickly moving over to Nicky. He still had a pulse, thank Christ, but he was bleeding out too fast for his body to heal.

"Damn it!" I barked, glancing around, searching for something to staunch the flow of blood. Juliet's wrap rested on the ground a couple of feet away where it had drifted to the floor. I snatched it up and pressed it hard against Nicky's stomach. He groaned in response to the pressure, his eyes briefly fluttering open.

"Don't you die on me, Nicky!" I ordered, undoing his belt with one hand and tugging it off him. I maneuvered it around until it was positioned over the makeshift bandage and pulled it as tight as I could. "Don't you dare. I'll hunt you down in the afterlife and kick your ass if you even try it, you bastard."

His fingers closed around mine and squeezed. I looked up from tending his wound to meet his stubborn gaze and knew he would do his damnedest to hang in there. Then he gave me a weak wink before slipping into unconsciousness.

I swiped my cheek across my shoulder, clearing away the blur in my eyes, then I spun around to reach for the phone, but a sudden blow to my left cheek sent me sprawling.

What the hell?

I rolled over and gasped when I saw Sebille, once more in human form, standing over me, the wounds in her chest sealing up before my eyes. "But I killed you!"

"You have no idea of the extent of my powers, you stupid little bitch," she hissed. "*You* can't kill me!"

Suddenly millions of particles of darkness swooped in

between us, forming a vortex of swirling black smoke that settled into a solid mass in the form of a man. A man in a trench coat and fedora.

"But I can."

Sebille's eyes grew wide, horror dawning on her bloodied face just before Nate struck. His hand drove forward, penetrating the wall of Sebille's chest, making her gasp. For one heavy second they stood silent and still in a horrific tableau. Then Nate jerked his hand out, taking with him a wispy white diaphanous strand. Sebille let out an airless gasp before dropping into a graceless heap.

Nate dropped down beside me and handed me his phone before pressing his lips to mine in a hard but brief kiss. "Call headquarters," he said. "I'll be back soon."

Then he was gone.

With shaking hands, I dialed the FMA emergency number. "This is Enforcer Little," I said, my voice barely above a whisper. "There's been an incident."

Chapter 39

At some point someone gave me coffee in a paper cup. I think it might have been Trish. She had shown up with the forensics team to process the crime scene sometime between when the paramedics had taken Nicky to the hospital and when the Investigators grilled me with the same damned questions over and over.

Most of the forensics team just gave me a solemn nod in greeting but Trish actually came and put an arm around my shoulders for a moment, giving me a comforting hug. Of course, I wasn't sure if it was for her benefit or mine. She'd seen worse, I know, but I could tell this one shook her up.

I could relate.

Nate returned at one point and had a quiet conversation with the Investigators, apparently convincing them to leave me the hell alone, before disappearing again. He showed up again sometime later when they were finally carting away Sebille's body and crouched down in front of me where I sat on the floor against the wall.

"Hi, sweetheart," he said softly. "How about I take you out of here?"

I nodded. "Okay."

He took hold of my elbow and gently helped me to my

feet. My bruised and battered body screamed in protest and I groaned involuntarily as the pain hit me. "Damn hell."

Nate slipped his arm around my waist, half holding me up as we navigated the blood on the floor on our way to the door.

"Looks like Nicky's going to make it," he said, slowing his pace so we could take the front steps one at a time.

My throat tightened and my eyes blurred, so I blinked rapidly and nodded. "Good. That's good." I cleared my throat a couple of times between winces as we made it down the steps. "What about Jules?"

I felt Nate's body tense at my question and clung to his arm a little tighter. I already knew the answer, but I'd needed to hear it. I needed to be sure.

Carefully, he eased me into the car and closed the door. It was at that point that I began to shake. My whole body trembled so violently my teeth chattered, clacking together hard enough to be heard over the drone of the car's purring motor.

Nate reached over and covered my clasped hands with one of his. "I'll take you home."

I shook my head. "I don't want to go home—not looking like this. Gran worries about me enough as it is."

Nate's head bobbed once. "Okay."

As Nate drove, I sat there, shaking, bemused, guilt ridden, and keenly aware of the blood splattered on my face and clothes and matted in my hair. I don't remember much else about the ride; the scenery went by in a surreal blur as I replayed Sebille's attack over and over. At some point, I squeezed my eyes shut, hoping that would banish the horrible images of Nicky and Jules, but it only seemed to sear them indelibly in my memory.

Eventually, the car slowed and we pulled into the driveway of a quaint little bungalow nestled in what I guessed was the Calumet Heights neighborhood. The house looked like it might be tan or beige stone, but it was hard to tell under the glow of the lone streetlight.

A moment later, Nate was taking my hand and leading me inside. Too dazed to question where we were, I hobbled along obediently beside him. We went through a living room that left me with a vague impression of quiet ease and on to a bedroom that was equally soothing.

Nate left me standing in the center of the room and disappeared. I heard water come on in the next room and the sound of cabinet doors opening and closing. Then Nate reappeared.

Gingerly, he removed the blood-soaked sweater, pulling it over my head and letting it fall to the ground. Then he slid the leggings down my legs, lifting my right foot, then my left to help me step out of them. My bra and panties followed, joining the other articles in the ruined, bloody pile on the floor.

Then, without a word, Nate took my hand and led me to the bathroom where the steam from the bubble bath he'd prepared had mercifully covered the mirror so that I didn't have to see how wretched I looked.

He helped me step into the tub, then knelt down beside me. With tender hands, he wet my hair and washed it for me, his fingers massaging away the gore in languid motions. I closed my eyes, not aware that tears were running down my cheeks until I felt their searing heat and tasted the salty sting on my split lip.

When my hair was clean, Nate picked up a thick washcloth and lathered it with soap, then wiped away the worst of the blood from my face, neck, arms. Then he rinsed the cloth and wrung it out, leaving it on the side of the tub, allowing me to do the rest.

Without a word, he rose and closed the door behind him.

Alone now, I pulled my legs up to my chest and rested my forehead on my knees, letting the warmth of the water ease the worst of my physical pain, all the while knowing it wasn't the kind of warmth I needed. When the water began to lose its heat, I scrubbed my body twice more with maniacal vigor until the skin was red and sore. But no matter how hard I scrubbed, the blood of my friends could never be washed away. It was seared into my skin, etched deep into my soul, just as sure as Nate's flames of penance were etched into his.

As new tears began to make their way down my cheeks, I got out of the tub and dried off, then ran my fingers through my hair to try to restore some semblance of order to the chaos enveloping me. There were no clean clothes awaiting me, of course, so I grabbed Nate's bathrobe from the back of the door and pulled it on, wrapping it tightly around me.

When I came out of the bathroom, Nate was rummaging through his bureau drawers wearing nothing but black boxers. His own clothes, bloodied from his gentle care of me, had been added to the pile with mine.

My breath caught in my chest at the sight of him.

When he heard my gasp, Nate turned around and tossed his clean T-shirt aside as he came toward me. He didn't say a word—just took my hand and pulled me into his arms, letting me hold on to him.

I closed my eyes and pressed my cheek against his bare chest, listening to the rhythmic pounding of his heart until mine kept time. Then I turned my face up to his, planning to offer an apology for intruding, a thank-you for his tenderness, but before I could utter a word, Nate's lips were on mine, soft, warm, and as hungry for me as I was surprised to find I was for him.

There was no hesitancy this time, no uncertainty. Nate kissed me like a man on a mission, his lips demanding to know every secret, every mystery of my own. And he wasn't about to be thwarted this time.

My fingers splayed out on his muscled back, holding him against me, letting him know that I was right there with him, that I needed the warmth of his body, that I wanted his skin pressed to mine.

A moment later, the bathrobe was on the ground and I got my wish.

His hands began to explore my body, questing and eager to know every curve, every hollow, but gentle and careful as he passed over the places where my pain still raged. At some point, his lips left mine to press a delicate kiss to the bruise on my cheek and jaw, then the mottled purple and green that had appeared on my shoulder, and the tender area along my ribs.

Now kneeling before me, he slowly smoothed his hands down my legs, then back up to brace my hips. I inhaled sharply when he pressed a kiss to the bruise there. And nearly collapsed when I felt the hot flick of his tongue on the sensitive skin between my thighs. The first wave of rapture came swiftly, making me buck against the heat of his mouth. I braced myself against his strong shoulders, letting each subsequent wave crash over me and wash away my agony.

Finally, eager to do a little exploring of my own, I took his face in my hands and drew him up. As he rose, I let my fingers glide along the intricate designs that marked his penance, giving in to my urge to follow where that mesmerizing conflagration led. My touch was light, teasing, and when I traced the flames along the inside of his thigh, his breath left him on a hiss.

I couldn't help but offer him a teasing grin at the hold I had over him—both figuratively and literally. But my smugness was cut short when his mouth crashed down on mine in a frenzied renewal of the earlier conquest. He lifted me up, and I wrapped my arms and legs around him so he could carry me the few steps to his bed.

Nate tore back the comforter with one hand, then eased me down gently on the mattress, stretching out with me. The warmth I had known that day in the woods, had craved ever since, washed over me now in full force, making my head spin with dizzying desire. Nate drew away just enough to look down at me. I met his gaze, so loving and certain as he tenderly smoothed my hair away from my face, and I realized I could drown in those dark depths forever. I took his face in my hands and drew him back down. Then, in one smooth motion, he joined our bodies.

Our lovemaking was exactly that—not just sex, but the joining of two troubled hearts, the easing of two battered souls. I was surprised by how amazing it felt to be in Nate's arms, to feel him inside me. I marveled at how perfectly right it felt as my hips rose to meet his. More surprising was that instead of feeling the usual urge to run far, far away and never look back, I reached for him, drew him to me, knowing I never wanted to let him go.

We moved together in unhurried rhythm, alternately devouring and savoring every moment of such perfect union. When one particularly hungry kiss ended, the full magnitude of what was happening between us hit me, stealing my breath and making my heart hammer in my chest with a mixture of fear and joy.

I was in love with Nate.

And it wasn't just a girl's first love, or a lust-fueled infatuation, or even the cautious love of one too afraid to follow where happiness might lead. This was the love of a woman whose heart had found its home.

Apparently sensing some change in me, Nate started to draw away, his expression darkening with concern. "Tess?" he asked warily, his brows knitting together in a deep frown. "Are you okay?"

By way of answer, I wrapped my legs around his waist, keeping him where he was, then kissed him with a passionate abandon that I'd never before dreamed possible.

At that moment, lying in Nate's arms, our bodies joined, our skin pressed together, I was completely and utterly *happy*. And this time, there was no *almost* about it.

Chapter 40

I awoke with a jolt and looked around the room in a panic, trying to figure out where the hell I was. I untangled myself from the unfamiliar sheets, throwing them off me and lunging from the bed. Then the horrors of the previous night came rushing back to me—the blood, the death, the fear, the sorrow. But then the aftermath of the bloodbath at Nicky Blue's home came back to me, and I couldn't help smiling.

Nate.

I located the bathrobe I'd worn briefly the night before and pulled it on, tying the belt around my waist as I made my way into the living room. I heard the unmistakable sound of a coffee grinder and felt a whole new rush of love for the man.

"Hey ya, Red," he greeted as I entered the kitchen. "Sorry if I woke you."

"Wasn't you," I assured him, coming up behind him where he stood at the stove. I wrapped my arms around his waist and rested my cheek against his bare back. "Good morning."

"You mean evening." He glanced over his shoulder and gave me wink. "You've been asleep all day."

My eyes went wide. "Seriously? I never sleep that long." And I sure as hell had never slept at the home of one of my lovers. But I didn't know if I was quite ready to divulge to

Nate that he was the only man who'd been able to keep me at his side until morning, the only man whose arms had ever held me through the night.

Nate turned off the burner and set aside the frying pan of sautéed veggies, then turned around and pulled me closer, tucking me under his chin. "Yeah? Well, you had a pretty rough night."

My arms tightened around him. "It wasn't all bad."

He smoothed my hair, then dropped a kiss on the top of my head. "If you want to get dressed, we can head in to head-quarters, fill out all the paperwork to get a warrant for Caliban. The hospital said he's starting to improve, so we should be able to take him into custody officially in the next day or two."

I nodded. "What about Seth? We can't leave him sitting in prison when we know he's innocent. His hearing is tomorrow."

"Already taken care of," Nate assured me.

My head snapped up. "What? When?"

"I called Mary Smith first thing this morning while you were still sleeping," he confessed. "She filed for Seth's release immediately."

"Thanks," I said with a grin, then pressed a kiss to his chest. "You have a good heart, Nate Grimm."

Nate's laughter rumbled deep in his chest. "Good thing, 'cause it's all yours, sweetheart."

Now, how could I not kiss him after a comment like that? And he kissed me back with such deliberate sultriness, I was ready to go in an instant. And, considering the hard length pressing against my belly, so was he. Nate was just pushing the bathrobe from my shoulders, when the familiar melody startled me, making me jump.

"What the hell?" I muttered. "That's my ring tone."

"Elizabeth had your things delivered here this morning," Nate explained, trying to press a kiss to my throat, but I pushed him back and pegged him with a suspicious glare.

"How'd she know I was here?"

"I called her this morning, too," Nate said, pulling the bathrobe back up on my shoulders with a sigh. "I thought you'd want her to know you were okay before she heard anything about what happened with Sebille."

I blinked up at him. "I honestly hadn't even thought of that," I admitted. "But thanks. I should call Gran, too. She's probably going out of her mind with worry!" I turned to where my belongings were piled up on his kitchen table, but Nate grabbed my hand and kept me from rushing toward it.

"I talked to Gran last night after I collected Jules," he assured me. "I figured she'd hear about it as soon as Nicky's people got a call. Eddie's Nicky's emergency contact."

I stared at him for a few seconds, wondering how I'd never before noticed what an unbelievable guy he was. And, apparently, he was now *my* guy.

How cool was that?

My eyes were ridiculously blurry when I stepped forward and pressed a lingering kiss to his lips. "Thanks," I said when the kiss ended. "I'm glad you brought me here."

Nate's eyes twinkled with mischief. "Me, too. Trust me."

I laughed, grateful for some much needed levity, and swatted at his arm. "Come on," I called over my shoulder as I headed toward the bedroom. I paused at the door and turned back around. "The sooner we get going, the sooner we can get back home."

Nate's brows lifted. "Yeah?"

I gave him a wink, then went into the bedroom. As I got in the shower, I heard the rattling of the frying pan and running water in the kitchen. And when I emerged from the bathroom ten minutes later, Nate was impatiently pacing his living room, fully dressed and wearing his hat and coat.

He gathered my clothes and held them out to me. "I thought we could grab some coffee and bagels on the way."

* * *

Nate gave me a quick kiss, then headed off down the hall to request the warrant for Caliban's arrest while I went looking for Trish. Seeing as how our murderer was lying on a gurney in the makeshift morgue, the results of Trish's investigation didn't really matter anymore, but I was still curious about a few things. Besides, Trish had been so shaken up at the crime scene, I wanted to see how she was doing.

Unfortunately, when I got to the conference room where she'd set up her temporary lab, she wasn't there. Frowning, I backed out into the hall, wondering where she might be. Hell, it *was* Sunday—maybe they'd released her from protective custody and she'd gone home to finally get some sleep.

"Hello, Red."

I felt my skin ripple with irritation and had to make a concerted effort not to snarl when I said, "Mary. If you came to give me shit about what happened last night—"

"I didn't even know you were here," Mary interrupted. "I was looking for Trish."

I eyed the prosecutor warily. "That makes two of us. What do *you* want with her?"

"She gathered a sample of genetic material and magical residue from Sebille Fenwick's body at the crime scene," Mary said. "I was hoping to get the results as soon as possible."

"Does it matter?" I asked, slightly annoyed that she'd be bothering Trish on a Sunday, demanding to know answers. My conscience gave me a little tap on the shoulder. *Hello, pot, meet kettle. . . .*

To my surprise, Mary actually squirmed a little at my question. "Imperative, as it turns out. Sebille's body has disappeared."

I gaped at her. "What?"

"Without the body," Mary continued, "I'll need Trish's test results for my case against Caliban."

I frowned. "Who would have taken Sebille's body?"

Mary squirmed a little more, making me uneasy. She

wasn't the squirming type. She was cool, calm, and collected—completely unflappable. "No one," she said, looking embarrassed by the answer. "She just vanished. The security tapes show her there on the gurney one moment and then gone the next."

"Huh." I turned away, my brows drawing together as I tried to process this unexpected development.

"Red?"

I halted with a huff. "Seriously, Mary, I'm not in the mood—"

"I was sorry to hear about Juliet," she said, cutting me off. "She was a good woman. It's a tragedy."

I blinked at her. "Yeah, it is. I guess some of us can never quite escape our unhappy endings, can we?"

"I hope Nicky pulls through."

I narrowed my eyes a little. "Thanks. I hope so, too."

"If you need anything—"

"Why are you being so nice to me?" I broke in, cutting through the bullshit. "You hate my guts. You piss me off every chance you get. So why are you suddenly being so . . . *nice*?"

Mary sighed. "I saw the photos," she said. "I heard what happened, what you did to try to save the Blues. I just wanted to tell you that I think you did everything you could."

"And?" I prompted, sensing there was more.

Mary took a deep breath and let it out slowly. "And maybe I was wrong about you."

What can I say? I was actually speechless.

Mary straightened to her full height, peering down at me haughtily, but I got the impression it was more for my peace of mind than any true condescension. "This doesn't mean I *like* you," she assured me. "It just means . . . well, I guess I *respect* you."

I nodded. "So noted. Thanks."

She turned on her stilettoed heel and tossed her head as

she strode away, her long strides carrying her around the corner in no time at all.

As soon as she was gone, I went in search of Nate, eager to find out if he'd heard anything about the disappearance of Sebille's body. But when I found him, he and the Chief were talking in hushed tones in Al's office. Their voices immediately ceased when I stepped into the room.

"What's going on?" I demanded. "Did you get the warrant for Caliban?"

Nate gave me a guarded look. "No."

"Why not?" I asked, my skin prickling with apprehension.

Al folded his hands and leaned forward onto his desk as if bracing himself. "Todd Caliban went into cardiac arrest and nearly died thirty minutes ago."

I blinked rapidly, too stunned by the news to believe I'd heard him right. "What the hell are you talking about? He was getting better." I turned to Nate. "You told me that when I woke up this evening."

Al glanced between Nate and me, his eyes full of questions I was sure he'd be asking later.

Nate cleared his throat, having caught the look, too. "Uh, yeah, I know. Apparently, someone slipped him a lethal dose of D. Luckily, a nurse happened to walk in just as he was coding and was able to save his life. Al sent a couple of Investigators over to question the medical staff and work the crime scene."

So that's where Trish was. . . .

That answered one question but left me with about a dozen more. Such as who would want Caliban dead now that Sebille was out of the picture? A certain drug lord with an ax to grind immediately came to mind.

"Let's go," I said, already stepping back into the hallway. "Something tells me this isn't over yet."

Chapter 41

When Nate and I ducked under the yellow crime scene tape, I felt my stomach turn. Caliban lay in the hospital bed, the white hospital sheet drawn up over his chest, which rose and fell in a slow rhythm thanks to the ventilator keeping him alive. I gave my head a quick shake, pushing away the surge of emotion I felt at seeing him this way. Nate's hand passed lightly down my arm, letting me know he was there if I needed him. I gave him a grateful look before he moved away to talk quietly with the Investigators who were taking a statement from one of the ward nurses.

I spotted Trish crouched down beside the bed, examining the floor, and came to stand beside her. "Find anything?"

Trish's head snapped up. "Red? What are you doing here? I figured you'd be taking the day off."

"We heard what happened," I said by way of answer. "Do you know anything yet?"

Trish rose from her crouch and put her hands on her hips. "Not much," she replied, her eyes still taking in details of the room as she spoke. "The nurse walked in and saw a woman injecting liquid D into Caliban's IV."

"A woman?" I repeated. "You mean it wasn't Tim Halloran?"

Trish shook her head. "Not unless he was in drag and has the ability to vanish into thin air."

"What?"

"When the nurse yelled for security, the woman vanished into thin air. Literally. She didn't leave a trace. There's absolutely *nothing* for me to go on."

"No residual magic?" I asked, thinking of Sebille Fenwick's missing corpse and wondering if fairy zombies could vanish into thin air.

(Hey, stranger things have happened. . . .)

Trish shook her head again. "Not even a hint. This place is way too clean."

I gave her a quizzical look. "What do you mean?"

She sighed and looked around again, surveying the room in a last-ditch effort to find answers. "Whoever came in here had to be able to move without leaving any footprint—magic or otherwise. Nothing has been disturbed at all, not even the air in the room."

"Who can do that?" I asked.

Trish turned her head toward me and met my gaze. "No one I know."

I scowled, my mind racing. Why would someone want to murder Caliban now? All the players in Sebille's carefully crafted play had already exited stage right. What unknown character was hovering in the wings, waiting to make an appearance for the dramatic conclusion?

"Red?" Trish said as if she'd said it a few times already.

I gave myself a quick shake. "Sorry—what?"

Trish glanced over to where Nate was absorbed in conversation with the Investigators, then took my elbow and ducked under the tape, pulling me along with her. When we were safely out of earshot, she said quietly, "The only time I've ever encountered a crime scene without residual it turned out to be a ghost. Do you think it could have been Sebille Fenwick's spirit?"

My brows lifted. Definitely an intriguing idea, but I told her, "No, I don't think so. I saw Nate take her soul. The only souls that hang around are those who wander off before the Reaper arrives. As far as I know, once they're delivered, there's no coming back."

Trish exhaled a long sigh. "I guess that would have been too easy, huh?" She started back into the room but stopped and turned toward me. "Oh—I almost forgot to tell you. I ran some tests on Sebille's body when they brought her in. Her ability to transform was definitely voluntary. She wasn't born a lycan, and there was no evidence of a curse like Seth's sample."

I wasn't entirely surprised by the information. "So, what kind of voluntary magic was she using?" I asked. "Was it sidhe?"

Trish shrugged. "No clue. I didn't get a chance to finish looking at the results before I was called here."

"When you get back to the lab, will you call and let me know?"

Trish sighed and gave me an irritated look. "You know, I do need to sleep at some point, Red."

I let out a little laugh. "Sorry, I'm just anxious to cross this one off my list. But I guess I can wait. I'm much more curious about our would-be assassin."

"You and me both," Trish rejoined. "I'll be here for a little while longer, but I'll see what I can do about getting those other results for you."

"Thanks, Trish!" I called as she went back into Caliban's room.

There was really nothing for me to do at the crime scene, so I leaned back against the wall and closed my eyes, waiting for Nate to come out.

A few minutes later, I felt his approach and opened my eyes. "Ready to go?"

"I need to stay close," he replied, giving me a pained look. "Just in case."

"Oh."

He put his arm around my shoulders. "Come on. I'll walk you out."

When we were in the elevator, I turned toward him and ran my index finger over his shoulder. "This still mine?"

Nate pulled me to him. "Anytime."

I wrapped my arms around him and clung to him as the elevator made its way up to the ground level, letting the warmth of him wrap itself around me. When the elevator doors slid open, Nate and I stepped apart and he tossed me his keys. "Take my car. Mind if I stop by later?"

This brought a hint of a smile to my lips. "I'd be pissed if you didn't."

Nate's laugh burst from him. "Then I'll see you soon. I still owe you dinner."

I checked my watch. "It might have to be a midnight snack at this rate. How about you bring tacos with you and we'll call it even?"

"You got it." He raised a hand to me in farewell as the elevator doors slid closed once more.

As I drove Nate's Zephyr toward Gran's neighborhood, I tried to shake the uneasy feeling I had hanging over me. Sebille was dead. I saw Nate collect her soul. And her partner in crime might soon be joining her in the great hereafter. So why couldn't I accept that it was all over? We'd figured it out. The ruthless scheme for building Todd Caliban's empire had been laid bare. And Seth was completely in the clear. I should have been relieved to have it all over and done with, but instead I felt like I was missing something.

I shrugged it off, forcing myself to focus on the road. Maybe if I'd had the chance to look at Hamelin's journal before everything went to shit, I wouldn't have had this nagging suspicion that there was more to the story.

The little devil on my shoulder gave me a prod with her pitchfork and whispered, "You know, Red, there's really no reason why the forensics team would have gone upstairs at Nicky's house. He was the only one besides Nate who knows anything about the flash drive. Odds are good it's still there. . . ."

Little Red Devil had a point. I'd be breaking some serious FMA rules about crime scene protocol, but it's not like I was going to traipse around and contaminate things. They'd probably already taken all the evidence they needed; keeping the scene secured for a few days was just a formality. What would it really hurt if I broke in and gathered a little more evidence on my own?

I took the next exit and headed toward Nicky's instead. When I pulled into his driveway, the sun was setting over the horizon, casting long shadows and making the abandoned mansion seem a little creepier than it would have been in the light of day. Squaring my shoulders, I shrugged off my uneasiness and went up the steps. Whoever had sealed the door had done a piss-poor job of it, so I was able to get inside without even having to disturb the crime scene tape.

"Score one for Red," I muttered. "Must be my lucky night."

Even in the waning light I could see that the forensics team had already cleaned up the blood and other signs of violence in the house, just as I'd anticipated. I could still feel the heaviness of negative energy hovering in the air, but at least I didn't have to *see* anything that I'd been too shaken up to observe the night before.

I hurried up the stairs to the guest room and found the flash drive sitting on the desk next to the keyboard where Nicky had left it. "Score again," I whispered. "Red's hot tonight, folks."

Hamelin's documents were a case study in how *not* to organize your hard drive, but thanks to what Nicky had already told me, I was able to find the journal without any trouble.

Unfortunately, Hamelin's thoughts weren't organized much better than his hard drive.

There were various rambling rants about how Sebille was blackmailing him and about how cruel and deranged she could be in her quest for power. He spoke of how Julie Spangle had seen through the ruse immediately and had been eliminated as a result. How Dale Minnows had threatened to pull his funding. How Alfred Simon had seen Sebille controlling the rats and had been murdered to keep him from blabbing.

Hamelin also made several comments about Caliban, calling him an "ignorant patsy" and a "tool" for letting Sebille control him. More than once, Hamelin said he almost felt sorry for Caliban for trusting such a manipulative woman.

I frowned as I reread the disjointed paragraphs. To hear Hamelin tell it, Caliban had been completely ignorant of Sebille's machinations to keep him on top and in the spotlight, and honestly knew nothing of the murders. If anything, he was only guilty of poor judgment when it came to his taste in women.

I continued reading, simultaneously rewriting the conclusion I'd mistakenly set aside as a final draft. If Caliban hadn't been in league with Sebille's plans, then who was the person she'd spoken of the night before? Who had warned her that I'd be a threat? Who had forbidden her to kill me in spite of the supposed threat I posed? Was this mystery man behind the attempt on Caliban's life even though it was a woman the nurse had seen?

The attempt on Caliban's life suddenly made sense. If Caliban was dead, he couldn't prove his innocence and the case would be officially closed. Who would think to look any further when both supposedly guilty parties were pushing up daisies?

Of course, if Mr. Mysterious found out Caliban had survived, he might come at him again to finish him off once and for all. Which meant if we played this right we could catch him in the act.

I grabbed my phone and called Nate, but he didn't answer. *Odd.*

I frowned, wondering if maybe Caliban had died and Nate was busy delivering his soul. I tapped my phone against my forehead for a moment, wondering who else I could trust with this information.

Trish.

I dialed Trish's number and was greeted with an exasperated huff. "You just don't give up, do you?"

"Trish," I said, ignoring her tone. "Is Caliban still alive?"

There was a slight hesitation. "Yeah. I mean, he was stable when I left the hospital. Why?"

"I can't reach Nate. Do you know where he is?"

"I think he said something about tacos."

I grinned a little. *God, I loved that man.* "I need you to do me a favor."

"*Another* one?" Trish drawled.

"I promise this is important," I assured her. "And I'll owe you."

"Fine, but that's two you owe me now. What do you need?"

"Can you request guards for Caliban's room? I need them to be from special ops with magical abilities. I don't have the authority to order something like that."

"Holy crap," Trish breathed. "You think someone's coming back to try again, don't you?"

"As soon as word gets out that he's alive, yeah."

"Okay," Trish agreed. "I'll call it in right now."

"Thanks, Trish. You're the best."

"Oh, hey, Red," Trish said quickly to keep me from hanging up. "Those other results just came back. Sebille was *ruvanush.*"

"Ruvanush?" I repeated. "Are you sure?"

"Positive."

"But she was from Arthurian legend," I pointed out. "Ruvanush werewolf transformation is Romany magic. How would she have learned that kind of magic in her story?"

"Maybe she learned it on this side," Trish suggested. "Are there any Tales who'd know how to transform into a werewolf using magic from that region?"

I swallowed hard, suddenly finding it difficult to speak with horror squeezing the hell out of my heart. "Just one," I whispered. "Thanks, Trish."

On a hunch, I did a quick search through Hamelin's diatribe for the word *Sarah* to see if Hamelin had had any info on the one murder that hadn't fit in with the rest. When I got the first hit, my mouth went dry. Sarah's murder seemed to have bothered Hamelin the most. He'd met the woman on the one occasion he'd visited Sebille's apartment. Apparently, she'd served as Sebille's housekeeper—until a falling out had resulted in Sarah's dismissal.

I blinked a few times and shook my head, not willing to believe the picture that was forming. I kept reading, hoping I'd find the explanation that would prove me wrong, but then a name caught my eye and turned my blood to ice water in my veins.

Jack Horner.

Sarah Dickerson's new employer.

Sebille had admitted that Sarah Dickerson's murder was personal—now I knew why. Sarah Dickerson was, in fact, Amanda's friend—the poor girl whose Mistress had treated her so heinously and had dismissed her out of jealousy for the man she wanted and couldn't have to herself. Hot tears stung my eyes as the rest of the story came into focus and the identity of Sebille's mystery man was suddenly clear.

"Oh, God," I groaned, crossing my arms over my stomach and bending forward as the agony of sorrow and betrayal hit me deep in my gut. "Vlad."

"Clever girl."

I whirled around and launched to my feet with a startled cry.

Vlad stood in the doorway, leaning nonchalantly against the door frame, his arms folded across his chest. He gave me a lazy smile. "I told Sebille you were not to be underestimated."

"You were behind all of this," I breathed.

Vlad shrugged. "Alas, 'this thing of darkness I must acknowledge mine,'" he replied, bastardizing *The Tempest.*

"Why?" I demanded, my heart racing. "Why did you do this?"

"The opportunity presented itself," he said, his expression bored. "When Sebille came to me to discuss investing in Caliban's endeavors, I agreed to assist her. For a price."

"And what was the price?" I asked, inching toward the desk where I'd left my phone.

"Well, aside from the obvious, I required her assistance in the elimination of some rather . . . bothersome competition," Vlad replied, strolling into the room.

"Who?" I demanded, my hip bumping into the desk. "Dale Minnows? Tim Halloran? Were you even taking on Nicky Blue?"

Vlad's mouth hitched up in one corner. "As it turns out, my ambitions and Sebille's dovetailed quite nicely. My only competitor not covered by her schemes was easy enough to resolve. All it took was a little instruction in the old ways of my homeland."

My fingers closed around my phone. "You taught her the spell to transform into a ruvanush," I deduced. "You wanted the murders committed by a werewolf."

"Indeed."

"And you wanted everyone to know it was a werewolf," I guessed. "You had Sebille destroy the forensics lab during the day so I would see the wolf and be more inclined to believe it was Seth."

"Right again, little one." In a sudden blur of motion, he was suddenly pressing into me, his fangs long and hungry. "He stood between me and my heart's one desire."

I kept my gaze averted, not daring to make eye contact. "And what was that?"

"Come now, my own," he growled, his speech distorted by his fangs, "you know how I crave you."

"What about Sebille?" I asked. "She was your mistress. She killed Sarah Dickerson to keep you to herself."

"As it turns out," he continued, a note of regret in his voice, "the sidhe enchantress's lust for me, for my bite, was more powerful than I'd anticipated. She grew greedy, sloppy. Caliban became suspicious when she came to his bed less often, and so it was necessary to treat his anxieties in a more aggressive manner. . . ."

"By upping his fairy dust," I deduced, trying to squirm out of his hold. "Did you order her to overdose him?"

"That was an act of her desperation," he murmured, his lips brushing against my neck with barely restrained hunger. "Had she followed my orders, our plan would have worked perfectly. Your little lapdog would have been behind bars, courtesy of your dedicated efforts to bring in the perpetrator of these *heinous* murders, and I would have consoled you, convinced you to be my own for eternity."

"So why steal Sebille's body?"

I felt Vlad's muscles tense at my words. After a fraction of a second's hesitation, he drew back, his expression betraying the merest hint of confusion. He hissed something under his breath and shook his head as if dismissing whatever thought had brought the curse to his lips.

He didn't know Sebille's body was missing, I realized. And, for some reason, that worried him. Which worried *me* even more than the body's actual disappearance.

Taking advantage of his distraction by the news of Sebille's disappearance, I pushed on. "And what about the assassination attempt in the hospital? How'd you pull that off?"

Vlad forced his attention back to me and offered me a smile that lacked its typical smug superiority. "As it turns out, the ghosts of Ordinaries are very pliable and quite useful for such purposes," he explained. "And it was really quite easy to find one willing to make such a sacrifice for me. In fact, my little love, it was you who put her in mind."

A sudden, horrifying thought struck me. "Amanda."

Vlad smiled, his eyes twinkling. "So clever. Is there any wonder why I *must* have you?"

He pulled back and opened his mouth to strike at the vein throbbing in my neck, but I darted to one side, narrowly avoiding the treacherous points. Trying to put as much distance between us as possible, I scrambled onto the bed in an attempt to make it to the door, but he was too quick. I felt him coming for me a split second before the impact took me down on the mattress. I tried to roll over to fight him off, but he pinned me down with his superhuman strength, keeping me where I was. A moment later I felt his hot breath on my cheek.

"My little love, why do you struggle so?" he mocked. "You know, in the end, you will give me everything I ask of you."

His fangs struck hard, making me cry out. But my cry faded to a whimper when I realized he was right. There wasn't a damn thing I could do. I went limp, letting him draw what he would from me. A fog began to descend upon me with each pull upon my vein, but I fought to remain in control of my mind, waiting for him to let down his guard. Finally sated, he ran his tongue along the wound in my throat and rose to his knees.

I remained completely still, allowing him to think he had me under his control. With surprisingly gentle hands, he rolled me over onto my back and grinned down at me, preparing to slake his thirst in other ways. I closed my eyes and gasped and moaned as he would have expected as his hands and mouth roamed my body. And when I felt him lift my shirt to press a kiss to my stomach, I opened my eyes to confirm that he was kneeling over me exactly as I'd hoped.

I jerked my leg upward, nailing him in the crotch, and

swung my hand holding the cell phone, catching him in the temple. The double assault was enough to stun him and knock him to one side. Without hesitation, I bolted to the bedroom door and down the stairs. I had just thrown open the front door, when a sudden jerk of my hair pulled me off my feet. I landed hard on the foyer floor, the impact knocking the breath from my lungs.

Vlad straddled me again, this time his face distorted with rage. "I tried to protect you, to keep you from harm," he snarled, his punishing grasp bruising the skin on my throat. "Had you just given yourself to me completely, I could have given you everything your heart desired, loved you for all eternity."

I glared at him. "And now?"

His grip tightened. "Now," he hissed, "you shall feel my wrath." He pressed a punishing kiss to my lips, his fangs cutting my skin and drawing my blood once again into his mouth. Running his tongue along my lips, he savored the final taste, then lifted his head. "But make no mistake, my little love, I *will* conquer you."

I spat in response, bloody saliva spraying his face. "Bring it on, asshole."

Vlad's chuckle was low and menacing. "Ah, my dear little Red," he drawled. "It appears the game is afoot once again."

He gave me a cocky smile and abruptly released me. Then he was gone, once more on the run, knowing I would pursue, that I wouldn't rest until he finally let me catch him. But this time there'd be no rehabilitation. There'd be a reckoning.

Feeling betrayed, humiliated, violated in more ways than I could count, I closed my eyes against tears of sorrow and anger, but they came anyway, trickling down my cheeks to pool in my ears and hair.

I was really getting into my pity party groove when my phone rang, making me nearly jump out of my skin. I sniffed a couple of times, trying to find where the phone had ended up when I'd hit the ground. I found it a few feet away and snatched it up.

"This is Red."

There was a slight pause, then, "What's wrong?" It was Nate's raspy voice, taut with anxiety and concern. "Where are you?"

"Nicky's." I covered my eyes with my forearm, hoping it would dam the waterworks, but the floodgates were jammed open. Cradling the phone against my ear, I curled up on my side, no longer able to hold back my sobs. "Oh, God, Nate— I need you."

I'd barely gotten the words out of my mouth when he appeared in the foyer, his shadows thick and menacing, his eyes blazing with smoldering fire. Without a word, he pulled me to my feet and into his arms, holding me until my tears finally subsided.

I lifted my face to his, feeling a twinge of shame for letting him see the confused, hurt, angry woman I tried so hard to keep buried. But to my surprise, there was no judgment or censure in his eyes. There was only . . . love.

He smoothed my hair away from my face and kissed me tenderly. "Come on, sweetheart," he said softly against my bruised lips. "Let's go home."

Chapter 42

I jolted awake to the sound of a heavy fist upon the door. Frowning, I glanced at the clock on the nightstand next to Nate's bed.

Six a.m.

"What the hell?" I muttered, wiggling out of Nate's hold and slipping from his bed. I glanced around, finding the bathrobe I was beginning to identify as my standard wardrobe when at his house, and pulled it on, tying the belt as I hurried to the door.

Without thinking, I threw open the door, ready to tell off the jackass on the other side, but the words stuck in my throat. I gaped at the man before me. "Seth?"

Seth gave me a self-conscious smile and shifted a little, adjusting the duffel bag he had slung over his shoulder. "Hey, Red."

I frowned at him, confused by my happiness at seeing him and my apprehension about what had brought him to Nate's doorstep. "How'd you know where to find me?"

Seth cleared his throat a couple of times. "Uh, your Gran thought you might be here. I stopped by there first. She makes really good blueberry muffins."

I blinked at him. "Yeah, I know."

"Anyway, I just stopped by to say good-bye."

My stomach clenched at his words. "What? Good-bye?"

"I need to get away. Clear my head." He glanced over my shoulder and gave a nod to Nate, who was coming up to stand behind me. "Anyway, I just wanted to say thanks for everything. All things considered, you could have left me hanging."

I gave him a sad smile. "All things considered, there's no way I could. So, where are you going?"

Seth shrugged. "Maybe out West. I've always wanted to see the mountains."

"Will you be back?"

He nodded. "Someday."

Nate's arm came around my shoulders and he leaned forward, offering his hand to Seth. "Good luck to you, Wolf," he said. "You need anything, just let us know."

Seth couldn't hide his surprise at Nate's words. "Thanks." He then jerked his chin in Nate's direction. "Is this the guy?"

I nestled a little closer to Nate and nodded. "Yeah."

Seth nodded his approval, then turned to go, but before he'd reached the first step he pivoted around and came back. "Sorry. Forgot to give you this." He handed me a simple white envelope. "Gran asked me to drop it off."

"Thanks."

There was an awkward pause with Seth glancing back and forth between Nate and me. Then he muttered something that sounded like "Fuck it," and darted forward, pressing a hard, but brief, kiss to my lips. "Take care, Red. I'll be seeing you."

Watching Seth walk away until he turned the corner at the end of the street, Nate and I then closed the front door, turning our attention to the envelope in my hands.

"Who's that from?" Nate asked, not mentioning Seth's kiss—much to my relief.

I didn't need to open the envelope to know the answer. "Nicky." With a sigh, I tore it open and pulled out the missive inside. The note was short:

*I know you're blaming yourself for Jules. Don't. It's not
your fault. I love you, kid. And I'll see you soon. Nate,
take care of our girl, or you'll have to answer to me.*
                                                    N.B.

"He's gone, too," I said, handing the note to Nate.

"He won't be gone long," Nate assured me. "He's got a
business to run. And friends who care about him. We'll get
him through this when he's ready."

I nodded, then took a deep breath, letting it out slowly.
"So, what now?"

Nate wrapped his arms around me. "Well," he said, peering down at me, "now we track down Vlad Dracula and bring
him to justice for what he's done."

"We?" I asked. "You want to help me bring him in?"

Nate gave me one of his cockeyed smiles that set my heart
to thumping. "Try to stop me."

"It's going to be dangerous," I told him. "Vlad's not going
to come quietly."

"I'm up to the challenge."

"And we still don't know what happened to Sebille's
body," I reminded him. "Something tells me we haven't seen
the last of her."

"Bring it on."

I arched a brow at him. "Think you can keep up with me?
Being an Enforcer requires some pretty strenuous physical
activity. . . ."

"I think you'll find my stamina equal to the task," he said,
bending a little to nuzzle my neck, and setting my head spinning. "Care for a demonstration?"

"God, yes," I breathed, wrapping my arms around his neck
and pulling him closer.

He untied the bathrobe's belt and let it fall open, making
me shudder with the sudden chill. But I wasn't cold for long.
The second his hands began to explore the curves of my body,
heat exploded from deep within the center of my belly,

spreading out through my limbs and warming me in the best possible ways.

As much as my body was ready to give in to Nate's not-so-subtle suggestions for passing the time, reason momentarily took control and I pushed him back.

"So, I guess we're really going to do this," I said, mildly shocked that the thought of giving things a go with him didn't make me want to hyperventilate.

Nate gave me a cautious look. "You okay with that?"

I cocked my head to one side, studying him for a moment. Then I nodded, feeling somewhat bemused by that remarkable truth. "Yeah, I'm okay with that." Then a sudden thought struck me. "But Al's going to be so pissed when he finds out about us."

"He's used to being pissed when it comes to you," Nate reminded me with a chuckle. "He'll get over it."

"But—"

He cut off my protests with a kiss that left me breathless and nearly sent me over the edge before things even got started.

"I forgive you, by the way," I told him, trying to hold on to my wits as he pressed a sultry line of kisses along my jaw. "For lying to me and all that. Just in case you were wondering."

Nate's teeth grazed my earlobe. "So I gathered." He moved lower, nibbling along my collarbone, then further down until he reached the valley between my breasts.

I closed my eyes, twining my fingers in his hair. "I just wanted you to know—oh, God!" I gasped as he took one of my nipples into his mouth and did something unbelievable with his tongue. I swallowed hard, trying to form a coherent thought. "I mean, I understand why you lied to me, and I—"

Nate abruptly lifted his head and gave me an exasperated look. "Red."

"What?"

"Shut up and let me love you."

When I blinked at him, momentarily stunned by his words, he chuckled, the sound echoing through every atom in my body and making me pulse with desire for the incredible man I loved, needed, didn't want to live without. He had given me everything I could ask for, restoring hope and happiness to a heart that had given up on such luxuries long ago.

And all he asked in return was that I let him love me.

So I did.

Read on for a sneak peek at the next
Transplanted Tales novel,
The Better to See You,
available in February 2013!

There was no point in trying to summon my magic now—
it had deserted me; that was pretty freaking clear. I just hoped
like hell my death would be quick.

The creature prowled toward me, its massive bulk a mercifully indistinct silhouette, and I swear I thought I heard it
chuckle, the sound sending chills down my spine. Then
from behind me came the whisper-soft padding of paws
on the underbrush. In the next instant, a great white wolf
leaped over me and slammed into the shadow-creature. The
two rolled end-over-end in a tangle of claws and teeth,
coming to rest with the wolf on top, its lips peeled back in
a vicious snarl.

I turned my head to get a better look just in time to see the
wolf grab the creature's throat in its teeth. The beast's howl
ended abruptly as the wolf gave a powerful shake of its head,
tearing out a large section of demon dog's throat.

The wolf flung the chunk of flesh into the underbrush,
then cautiously padded toward me, its head down between its
shoulders, sizing me up. As it came closer, I realized it wasn't
an ordinary timber wolf. This animal was easily twice the size
of any wolf I'd ever seen and had a distinctly human intelligence shining in its eyes.

I didn't stand a chance.

It bit through the pine needle rope and shook its head,

scattering the needles all over the ground. The rest of the needles instantly fell away and the trees halted their brutal assault.

I raised a bloody, trembling hand, not sure if I'd just exchanged one predator for another. "Please," I managed to gasp between the quick, shallow breaths that were all my punctured lung would now allow. "Please . . ."

In response, a soft shimmering light encased the wolf, and where the beautiful creature had stood, now crouched a man, his ice-green eyes still glowing. As he gently lifted me into his arms, I cried out, pain engulfing me.

"It's all right," he said softly, cradling me against him. "You're safe now."

I looked up into the grim face of my rescuer, now recognizing him. How could I not when I'd seen his face on WANTED posters and in the Tale news so often over the centuries?

As pain and nausea sent me careening toward a dark abyss, his name drifted to me.

Seth Wolf.

ABOUT THE AUTHOR

Kate SeRine (pronounced "serene") faithfully watched weekend monster-movie marathons while growing up, each week hoping that maybe *this* time the creature du jour would get the girl. But every week she was disappointed. So when she began writing her own stories, Kate vowed that *her* characters would always have a happily-ever-after. And, thus, her love for paranormal romance was born.

Kate lives in a smallish, quintessentially Midwestern town with her husband and two sons, who share her love of story-telling. She never tires of creating new worlds to share and is even now working on her next project.

To learn more about Kate and her novels, please visit www.kateserine.com.

Don't miss the newest eKensington releases!

If you liked this book,
check out TUCKER'S CROSSING by Marina Adair,
available now!

**Sweet Plains, Texas, wasn't so sweet to
Cody, Noah, and Beau Tucker. But now
the Tucker boys are men, ready to take on
the questions that have haunted them
since they left home . . .**

Cody Tucker shook the dust of his two-bit hometown off his
boots ten years ago—right about the time his college sweetheart, Shelby Lynn Harris, married his so-called best friend.
But when his dad dies, Cody finds himself home again and
knee deep in the past. Except now his rowdy beer buddy is the
sheriff, his housekeeper is a blue-ribbon chili chef, and the
family ranch is in the red. The only thing that hasn't changed
is Shelby Lynn . . .

Shelby Lynn has gone through a lot of heartache thanks to
Cody. But that's all over now. She just wants a chance to live
the life she's made for herself in peace. The trouble is, the
Sweet Plains chili cook-off is heating up, the Ladies of Sweet
are as riled as hornets, and as soon as Cody gets near, she
forgets all about peace. Cody is pure temptation—and she
knows just how good it feels to give in . . .

The only thing hotter than a Texas summer is a cowboy's love...

Tucker's Crossing

"A perfect mix of heart and heat, Adair keeps the pages turning."

—*New York Times* bestselling author Jill Shalvis

Marina Adair

❖ SWEET PLAINS, TEXAS ❖

"A master of her craft."
—Maggie Shayne

NEW YORK TIMES BESTSELLING AUTHOR

AMANDA ASHLEY

BENEATH A MIDNIGHT MOON

Printed in the United States
by Baker & Taylor Publisher Services